BUTTERCUPS AND DAISIES

In *Buttercups and Daisies*, the author describes the hilarious adventures of Mr Waterall and his family when they buy 'a place in the country'. Surrounded by a host of the maddest of Mackenzian characters, Roger and Ralph Waterall savour the delights of rustic simplicity, while Mr Waterall suffers, in a far from stoical fashion, the escapades of his two high-spirited sons and the machinations of his fellow refugees from suburbia. When Mr Waterall decides to take a hand in local affairs, the fun is fast and furious for the boys and their friends, Texas Bill, Uncle Gus and Peter the dog, and the author's description of the meeting, resulting from Mr Waterall's crusade for a new name for Oak Farm Estate, is a gem of humorous narrative.

BUTTERCUPS
AND
DAISIES

Compton Mackenzie

LONDON
ROBERT HALE & COMPANY

Copyright Compton Mackenzie 1931
First published in Great Britain in 1931
This edition 1973

ISBN 07091 3791 5

Robert Hale & Company
63 Old Brompton Road
London, S.W.7

HERTFORDSHIRE
COUNTY LIBRARY

823/MAC

6155224

Printed in Great Britain by
Redwood Press Limited
Trowbridge, Wiltshire

To
Ethel and Fisher Dilke
in memory of
June, 1904

CHAPTER ONE

'THIS,' Mr Waterall announced, on a fine Saturday morning in late September, as he gazed over the top of his paper at his wife, 'this is what I have been looking for for years.'

Mrs Waterall's impulse was to suppose that her husband was enjoying one of those little triumphs to which he was periodically addicted. He had a habit of putting articles away in safe places, forgetting the place immediately afterwards, and accusing every member of his family, from his wife to the boy who came in to do the knives, of having interfered with his arrangements for security. Mrs Waterall could not be blamed for assuming that this was one of the mislaid treasures.

'For years!' Mr Waterall portentously repeated. 'Have the goodness to listen, my dear.'

Mrs Waterall, realizing that her husband wanted to read something from the *Daily Telegraph,* jumped to the conclusion that he had discovered another cure for baldness. She hoped it would not be so complicated a cure as the last one he had tried, when he had sat for two hours in the bathroom every Sunday morning, wearing upon his head a hemisphere of indiarubber which was kept firm by the vacuum and was connected by a long tube to an electrical apparatus emitting fizzes and blue sparks.

Mr Waterall read solemnly from the advertisement columns:

CANADIAN COTTAGE, GALTON, HANTS.

FOR SALE. *Two-roomed wooden bungalow with lean-to shed easily convertible into kitchen. Quarter acre of land planted with apples, pears, peaches, plums, cherries, currants, gooseberries, strawberries and vegetables. More land obtainable adjacent. Price £125.*

'For years!' repeated Mr Waterall.

'And what would you do with it?' his wife asked.

'Do with it?' he repeated scathingly. 'What do you suppose I should do with it?'

7

'I really don't know, dear,' said Mrs Waterall. 'I can't guess.'

'Do you mean to say we've been married all these years without your having realized that I wanted a place in the country? Haven't I continually pointed out how bad it is for the children to be cooped up in London? For what other reason do you suppose I insist on giving them the money to go to Kew or Richmond Park every Saturday afternoon?'

'Oh, I know, dear,' said Mrs Waterall to pacify him. 'You are always thinking about the children.'

'I think about the children too much,' said Mr Waterall. 'If I thought about myself a little more sometimes . . .' He broke off, leaving in the air an illimitable apodosis. 'Peaches!' he murmured. 'Do you mean to tell me you wouldn't like to have your own peaches every morning?'

'Of course, I think it would be lovely,' she assured him.

'We could keep chickens,' he went on. 'Those eggs this morning, for instance – that sort of thing couldn't happen if we had a place in the country.'

'I think they were Danish, dear,' Mrs Waterall apologized.

'Danish?' echoed her husband. 'They might have been Anglo-Saxon!'

Mrs Waterall was almost sure that he was making a joke; but she could not be perfectly sure, because one of the shops at which she dealt was called The Anglo-Saxon Stores, and it might be that he was criticizing the eggs from there. So, she sighed with the intention of giving an impression, if he had made a joke, that she was helpless with inward laughter or, if he had not made a joke, that she was sorry about the eggs and would give up frequenting The Anglo-Saxon Stores.

'And of course,' Mr Waterall added, 'the time has come to keep a dog!'

Mrs Waterall stared at her husband. Ever since their engagement fifteen years ago, when Robert had gently insisted that her favourite Yorkshire terrier should be left with her mother, she had supposed that a dog was the one thing that Robert would never allow in his own house.

'I think,' he went on, apparently oblivious of any break with the traditions of fifteen years, 'I think that on the whole the most suitable dog would be an Airedale terrier, and as I don't want to give an excessive price for a dog I think, my dear, you had better go to the Dogs' Home at Battersea this afternoon and choose some unclaimed dog there, because I understand that dogs can be obtained there for anything from ten shillings down to half a crown.'

If Mr Waterall had told her to buy an elephant, the poor lady could not have shown more dismay.

'You can take one of the boys with you,' he added.

'But hadn't we better wait, dear, until we know more definitely about this cottage?'

Mr Waterall looked at his wife in astonishment. 'I should have thought,' he said severely, 'that by this time and after all these years you would have grasped that I do not allow myself to be carried away by momentary impulses. Can you look back on the history of our married life and recall one single momentary impulse?'

His wife could recall at least a thousand, including one momentary impulse to become a vegetarian which had lost her the best cook and the best housemaid she ever had.

'Had,' went on Mr Waterall without waiting for an answer, 'had you waited one second, you would have heard that I am going down to Galton this very afternoon to occupy myself with the purchase of this' – he was on the point of saying 'estate', but compromised with 'property. 'In order not to waste any time, you and Ralph, and, if you like, Roger . . . yes, you can take Roger too . . . I have no objection . . . while you are all occupied with the dog, I shall be going into matters at Galton. I shall certainly grow melons next year. I'm tired of these pale yellow Easter eggs miscalled melons with which Covent Garden is flooded. Suppose we buy two frames six feet by four, that should allow two plants in each frame. And I assume I can obtain the requisite manure from a neighbouring farmer. That would give us at least thirty melons . . . but I mustn't waste time talking about melons when I have to catch my train. Now then, forward the Light Brigade!' he shouted.

This was a facetious formula for summoning his two sons. Ralph and Roger, who were at the age when facetious fathers are not esteemed by their sons, made a point of resisting the summons whenever it was couched in this detestable hyperbole, and it was not until their father called them by name that they put in an appearance at the breakfast-table.

'Boys,' he inquired, when his two sons were louringly

eating their porridge under the paternal eye, 'boys, how are you going to spend this beautiful autumn day?'

Ralph looked at Roger; Roger looked at Ralph. They had a dozen alternative schemes for passing their Saturday afternoon; but, since even the least innocuous of them would not have won their father's approval, they muttered an incoherent reply to the question and filled their mouths with porridge.

'No plans, eh?' Mr Waterall chuckled with that maddening joviality which they felt portended a vile paternal plot to enslave the precious hours of a holiday. 'How would you like to go with your mother to pick out a dog at the Battersea Home?'

The brows of the two boys cleared. For a holiday task this was very much better than anything they could have expected.

'Pick out a good Airedale,' said their father grandly. 'You can go to ten shillings. I shan't be back till this evening, and when I return I shall have some interesting news to tell you. Where's my little Phyllis? Isn't she going to kiss her father good-bye?'

Ralph, a lanky boy of thirteen, made a grimace, an exquisitely modulated grimace of disgust at his father's sentimentality, whereupon Roger, a fat boy of twelve, unable to contain his merriment or the porridge with which his mouth was filled, exploded over the table.

'Roger,' said his father sternly, 'if you wish to eat like a cannibal, you must eat elsewhere. Remove yourself from the table and finish your breakfast in the passage.'

'Well, Ralph made me laugh,' Roger grumbled.

'No, I didn't, you dirty liar,' said Ralph.

'Ralph,' interposed his father, 'if you cannot use decent language before your mother, you must leave the room too. Remove yourselves. It's a pity I cannot be at home all the time,' he said to his wife when his two sons had dragged themselves out of the room. 'Those boys require my supervision. That is one of the very reasons why I want to buy this little place in the country. I intend to make the country an influence in their lives. I intend to remove them from these urban surroundings by which at present they are contaminated. Ah, my little darling,' he exclaimed, turning to his daughter Phyllis, a fair-haired child of ten, 'come and kiss your poor old father who is going on a journey to get something for his little daughter – something that she'll never guess.'

'Oh, Mother,' said Phyllis, 'those greedy boys have eaten all the jam.'

'No, we haven't, you liar,' declared the two boys, putting their heads round the door to contradict the assertion.

'Great heavens,' Mr Waterall exclaimed, 'it is indeed high time something was done! But I cannot stop now to deal with Ralph and Roger as they should be dealt with. I have only just time to catch my train, as it is. Besides, I want to buy a new straw hat on my way to the station.'

Mr Waterall was a chartered accountant, the junior partner of an old-fashioned firm; but when he paused upon his front door steps on this fine September morning and looked first to the right and then to the left along Orange Road, Kensington, he felt some of the emotions that may have stirred the breasts of mundane conquerors on the threshold of their greatest victories. There really was in the length and straightness of Orange Road a hint of Rome, and Mr Waterall, who lived exactly midway between Uxbridge Road and Hammersmith Road, felt that he had contributed something to the personality of the thoroughfare by his habit of alternating every morning his route to the city between the green omnibus of Bayswater and the red omnibus of Hammersmith. And now to crown his civic valour, he was going to confer on Orange Road the dignity of a place in the country. Regarding the houses belonging to his nearest neighbours, he wondered with some complacency how many of them could boast of a rural annexe. At this moment a hansom-cab plying for hire came past at a walking pace, and Mr Waterall suddenly felt that the occasion could not be more fitly celebrated than by driving in a cab from Orange Road to Waterloo Station. Moreover, he should be able to stop at Heath's to buy himself that straw hat.

'Hansom!'

The cab pulled up.

'Waterloo. Stop on the way at Heath's,' said Mr Waterall grandly.

As with dignity he mounted the step of the hansom, Mr Waterall was sure that there was neither a blind nor a curtain in the adjacent houses that did not quiver with envy. It was Dr Johnson who said that if he had no reference to futurity he would spend his life driving briskly in a post-chaise with a pretty woman, and Mr Waterall might have said this morning that if he had no reference to the City he would spend his life driving briskly in a hansom-cab and never mind the company of women. What could the company of women add to his pleasure? Did his wife for instance appreciate what he was doing now? Had she ever appreciated what he was doing? Would she ever appreciate what he was doing? Never.

The hansom-cab gradually turned itself into a dog-cart with a high-stepping mare in front and two Dalmatian hounds behind. His crops were looking well; that field of oats in Kensington Gardens, that clover lea in Hyde Park were splendid; and what a magnificent head of pedigree shorthorns was his in Green Park. That bull should fetch at least five thousand guineas. Some American would buy him. Or should he keep Herefords? He remembered reading somewhere that in the Argentine Republic there was a great demand for Herefords. 'Mr Waterall's famous Galton herd of Herefords!' Or why not invent an entirely new breed? 'Black Waterall's!' Damn! That fool of a cabman had forgotten to stop at Heath's. The stockbreeder decided to say nothing about it, and while he was driving over Westminster Bridge he flung a March-brown and hooked the largest trout ever caught in that stream.

At the booking-office he was seized with an overwhelming temptation to travel first class; but he resisted this partly out of economy and partly out of prudence, inasmuch as it might give a false impression at Galton of his capacity for spending. One more extravagance, however, Mr Waterall did allow himself. He bought a copy of *Country Life*, which smelt very nearly as rich as the cushions of a first-class carriage.

It were idle to expatiate on the emotions Mr Waterall derived from the various aspects of nature beheld from the windows of the train on that fine September morning: they are emotions common to mankind; and they have been perfectly expressed by Keats in his ode to Autumn, and by Mr Pickwick when he was being trundled along in a wheelbarrow to watch the sportsmen after partridges. The train passed through Wimbledon and Surbiton, suburbs that Mr Waterall regarded with contemptuous compassion. To think that, if he had listened to his wife in the early days of

12

their married life, he might have bought a miserable little villa in a suburb and there existed content with one of those ridiculous back-gardens so painfully visible from the train. Instead he had insisted upon buying 315 Orange Road, and he was now on the verge of acquiring a place in the real country.

The train reached Weybridge, went on to Woking, passed the innumerable dead of Brookwood, trickled through Aldershot, and at Farnley acquired the authentic flavour of rusticity. The golfers, the river-excursionists, the soldiers returning from furlough, had alighted by now, and their places were occupied by farmers who pulled out of their pockets handfuls of corn or hops which they invited one another to smell and taste, even extending to Mr Waterall himself an invitation.

'That's some fine barley,' said one, offering a gnarled fistful to Mr Waterall who wondered what on earth he was to do with it. He accepted two grains as timidly as a chicken, chewed them very carefully, and pronounced them remarkable samples of barley.

'I am intensely interested in farming,' he said. 'Intensely interested. I never remember a finer sample of barley.' This was strictly true; he had never seen a sample of barley before.

'Travelling far, sir?' asked another farmer.

'To Galton.'

'Some fine land around Galton,' interjected a third.

'Ay,' said the man with the barley, 'there's good land round Galton, and there's bad land, some of it danged bad land, b'Job.'

'Ah,' the others grunted with slow headshakes.

'As a matter of fact,' said Mr Waterall, 'I am going down to look at a little property in the neighbourhood.'

'Farming?' asked one of his fellow travellers.

'A little,' said Mr Waterall.

'Stock?' inquired another.

'That was rather my idea,' said Mr Waterall.

'Well,' the man with the barley declared once more, 'there's some of the best land and some of the worst land around Galton. Some of the worst there is, and some of the best.' Then looking out of the window at the fields the train was passing, he went on; 'Now there's that there farm, for instance, which belonged to old Runciman. It looks good land. Is there anybody in this carriage as'll tell me that don't look good land?'

'It looks good land,' another agreed.

'And yet there's no land grows bigger rubbish in Hampshire. Poor old Runciman! He farmed it and farmed it and never grew nothing but rubbish on it till he up and died.'

'Ah!' ejaculated one.

'Eh!' ejaculated another.

'Ay!' ejaculated the man with the barley. And then he continued with a hoarse chuckle: 'Well, he won't grow no more rubbish where he is now.'

All his companions with delighted appreciation agreed that where he now was he undoubtedly would not grow any more rubbish; after which they returned to smelling each other's hops and tasting each other's barley.

'Real sons of the soil,' Mr Waterall assured himself fatuously. 'No false sentiment. A cockney would have elaborated that story about Runciman. But what is Runciman to them? A failure. A dead man who has failed to farm his land well. The bone and sinew of the country. That's what these fellows are.'

At the next station the farmers got out, and Mr Waterall was left alone in the carriage as far as his destination. He alighted on the pleasant little platform of Galton perfumed with lingering roses and gay with dahlias and other autumn flowers. He liked the friendly way, the almost personal way, in which the porter took his ticket; he liked to hear the greetings of people who had been intimate since childhood; and while he was half lost in a dream of sentimental self-congratulation, a tall cadaverous man with drooping grey moustaches and wild light blue eyes approached him to ask if he were Mr Waterall.

'Blackham is my name,' the newcomer announced.

'Mr Frederick Blackham, the owner of Canadian Cottage?'

'That's right. I've got a fly waiting for us. We're right out in the country, you know, at Oaktown.'

'The farther the better,' said Mr Waterall fervidly.

'And they charge half a crown,' Mr Blackham went on pensively. 'Say you give sixpence to the man: that makes three shillings.'

'And is not excessive, I think,' Mr Waterall opined with a judicial demeanour.

14

'Of course I usually walk myself,' said the owner. 'There are one or two short cuts I know of.'

'*I* hope to do a certain amount of walking as well. There must be some magnificent walks round here.'

'The finest in England,' affirmed Mr Blackham, who until the purchase money for Canadian Cottage was in his pocket did not intend to deny any amenity to the neighbourhood. 'Unfortunately I'm too much of an invalid myself to walk very far. Sometimes when I've walked into Galton I've been so exhausted that I've had to spend the whole afternoon in the Market Hotel instead of getting my business done. Perhaps we'd better stop at the Market Hotel now on our way out. I expect you'd like to meet the proprietress. Then when you come down here, all you'll have to do is to send a post-card and she'll know who you are. Mrs Camberley her name is.'

Mr Blackham leaned forward and tapped the driver of the fly on the fourth rib. The driver nodded his head without turning round. Shortly afterwards the fly pulled up at the Market Hotel. Mr Waterall, who was determined to be optimistic about everything, thought what an intelligent fellow the driver seemed.

'A most intelligent fellow,' he said to Mr Blackham. 'Don't you think we might send him out a pint?'

'Well, perhaps as you're a newcomer here, it mightn't be a bad thing,' Mr Blackham agreed. With this he raised one eyebrow to the driver, who said, 'Thank you, Mr Blackham, I don't mind if I do.'

Mr Blackham piloted Mr Waterall through a number of horsey-looking men who were buzzing in and out of the hotel like bees, and thrusting his long neck over the counter he whispered to the barmaid: 'Ask Mrs Camberley to give me a moment, there's a good girl.'

The landlady, a florid, crimped, upholstered woman of about forty-five graciously accepted the presentation of Mr Waterall, who, still in an optimistic mood, felt what a difference there was between the simple manners of the country and the critical suspicion of the town.

'Come to live down here, have you?' said Mrs Camberley graciously. 'I see.'

'I hope so,' said Mr Waterall. 'What is yours, Mr Blackham?'

Mr Blackham's was a double brandy neat.

'I cannot drink anything else,' he confided, 'on account of my complaint. You'd be surprised if I told you how many times His Royal Highness the Prince of Wales has said to me, "Blackham," he said, "there's only one thing for your complaint, and that's brandy, Blackham." Yes, I used to be one of His Royal H's couriers, and now here I am stuck down in this . . .'

Mr Blackham remembered himself in time and explained that he wasn't saying a word against Galton or its neighbourhood, which if you liked a quiet life was the finest neighbourhood in Great Britain. 'But you see, I've been used to getting about more. Royalty doesn't stand still, Mr Waterall. And I've been everywhere. But I mustn't stay here spinning yarns. Now, one moment. You see that man in the corner?' he whispered.

Mr Waterall gazed in the direction he indicated, and perceived a pale worried-looking man who was staring intently at the glass in front of him.

'That's a neighbour of mine, Edward Lightfoot. A splendid solicitor. He's just built himself a house at Oaktown. Would you like me to introduce him, supposing we do business together? He's a first-class lawyer who held a splendid position in Hampshire till his wife left him.'

Mr Waterall's optimism was not equal to echoing Mr Blackham's praise of Mr Lightfoot, whom he considered one of the dingiest individuals he had ever seen. At the same time, if Mr Blackham chose to employ him for the conveyance, it would be scarcely worth while calling in his own solicitor.

'Now look here,' said Mr Blackham, 'I have no manner of doubt in my mind at all that you are going to buy Canadian Cottage. I said to myself this morning as I walked into the station, "There's no manner of doubt that this gentleman's going to buy Canadian Cottage. What's more, he's going to jump at it. The moment he puts eyes on it, he's going to say to himself, 'This is what I've been looking for for years.' Well," I said to myself, I said, "what's the good of delay? I'll tell my friend Lightfoot to be about, and the sale can go right through this afternoon." Yes, that's what I said to myself.'

'I must admit,' allowed Mr Waterall, 'that I've come with my mind more than half made up.'

'I knew it,' Mr Blackham cried. 'In fact, I'm so certain

you are going to buy Canadian Cottage that if you said to me now right here, "Where's the sense in driving all that way to look at it, why not complete the purchase right here where we stand in the Market Hotel?" I shouldn't have the slightest hesitation in agreeing. I want you to have this place. I knew the moment you got out of the train this morning that you were the very man for it. You deserve to have Canadian Cottage. Mrs Camberley'll tell you, and Mr Lightfoot here'll tell you that there have been dozens of people who have gone down on their knees to me almost to sell them Canadian Cottage, and I've said to 'em "No, when I see the man, the right man, I shall know him. It's not a bit of use you coming out with me," I've said to 'em, "because I'm not going to sell it to you. *You* don't appreciate the country. *You* don't appreciate what you're getting." Isn't that right, Mr Lightfoot? Haven't I said that many a time in front of you?'

'You have, Mr Blackham,' the solicitor confirmed.

'Haven't I said that in front of you, Mrs Camberley?'

'Oh, go on with you,' said the hostess. 'I don't know what you haven't said in front of me.'

'Woman, lovely woman! However, don't let me force the place on you. Only this morning I said to myself, "Why should I sell it, why should I come down here and make the wilderness blossom like the rose, and then go and give it away to the first man who asks me for it?" And I wouldn't sell it if my wife liked the country better. But Mrs Blackham complains she's lonely. And it's no use keeping a woman in a place against her will.'

'Not a bit,' Mr Waterall agreed.

'So you're quite sure you'd like to take the trouble and drive out as far as Oaktown? Because if you don't want to come, I'm quite ready to do business here. You can be very comfortable at the Market Hotel for the whole afternoon if you like, and spare yourself any trouble as far as I'm concerned. That's one of the things the Prince of W. used to like about me. I never considered myself. If he wanted to go anywhere in a hurry I was off in front of him like an arrow from the bow. Whizz! Bang! There I was waiting for him when he arrived with everything ready, and I never remember he once went away without first saying to me, "Blackham," he'd say, "what you want for your complaint is brandy, Blackham." '

'Will you have another brandy now?' asked Mr Waterall anxiously.

'No,' said Mr Blackham firmly. 'No, by Gad, I won't touch a drop of brandy until the completion of the purchase. You might think I was cracking up my little home on brandy, Mr Waterall. I wouldn't like you to think that. I've been here now nine months which is a long time to be in any place, and I'm so fond of it that if I drank any more brandy I might turn obstinate. I might say, "No I'm damned if I sell. Get back to London and don't come down here disturbing our country peace and tempting me to destroy nine months' work." There's no knowing what I won't do on a drop of brandy.'

And then, as if to avoid further temptation Mr Blackham crammed his hat on his head and rushed out of the Market Hotel.

During the drive out from Galton to Mr Waterall's proposed estate, Mr Blackham explained the genesis of Oaktown.

'I want you,' he said, 'to imagine a farm of some hundreds of acres gone to seed. Thistles everywhere. Docks, brambles, groundsel, nettles. A man comes down here one day, sees this derelict farm, and asks who it belongs to. St Mary's College, Oxford, he's told. Does he hesitate? No. He goes up to Oxford, and he says "I'll give you £2,000 down for the Oak Farm, Galton, Hants," and he buys it, and he cuts it up into lots from a quarter of an acre to five acres or more if required, and the first man that answered his first advertisement was me, Frederick Blackham, ex-courier to His Royal Highness the Prince of Wales, and when he saw me he said to me, "You shall have the pick of the whole estate," he said. So I drove out with him the same as you're driving out with me now and I picked the finest quarter of an acre on the whole farm. Lots of 'em have come after me, but there's not one of them that hasn't said, "Blackham got the best plot." There's old Joe Gnathead and his beady-eyed wife opposite. They bought six acres and thought themselves clever and laughed at me with my quarter acre; but they bought their six acres on the wrong side of the road. They're in the shade till one o'clock. And that silly old juggins gave up a confectioner's business in Blackheath to come down to Galton and grow fruit on the wrong side of the road. You'll see him there every day digging and digging, but he'll never make any money at it. The Oak Farm Estate! But we don't call it that. We call it Oaktown, and we shall continue to send a deputation twice a year to the Rural District Council of Galton until we get the name Oaktown accepted. Oak Farm Estate! Anybody would think we were a lot of farm-labourers.'

'It certainly seems monstrous that colonists shouldn't be allowed to name the land they have colonized.'

'Mr Waterall, you're a sensible man: it *is* monstrous. Well, I shan't be here much longer, and you'll be taking my place in the dear old village, and I shall be glad to think wherever I am in the wide world that there's somebody down in Hampshire who is fighting for the rights of us all. You probably think I'm talking a great deal. I don't often talk like this. I haven't talked liked this since I left His Royal H. the P. of Wales. But there's something about you, Mr Waterall, which draws a man out. I suppose it's a kind of sympathy. I often think that sympathy's a very wonderful thing. Well, we shall soon be there. Splendid year for nuts. Look at them.'

Mr Waterall gazed eagerly out of the carriage at the hazel-hedges, between which they were jogging along.

'And those nuts, of course,' he said, 'are public property?'

'Anybody can go and pick those nuts,' Mr Blackham declared. 'If we like to stop the fly now and get down and pick a few mouthfuls of nuts, there's nobody to stop us. That's country life. You couldn't go into a greengrocer's shop in London and pick a handful of nuts, could you?'

'You certainly could not,' Mr Waterall agreed.

'I don't believe I shall be able to sell. I don't think I can bring myself to part with all this,' Mr Blackham sighed. 'I've been watching these nuts all the summer through. I'm a great lover of nature, Mr Waterall. But one touch of nature makes us wondrous kind, you know. And so in the end I suppose I shall let you have the little place.'

'I am a great lover of nature, too,' Mr Waterall announced.

The hedges were getting higher on both sides of the road, and presently without any warning that they were approaching a human settlement the fly pulled up before a white gate on which was painted in black Gothic letters CANADIAN COTTAGE.

19

CHAPTER TWO

MR WATERALL was disappointed by the first sight of Canadian Cottage, until he reminded himself that after all it answered exactly to the description in the advertisement and that it was ridiculous to expect anything more for £125. At the same time, he wished that Mr Blackham had not chosen cobalt blue as the colour for the woodwork and he wished that he had not chosen electric blue as the colour for the corrugated iron roof. His first impression was of a temporary stand erected at Putney to view the Oxford and Cambridge boat-race, and he perceived at once that many alterations would have to be made before his country estate took on even a remote resemblance to his dreams. He did not altogether like the effect of somebody's having left an old packing-case on a piece of waste land, which was the first impression Canadian Cottage made upon him. Mr Blackham probably recognized the traces of disappointment on Mr Waterall's countenance from his experience with other prospective purchasers.

'Beautiful little place, isn't it?' he exclaimed.

Mr Waterall qualified a hesitating agreement by thinking it seemed rather small.

'It is small,' Mr Blackham agreed. 'Which is what makes it so convenient. Seasoned pitch-pine outside. Match-boarding inside. And felt between. When I was building it, they said to me, "Do you want felt between? It's going to cost you more, but you're going to be glad you've had it." "What is the advantage of felt between?" I asked, for you'll probably have seen enough of me by now, Mr Waterall, to understand that I'm a man who wants value for his money. "What is the advantage of felt between?" I asked. "The advantage of felt between," they said, "is that you're warm in winter and cool in summer." And by Gad, sir, they were right. I want you to notice also that the outer walls are wood. That is another great advantage. There's a regulation here made by those pompous imbeciles of the Galton Rural District Council that no wooden buildings may be erected in their jurisdiction. But did I pay any attention to that regulation? I paid no attention whatever to it. What was the result? They threatened to prosecute me. I said, "I'm a poor man," and they made an exception in my favour. What is the result? The result is that if you buy Canadian Cottage, you'll be able to pat yourself on the back and boast that you've got the only cottage with wood inside and out for seven miles. But what do I see? I see Mrs Blackham beckoning us to say that dinner is on the table.'

Mrs Blackham was a small shy woman with a pale face and a receding chin, evidently frightened to death of her husband, and as Mr Waterall afterwards found out, with some cause, because it was his habit every Saturday night to chase her round the garden with a carving knife. On the present occasion, however, Mr Blackham was on his best behaviour, and beyond grinding his teeth at her once, when she passed the salt instead of the pepper to the guest, he seemed as proud of her as he was of his cottage.

'It's something to be able to invite a friend, if you'll pardon the familiarity, Mr Waterall. But the moment you got out of that railway carriage, I said to myself: "Blackham," I said, "there's a friend for you." It's something to invite a friend in to a bit of dinner and to be able to say that you've grown every vegetable on the table yourself.'

'It is, indeed,' Mr Waterall agreed.

'I don't want to boast, Mr Waterall, but I doubt if you've ever tasted finer peas than these.'

'I don't believe I ever have,' said Mr Waterall.

'And when you think I wasn't brought up as a gardener, you'll understand the quality of the soil here. Marl!'

'Oh, marl, is it?' said Mr Waterall, who had not the faintest idea what marl was. 'And your water?'

'Ah, now you've touched on one little inconvenience. At the moment there is no water. Owing to the dry season the water-butts are empty; but all we have to do is to walk a little way down the road and get all the water we want from the well belonging to the brickworks.'

'Are there brickworks here?' Mr Waterall asked, frowning.

'Well, there are and there aren't. They used to be very good brickworks about a hundred years ago, and I believe a fellow from London has bought them and is going to try again. But he is too far from the station. They'll never pay.'

The home-grown vegetables acted upon Mr Waterall's mind like magic herbs. As he sat over his dinner in this little wooden room, listening to the song of a robin in the hedge, to the buzz of bees and the distant lowing of cattle, he was filled with compassion for the myriads of toilers in the great city. He yearned to bring his family down here and to say to them, like God to Moses, that here was a land overflowing with milk and honey. The difficulty of obtaining water, the necessity for constructing a proper kitchen, the urgency of building at any rate one extra bedroom for the boys – all these drawbacks were swallowed as smoothly as the peas.

'There's no doubt,' he declared, 'no doubt whatever, that the only life is a country life.'

Mr Blackham was quick to observe his guest's frame of mind, and he chose that moment to clinch the favourable impression by taking him round the garden.

The garden of Canadian Cottage was a strip of land some eighty yards long and about twenty yards wide, full of diminutive fruit trees and plants and irregular rows of vegetables. But its principal feature was a kind of sentry-box half way up the slope.

'Is that a summer-house?' Mr Waterall inquired.

Mr Blackham leaned over and whispered something in his ear.

'Oh, I see,' said Mr Waterall rather embarrassed.

'You can, of course, put it nearer the cottage, if you like. Well, now, if you'll walk with me to the top of the garden, you'll get an idea of the lie of the land, and I can explain to you about some of your neighbours.'

'*My* neighbours?' repeated Mr Waterall quizzically.

'There I go again,' said Mr Blackham. 'Of course, I oughtn't to have said that, ought I? I ought to have said "*my* neighbours." But it's no use pretending I'm to be allowed to keep this place. I know you aren't going to let me go on living here. In fact I've already asked a friend of mine in Galton to cast his eye around for a couple of rooms in the town until I can look about me a bit and settle where I *am* going. But there's this complaint of mine. I suppose I ought not to talk in this way, but do you know into whose pockets the purchase money for Canadian Cottage is going? Into the pockets of doctors. You know, I've taken such a fancy to you, Mr Waterall, that if I hadn't got to have a serious operation I should *give* you Canadian Cottage; I wouldn't take a halfpenny for it. Do you think I haven't been watching you hard all through dinner? Do you think

I didn't observe the beautiful way those peas were going down your throat while they were sticking in mine like pills?'

Overcome by emotion, Mr Blackham paused for a moment, took a large bandanna handkerchief out of his pocket and dabbed his eyes.

'The pioneer of Oaktown – yes, that's what they call me. I had reckoned on spending my old age here. I had reckoned to have people come and look at me and nudge one another and say, "There's the man as made Oaktown!" You're a younger man than me,' Mr Blackham continued, 'and I hope when fifty years from now you stand where we're standing now and look around at the beautiful gardens and houses of Oaktown – I hope you'll think of poor old Blackham as the pioneer. But I mustn't talk about myself any more. You know what I'm feeling. If I was to say you were feeling what I'm feeling, I wouldn't be indulging in exaggeration.'

By this time they had reached the top of the garden whence Mr Waterall could observe the view. He saw a distance of blue woods and hills, a middle distance of glittering stubble backed by woodland, and in the foreground the first habitations of the Oak Farm Estate.

'Now then,' Mr Blackham began jocularly, 'let's give you a bit of a lesson in geography, as my poor old father often used to say to me. And he'd give me such a slosh on the jaw if ever I went wrong over as much as a cape. Well, it did me good, for many's the time His Royal Highness has said to me, "Blackham," he's said, "I believe there's nobody can catch you out over geography. If ever a man had the bump of locality, I'm bothered if you haven't got it, Blackham," he's said. And then if I thought His Royal H. was in the mood for a joke, I'd tell him it was the bump I got from being thumped over geography by my poor old father. Now then, if you'll turn to the left, you'll find yourself on the Basing road. If you turn to the right, you'll come to the village of Medworth about two miles farther on. But what's the good of me telling you about Basing and Medworth? I know perfectly well that when you're the owner of Canadian Cottage you're never going to Basing or Medworth.'

'But I am very interested in the lie of the country,' said Mr Waterall encouragingly.

'You'll hop into the fly at Galton,' proceeded Mr Black-ham, 'and you'll drive out here for half a crown which with sixpence for the man will make three shillings, and you'll hop out of your boots and hop into your slippers, and you'll hop up here where we're standing now and smoke your pipe of an afternoon and you'll say, "This is mine." Yes, you'll have your roses and your marrows and your plums. Don't forget that in about ten years from now this is going to be an orchard. There's the beauty of living in the country. You're always living in the future, as you might say. All the nasty little worries of the present fade away in the country, thinking about the future. Now, if you'll take my advice, the first thing you'll do when we get back to Galton tonight and the legal business is all fixed up – the first thing you'll do is to buy the plot on each side of you. Then you won't be overlooked.'

'Well, to tell you the truth,' said Mr Waterall, 'I hadn't thought of taking so much land as that.'

'I know you hadn't,' said Mr Blackham, 'but I'm advising you for your own good. You'll want a bit of land on each side. Well, you can have the half acre on the left for £80 and you can have the quarter on the right for £40. The men who own these plots are waiting for you in Galton now. What would it mean? £120! £125 for Canadian Cottage. £245. Legal expenses say £15–£260. Fly, three shillings. For £260 3s. od. you can go up to any man on earth and snap your fingers in his face. Now then, I suppose I ought to explain some of your neighbours. You see that small shanty over there?' he asked pointing to the left. 'That belongs to the Chilcotts. Their father's a minister of the Reformed Children of Israel. Fine old boy. He set up his two sons with a bit of capital, and they're poultry farming. Up be-yond them, there's the big stucco house of Lightfoot, the lawyer I introduced you to in the Market Hotel. He wants to sell. There's about twelve acres goes with that though. And then there's four plots of land between you and the Chilcotts; then comes the bit of land you're going to buy; then there's you; then there's the other bit of land you're going to buy; then there's a bit of land belonging to a fellow called Hobday. He's going to open a grocer's shop when he can raise the money to build one. That's going to prove convenient, you know. The other side of the road is old Gnathead who I told you about. Next to Hobday on the other side there's old Poley. He used to be a butcher at Maidstone until he came to grief, and he's living here on what's left. Beyond him, there's Floral Nook. A man called Paterson lives there, who used to be a tax collector in Trinidad. And so it goes on for a mile or more. In some places you'll find gardens without houses, and then again you'll find houses without gardens. One man's only got a gate. He put up this gate with Elizabeth Place upon it, and he hasn't been seen since. But it's no good me telling you about everybody. You'll find them out for yourself. There's only one thing, I will say: Beware of the blessed lot!'

Had not Mr Waterall already made up his mind to become the owner of a little place in the country, he might have been deterred by the menace of this warning. As it was, he paid but small attention to it, and before he went back to town that afternoon, the transfer of the property had been completed.

'I suppose,' said Mr Blackham, as he stood outside the compartment of which Mr Waterall majestically occupied a corner with the *Farmer and Stockbreeder,* 'I suppose you have no objection to my cutting a few vegetables until I'm able to move out?'

Mr Waterall had the greatest objection to Mr Blackham's doing anything of the kind; but he did not like to appear stingy, and he begged him heartily to cut as many as he liked.

'I shall get down next week-end,' he announced, 'with my wife and little daughter. You have no children, I believe, Mr Blackham?'

Mr Blackham applied the large bandanna handkerchief to one eye.

'Ah, if things had happened otherwise,' he said, 'you wouldn't ever have had Canadian Cottage, Mr Waterall.'

'Children add greatly to the pleasure of life,' said the new proprietor. 'My own little daughter is an unfailing source of gratification. Last week she was head of her class in history.'

'Was she indeed? She must be a sharp child,' said Mr Blackham.

'She is a very industrious child,' said Mr Waterall. 'A real little worker.'

The guard gave the signal; the train moved forward. Mr Waterall, torn like Cincinnatus from the plough, settled down to read his agricultural paper, while Mr Blackham went back to cut as many vegetables as he could before next Saturday.

Mr Waterall arrived home at about eight o'clock. When he was walking along from the station to his house, he felt an overwhelming compassion for the toilers of the great city who must depend on greengrocers for their greenery. He thrilled with paternal pride to think how his children in years to come would look back with gratitude to this day. He saw himself in the old place as an old, old man sitting beneath the shade of the spreading chestnut tree he intended to plant this very autumn, sitting there surrounded by his children and grandchildren, and even a few great-grandchildren.

'The old place,' he repeated aloud.

He thought how delightful it was going to be on Monday morning when he went down to the office to tell his partner of his enterprise, to tell old Wickham, who had been bragging for two years about his detached house and acre of grounds at Wimbledon, who had flaunted gardening-papers and poultry-papers and behaved as though Wimbledon were the Dukeries.

'Tonight,' thought Mr Waterall, 'we will choose a name for the little place, for it obviously cannot go on being called Canadian Cottage.'

Upon this anticipation of a pleasant evening to wind up a wonderful day Mr Waterall reached the steps of his own front door.

'Poor old house,' he apostrophized sentimentally. 'Poor old house of which I was once so proud, how dingy you look! But why the deuce have they got all that gas burning upstairs? How extraordinarily careless of Mary to let the maids waste gas in that way! And why is there no light in the front hall?'

While he was fumbling irritably with his latchkey, an upper window went up and his wife's voice asked: 'Is that you, Robert?'

'Of course it's me,' said Mr Waterall. 'Who did you think it would be?'

'Don't go in. Don't open the door.'

'What do you mean, don't go in? Do you suppose I'm going to stay out here all night?'

'Please don't go in, Robert. It's in the hall.'

26

Mr Waterall wondered if the excitement of a house in the country had turned his family's heads, and he addressed himself more sternly to the task of opening the front door.

'Robert!' screamed his wife in accents of such emotional intensity that Mr Waterall forgot his irritation and drew back in alarm. 'I entreat you, Robert, not to go in. It's the dog.'

'Dog? What dog?'

'The dog you told us to get at the Battersea Dogs' Home. We've had to stay up here since five o'clock. That is why it's all so dark. Cook is waiting in the kitchen till her young man comes, and when he does, she's going to whistle up to me and tell him to fetch a policeman.'

'What is the matter with the dog?' demanded Mr Waterall. 'Has it bitten anybody?'

'Only your hats and coats, dear, which were hanging in the hall,' said Mrs Waterall. 'While he was doing that, we all hurried upstairs. I thought you'd rather lose a hat than have any unpleasantness with the maids.'

'Where are Ralph and Roger? A fine help they'll be to their poor father in the country, if they're going to be frightened by the first stray dog they meet.'

'Ralph and Roger have been very brave,' the distracted mother declared, 'but I had to stop them.'

'Stop them from what?'

'Stop them from pouring water down on the dog. We found it really didn't do any good, and it was making such a mess of the hall.'

'It's a most extraordinary thing,' said Mr Waterall, 'that I cannot go away for an afternoon without coming back to find my house turned into a bear-garden. It's most discouraging. I come home to tell you all about my day in the country. I arrive back tired and hungry to find one half of the house lit up like a Jubilee procession and the other half as dark as a coal-hole. And finally I'm forbidden to come into my own front door. Where is this dog?'

'In the hall, dear.'

'Well, who put him in the hall?'

'He put himself there,' said Mrs Waterall.

'Why was he ever unchained? He must have been on the chain when you brought him back.'

'Yes, but he wound the chain round poor little Phyllis, and Roger had to let go or he'd have broken her leg. Then he attacked Dodsworth, and when we all ran upstairs, he stood on the mat at the bottom and growled at us, and if anybody moved on the landing above, he'd run half-way up the stairs making the most dreadful noises. If you'd seen the way he tore your coat to pieces, I'm sure you'd agree it wasn't safe to let him come near any of us.'

'Where's Ralph?'

'Here he is, dear, with me.'

'Ralph,' said his father angrily, 'what have you and Roger been doing to that dog? Now don't prevaricate, my boy. I am determined to know the truth.'

'Oh, of course we get the blame,' Ralph grumbled in a whisper to his brother.

'When I do get in,' Mr Waterall went on, 'I shall probe this business to the bottom, and if I find that either of you boys have been monkeying with the dog you'll go straight to a boarding-school next term. Dogs don't behave like that if they're not badgered.'

Mr Waterall wished that he could muster up enough courage to open the door, march into the hall, soothe the dog with appropriate flattery or intimidate it with suitable threats, and thus establish himself for ever in the eyes of his family as a hero. He rattled the handle of the front door to try the effect of the noise; but the answering growl on the other side did not encourage him to proceed.

'If you had any sense,' he said to his wife, 'you would have whistled down to cook and told her to go to the Dogs' Home and insist on their sending one of the keepers to remove the animal. It's monstrous that an institution like that which only exists by charity should be allowed to sell ferocious brutes to their customers. Look at the ridiculous position in which I'm placed. I suppose I shall have to go in by the back door and spend the rest of my evening in the kitchen. How much did you pay for the dog?'

'Only ten shillings, dear. You said an Airedale, and it was the only Airedale for sale.'

'I said an Airedale, yes,' Mr Waterall agreed. 'But I naturally assumed that you would be guided in your choice by the animal's suitability. I didn't ask you to go to the Zoo, did I? I didn't ask for a lion or a wolf, did I?' he inquired with elaborate sarcasm. 'However, this nonsense must come to an end. Dog or no dog, I am not going to be kept out of my own house any longer.'

In the desperation of extreme irritability Mr Waterall turned the key in the lock, and flinging open the door shouted, 'Lie down, you mangy brute!'

A dark form rushed past him in the gloom. A few moments later the clank of the heavy chain the dog was dragging behind him was lost in the murmurous darkness of the London night.

'Perfectly simple, you see,' said Mr Waterall. 'I wonder why one of you couldn't have done that? However, it was absurd to buy a full-grown dog like that. We must get a puppy and train it ourselves. And now for goodness' sake, hurry up and get my dinner. I am worn out by my day in the country.'

'As I grow older,' Mr Waterall thought to himself just before falling asleep, 'as I grow older I am beginning to realize that there *is* something in palmistry after all. That woman who told me that I required an emergency to bring out my best qualities was perfectly right. The situation with which I was faced required lightning judgement.' He turned over and nudged his wife. 'I think I shall get a bloodhound,' he announced. 'I realize now what I have never realized before, that I have got a natural instinct for dealing with dogs.'

CHAPTER THREE

WHEN the irritation of Sunday morning had evaporated in the odour of hot roast beef, Mr Waterall gathered his family round his cigar, which was the focus of their family life, and invited suggestions for a name that might replace Canadian Cottage.

'What is your own suggestion, dear?' asked his wife.

'Well,' said Mr Waterall with considerable complacency, 'I flatter myself that this time I have really hit it.'

Mrs Waterall hastily assumed from the conjugal make-up box an expression of acute conjugal interest.

'I knew Father would think of something clever,' she exclaimed, turning to the two boys with entreaty in her eyes. The two boys were winking at each other behind their father's back and, as Mrs Waterall divined, forming an alliance to oppose any name he suggested.

'I think,' repeated Mr Waterall, looking modestly at the long ash of his cigar, 'I think that this time your poor old father has hit it.'

Ralph and Roger glared at the floor; the chosen name might exceed their gloomiest apprehensions. When their father prefaced himself as 'poor' or 'old', bitter experience had taught them that it was the inevitable prelude of paternal behaviour that would expose them to the ridicule of their friends. They waited in despair.

'Yes,' said Mr Waterall, 'I hardly think that my name can be improved upon.'

'They're all longing to hear it, dear,' said his wife, trying to prevent her husband's perceiving that she was patting the knee of her eldest son to implore his enthusiasm for the revelation.

'It is such a splendid name,' Mr Waterall went on, 'that I've a very good mind not to tell any of you what it is until you see it on the gate.'

Ralph and Roger sat in sullen determination not to gratify their father by the least glimpse of inquisitiveness, and poor Mrs Waterall in growing distress plucked at her daughter's pinafore. The little traitress, condemned later in the day to pay the penalty of her base toadyism, tripped forward with an affectation that set her brothers' teeth on edge, threw her arms round her father's neck, and said:

'Oh, Daddy dear, don't keep us waiting any longer for your lovely name.'

'Well, my little pet,' said Mr Waterall, while Ralph and Roger ground their teeth, 'since *you* ask me, I'll tell you.'

Mrs Waterall had by this time managed to seize with her left hand her elder son's right and with her right hand her younger son's left, so that while the assembled family awaited the revelation, their attitude resembled that of people about to play a parlour-game, or cross an Alpine ledge.

'But before I tell you my name,' said Mr Waterall, who was determined to wring the last drop of satisfaction from the orange of his complacency, 'before I tell you my name, let me hear some of your suggestions.'

'Look out, Mother, you're hurting my finger with your rings,' Roger grumbled.

'Roger,' his father demanded severely, 'how many times have I told you not to speak to your mother in that manner? If you're not very careful, my boy, you'll be sent out of the room.' Mr Waterall was going to add 'and never hear the name I have chosen for the cottage.' But he realized on second thoughts that in order to carry out his threat he would have to abandon his choice, and he substituted, 'If you're not very careful, you'll be sent to a boarding-school.'

'I saw a nice name, Daddy, the other day,' Phyllis gurgled.

'Did you, my little honeypot? What name did you see?' The two boys writhed in disgust.

'When Mother took me to see cousin Gilbert, I saw a house called Glorinda House. Don't you think that's a nice name, Daddy?'

'A beautiful name, my little pussy-cat. But not so good as your poor old daddy's.'

'Glorinda House,' sneered Ralph. 'I call that a stinking name.'

'Ralph, have I or have I not forbidden you to use that detestable epithet in the presence of your mother and sister? Look here, my boy,' he went on, seizing his younger son, 'if you laugh when I'm talking to your brother, you'll find yourself in a very unpleasant position.'

Mrs Waterall had aged about ten years since her husband had proposed this assembly to choose the name of the cottage, and now with a convulsive clutch of their hands she begged her sons to be pleasant for her sake.

'Do not waste your time on such ungrateful little savages,' Mr Waterall advised.

'Well, you keep us waiting such a long time,' said Ralph, whose heart, though he would never have admitted it, had been touched by his mother's appeal and who thus, awkwardly, for her sake, tried to express an interest in their father's announcement.

Mr Waterall coughed heraldically.

'As I was coming back from Galton yesterday afternoon, I saw a book at the station bookstall called *Dream Days*. Very well, then, in future Canadian Cottage shall be known as "Dream Days".'

'How clever of Father!' Mrs Waterall rhapsodized.

'Isn't Father clever? Isn't he clever?' echoed Phyllis. 'I think Dream Days is a lovely name.'

Ralph and Roger gazed at each other in horrified incredulity. They had expected their father to choose a ridiculous name; but their gloomiest anticipations had not foreshadowed anything so ridiculous as 'Dream Days'.

'What will all our friends say?' Ralph gasped.

'What will all your friends say?' repeated his father. 'If any of your friends are ever lucky enough to be invited to Dream Days, you may depend upon it from me, my boy, that they'll be wishing that they had fathers like yours. Have you no appreciation of what I am doing for you? Do you suppose I am buying this place for my own pleasure? Do you think I went toiling down into the country to amuse myself yesterday? You fancy you're so very clever, but the only thing I've asked you to do so far was to get a dog, and that wasn't very successful, was it? You couldn't even manage to keep your dog long enough to give it a name. Well, inasmuch as you and your brother are so contemptuous of your father's present to you, you shall neither of you see it till November. I had intended to take you both down there next week-end. I shall take Phyllis instead.'

'Oh, thank you, Daddy,' cried Phyllis, dancing in exaggerated gratitude and clapping her hands. Her brothers would have thrown her out of the window, had they dared.

Being unable to do this, they went upstairs and threw one of her dolls out of the window.

Mr Waterall was secretly rather glad of an excuse for not taking either of his sons to Oaktown. The problem of accommodating himself, two sons, and a daughter in two rooms and an out-house taxed even his optimism.

'The best thing to do,' he told his wife that night, 'will be for me to take you and Phyllis down there on Friday evening, and for you and her to stay there until the extra room for the boys is built. It'll do her no harm to be away from school for a week or two. I drew out a rough sketch in the train for what I want. The place requires repainting for one thing. At present it's bright blue. I rather thought of painting it white with black lines to simulate old English woodwork. The roof can be painted the colour of tiles. You'll find it a bit uncomfortable at first; but by the time the boys get their November exeat and we all go down for two or three days we shall be quite comfortable.'

On Friday, therefore, Mr Waterall introduced his wife and daughter to the cottage.

'We will buy our furniture locally,' he proclaimed. 'It will cost very little more and will create a good impression in the neighbourhood. You and Phyllis won't require much at first, and I shall look out in town for any picturesque bits of furniture to supplement what we buy in Galton.'

The first picturesque bit of furniture that Mr Waterall discovered was a Toggenberg nannygoat which was guaranteed milkable by a little girl of ten. With the goat he sent the following letter to his daughter:

> 315 *Orange Road,*
> *Kensington, W.*
> *October 2nd.*

My dear little Dairymaid,

I am so glad to hear from Mother that you are being such a help in getting Dream Days comfortable for Daddy. I have just bought you a beautiful little goat, so that when Daddy arrives in November you'll be able to give him your own milk. For the present the goat can be put in the out-house. It will eat anything, I am told.

> *Your loving Daddy.*

Will you tell Mother from me that the chalk from the well must be carried away and the price contracted for. I

*am going down to a nursery to order some plants for
November planting, and I cannot have the whole garden
covered with chalk.*

Three days later Mr Waterall received a long letter from
his wife:

> *Dream Days,
> Oaktown, Galton,
> Hants.
> October 5th.*

My dearest Robert,

    *Phyllis and I were both delighted to hear of the arrival
of the goat, and we both agreed how sweet it was of you to
think of such a nice present. It seems ungracious to grumble
in any way when you are so thoughtful and are doing so
much for all our comfort and happiness, but I think, dear,
that perhaps it would be better if you superintended the
arrival of any more animals yourself. Probably the goat
was excited by the railway journey – at least that is the
explanation that all the neighbours give. They have been
most kind, although it has been rather destructive. I know
that you warned us it would eat anything, but we somehow
didn't expect that it would eat one of Mrs Gnathead's hats.
She has been most kind about it, and assured me that it was
an old hat and didn't matter, but of course I considered it
necessary to go into Galton and buy her a new one, with
which she is delighted, I am glad to say.*

    *Poor little Phyllis is going to write to you when she is out
of bed. It is nothing to be alarmed about, as the men had
not got very far with digging the well, and so she only fell
about seven feet. I expect it was entirely Phyllis's fault,
but you mustn't blame her, as of course she doesn't know
much about milking yet. The two young Chilcotts who have
the poultry farm at the corner have most kindly taken
charge of the goat till you come down. They are both very
nice young men, and dear Ralph and Roger are sure to like
them extremely. But please don't tell Ralph and Roger this,
because they are a little inclined to be contradictory. Since
being with the Chilcotts the goat has apparently gone dry,
but please don't allude to this when you next write to
Phyllis, as I think it might put ideas in her head. The boys'
room is getting on splendidly, and Mr Donkin the builder*

*thinks that your idea of two wooden bunks instead of beds
is admirable. You are always so clever, dear, I wonder where
you get your ideas from. Unfortunately your idea of having
a spring worked from our room by which you would be
able to empty the boys out of bed in the morning would
cost too much, Mr Donkin says, and down here in this
beautiful country air I am sure they both will make an
effort to be punctual for breakfast in the morning. They
are carting the chalk away, as you said. I shall be glad
when this well is finished, as I find it very tiring to carry
a bucket of water for half a mile from the brickworks. Mr
Blackham was very pathetic about that small easy chair
you sent down. He said it was the only comfortable chair
he had ever known, and as the poor man is really ill, I
thought you wouldn't mind my lending it to him until he
can buy one for himself. He's been most helpful and has
shown me how to cut the vegetables. I think we shall have
to have the kitchen strengthened rather. The rain was so
heavy last week that it actually put the kitchen fire out.
Mr Blackham tells me that it was never intended to be
anything but a temporary erection, and I have authorized
Mr Donkin to put in a new roof, a new floor, and some
sides. I know you've been put to great expense in order to
give us pleasure, so I want you to let me pay for the new
kitchen out of my own little hoard. The painting has been
rather interfered with by the weather, but Mr Donkin
assures me it will be finished by November. Phyllis and I
are very excited to hear of plants being bought. Dear little
child, she's been so patient about her bruises and made
so light of them that when she heard about the plants she
whispered to me: 'Do you think Daddy will buy me a
mulberry bush?' I don't know whether there is such a thing
as a mulberry bush to be bought, but if there is, I know
Phyllis will appreciate one. I hope the boys are being good
and are showing some appreciation of your kindness to
them. I am really glad that they have this opportunity of
getting to know you a little better. I always felt that perhaps in my desire to keep the peace I have often unneces-
sarily irritated both you and them. I am so sorry that for a
week you have had no letters from me. I find that I posted
them by mistake in a small letter-box which the Chilcotts
put up on their gate to save the postman trouble. As they
weren't expecting any letters, they didn't open this box for*

a week, which explains why you didn't hear from me. I have only spoken so far to our immediate neighbours, Mr and Mrs Gnathead opposite, and the two Chilcott young men. I thought it wiser to wait until you came down and could give me your advice about some of the people here who seem a little odd. There's a certain Lieutenant Green, formerly in the Royal Navy, who seems to drink rather heavily. I met him the other night just after dusk accompanied by seven fox-terriers, but luckily his housekeeper, a Mrs Rellie, appeared and I was spared any further annoyance. Mr Lightfoot the solicitor has sold his house to some people called Gateacre who have not arrived yet. Mr Lightfoot himself they tell me has left rather suddenly for South America. I believe there has been a little unpleasantness. Some people even say that his wife doesn't know where he is, but of course in a country place one must make every allowance for gossip.

Phyllis and I never do anything or say anything without thinking about you. Thank you again, dear, for the great pleasure you've given us.

Your loving

Wife.

Mr Waterall was much moved when he heard of the accident to his little daughter, and in order to console her, lost no time in sending her a canary about whose temper he made the most careful inquiries beforehand. Even this attempt to purchase live stock was a failure, for a railway porter took a fancy to the bird, and only an empty cage arrived at Galton, which kicked about the house until Ralph and Roger tried to keep bats in it. To his wife, in order to mark his appreciation of her action about the kitchen, he sent a small stained-glass window with the arms of some noble family, with which he proposed to shut out from the dining-room the horrid intimacies round the kitchen door.

The boys were inclined to regard Oak, as their father insisted on calling it in distinction to the Oak Farm Estate or Oaktown, as an Eldorado or Utopia. Sometimes they openly doubted its existence and supposed it to be a device to give their sister a holiday which she didn't deserve and which could only make her, when she came home, more affected than ever. In the eyes of Ralph and Roger nine-tenths of the life of Phyllis was spent in acquiring new affectations, of manner, speech, thought, behaviour, feeling, and gesture. Their own lives were one long crusade to combat this affectation. Anything that encouraged her affectation was deplorable, and this removal to the country might mean the undoing of the labour of years. When their father told them of Phyllis being butted into the well by the goat, they even found that that was an affectation. When they heard she was lying in bed severely bruised, they expressed doubt, alleging that Phyllis was notorious for exaggerating the effect of the slightest knock.

At last, however, the slow hours of school crawled into November, and exhausted by seven weeks of consecutive work, Ralph at St. James's, Roger at Randell's, the Preparatory School, broke up for the November exeat. They were to go down by train on Thursday evening, and they would not get back till the following Tuesday morning. Before they went to school in the afternoon, their father told them to hurry back and not to dally about, as though they wanted to dally about. Their mother had sent minute instructions what they were to wear and what Dodsworth was to pack for them. Roger was to be sure to help with the packing when he got back from Randell's soon after four so that Father was not kept waiting. At eight minutes past five, Ralph having made a record journey from school arrived home in that state of elation which is proper to the vigil of a holiday however short. He was met in the hall by his brother with – as far as it is possible to apply the adjective to one so fat – a long face.

'What's the matter?' Ralph asked anxiously. 'Aren't we going?'

'It's Father.'

'Isn't he going to take us?'

'Oh, Ralph, he looks the most frightful ass. You've no idea what clothes he's got on, and he's as cocky of them as anything.'

At this moment Mr Waterall, attired in a brown Norfolk suit and box-cloth gaiters, appeared in the hall. Ralph groaned. His father's costume was even more conspicuous than Roger had led him to believe. Mercifully it was a dark wet afternoon, and under an overcoat, his father might not attract so much attention.

'Now, boys, don't stand mooning about like that. We've

37

only got a few minutes before we start. Have you got your things? You must carry your own bags, you know.'

'Aren't you going to put on a coat?' Ralph suggested, when a few minutes later they were mustered on the front door steps of the house in Orange Road.

'My coat's down at Oak.'

'Won't you catch cold?' Ralph asked.

'Catch cold? Good gracious me, one doesn't catch cold in the country.'

'Well, don't shout so much, Father,' Ralph replied. 'People are turning round to look at us.'

'Great heavens, you boys are more self-conscious than a pair of schoolgirls. What does it matter if people are turning round to stare? Let them stare!'

And then, just to put the seal upon his behaviour, their father began to sing:

> 'For to-night we'll merry, merry be,
> For to-night we'll merry, merry be,
> For to-night we'll merry, merry be,
> To-morrow we'll be sober.'

Mr Waterall was not content with song, but to the horror of his two sons he had no sooner reached the pavement than he began to trip and skip in the direction of the railway station like some dreadfully volatile and hideously demonstrative schoolgirl.

'People will think he's a lunatic,' said Ralph.

'We might pretend he wasn't with us,' suggested Roger.

'You ass, how can we do that when he buys the tickets?'

'Perhaps people won't think he's our governor anyway,' Roger theorized hopefully.

'You ass, nobody except a fellow's pater would show off like that,' said Ralph.

'An uncle might,' said Roger. 'I say, Ralph, look at him now!'

Mr Waterall had just bumped into a pillar-box on his capers and was filling the cup of his sons' humiliation to the brim by pretending it was a real person and bowing his apologies.

'I suppose,' said Ralph in the voice of one in whose mouth all worldly experience had turned to Dead Sea fruit, 'I suppose he thinks he's being funny.'

'I suppose he does,' Roger agreed tonelessly.

'I wonder why chaps' paters are such asses,' Ralph speculated. 'A chap in my class told me last week that his pater wears a hat like an organ-grinder. He's a journalist.'

'What's a journalist?'

'Fish and find out,' replied Ralph, who was in no mood to be pleasant to anybody and who was moreover not quite sure himself of the correct answer.

'Anyway, I know,' said Roger. 'So sucks to you!'

'What is it then?' Ralph challenged.

'Fish and find out,' Roger replied.

Upon this cheeky answer Ralph swung his bag and caught Roger behind the knees, almost upsetting him in the gutter. Roger thereupon swung his in a frontal attack and winded Ralph, after which they manœuvred round one another, waiting for an opportunity to give a knock-out blow. They might have continued like this for ten minutes, if from ahead in the November mist the voice of their father had not been heard yodelling:

"Boy-oys! Boy-oys! Tra-la-la-la-la li-hi-ti!'

Reunited by a sense of common danger the brothers hurried on to prevent their father's finding an excuse for even worse vocal excesses than he had hitherto committed.

'It's frightfully light by the station,' said Ralph in the hollow voice of despair.

'Well, anyway *we* don't look asses,' Roger proclaimed.

Without the menace of paternal eccentricity Ralph would have replied: 'Speak for yourself, you silly little fool!' As it was, he hailed with relief Roger's estimate of the total impression likely to be made on the minds of critical observers. He felt that the house of Waterall was saved from utter ignominy by the sane exterior of himself and his younger brother.

'I've got two ounces of rather decent fruit pastilles,' he announced gratefully.

'Have you? How decent! What flavour?'

'Greengage, lime and strawberry.'

Roger sighed voluptuously.

'And some cigs,' added Ralph, looking over his shoulders as Guy Fawkes may have looked over his in the cellars of Westminster Hall.

'What kind?' Roger whispered in awe.

'Guinea Gold.'

At this moment they heard their father asking the booking-office clerk for two returns to Galton.

'Two?' muttered Ralph.

'We're going as halves,' said Roger.

'Halves!' Ralph growled. 'Why even you ought to have a ticket to yourself. Well, I suppose if he gets run in, they'll let us go on with a ticket each. They won't run *us* in, I shouldn't think.'

To the guilty consciences of the two boys the ticket collector's eyes resembled augers. He really seemed to clip them at the same time as he clipped the tickets. However, he did not summon a policeman, and when they were seated in the train Ralph felt safe enough to remonstrate with his father on the risk he had run.

'Perhaps you'd like to get out right away and walk back?' Mr Waterall suggested with what went beyond sarcasm into foolishness, his sons felt, inasmuch as the train was in the middle of a tunnel. 'If you feel so nervous about travelling as a half-fare, no doubt you won't want to come any farther.'

'Well, I don't look under twelve,' Ralph protested.

'You'll look exactly what your father chooses you shall look,' Mr Waterall declared. 'And if you're going to suck sweets all the way down to Galton, you won't look like a boy at all by the time you arrive.'

'What shall I look like then?' Ralph challenged.

Mr Waterall had forgotten how to fend off an awkward question with the magical phrase, 'Fish and find out.'

'Never mind what you'll look like,' he said. 'And don't keep talking so much, I want to read the evening paper.'

'Do they think West Bromwich Albion will beat Aston Villa to-morrow?' Roger asked.

Mr Waterall glanced hurriedly at the leading article and said there was nothing about Aston Villa in the paper. Ralph doled out three fruit pastilles to his brother, and the two boys tried to peer over the edge of their father's paper to find out the prospects of to-morrow's football. They might at the expense of nothing worse than cricked necks have gradually acquired the information they wanted, if Roger in the excitement of catching sight of his favourite club, had not coughed out a greengage pastille on Mr Waterall's boot which he had to remove with his paper.

'If you two boys move another muscle,' he declared, 'you

shall spend your holiday in London. Haven't you had enough tea? What do you want to guzzle sweets for at this hour of the day? If I hadn't the patience of Job, I should get angry. What you want is a couple of babies' bottles. I was just going to let you try and find out about this wretched football match; but Roger has made my paper in such a loathsome mess that I must now throw it out of the window.'

However, when the agitation of changing trains at Clapham Junction had subsided and every minute was bringing him nearer his little place in the country, Mr Waterall's good humour returned.

'Seven o'clock,' he said. 'Well, Ralph, I'll try one of your sweets. Which do you recommend? Strawberry flavour? Haha! next year we shall be having our own strawberries.'

'Shall we be able to eat them?' Roger inquired tentatively.

'Eat them? Of course you'll be able to eat them,' Mr Waterall explained. 'What did you think you were going to do? Wash your hands with them?'

Both boys exploded with laughter, and their father who was not used to making successful jokes outside his own office expanded under the flattery of filial appreciation.

'I might even go so far as getting a pony, which you boys could learn to ride and drive.'

'That would be spiffing,' said Ralph.

'Fizzing,' Roger agreed.

'Will you try a greengage pastille?' Ralph asked politely. 'They're easier to chew than the strawberry- and lime-flavoured ones. The only other kind soft like that is black-currant, but I didn't get them because they're a bit like throat medicine.'

'So are raspberries soft,' said Roger.

'No, they aren't, you liar.'

'Yes, they are.'

'Not the penny an ounce ones. And the two ounces a penny aren't flavoured with real fruit. A chap in my class told me you've no idea what awful muck they put in them.' Then after a pause Ralph added solemnly: 'Chemicals.'

'Good lummy,' exclaimed his brother, impressed in spite of himself.

'Now don't start arguing,' said their father. 'When I was your age I had to be content with sticks of liquorice at eight

41

a penny, and what's more I had to make them last a week. But then of course I hadn't an indulgent father like you.'

In ordinary circumstances the two boys would have glowered at this, but the possibility of that pony made them tactful. Indeed they actually tried to look sympathetic over the legendary figure that was their grandfather. They continued to rule themselves for the rest of the journey, and by the time they alighted on the platform in the dampness of a November night, Mr Waterall was beginning to think that after all it was not a bad thing to be the owner of two growing boys. During the drive out to Oak he tried to call their attention to the features of the landscape; but owing to the fact that he did not remember them very clearly himself, that the blackness without was impenetrable to human vision, and that Roger on being bidden to look out of the window at the largest poplar in Hampshire was scratched on the nose by a bramble spray, the drive as an exposition of the beauties of the neighbourhood was not a success. At last the fly pulled up in front of Dream Days. Then the name was true, the boys realized. They exchanged a brief shudder at the sight of the Gothic letters on the white gate; but they were immediately distracted from their nausea by the appearance of their mother in the doorway, holding high a lamp and supported by Phyllis in what they censured as the most affected attitude even she had dared to assume.

'Look at Phyllis!' Roger growled hoarsely.

'I knew living in the country would make her more affected than ever,' said Ralph. 'I told you it would.'

Mr Waterall had finished exchanging rural civilities with the driver while he was looking for the supplementary sixpence, and was close behind his sons. They, with pony still in view, managed to refrain from hurling themselves upon their sister and forcing her to resume the normal attitude they would have demanded in London, while Mrs Waterall who had been mentally rehearsing for this moment all day, exclaimed or rather wished to exclaim, but actually whispered:

'Welcome to Dream Days!'

CHAPTER FOUR

'I'M afraid Phyllis and I have not been able to manage a very interesting supper for you to-night, dear,' Mrs Waterall apologized, when her husband and children sat round the table about half-past eight. 'But some important part of the chimney didn't arrive as Mr Donkin's men hoped it would, and so we may not be able to cook anything till Monday, except of course your shaving water. I mean to say we have the little Beatrice. The little oil-stove that is.'

'Never mind,' said her husband with the gracious acquiescence of an old patrician in simplicity. 'When in Rome we must do as Rome does. What have we?'

'This is a tinned tongue, dear,' Mrs Waterall told him, as she regarded nervously the large chilblain of preserved meat on an ungarnished dish.

'Good enough, good enough,' exclaimed paterfamilias, waving cheerily the carving knife and fork. 'We're as hungry as three hunters. Aren't we, you boys?'

Ralph and Roger, who were still clinging optimistically to the thought of that pony, made an effort to give enthusiastic assent by muttering, 'Oh rather!' but such weak truckling to paternal imbecility outraged their manliness, and they relapsed into a shamefaced silence.

'Come along now, don't moon,' their father went on. 'You, Ralph, get busy and cut some bread, and you Roger take these plates of tongue to your mother and sister. We've got to learn how to wait on ourselves down here. This is the simple life, you know. So let's see some of the old pioneer spirit.'

The two boys exchanged glances which inquired each of the other when, since they emerged from long clothes, they had ever not been expected to wait upon themselves. The result of this exchange was that Ralph narrowly escaped cutting off a large piece of his thumb with a slice of bread, and that Roger tripped over his own foot and shot three slabs of tongue into the bowl of tinned peaches and one into his mother's lap.

'Look here,' said their father sternly, 'if you two boys are going to behave like a couple of awkward bumpkins, you'll stay in London instead of coming down here and enjoying the simple life of the country. Take a fork, Roger, you booby, and don't start picking the tongue out of your mother's lap with your filthy fingers.'

'There's one slice on the floor,' Phyllis informed the world in that tone of self-satisfaction and superiority which her brothers found so intolerable.

'No, there isn't, you liar,' exclaimed Roger, turning round so quickly that he jabbed the fork into his mother's leg instead of into the tongue.

'Look here,' said Mr Waterall, 'once and for all I will not have these epithets bandied about at meals. Leave the room, Roger.'

But when Roger was preparing to withdraw with a stock of provisions into the kitchen, Mr Waterall remembered that the banishment of his sons would punish himself more than them, since he would be deprrived of their attendance for the rest of the meal, and he called Roger back.

The rest of the supper passed by to a long recitative by Phyllis in her most affected voice about the various excitements of life in the country during the autumn. Ralph and Roger, still clinging desperately as it were to the tail of that pony, managed to choke back the criticisms they longed to utter of their sister's self-importance, and contented themselves by scowling at her threats of stern disciplinary measures on the morrow.

'What on earth is the matter with you two boys?' their father asked. 'Aren't you enjoying yourselves down here?'

'Of course they're enjoying themselves, dear,' Mrs Waterall intervened anxiously.

Ralph and Roger sighed. Such discussions of their emotions in public always acutely embarrassed them. To them one of the mysteries of life was the way the feminine mind had to proclaim its feelings aloud. If Ralph was enjoying himself he showed it by pushing his brother over. If Roger was enjoying himself he showed it by shooting through a window from a catapult. The more intimate and exquisite the emotion, the more coarsely paradoxical should be the expression of it. But at this moment they were not enjoying themselves. At this moment they would have been glad to be back in London, celebrating the Fifth of November by pushing Dodsworth into the larder with half a dozen jumping crackers and listening to her screams mingled with the explosions inside. However, life in the country surely would not mean sitting eternally round a table passing slices of tinned tongue to their father, and anyway there would be no school until next Tuesday morning.

A pleasant interval in what threatened to be the monotonous oppression of rural existence was provided by the oil-stove.

'Can't I smell something burning?' Mr Waterall asked.

There was a brief silence while everybody sniffed the air.

'Phyllis, run and see if the lamp is smoking in the kitchen, darling.'

Phyllis rose primly from the table and opened the kitchen door.

'Oh, Mother, you can't see for smoke,' she cried, as a dark grey fog came sweeping out of the kitchen into the dining-room, the component smuts of which settled down on everything like aphides.

'Shut the door!' shouted Mr Waterall, flinging a napkin over the dank crimson of the tongue which was being heavily peppered with greasy black.

The two boys, secure of their innocence in this calamity, made the most of it by coughing and choking.

'Open the windows, you young idiots,' shouted their father; but when they advanced to do so their father shouted again, 'Turn down the stove first, you duffers.'

'Well, we can't do everything at once in this awful stink,' Ralph protested indignantly.

'Don't stop to argue with me when a lamp is smoking.'

'I'm not arguing,' Ralph called back over his shoulder, as he opened the window.

What his father would have replied was never to be known, because the moment the window was opened both curtains leapt forward into the room and wrapped themselves round him.

'Good heavens!' he exclaimed. 'We'll have the place blown inside out in a minute.'

'I didn't turn up the stove,' Phyllis announced virtuously.

'Yes, you did, you liar,' her brothers declared.

By this time Mr Waterall had disengaged himself from the curtains which were now lashing at the ceiling as waves lash at the foot of a cliff.

'Shut the window,' he commanded. 'I can't hear myself speak. Shut it, I say.'

'Well, you just told us to open it.'

'I told you to turn down the stove, you obstructive young vagabonds.'

Mrs Waterall, her face streaked like a peppermint bull's eye, emerged from the fog of the kitchen.

'The little Beatrice was smoking,' she explained. 'But I've turned it down now.'

At this moment Phyllis was heard to utter a piercing scream.

'There's a cow in the kitchen, Daddy,' she came rushing in to announce.

'A cow in the kitchen?' Mr Waterall repeated indignantly. 'But how can there be a cow in our kitchen, Phyllis? My little girl mustn't exaggerate like that.'

But Phyllis had not been exaggerating, for the cow arrived in the dining-room by the same door as herself, and it was now benevolently eyeing the company through the haze.

'Get out, you brute,' Mr Waterall shouted. 'Whose cow is this, Phyllis?'

But there was no answer from Phyllis, for she had retired into the bedroom with her mother, and they had locked the door behind them.

'Don't stand there staring at the brute. Put it out,' Mr Waterall commanded his sons.

The first missile that appealed to Ralph as suitable for an offensive was his father's cap which he picked up and threw at the cow. She tossed her head as it rebounded from her nose to the floor, and then bent down to see if it was worth eating.

'What are you playing at?' Mr Waterall asked. 'That's the only cap I've brought down here, and I don't want it eaten.'

'Well, cows don't eat caps,' Ralph protested.

'Look here, my boy, if you start arguing with me about the diet of cows back you'll go to London by the first train to-morrow morning.'

'Well, there wasn't anything else to throw,' said Ralph sullenly.

'There wasn't any need to throw anything at all. If you lose your heads at the sight of the first domestic animal you

46

see in the country you'll be the joke of the whole neighbourhood. You should keep perfectly cool, and the cow will recognize that you are used to dealing with cows.'

'Well you do it then,' Ralph challenged his father; and Mr Waterall braced himself for the demonstration.

'Get out, you brute,' he shouted, rushing across the room and waving his arms at the cow who merely eyed him with a mild and apparently still benevolent curiosity. 'This is getting a little ridiculous,' he declared. 'We can't spend the rest of the night, looking at a cow in a thorough draught.'

Perhaps the cow was beginning to feel the draught as keenly as Mr Waterall, for she turned round and retreated. There was a clatter of broken dishes as she upset the kitchen table with her haunches, and then a silence.

'Of course, as usual,' said Mr Waterall, 'I have to do everything. You two boys talk a great deal about your football and your cricket and what not, but when it comes to turning a cow out of the house it's your father who has to show you how to do it. The brute was dribbling all over my cap,' he added, as he stooped down indignantly to pick it up. Then he turned to the locked door of the bedroom. 'It's quite safe now,' he shouted to his wife and daughter. 'I've driven the brute off. But what I want to know is who left the kitchen door open?' he asked severely when they emerged.

'I'm afraid, dear, I can't have made it quite clear in my letters that there isn't a kitchen door yet. That's probably what made the lamp smoke.'

'No chimney, no kitchen door?' Mr Waterall exclaimed. 'What's been going on here for the last two months?'

'Mr Donkin has finished the boys' bedroom, and he hopes to finish the kitchen in another week. I didn't like to disappoint you, and I thought we could manage just for a few days,' said Mrs Waterall.

'But does this cow make a habit of coming in here?' her husband asked. 'Whose is it? Who does it belong to?'

'I think it belongs to the Chilcotts,' said Mrs Waterall 'They are the kind young men I told you about who took charge of the goat after poor little Phyllis's accident.'

'And because they have taken charge of a goat which you and Phyllis were evidently incapable of managing, that is no reason why they should expect us to feed their cow. I shall go and complain about its unpleasant behaviour tomorrow morning. There is nobody more bohemian than myself; but there is a limit to being free and easy. When people's cows start walking into dining-rooms at nine o'clock at night, it's time something was done about it. Now look here, you two boys, if I find you encouraging that brute, there'll be trouble. You may think it's very clever to stand there grinning like a couple of zanies. What are you both laughing at now?'

'I'm sure they're only smiling, dear, because they are both so happy at being down in the country,' Mrs. Waterall put in. 'And Robert, dear, I think you managed to get a little of the mustard in your hair.'

Mr Waterall clapped his hand to his head, and when it encountered the mustard to his obvious disgust, his two sons could contain themselves no longer, but gave way to loud laughter.

'I wish you boys would learn to appreciate real humour,' said their father. 'When you get something really worth laughing at you sit there like a couple of stuffed owls; but let something a little unpleasant happen and you'll hoot like a pair of Zulus. How on earth did all this mustard get into my hair?'

The rest of the evening passed away uneventfully except for a brief fracas between Ralph and Roger after they had gone to bed, because Ralph after choosing the lower bunk for himself decided ten minutes later that he would prefer the upper one. Roger, however, declined to move, and claimed that he had already been asleep.

'Well, if you don't move, I'll jolly well pull you out,' his brother threatened.

'You cad,' cried Roger, when Ralph seized his leg and began to pull. The struggle ended in both boys falling from the top bunk and only just missing the circular bath, after which they slept, this time Ralph above and Roger below.

CHAPTER FIVE

RALPH was the first awake in the dimness of a drenched November morning. From the top bunk he surveyed the minute kingdom belonging to his brother and himself. He gazed down into the cold shallows of the circular tin bath which occupied most of the floor space, and shuddered. He looked across to the door that communicated with the parental bedroom and scowled at the threat such proximity as this offered to the freedom for which his soul yearned. He gazed up at the wooden ceiling. A long insect with a quantity of legs emerged from a crack, ran rapidly across one of the matchboards, and disappeared down a crack on the other side. Ralph blinked. Perhaps he had made a mistake in choosing the upper bunk. When a large spider emerged from the farthest corner and started off on a tour of the ceiling Ralph was convinced that he had made a mistake. To-morrow night he should claim the privilege of the elder brother to sleep in the lower bunk. Looking round anxiously for the advance of insects from the rear, Ralph caught sight of a dark pulp upon his pillow. 'Good lumme!' his heart cried within his breast. He had actually been lying on a spider all night. In the violence of revulsion against such knowledge Ralph slung himself over the edge of the bunk, his right foot sinking up to the ankle in the fat cheeks of his sleeping brother, who uttered a bellow of alarm which stilled the snores of their father within and brought their mother fluttering out of bed to the door to ask if the Chilcotts' cow had got into the cottage again.

'It was only my foot slipping,' Ralph explained.

From the darkness of the parental bedroom the voice of Mr Waterall was heard threatening to send his sons back to London by the first train if they could not behave themselves.

'You put your stinking toe in my eye,' Roger grumbled.

Ralph had only just managed to save himself from the humiliation of confessing that he had been frightened out of his bunk by the thought of having overlaid a spider during the night, through perceiving in time that what he had supposed to be a spider was in fact a squashed fruit-gum

49

that his brother must have left behind in the struggle for the upper bunk.

'Serve you jolly well right, you cad,' said Ralph. 'You shouldn't leave your stinking tuck on my pillow. But pax now, because I put something of mine under your mattress, and I want to get it.'

Roger eyed his brother suspiciously.

'No you didn't, you liar.'

'I did. I left an air-gun there,' said Ralph.

'An air-gun?' Roger exclaimed in astonishment.

'Well, don't shout about it, you ass,' Ralph went on in a fierce whisper.

'Ha-ha! Very clever,' Roger jeered. 'You're just trying to make me get up.'

'No, I swear I'm not.'

There was something in Ralph's accents which half convinced a justly suspicious younger brother.

And sure enough when Roger evacuated his bunk and the mattress was lifted, the air-gun was revealed.

'I say, how *did* you get it, Ralph?' the younger boy asked, a note of such genuine reverence in his voice that Ralph's indignation at being disbelieved was mollified.

'I swapped two unused British Guianas, my ammonite's horn, and the bigger of the vertical engines. It was Hartfield's air-gun, and his governor said he'd got to get rid of it, because he shot their cook in the leg and she gave notice. It was a good swap,' Ralph concluded with simple pride, 'because the piston of that engine is bent, and I think one of the stamps may be a fudge.'

By this time Ralph had taken the air-gun from under the mattress and was stroking lovingly its nickel barrel. A respectful younger brother asked what he would shoot with it.

'Slugs.'

'Slugs?' Roger repeated in astonishment, for they struck him as poor game. 'Won't it kill birds?'

'Slugs are bullets, you ass! Of course, it'll kill birds. The chap who swapped it with Hartfield shot his kiddy sister's canary with it.'

'But how did you bring it down without Father's seeing it' Roger asked.

'I wrapped it up with those gardening tools he brought. Dodsworth helped, and she swore she wouldn't tell.'

'Can't you go out and shoot something with it now?' Roger suggested.

Ralph was genuinely touched by the recognition his brother's use of the second person implied.

'You can have a shot sometimes,' he offered.

'Thanks frightfully, Ralph. I say, I vote we dress and go out shooting before breakfast.'

Ralph looked down distastefully at the cold water in the circular bath.

'I'll slosh the water over on to the floor and you mop it up with the towel,' he suggested.

By the time the boys were supposed to have had their baths the floor of the diminutive room looked like the wallowing pool of a hippopotamus. Then they dressed themselves and climbed out of the window into the murk of the November morning. They walked up to the top of the narrow garden, gathering so much clay with every footstep that by the time they reached the northern boundary of Dream Days they could hardly lift their legs for the weight of it. To the left of them as they trudged up was the extra quarter of an acre which Mr Waterall had bought, to the right of them the extra half-acre. Both these plots had been dug over, but as yet they were unplanted and their present appearance added to the general air of desolation. Even on the bright September morning when Mr Waterall had been granted his first view of the Oak Farm Estate his impression had been of a piece of waste ground scattered with large packing-cases, and in the wet twilight of this November dawn when the rich woods that surrounded the derelict farm were almost invisible in mist the prospect was not so rural as the boys had been led to expect.

'I say, is this real country?' Roger asked doubtfully.

But Ralph did not answer. A chaffinch had just perched upon a clothes-prop ten yards away, and he levelled the airgun with a muttered demand for silence. He pulled the trigger. The bird flew away; but the slug was embedded in the wood just below where it had been sitting.

'It would have killed it,' Roger whispered in awe.

'Hartfield didn't say it stuck in their cook's leg, but perhaps it did,' Ralph said, gloating in the power of his new weapon.

A blackbird flew over and alighted for a moment on the bough of a young plum-tree. Ralph fired again, and a sharp

51

ping declared that the slug had hit the corrugated iron roof of their bedroom forty yards away.

'Even if one of those British Guianas wasn't a fudge, it was a jolly good swap,' Ralph decided.

'Can I have a shot?' his brother gulped.

'Shut up, shut up, you ass. I can see a rat. Don't move.'

Ralph fired. The rat leapt in the air and collapsed upon its side.

'You've killed it!' Roger shouted, and, their hearts beating with triumph, the two boys plunged down the muddy path to confirm the miracle. Yes, the rat was undoubtedly dead. Ralph prodded its light belly with a twig. It did not twitch. Roger pulled it along a few inches by the tail. It did not resist. Ralph pointed to an exquisite drop of blood above one eye. Roger discovered another which had trickled down to the tip of its nose.

'What a swizzle you can't eat rats,' Roger sighed. 'We might have cooked it for breakfast.'

The rain pouring mercilessly down upon the rat filled Roger with compassion for its carcass. He looked round for a place of shelter and noticed a cupboard with a door of perforated zinc hanging up beside the kitchen door. He picked up the rat by the tail to put it inside. This time the tail seemed to twitch with returning life, and in a sudden disgust he flung it inside and slammed the door.

Then Roger who had been exploring the high hazel-hedge which separated Dream Days from the road announced that it was absolutely packed with birds. So the two boys slid down the bank into the damp lane to avoid calling attention to themselves by opening the garden gate; and, turning to the left, they advanced cautiously to the slaughter. After firing off half a box of slugs without success they reached, about three hundred yards down, the spot where the road from Galton forked, the left-hand branch being the one along which they were walking, and the right-hand branch going up hill to disappear over an attractive slope under a grove of high beech trees. The wooded tongue of land that divided the two roads revealed the beginning of a carriage-drive beyond a massive gate of wrought iron slung between two stone pillars, each surmounted by a rusty cannon-ball. The rain had stopped, and the mossy drive was a-flutter with blackbirds, and thrushes hoicking worms out of the moist ground.

The two boys gazed covetously through the gate at this plenitude of game.

'I wonder who lives in there,' said Ralph. 'I've a jolly good mind to rest my gun on the gate and take a pot.'

'I say, but wouldn't that be poaching?' Roger objected.

But the notion of being a poacher was not unpleasant to Ralph. When he returned to school next week after the all too short November exeat and was asked by chaps what he had been doing, it might create a bit of a sensation to announce that he had spent most of the time poaching. And at that moment round the curve of the wooded drive a rabbit came lolloping slowly. The temptation was too strong. The rabbit had stopped and was actually sitting up. Ralph balanced the muzzle of his gun on the gate and took deliberate aim. Just before he pulled the trigger the rabbit plunged across the drive into the undergrowth, and Ralph fired wildly after it.

'What the blazes is that?' a hidden voice exclaimed.

Roger went very white and turning round ran as hard as he could in the opposite direction. Ralph went white too, but his gun was stuck in the scroll work of the gate and before his shaking hands could disentangle it a slim young man with florid freckled face and bright red hair appeared round the curve of the drive.

'Hi!' he shouted. 'You got me in the leg then.'

'I'm frightfully sorry,' Ralph quavered. 'I didn't mean to, I didn't really.'

'Who are you?'

'My name's Waterall.'

'Oh, you live down at Canadian Cottage. Let's see, you call it Dream Days now, don't you?'

Ralph blushed hotly.

'My governor called it that,' he explained apologetically.

'Who's the other kid that bolted?'

'That's my brother Roger.'

'Well, call him back. We won't eat him.'

'Thanks awfully,' said Ralph, who took this to mean that he was forgiven for that reckless shot. Then he shouted after his fugitive brother to come back. But Roger fancying that the cries betokened the arrest of Ralph put his head down and ran faster in the opposite direction.

'I think he must have bunked,' said Ralph.

'Well, come on in and have a cup of cocoa in the shack

53

and meet my brother Micha. We're looking after your sister's savage goat. You were properly had over that goat.'

'It was my governor who bought it,' said Ralph. He was most anxious to dissociate himself from all his father's activities, which were evidently as foolish as he had suspected.

'She's been as dry as a dog-biscuit for the last month. She's too old. You want to know something about goats before you start buying them, tell your father.'

'I wish you'd tell him. He was awfully cocky about this goat. And I say, is that your cow which came into our place last night?'

'White with black spots?'

Ralph nodded.

'That's her. She gets over the fence at the top of our place,' said the red-headed Chilcott, whose name presently turned out to be Rehob.

'She came in while we were having supper.'

'Yes, she's a sociable old thing. She'll often poke her nose round the door of the shack when we're grubbing.'

Ralph decided not to say anything about the annoyance the cow's visit had caused his father. The Chilcotts evidently regarded their cow as a privileged female retainer.

By this time the drive through the copse had come to an end in a large untidy field dotted with fowl-houses, fowls, piglets, bricks, planks, rolls of wire netting, buckets, tools, and chimney pots.

'Is that where you live?' Ralph asked, pointing to a stucco house which stood at the top of the slope of which this untidy field formed the lower portion.

'No, that's Edward Lightfoot's house. He's sold it to some people called Gatacre and bolted, owing a good deal of money in Galton. Bit of a wrong 'un. I don't know what the Gatacres are like. We haven't built our house yet. For the present we're living in that shack.'

Ralph looked in the direction indicated and perceived a wooden erection slightly longer than the largest fowl-house.

'I suppose,' said Rehob Chilcott, 'you expected something tremendous after that drive and entrance-gate? But we bought the gate very cheap at a sale, and it seemed a pity to let it lie about.'

'Oh, rather,' Ralph agreed.

By this time they had reached the shack, where Ralph was presented to Micha Chilcott, who was a genial young man with very fair hair and a face not unlike an extremely pleasant middle-white pig's. He was sitting in his shirt-sleeves before the stove and watching the progress of some sausages in the course of being fried.

Notwithstanding Ralph's hostility to feminine affectation, his disapproval of his father's exuberant romanticism, his stern stoical schoolboy's mind, and his ambition to kill small birds, he was not without a vein of poesy, and the Chilcotts' shack struck a chord in the most solemn and intimate depths of his nature. Had he been given to building castles in Spain, this was the very castle he would have built for himself. He looked round it, his eyes shining as Ali Baba's may have shone when he found himself in the cave of the Forty Thieves and before he realized he had forgotten the name of the particular cereal which would let him out.

The shack was not large. It was indeed not more than twelve feet by seven. The walls were of wood. The roof was corrugated iron. The bed of Micha Chilcott, under a small window, occupied one end. The bed of his red-haired brother under another small window, occupied the other end. There was a door in the middle, and a small cooking-stove opposite. There were two cane chairs with comfortably broken seats. There was a table covered with white American cloth to which the stains of a year's eating, cooking, washing, writing, doctoring animals, plucking fowls, and mixing chicken's food had given a polychrome more rich than a painter's palette. The floor was littered with feathers, old magazines, slippers, dirty clothes, pots, pans, kettles, and baking-tins. Books on all sorts of interesting subjects like phrenology, the interpretation of dreams, the treatment of female ailments, the breeding of rabbits for show and profit, conjuring, mesmerism, and the bicycle from A to Z, supported one another on shelves of packing-case wood hanging from the walls by triangles of string. Bunches of herbs hung from the roof. Guns of various degrees of rustiness, fishing-rods, rakes, and strange walking-sticks, were stacked in corners. A bicycle was suspended over each bed, and the beds themselves were just a muddle of patchwork rugs, grey blankets, boxing gloves, and overcoats on top of sagging iron bedsteads and mattresses sprouting with great cauliflowers of flock. On one window-sill were large medicine bottles for curing domestic animals of every complaint, and on the other window-sill were tiny little bottles of homeopathic medicine for curing human beings. Cans of paint oozed everywhere. Oil-lamps were leaking. There was a clothes-basket full of coal and a coal-scuttle full of boots. Whatever one touched was either greasy or sticky, and the combined smell of the interior was prodigal both in variety and intensity. The shack was indeed the contents of a schoolboy's pocket in the nth degree, and Ralph as he looked round this ideal home promised himself many long happy hours of inquisitiveness, cogitation, and languorous enjoyment therein.

'I say what's that?' he asked, pointing to a contraption of wheels, troughs, treadles, and tubes which stood by the door.

'Crammer for fowls. When you want to fatten them for market you can push as much food into them with that as you like. But we don't use it,' said Micha.

'We don't approve of treating fowls like that. We think it's as bad as vivisection,' said Rehob. 'That crammer was thrown in with two incubators we bought cheap at a sale.'

'Don't you ever use it?' Ralph asked.

The brothers shook their heads.

'What will you do with it then?' he pressed.

'Nothing. Do you want it?' said Rehob.

'Can I really have it?' Ralph exclaimed in joyous amazement. 'Will you show me how it works?'

'Hold his head, Rehob,' said Micha. 'What can we cram him with?'

'No, I say, you're only fooling, aren't you?' Ralph protested nervously.

'The sausages are ready,' Micha announced. 'Find yourself a plate, youngster, and sit on the bed.'

Ralph still hoped he might be presented with the crammer, but he was glad to let the subject of its proper manipulation drop for the present, for although the Chilcotts were probably only ragging, prudence was best. He was feeling too a little doubtful about the wisdom of sitting down to breakfast away from the family table. He had in his day ventured to accept invitations to tea without reference to his parents. He had even on one occasion accepted a schoolfellow's invitation to lunch, but breakfast taken like this was a revolutionary step. He was feeling too a little worried on

Roger's account. At the rate he had been running in the opposite direction he seemed unlikely to get any breakfast at all. In spite of Ralph's doubts the sausages tasted delicious, and when in the middle of his self-questioning the noise of a penny whistle sounded from the field, Ralph finally abandoned himself to the pleasures of the moment.

'There's Texas Bill,' Micha Chilcott observed to his brother, who at once went to the door and beckoned. A few minutes later a boy of about fourteen in a much worn knickerbocker suit of navy blue broad-cloth appeared in the doorway. After playing the first few bars of 'Annie Laurie' he flipped the spittle from his pipe and shook hands with everybody in turn.

'Have a sausage, Texas?' Micha invited.

The newcomer sat down at once on a packing-case and ate with extreme rapidity, uttering not a word between the mouthfuls. When he had finished he took out his whistle and expressed the satisfaction of his inside by tootling 'The Keel Row'. Ralph looked at him with curiosity and respect. The cool manners of Texas aroused his admiration. He wished that he could arrive in this free and easy way at the shack and converse by means of a penny whistle. And when this self-assured youth winked in his direction and asked who the kiddo was, Ralph did not resent it. On the contrary he felt proud that Texas should have noticed him at all, and he smiled in modest embarrassment at this shabbily dressed contemporary with that large head and pale face, that impudent snub nose, and those mocking green eyes. He recognized in Texas Bill the natural leader of men, and he hoped that Texas would recognize in himself the devoted follower. Texas was told that the kiddo was Ralph Waterall who was one of the family now living in Blackham's place.

'Blackham's hopped it,' Texas announced. 'Hopped it last night, it seems, without paying a blooming penny of what he owes in Galton. That makes the sixth who's hopped it from Oaktown since August. And they aren't getting half ratty about it in Galton, I give you my word. Hilton Jones, the ironmonger, said he'd put his dog on the next fellow from Oaktown who came in and gave an order without laying the money down on the counter.'

'How's your uncle, Texas?' Micha asked.

For answer the boy played 'The Last Rose of Summer', and Ralph who was not deaf to the emotional suggestion of

57

music like this and who, away from familiar surroundings, did not fear to be accused of feelings unworthy of masculinity, felt a romantic yearning to meet such an uncle.

'Has he been sober at all this week?' Rehob pressed.

'He was as sober as a kipper on Monday morning, because he ran out of booze on Sunday through him slinging the full bottle at the cat by mistake. And then he cut his tongue, trying to save the last drop. He said if he ever did such a thing again he'd learn me not to be so careless. So I took my hook out of it and slept with Harry Gibbs down at the brick-kiln, and when I came in on Monday Uncle Gus didn't know which end of himself *he* begun, leave alone me. So I shoved the grandfather-clock out into the middle of the room, and when he'd knocked it down for giving him back answers which was when it struck seven o'clock, he went to sleep for two days and all was peace till he woke up with his head inside the pillow and his mouth full of feathers, which he said was through me bringing him the wrong whisky, because it always gave him a mouth. He didn't half carry on when he found it was feathers. He says he can still feel them tickling his inside. He says he's never felt anything like it since he swallowed a caterpillar once, which a kid put in his whisky for a lark. They kidded him up it would hatch out into a butterfly, and he said if he hadn't have known that butterflies only lived for a day he'd have gone off his onion when he felt it flutter about inside him. Wonderful what anybody can believe on drink! Last summer Pluepott's bees swarmed in our place, and blessed if Uncle Gus didn't think as some of the little blighters had hived inside of him. He bought a lot of bee-skeps in the hope they'd find a new home. He used to mooch about, snapping his teeth to try and catch them as they flew in and out of his mouth, and he give up sweetened gin because he said he was so full of honey that anything sweet turned on him. But I reckon a fellow who used to earn a living by writing mottoes for crackers gets fanciful. You can't blame him in one way. He never had a chance to be sensible. Well, I can't stop here quacking all the morning. I'm going into Galton. Want anything, you two?' he asked of his hosts at breakfast.

Ralph, who had been listening in fascination to Texas Bill's narrative and enjoying, in fancy, a freedom that allowed him to sleep in brick-kilns, came back to earth.

'I say, what's the time?' was his anxious inquiry, and on

hearing that it was nearly half-past nine he declared that he must bunk home at once.

'I say, couldn't we – I mean I'd awfully like to see the brick-kiln,' Ralph gulped forth in embarrassment.

'Right-o. I'll pop round for you to your place to-morrow night and we'll go round and stir up old Harry Gibbs. Round about eight. Your old man doesn't drink, does he?'

'Oh, rather not.'

And before Ralph could explain anything more about his own domestic milieu, Texas Bill was off down the road piping 'Say au revoir but not good-bye' on his whistle.

Ralph turned, a little doubtfully, in the direction of Dream Days.

CHAPTER SIX

At half-past eight Mr Waterall had sprung from bed with all that zest in the beginning of a new day which he believed should celebrate the act of rising from a rustic couch. Unfavourably for this mood of Arcadian bliss he landed with bare feet in the rills of cold bath water which were babbling across the cork linoleum from under the door of his sons' room. This was not the worst. In leaping for dry linoleum he slipped and sat down with some force upon a small lawnmower, he and the mower both emitting the same kind of grinding noise that indicates acute pain. Nor could he alleviate his hurt by demanding in a loud voice who on earth had been stupid enough to leave a lawn-mower kicking about in a bedroom. It was he who had insisted on putting it there. No hero of romance could have been more solicitous over the bestowal of his gallant steed before attending to himself than Mr Waterall had shown himself over the comfort of that lawn-mower.

'Now don't either of you two boys start monkeying about with my lawn-mower,' he had warned them. 'I don't want the whole house ploughed up. It can stay in my room to-night, and I'll unwrap it myself to-morrow.' Then he had added to his wife, 'I'm going to take to mowing and that sort of thing when I'm in the country instead of doing physical exercises.'

'Yes, dear, what a splendid idea! And I do hope there'll be enough grass,' she had murmured anxiously.

'Enough grass? Why, there was a quantity of grass when I was here last. If that cow . . .'

'No dear, it wasn't the cow. It was the workmen. You'll see in the morning that they've trampled a good deal of it away during the building.'

'Well, whatever the workmen do I don't want anything to happen to the mower. It's a regular little beauty.'

'I'm sure it is,' Mrs Waterall had agreed fondly. She had been tempted to express her appreciation of the new pet by stroking it or patting it, but she had refrained in case her husband should think she was fiddling with it. Now in response to his groans she hurried along from the preparation of breakfast to condole with him.

'We must get a shed built for this confounded lawn-mower at once,' he said. 'I only put it in here for the night. We can't keep it in our room permanently. I tripped over it just now and might have given myself a nasty gash. It was lucky I didn't let anyone unpack it last night.'

Then Mr Waterall remembered the ultimate cause of his accident.

'What are you two young blackguards doing with the water in there?' he shouted.

There was no response, one young blackguard being at that moment engaged with his second sausage, the other still running head down in the opposite direction from Dream Days.

'Answer me,' their father adjured. 'Where are my slippers, Mary?' he continued fretfully. 'Can't you see I'm standing here in a puddle of water?'

'Yes, dear, here they are. I am so sorry Ralph and Roger were so careless. Boys, boys,' she pleaded, tapping on the door of their room. 'Can't you hear Father calling?'

By this time Mr Waterall had pushed past her and flung open the door.

'They've gone out,' he gasped. 'They've actually had the audacity to dress and climb out of the window and go off leaving the room like a marsh.'

'And it's such a wet morning,' a tender mother sighed.

'It's not so wet outside as it is inside,' the indignant father growled. 'A polar bear having a bath would make less mess than those two boys. I'll make them have their bath out in the garden if they can't behave in a more civilized way.'

'Oh, Robert dear, not in this bleak November weather.'

'They want a little really Spartan discipline,' he growled. 'I wasn't coddled like them when I was young. What would happen to them if I lost everything and had to go into the workhouse?'

However, gradually the peace of the country shed a benison upon Mr Waterall's vexed spirit, and as he sat beside the Tortoise stove in the sitting-room and warmed his chilled toes while Phyllis laid the table for breakfast and his wife frizzled away with eggs and bacon in the kitchen he congratulated himself for the hundredth time upon his acquisition of that little place in the country.

By half past nine, when Ralph arrived back, Mr Waterall had lighted his after-breakfast pipe and was feeling well disposed even toward prodigal sons. Still, he had a duty as a father to perform and he told Ralph sternly that neither he nor Roger could expect anything more than bread and butter if they could not be in to breakfast more punctually. Ralph being full of sausages bore his punishment so temperately that his mother began to hope that the better nature in which she firmly believed, against all evidence, was taking possession of her eldest child at last.

'Where's Roger?' Mr Waterall asked.

'I don't know. He was running the other way,' said Ralph.

'What do you mean, he was running the other way? You come in three-quarters of an hour late for breakfast, and then calmly inform me that your brother is running the other way.'

'Well, he was. He got in a funk.'

'Do you mean he was afraid to face me when he was so late?' Mr Waterall asked, a note of complacency damping down his voice like the soft pedal.

'No, he thought somebody thought we were poachers, and he bunked because he was funky.'

'Speak English, boy. Don't keep muttering to yourself about bunking and funking. Who thought you were poachers?'

'A chap called Rehob Chilcott.'

'Rehob? A man can't be called Rehob. You've got the name wrong.'

'No, dear,' put in Mrs Waterall soothingly. 'Ralph has the name right. Mr Rehob Chilcott is one of the pleasant young men at the corner who are kindly looking after Phyllis's nannygoat.'

'Rehob?' Mr Waterall ejaculated. 'But there's no such name.'

'Yes, dear, really. It's in the Bible.'

'Well, there are lots of idiotic names in the Bible. There's Nun for instance. Joshua the son of Nun. I remember it was a favourite old riddle when I was a boy. But you wouldn't find anybody called Nun.'

Mrs Waterall pulled a face of agonized entreaty. She could not bear her husband to laugh about the Bible in front of the children.

'Really, dear, that is his name, and the brother living

down here with him is called Micha, and there's another brother called Hashabiah. Their father is a minister of a sect called the Reformed Children of Israel.'

'Children of Idiots more like,' said Mr Waterall, and Ralph with a rare spontaneity laughed at one of his father's jokes.

'Robert! Robert! Please, dear,' his wife begged.

Mr Waterall turned to his son.

'Why should this young man with a ridiculous name think you and Roger were poachers? Did you tell him their cow had come charging into our kitchen last night? They may be Reformed Children of Israel themselves, but they don't seem to have reformed their cows yet,' he guffawed.

Mrs Waterall, anxious for the ears of a ten-year-old daughter, bade her run out to the larder and bring in more butter for Ralph's breakfast. She diverted the course of the conversation even more successfully than she had expected, for there was a wild scream from Phyllis, who came rushing back into the room with the news that there was an enormous animal in the butter.

'Not the Reformed Children of Israel's cow, I hope.' Mr Waterall inquired sarcastically.

His wife hurried away to verify Phyllis's assertion and immediately began to scream herself.

'It's a rat! A huge rat!' she cried.

'And it looked at me, Daddy,' Phyllis moaned, clutching her father's coat.

Mr Waterall advanced boldly to the rescue.

'Why, it's dead,' he exclaimed. 'And the brute has been bleeding all over the butter.'

Ralph was in a quandary. He did not like to admit to the ownership of the carcass, because he dreaded restrictions for his air-gun, possibly even the confiscation of it for having brought it to Dream Days without permission. He might indeed claim that he had shot the rat in the very act of eating the butter; but it would be difficult to explain satisfactorily why he had allowed it to remain on the butter. On the other hand he did not want to lose the carcass. He might never succeed in shooting anything again, and should the Chilcotts decide to present him with that crammer, the rat would provide such splendid material for an experiment, as successful an experiment perhaps as when he and Roger had put a dead mouse through the mincing-machine at home in Orange Road, and Cook had fainted.

Fortunately for Ralph he was not called upon to make this difficult decision. Fate intervened in the shape of a large wagon loaded high with trees and shrubs of every shape and size which had stopped outside the front gate of Dream Days, obscuring with its bulk the dim November sky, and presenting an impassable barrier to all traffic coming from Medworth in the opposite direction. Its arrival threw Mr Waterall into almost as acute a state of agitation as the arrival of Birnam Wood threw Macbeth. His family supposed at first that he was annoyed at the way the wagon was blocking the lane outside Dream Days. Presently, however, it transpired from his manner that he must have been expecting the arrival of this great mass of dormant vegetation, for when a large man wearing an apron of sacking crept out from the heart of this moving wood followed by two other men also in aprons of sacking, and inquired in loamy accents if this was Mr Waterall's place, the owner of it replied that it was and went on to ask if the stuff he was expecting from Bocock's Farnley Nurseries was on the wagon.

'Yes, sir,' said the large man, lifting his apron and wiping away with the end of it a few twigs that were still adhering to his loamy countenance. 'Yes, sir, this here be your little lot, and the rest of it be in the second wagon which will be along in another half an hour.'

'The rest of it?' Mr Waterall echoed a little nervously. 'Is there much more then?'

'We put the bigger stuff on the second wagon.'

'The bigger stuff? Is it bigger than this?'

'Yes, there's some handy-looking trees on the other wagon,' the large man assured him. 'Very handy-looking trees. I expect you'd like us to get this lot unloaded first. The way we are now nothing will be able to get by. The road's a bit narrow just here.'

'Yes, perhaps it is a little on the narrow side,' Mr Waterall agreed. He did not altogether like criticism of the Oaktown landscape, but an impatient bicyclist who had had to dismount was ringing his bell persistently, and if a bicyclist could not pass the wagon . . .

'Now, Ralph,' said his father, 'can't you find something more useful to do than to stand about gaping. Come along, my boy. Remember what I said last night. When in Rome we must do as Rome does. Put you back into it and help un-load these shrubs. Look at your father.'

Mr Waterall seized the first piece of vegetation that offered itself; and as this happened to be a berberis of ferocious prickliness he dropped it smartly and changed the burden of his refrain.

'Now, Ralph, don't get in the way of the men while they're unloading. Too many cooks spoil the broth. I may want you to help me in a minute. I've got to arrange where all these trees and shrubs are to be planted.'

The truth was Mr Waterall was growing nervous. He could not believe that a reputable firm of nurserymen like Bocock's of Farnley would deliberately saddle him with a lot of trees and shrubs he had never ordered, and yet . . .

His mind went back to that sunny October day when he had walked round Bocock's Nursery, full of pride in his successful acquirement of the quarter-of-an-acre plot on one side of Dream Days, and the half-acre plot on the other. His sense of property had perhaps been unduly stimulated by the attentive young man who had accompanied him round the nursery and helped him to plan out the little para-dise he hoped to create. He certainly had admired a large number of beautiful shrubs, and he certainly had, under the earnest advice of the young man with a pencil, ordered half a dozen and sometimes a dozen of what were being recommended to him. Perhaps he had been confused by the long Latin names and by the habit the young man had of telling him that he ought to grow this and that as well. There had been a suggestion of a moral duty about his planting which he had found it hard to resist. Many plants too had had such long names that, even if he could have remembered them and remembering them pronounced them correctly, it would have seemed unfeeling to cancel the purchase of them after the young man had taken so much trouble to write them down in his notebook.

'You'll want a representative collection of the cratae-guses,' the young man would say.

'Will I?' Mr Waterall would reply.

'The orange-fruited species blend so exquisitely with late teas.'

'Do they indeed?'

Mr Waterall could not recall that he had ever heard of a fruit called crataeguses eaten at tea or any other meal;

but he had not liked to admit as much, and a representative collection of the family had been rapidly entered up.

'You won't be able to do rhododendrons, I'm afraid,' the young man had said, shaking his head gravely. 'Too much chalk.'

'A little too much, I'm afraid,' Mr Waterall had agreed with an insincere break in his voice, for by this time he was beginning to think that the presence of chalk had a definite economic value.

'But you'll be able to do clematis. They'll riot with you.'

'Will they really?'

'Oh, absolutely,' the young man had proclaimed with enthusiasm. 'I think perhaps three of each type will be enough for a start. We can make you up a very good representative collection. But I shan't put you in any doubles.'

'No, one of each will be enough.'

The young man had looked sharply at Mr Waterall and, apparently realizing that he knew even less about horticulture than he had thought, had immediately proposed a representative collection of the flowering crabs, some of the names of which sounded to Mr Waterall as if a train had gone off the line and was tearing up the permanent way, others like a man with asthma trying to dictate his will. At this point, he had felt that it was time to assert what little knowledge of trees he had.

'I want some of the old favourites, you know,' he had then told the young man with a pencil, who in subsequent correspondence with Messrs Bocock turned out to be called 'our Mr Rigmaiden'.

'Well, of course a really representative collection of the roses of long ago would undoubtedly be very suitable. As a matter of fact Mr Bocock Junior has made rather a speciality of the sweet old-fashioned roses of long ago, and we have some very choice items which are not to be found anywhere nowadays except in our nurseries. A really representative collection of say fifty . . .'

'No, I think I have all the roses I want for the present,' Mr Waterall interrupted quickly. 'The old favourites I had in mind were such trees as an oak, and an . . . an ash, oh yes, and a horse-chestnut . . . and my little daughter is very anxious to have a mulberry bush. Then perhaps you might add a weeping willow and a walnut and a poplar

66

and a laburnum. And I think that will be enough for this year.'

'Certainly, Mr Waterall. I understand exactly what you want.'

Whereupon our Mr Rigmaiden had muttered over the Latin names to himself and, having thus securely fixed in his own mind the identity of these common objects of the English country, he had expanded again.

'I take it you'll require the American oak as well as the English oak?'

Mr Waterall had felt inclined to resent the existence of oaks in America.

'The foliage in autumn turns to a rich glowing red,' Mr Rigmaiden had gushed persuasively. 'Unfortunately you are a little too early to see our American oaks in the full glory of their autumnal tints.'

But this time Mr Waterall had been firm.

'No, I just want a plain English oak.'

'We can do you some very fine quercus robur from fifteen to twenty feet. Shall I put you down a dozen?'

'No, no. We're not a family of Druids. One oak will be ample.'

The young man had smiled so obsequiously at his client's humour that Mr Waterall had felt more sure of himself.

'And one ash,' he had said firmly. 'And one horse-chestnut.'

But this had evidently pained Mr Rigmaiden too, who had shaken a reproachful head.

'Oh, but you must have one white and one red.'

'Very well, two horse-chestnuts.'

'Two aesculuses, yes, certainly. One albus and one ruber. About twenty feet, I suppose? That is if we can manage them. But you wouldn't object if we can't manage more than fifteen? We have been planting an avenue of aesculuses for Mrs Cudworth-Pym, and so we may be unable to manage just the height you require. And what was the next? Oh, yes, one salix dependens. The weeping willow so called. Some of the salices from . . .'

'No, no, one weeping willow will be ample.'

'And a mulberry? One will be sufficient?'

'Yes, yes. I just want it for my little daughter to play round. And I only want one walnut.'

'Which variety?'

'The ordinary walnut you eat after dinner.'

'Certainly. And now we come to the populuses.'

Mr Waterall had guessed in desperation.

'I only want one poplar. One of those trees that look like large egg-whisks.'

Mr Rigmaiden had smiled encouragingly.

'That would be the Lombardy poplar. Now if I might suggest as a possible screen against unwelcome neighbours a line of Canadian poplars. No tree grows so rapidly and while it creates a most effective barrier, the shade is not heavy and . . .'

'I'll have a dozen,' Mr Waterall had declared. He had just remembered that Albert Hobday who owned the land beyond the extra quarter of an acre he had bought on the western side of the original domain, was threatening to erect a general store thereon. It might be convenient to have a general store so close at hand, but with twelve Canadian poplars he would obliterate from the poetic seclusion of Dream Days that materialistic and plebeian erection.

'About twenty-two feet?'

'Yes, and that will be enough,' Mr Waterall had decided.

'You will not be requiring a laburnum?'

'Oh, very well, put down one laburnum.'

'You'd prefer a Scotch laburnum, of course?'

'No, I just want an ordinary laburnum. The thing with yellow flowers you see all over the place.'

'The Scotch laburnum has superior racemes,' Mr Rigmaiden had insisted gently, and Mr Waterall had begun to feel aggressively patriotic.

'American oaks and Scotch laburnums may be considered better by people who always think everything outside their own country is better. But English oaks and English laburnums are good enough for me.'

An English laburnum would certainly have been Mr Waterall's final order if Mr Rigmaiden had not cleverly steered him within the zone of temptation from Bocock's famous herbaceous borders.

'Though it's really a shame you should see them now, Mr Waterall, when of course they are really over. Still, I thought you would be wanting some herbaceous stuff, and we rather pride ourselves on our herbaceous stuff. We won another gold medal this year with our delphiniums, which are unquestionably superior to any.'

68

But Mr Waterall had resisted the delphiniums, in which resistance he had been considerably helped by not having the faintest idea what a delphinium looked like. He had fallen, however, to the Michaelmas daisies, and he had made an absolute ass of himself over the dahlias, ordering them as recklessly as women order cushions at a sale.

'And then,' Mr Rigmaiden had said, 'there are bulbs. Normally, of course, you would have most of your bulbs in by now, but it struck me that you might care to avail yourself of our special offer of surplus bulbs, subject to their being unsold at the time of ordering. They are really ridiculously cheap, and though we do not advise such late planting to obtain the best results the following season, you will find that it is a most economical method of stocking your garden. For instance we could do you ten thousand crocuses for . . .'

'Ten thousand? Did you say ten thousand?' Mr Waterall had gasped. He thought Mr Rigmaiden must have forgotten he was talking about bulbs and suddenly become astronomical. 'But I'm afraid you have a wrong idea of the size of my garden. The whole of it hardly covers a full acre.'

And Mr Rigmaiden had let his customer off with a few daffodils, hyacinths, tulips, and anemones. He had been afraid Mr Waterall might reconsider the trees and shrubs.

And Mr Waterall most certainly would have reconsidered them if he had had any prevision of those two wagons loaded up with dormant vegetation which would draw up a month later in the narrow lane outside the front gate of Dream Days.

Three carts on the way to Galton were held up on one side. Two carts, a doctor's gig, and a farm-wagon on the way from Galton were held up on the other. Cries resounded of: 'Can't you pull in a bit more to the left?' 'Get hold of his head!' 'Back her another two foot into the hedge!' 'Mind you don't get your wheel jammed!' 'Whoa back there!' Whips were being cracked. Bicycle bells were shrilling. Horses were pawing the road. Half a dozen idlers had gathered by the stile opposite, at the start of the short cut for foot passengers to Galton over the fields by Wyatt's Farm. The rain came drenching down again, but that did not deter the idlers who sat on the stile absorbed by a scene that appeals to idlers more than any other, the spectacle of other people hard at work. And the three men with sack aprons from Bocock's Farnley Nurseries tramped back-wards and forwards, carrying trees and shrubs, until the whole of the freshly dug and newly acquired plots on either side of the original Eden looked as if a cyclone had passed over a jungle and laid it low.

In the middle of the unloading, Roger, creeping cautiously back to reconnoitre and hearing from afar the sounds of congested traffic and the hoarse cries of congested drivers, decided that all the members of his family were being arrested. He had had an adventurous morning. While run-ning head downwards as fast as he could along the Basing road a dog belonging to a lodge-keeper of Squire Melville had rushed out and seized him by the seat of his breeches. The lodge-keeper's wife, a kindly soul, had hurried to the rescue and brought him into her humble abode. There she had given him food and shelter and with deft fingers had stitched up the rent seat of his breeches, speeding him upon his way again with a pot of home-made raspberry jam. Now he was faced with the melancholy prospect of arriving back at Dream Days to find that his father, mother, brother, and sister had been dragged off to prison. Small wonder that the wretched boy stood rooted to the muddy lane far more firmly than any of Messrs Bocock's trees were as yet rooted to the soil of Dream Days. Small wonder that his appre-hensive tears mingled themselves with the torrential Novem-ber rain. And thus he might have stood for a very long time if he had not caught sight through a gap in the hedge of his father and brother walking about on the nearer plot of unplanted ground linked by a measure of yellow tape.

'Come along, Roger, get hold of the other end of this tape-measure,' said his father, who was too much overcome by the problem of finding suitable sites for all the Bocock shrubs and trees to carry out an inquisition at this moment into the behaviour of a younger son.

In spite of the chalk and in spite of the flints which be-strewed it, the soil of Dream Days appeared to be an unmiti-gated clay as adhesive as a club bore. Mr Waterall and Ralph had by now gathered so much of it on to their boots that they both seemed to have grown about six inches. The more they measured, the slower they moved and the taller they grew. At last Ralph kicked his leg in desperation, whereupon a large lump of clay left his boot with the velocity of a projectile from a medieval catapult and caught his father full on the forehead. Mr Waterall staggered by the blow, reeled, caught his own clay-impeded legs in the branches of a prostrate quercus robur, and crashed heavily among a representative collection of lilacs.

To do him justice, Ralph waited to see if his father was seriously hurt before he started to escape from the paternal wrath. The amount of clay he had discharged from one boot enabled him to gain rapidly, and half-way up the garden Mr Waterall gave up the pursuit, for by that time so much clay was sticking to his boots that he was rendered as inactive as a Kanaka with elephantiasis. Forgetting the example he should have set, he now launched out with his own leg and propelled a lump of clay into the stomach of the large man from Bocock's, who was trudging up the slope with a weeping willow over one shoulder and a copper beech over the other. However, the large man was quite pleasant about it, and merely asked his assailant where he wanted the weeping willow planted.

'Just where you're standing,' said Mr Waterall.

The large man looked doubtful.

'Isn't this the middle of a path?' he suggested.

'Yes, so it is. By Jove, I didn't notice it for a moment,' said Mr Waterall, for which he could hardly be blamed, because the paths of the Dream Days garden were nothing more than a slightly denser accumulation of flints running in a straight line through the flint-strewn clay of the beds. It began to look unlikely that the shrubs would ever be planted, and he inquired a little anxiously how long it would take to plant them all.

'Well, sir, I don't see getting through with the job under three days,' the large man replied.

'That means you'll be here over Sunday,' said Mr Waterall pensively.

'Well, if we could get an extra couple of hands we might finish it off by Saturday. But this rain makes it rare heavy going, and there's a handy pile of stuff here. You come to look around you there's a powerful lot of shrubs. And some of these trees really take three pairs of hands to get them in proper. Still, if we could get one extra, we might manage to finish the job by Saturday.'

'I shall take immediate steps to secure an extra hand,' Mr Waterall announced grandly.

CHAPTER SEVEN

DURING October an aged man called Snell had been engaged to come to Dream Days and dig away at the two new plots Mr Waterall had acquired, to bury what he called the plaguy twitch, and to deposit basketfuls of flints upon the paths. Snell was the last surviving labourer of the old Oak Farm, and he still lived in one of a row of ancient thatched cottages whence not even the purchaser of the derelict farm had been able to evict him. He was bent with rheumatism, and fifty years of ploughing, sowing, harrowing, reaping, and threshing in their seasons had marked him so heavily that, although actually he was not yet seventy, he was credited by none of the colonists of Oaktown with less than eighty years and by some with over ninety. They were proud of old Snell. He seemed to provide amid all this eruption of new tin dwelling-houses, a pledge of permanency. When they saw him digging that small garden of his in front of the ancient cottage where he had been digging for so many years, they began to fancy that with practice they might really be able, one day, to earn a living from the land themselves. They addressed him respectfully as Mr Snell and vowed he was a fine old type the like of which would soon be extinct all over the country. Old Snell himself, who was as deaf as an adder, could not hear the nonsense talked to him, and if he had he would have regarded his new neighbours with even greater contempt and aversion than he felt already.

'Go and fetch old Snell,' Mr Waterall commanded his sons. 'Tell him I want him to put in a couple of days for me at planting my shrubs and trees.'

So Ralph and Roger turned up to the right along the farm road until they reached the row of thatched cottages where the old man lived with a granddaughter.

But when this granddaughter had succeeded in screaming into the ancient's ear the demand for his services, old Snell **shook his head.**

'I won't do any more digging down there not if they pay me a guinea a minute,' he declared obstinately. 'I said I'd dig 'un and I digged 'un, and I'll be danged if I dig 'un again. I be too old, and my rheumatics be too bad, and that 'ere plaguy twitch have bested me at the last. I fought 'un for fifty years and more, but it have bested me, and the sooner I turns over and dies, the better for all and sundry.'

'Don't talk so silly, Grandpa,' his granddaughter screamed. 'Mr Waterall only wants for you to help with some trees.'

'Well, I won't. I won't help wi' naught.'

And not all his granddaughter's screaming could induce the old man to change his mind.

'Won't come?' exclaimed Mr Waterall indignantly, when his sons returned with the news. 'Did you make him understand who it was that wanted him? I suppose you just mumbled something to the old fellow, and he never understood the message was from me. Old Snell's very fond of me. I've had many a crack with the old veteran. Of course, as usual, you two boys have made a complete muddle of a simple errand. I wish I'd sent Phyllis now.'

'Oh, do let me go, Daddy,' cried Phyllis. 'I'm sure Mr Snell will come when I ask him.'

'You cocky little ass, why should he come for you any more than for us?' Ralph ejaculated.

Secure in the support of her father Phyllis tossed her head defiantly, and both brothers glaring at her coldly resolved to take the first opportunity that occurred of tying that odious head of hair to the back of a chair by one of its own exaggerated ribbons.

'Well, we must get somebody to help with this planting,' said Mr Waterall. 'I'll go over and ask our neighbour opposite if he can spare me a couple of days from his own garden. And you two boys had better come with me. I can't trust you here by yourself with all these rare shrubs.'

So Mr Waterall and his two sons crossed the road and entered the six-acre field which was ultimately to provide Mr Joseph Gnathead, late of Blackheath, with a living from the soil.

Mr Gnathead was a wizened little man with a goat's beard who shuffled about his domain in an apron of crimson baize and a confectioner's white cap. Whether he wore such caps out of long habit or out of economy to save himself buying new caps was not known. But he could hardly have chosen a form of headgear less suitable for gardening, since the lightest wind would blow them from his head, and the old confectioner was often to be seen chasing these white caps across his territory with a rake or a hoe. His wife was a ferrety-faced little woman with eyes like boot-buttons and a passion for floral bonnets, one of which had been devoured by Phyllis's milkless nannygoat. Mrs Gnathead ruled her husband with some severity, and it was always a matter for surprise that she had ever allowed him to escape from confectionery into what she described as an existence hardly fit for a heathen.

'Mr Gnathead,' she declared, 'always had his heart in gardening, and he came to regular loathe the sight of a cake. I tried to persuade him to sell his business and buy a greengrocer's shop. But no, nothing would content him, once he'd seen this blessed advertisement of land for the million but he must come down here and start off being one of them. And I will say one thing. Mr Gnathead has worked. That man has worked himself to the bone, you might say. And many's the time I've said jokingly that it was really a pity he wasn't a convict he was so fond of hard labour. I can't hardly make him come in for a snack, and even in his sleep you'll hear him muttering about the weeds. Well, if he'd have thought a quarter as much about his cakes as he thinks about weeds, what a business that man would have had. Weeds are on his mind night and day. Why, one night I woke up with him tugging away at my hair, him thinking I was a dock. Oh, it was a real nightmare. And it's all I can do now to keep him from weeding of a Sunday, and when we lived in Blackheath there was nobody more strict than Mr Gnathead about Chapel. Used to read his Bible regular and almost be afraid to twiddle his thumbs for fear of breaking the Sabbath. But now as soon as he gets to the bit where Adam and Eve are turned out of the Garden of Eden his interest in the Bible seems all gone, and he begins looking out of the window and wondering if the mice have been at his peas again.'

One of Mrs Gnathead's peculiarities was that she never invited anybody over the threshold of Blackheath Villa, though she would gossip gladly, even hungrily, with a caller for as long as he or she was content to remain under the rustic porch of her front door. So, now, when Mr Waterall and his sons presented themselves, while Mrs Gnathead expressed her intense pleasure at the visit, she made not the slightest sign of inviting them to step inside her villa, which by the way unlike most of the Oaktown habitations was built of red brick.

'Well, and if this isn't a pleasant surprise, I'm sure,' she declared, her black beady little eyes darting from one to the other like the eyes of a thrush choosing between three plump worms. 'Well, I really am delighted to see you, Mr Waterall. I often look across to Canadian Cottage, but I mustn't call it Canadian Cottage any more, must I? . . . that Blackham! Well, I shall always say if ever there was a black villain on this earth it was that Blackham. I've seen him chase his poor wife all round the garden with a carving knife and I've stood petrified to the ground in a condition I can only describe as chronic, petrified I've stood and unable to so much as call out to Mr Gnathead, I've been that petrified. And the insulting postcards that man used to send us! Yes, as sure as I'm standing here he'd walk all the way into Galton, and which is two miles if you go round by the road or a mile and three-quarters if you take the short cut by Wyatt's Farm – he'd take all that walk just to send us an insulting postcard. He wrote to us once, "Adam and Eve Gnathead, The Garden of Eden, Oak Farm Estate." And Mr Gnathead felt that very much because even if he doesn't read his Bible now the way he used to, he doesn't like for anyone to laugh at sacred things. And that wasn't the worst of it. He actually drew a disgusting picture of me and Mr Gnathead on the back in a couple of fig-leaves, excuse me mentioning such a thing in front of your two boys. That man was bad through and through. He was bad to the very core, as they say. Well, they tell me he's left Galton for good now, and left a lot of money owing by what I hear."

'Left Galton, has he?' said Mr Waterall indignantly. 'Why, I lent him a chair of mine. I wonder if he's taken it with him.'

'He'd take anything he could lay his hands on,' Mrs Gnathead averred. 'Well, I know I warned Mr Gnathead to be careful of his agates.'

'His agates?' Mr Waterall repeated.

'Yes, he has a boxful of agates which he's very proud of. As a matter of fact he got them in a bad debt for a wedding-cake he made once. But what with fingering them and turning them over Mr Gnathead grew very fond of these agates, and there's nothing he likes better than fingering them quietly of a Sunday afternoon to himself. Well, I say likes, but liked would be more correct, because he hasn't liked anything since he came down here except digging.'

She paused a moment for breath, and Mr Waterall thought this was a good chance to introduce the business which had brought him to Blackheath Villa.

'I wonder if Mr Gnathead would . . .' he began; but Mrs Gnathead did not give him a chance to develop his theme.

'Yes,' she broke in, 'I said to him, "Joe," I said, "you be very careful of those agates when that Blackham is about, for you mark my words he'll lay his hands on them if he can. Perhaps you noticed his expression, Mr Waterall? I know the first time I saw his expression I shivered all over inside. Oh, what a cruel mouth! And those nasty, mean, hungry-looking eyes. Well, I know when I heard he'd been a courier to the Prince of Wales, I asked myself what the world was coming to. A shark, I called him. And in fact, after we'd had some of those insulting postcards I was telling you about, I wrote him one myself, and I addressed it, "Mr Frederick Blackham, The Shark's Den, Oak Farm Estate." Yes, and he knew it came from me. He knew it. He actually stood there by the gate, and when he saw me coming up to empty a few scraps for the fowls he made a rude gesture in my direction. I couldn't bring myself to repeat what he did; but I know after he did it I could never again bring myself to think of him as civilized.'

Mrs. Gnathead paused for breath, and Mr Waterall began once more.

'I wonder if your husband would contemplate . . .'

But she broke in relentlessly.

'And of course between you and me there's too many uncivilized people in Oaktown. We keep ourselves to ourselves. I just nod to Mrs Poley opposite when I'm emptying my rubbish and she's emptying hers, but beyond that I don't have anything to do with anybody. Not that I've anything against the Poleys. He was a butcher in Kent and made a mess of his business I've heard it said, though I never gossip myself. He sold up and came down here and bought two plots and put up a two-roomed cottage from Humphrey's Iron Buildings, though I will say the foundation is brick, and which is something. Mrs Poley, she was a lady's maid once, but she lost her voice in Kent and has never spoken out of a whisper since. That's the sort of thing to teach anybody there's a

God above us. Blackham, us and Poleys, we were the first of the million, Blackham used to lead the Poleys a worse life than he led us. In fact he chased his wife right up the road in her nightdress once, and Mr Poley got out of bed in his slippers and let her in, and I've heard it said that the language Blackham used through the keyhole was something shocking. Well, if I'd have liked to gossip, the things I might have heard! Of course, Blackham's trouble was drink, and it's been the trouble of half the people that have come to Oaktown. Yes indeed. There's that Ryan who lives up the road on the right beyond the farmhouse. He has a young rapscallion of a nephew they call Texas Bill.'

Ralph pricked his ears at this.

'Well, I wouldn't like to say that boy drinks himself, but he's the wickedest, mischievousest impudentest young rascal I ever did see. But perhaps the boy can't be blamed, because they tell me his uncle with whom he lives hasn't been sober for two whole days since he came here, and what is more used to earn a living writing songs for the music halls and motters for crackers. What a misspent life! Oh dear, oh dear, it makes one's heart bleed I'm sure. And then there's that Lieutenant Green who lives up beyond where Major Kettlewell is building. They tell me he walks in every evening two miles to Galton just for the pleasure of walking out again dead drunk. I've seen him myself with a lot of fox-terrier dogs and a person who calls herself his housekeeper. Well, they always say that one half of the world doesn't know how the other half live, and when you've heard some of the stories you can't help hearing about people in Oaktown, you realize how true it is.'

Mrs Gnathead would no doubt have gone on to supply a full history of Oaktown and all its inhabitants if the stream of her information had not been abruptly dammed by the arrival of Phyllis with a request from Bocock's large foreman to know just where Mr Waterall wanted to plant the poplars.

'Well, good morning, Mrs Gnathead, I'm afraid we must be going,' said Mr Waterall as he turned away from the threshold of Blackheath Villa, across which, throughout Mrs Gnathead's monologues, he had not put a foot.

'Good morning, Mr Waterall, and I hope you'll look in again and give me some of the news, for really, as I sometimes say to Mr Gnathead, I might be living at the back of

77

beyond for all I ever hear from one week-end to another.'

'Why didn't you ask her if Mr Gnathead would come and help with the trees?' Ralph wanted to know, his countenance innocent of the least impression of trying to score off his father.

'Because he was evidently too busy to come,' Mr Waterall replied sharply.

'But he never knew you wanted him,' Ralph pointed out.

'Look here, my boy, I wish you'd cure yourself of the habit of arguing with people who came into this world a long time before you did. You think yourself very smart, but you've a lot to learn yet.'

'Shall Roger and I go round and try to get Mr Poley to come?'

It was not that Ralph had the least hope of securing his services; but he was anxious to hear more about their neighbours, and he was not anxious to tramp about any longer in the mud with a tape-measure.

Next to Dream Days on the road to Medworth were the two quarter-acre plots of Albert Hobday, the foundations of whose general store were beginning to rise from the soil. The prospect of Hobday, who had a family of twelve between the years of eighteen and one, did not enchant Mr Waterall. He wished that before Hobday, who was a carrier on a small scale on the other side of Galton, had perceived the commercial possibilities of Oaktown he had made an offer to buy him out of his two plots and thus guarded himself against being intimately overlooked by Hobday, Mrs Hobday, and their large family. Beyond Hobday's land were two plots as yet unbuilt upon, and then came Fernbank, the half-acre estate of Mr and Mrs William Poley.

Ralph and Roger climbed up a meandering path cut in the bank between two high hedges of untrimmed hazels which shielded the corrugated iron residence of the Poleys from the eyes of passers-by, and when they reached the top they rattled a green gate. From where they stood they could see that the residence consisted of two rooms; but they could perceive no sign of life within. They rattled the gate again so vigorously that at last the curtain of one of the rooms was pulled back, and they were regarded by a large white face with an expression upon it remarkably like that of the old lady of Sweden who in Lear's *Nonsense Book* went by slow train to Weeden. As they continued to rattle the gate, the face at last retreated from the window, and presently the door opened with extreme caution for a very fat woman to peer out and ask in a hoarse whisper what they wanted.

Ralph managed to explain that they lived at Dream Days without choking himself into incoherence over the detestably affected name their father had chosen, and the fat woman shuffled along the narrow path towards the gate with the key of the padlock in her hand. She was wearing a man's cap which was pinned to her sparse grey hair by half a dozen black-headed hatpins, and in addition to the key of the gate she was carrying a rolling-pin which, since it bore no marks of fresh dough, was probably intended to protect herself against invasion.

'Can we speak to Mr Poley, please?' Ralph inquired.

'Mr Poley's digging at the top of the garden. What were you wanting?'

'Well, we were going to ask him if he could come to help us put in a lot of trees.'

'Come along in, my dears, and one of you shall go up and ask him. I can't shout for him. You may notice I've lost my voice? I lost it when Mr Poley and me were living in Maidstone in Kent, and I won't ever get it back here. You may depend on that. I'll carry my hoarseness to the grave. You may depend on that.'

The interior of Fernbank was of varnished matchboarding; but the walls were almost entirely covered by four portraits, one in oils of a woman not unlike the notorious murderess Mrs Manning, and the others coloured enlargements of photographs.

'Yes, that's me,' Mrs Poley breathed heavily, as she nodded in the direction of the female like Mrs Manning. 'It was painted by a travelling artist on the Whit Monday of 1877. And it was considered a speaking likeness at the time. There was a time when people used to come into a room and get a regular shock when they saw me sitting there. My old mother-in-law used to say it was the walking spit of me. That's her,' Mrs Poley continued, pointing to the other female on the wall. 'And that's Mr Poley. But his collar stud was sticking into the back of his neck when he was took, and I think that give him rather a staring look. And the other is Mr Poley's father who was laid to rest in 1882. We saved those pictures from the wreck.'

'Were you shipwrecked?' Roger asked, his eyes bulging.

'Shipwrecked? No. I was referring to the wreck of Mr Poley's affairs as a butcher. The trouble was Mr Poley never had his heart in butchering. It was his father who drove him into it. Mr Poley wanted to be a fishmonger, and if he'd have been a fishmonger, it's my belief there never would have been a wreck. But there, what's the use of repining? Look at me, I've travelled the world round with the late Lady Devizes. We visited Rome, Naples, Vienna, Madrid and hundreds of places, and now here I am in this two-roomed cottage and never likely to move out of it again. But I don't repine.'

All this history was uttered in the same hoarse whisper, and Ralph was much relieved when Mrs Poley bade him go up the garden and fetch Mr Poley, for the strain of avoiding his brother's eye during the tale had been acute. He rushed away now, aching with inward laughter.

Mr Poley was a thin man of about fifty with sandy hair turning grey and a very long upper lip. His merry blue eyes were twinkling with fun, and his movements gave the impression of intense energy. He was digging away in his shirt-sleeves, wearing an apron of sacking and round his neck a decayed otter-skin stole which had presumably belonged to his wife. The battered straw hat too, which was perched on the top of his head, was a woman's straw hat. Probably when she took to wearing his cap he had borrowed her old hat. Ralph's proposal that he should come over and help with the planting of the new trees and shrubs evidently appealed to Mr Poley. It might have been conjectured that he had sallied out to dig at the top of his garden on this wet morning at least as much to find a post of vantage for his curiosity as to perform any useful horticultural service on his own account.

'If Mrs Poley doesn't mind being left I'll come,' he promised.

Mrs Poley who was no doubt as curious as her husband to ascertain something about their new neighbours gave it as her opinion that it was his duty to go.

'We've never not helped neighbours all we could, Will. And we aren't going to begin not to help them just because we've had a few nasty experiences since we came to live in hoggish Hamshire.'

While she was talking she was busying herself with a

80

bottle and glasses, two of which brimming with a darkish yellow sticky liquid she now offered to the boys.

'Do you know what it is?' she asked when they had sipped it.

Both boys thought it tasted suspiciously like medicine; but neither of them could bring himself to believe that Mrs Poley would commit such a breach of hospitality as to offer medicine to a guest. So they gave up the riddle.

'It's cowslip wine,' she breathed hoarsely. 'It'll do you no harm. Mr Poley and I never had any little ones of our own, but if we had have had I wouldn't have thought twice about giving them a glass of this cowslip wine the same as I'm giving you. And next time you come you shall taste my elderberry, which I've known people say was better than any port they'd ever drunk. And we have our own home-brewed too.'

'Beautiful,' said Mr Poley, smacking his lips. 'Better than cream. But then Mrs Poley has such a lovely light hand. And if anybody tells you a light hand ain't required for brewing, you can laugh in their face. Mrs Poley will be brewing again soon, and you shall taste it. I reckon after you've drunk her home-brewed you'll say you've never tasted ale before.'

'Yes, if it wasn't for some of the people round us Mr Poley and I would be very happy here,' his wife put in, for even to indulge in encomiums of herself she grudged Mr Poley freedom of speech. 'But there's one thing, I'm glad Blackham's gone.'

'He was rather a rotter, wasn't he?' Ralph suggested.

Mrs Poley looked at her husband.

'Will, did you hear what he said?'

'I did, Maria.'

'And did you ever hear a truer word spoke by a child? Rotter he was. And the way he treated that poor wife of his! She's come to me, my dears, with bruises on her limbs that made you wonder how the Lord ever came to create such brutes. The summer just before your father bought Canadian Cottage, Blackham grew a row of tomatoes, and these tomatoes not ripening in the open air, he gathered them and laid them along the window-sills to ripen indoors. And Mrs Blackham, poor soul, told me with her own lips that he never used these tomatoes for anything except to throw at her. He'd say something. Then she'd say something, or not say something. It didn't matter which. And then she'd have to dodge under the table while he started pelting her with those unripe tomatoes. Oh, that man, what a vile nature he had! Well, to give you an example of what he'd do. Poor old Gnathead opposite grew a vegetable marrow which he thought the world of, and one night after he and Blackham had had their quarrel, what does Blackham do but go into Gnathead's place and deliberately carve that vegetable marrow up into the living image of old Gnathead himself. Did it with a penknife, he did, for the man was clever with his fingers, there's no denying it, too clever indeed. Yes, he did it with a penkife by the light of the moon, and stuck it up against the Gnatheads' door. And it gave poor Mrs Gnathead the turn of her life when she opened her door and saw this ghashly likeness of her husband glaring up at her, beard and all, for that Blackham had actually made a beard out of some horsehair he'd took from one of the grates in the Market Hotel. Yes, that man was a living terror. Brandy and Brag, that's what I called him. Yes, you two boys want to be very careful who you talk to round here. Now come along, Will, don't keep Mr Waterall waiting. If he wants you to help plant his trees, it's your duty as a neighbour to lend a hand.'

So Ralph and Roger presently arrived back home triumphantly with Mr Poley; and all day for two days in the drenching November rain the three men with their aprons of sacking and loamy accents and Mr Poley's help, planted the representative collections of trees and shrubs that Mr Waterall had chosen at Bocock's Farnley Nurseries.

CHAPTER EIGHT

WHEN Mr Waterall sat down to supper on Saturday night, he felt at such peace with the world that not even the thought of Bocock's bill could disturb the serenity of his mind. When he had presented Bocock's large foreman with half a sovereign as a token of appreciation for the way he and the two other men had worked away in the November rain to finish the job by Saturday, the large loamy foreman had remarked that in a couple of years he would have as pretty a little garden as could be seen anywhere.

'I'm glad to hear you say that,' Mr Waterall had almost simpered. 'Very glad. Because I was a little doubtful at first of my ability to plan a garden. However, I've learnt a great deal in watching you at work. And though Rome wasn't built in a day, it was built finally.'

And to Mr Poley he had said:

'I am relying on you, Mr Poley, to come in two days a week from now on to keep the place up.'

'Very glad to do anything I can,' Poley had replied in his quick jerky voice. 'Neighbours must help one another. Yes—yes—yes. Mrs Poley always says that.'

And then, perceiving Ralph and Roger eyeing him, Poley had winked at them with evidently such a keen appreciation of their father's assish way of talking that they had been forced to stagger round the corner of the bungalow to hide the exuberance of their response.

'Well,' Mr Waterall looked round at supper to proclaim with a smile of immense complacency, 'I think you'll all agree with me that when your poor old father sets his mind on doing something he does it pretty well.'

A smooth stream of wifely flattery gushed from Mrs Waterall; and his small daughter played up to this mood of self-congratulation:

'Oh, Daddy, I think you're the cleverest daddy that ever lived, and I'm going to dance round that lovely mulberry bush every morning, and when summer comes I'll get up ever so early and perhaps I'll see the fairies.'

Ralph groaned hollowly. Roger's fat cheeks were corrugated with painful disgust.

'Haven't you two boys got anything to say in appreciation of our garden?' he inquired.

'It's quite decent,' Ralph muttered with difficulty.

'It's quite all right,' Roger mumbled.

'Well, don't sprawl all over the supper table, but sit up and pass me the bread,' said their father sharply. 'I didn't buy this place in the country for you lads to turn into a couple of hobbledehoys. It is discouraging to find you both so utterly blind to the beauties of nature.'

'Well, there isn't anything particularly beautiful in standing about in the wet all day,' Ralph argued.

'And remember, dear,' Mrs Waterall put in tactfully, 'the boys don't know so much about trees and shrubs as you do. When they see all the lovely things beginning to come out in the spring, they'll appreciate better your kindness and the wonderful opportunity you have given them of learning something about nature.'

'But they seem incapable of taking an intelligent interest in what is going on,' Mr Waterall complained. 'I had always understood that Ralph was reasonably advanced in Latin, but he couldn't translate a single one of those labels into English. He was completely flummoxed every time.'

'We don't learn that kind of Latin in school,' Ralph protested. 'Besides, half the writing on those labels was smudged out.'

'Which reminds me,' said Mr Waterall, 'to-morrow I want you and Roger to go round all the plants and carefully pencil over any labels that are all faint. I myself intend to make a plan of the garden in a note-book and enter the names so that we shall have a permanent record of them. It's no use my spending all this money on representative collections of the best shrubs if you boys are never going to be able to tell one kind from another. I only wish I'd had the advantages you had. But I had to be earning my own living when I was hardly any older than you, Ralph. You don't grasp your luck.'

The boys sat in dumb resentment. If their holidays were going to be entirely taken up by the performance of menial horticultural tasks, better by far they had remained in London.

While they were sitting thus, there floated in from the darkness of the November night the strains of a penny whistle. In the stress of the last two days Ralph had forgotten Texas Bill's promise to call in for him on Saturday night and take him to the brick-kiln. He looked nervously towards the window. He was wondering what effect Texas would have upon his father.

The whistling stopped. There was a click of the gate. There was a crunch of steps along the path. There was a confident rap on the door.

'Go and see who it is,' Mr Waterall demanded a little irritably. Country life was most delightful, but he rather wished that people would not rap on the door while he was still at supper. He disliked the idea of being discovered in the middle of his food without any chance of escape.

'I think it's a friend of mine,' said Ralph.

'A friend of yours?' his father repeated. 'What friends have you got down here?'

'It's a chap I met the other morning.'

'What's his name?'

Ralph hesitated. To announce his friend as Texas Bill might prejudice his father hopelessly. It would be more tactful to say that he did not know what his name was.

'Don't know his name?' Mr Waterall repeated. 'How on earth can he be a friend of yours if you don't know his name?'

Ralph was spared the solution of that riddle by the appearance of Texas Bill himself, who tired of waiting outside had walked in, inquiring cheerily as he entered if there was room inside for a tiddler.

'And who may you be?' Mr Waterall asked in accents of majestic frigidity.

For answer the boy in the shabby blue broadcloth suit piped upon his whistle the melody of 'The Dandy Coloured Coon', to which Mr Waterall listened with an expression of grave disapproval, which was not mitigated when the newcomer inquired of Ralph in a cheery voice:

'Is this your old man, kiddo?'

'It's my father, yes,' Ralph mumbled sheepishly, the embarrassment of the introduction choking him into incoherence.

'Pleased to meet you,' Texas Bill declared cordially, as he thrust out a grimy paw and shook Mr Waterall's hand warmly. 'And this'll be the missus, eh?' he continued, beaming at Mrs Waterall and shaking her hand with equal warmth.

'And who may you be, sir?' Mr Waterall repeated in what he hoped was a quelling voice.

This time he was not answered upon the whistle.

'William Walter Ryan. Known to all in these parts as Texas Bill, the Terror of Blindman's Gulch,' the youth announced. 'Are you in the middle of your grub? Never mind, I can tuck away another plateful before we go round and wake up old Harry.'

Ralph tried with agonized grimaces to deter Texas from alluding to the object of his call. Not that he had much hope now of escaping for the rest of the evening, whatever excuse he made. His father was showing too obvious signs of disliking the free and easy breezy manner of Texas, who was pointing with his thumb in Phyllis's direction.

'This your sis?' he asked, whereat Phyllis with a toss of her head turned her most affectedly wide open eyes in shocked surprise at her father.

Ralph knew that something must be done quickly.

'I say, can I speak to this chap a minute, Father?' he asked. 'I meant to say can I take him outside and speak to him?'

Mr Waterall would not ordinarily have agreed to such a proposal; but he was beginning to feel incompetent to deal with William Walter Ryan, and Ralph's request indicated an easy way to get rid of him.

'You may speak to him for a minute outside and you can explain to him that we are at supper,' he said.

Ralph blushing for his father's obvious lack of hospitality, retired through the front door with Texas. By the light of a watery moon he stood in colloquy with Texas amid the innumerable labels that fluttered feebly in that thicket of newly planted shrubs, not one of which had as yet succeeded in looking as real as a besom stuck handledown in a mound of soil.

'I say, you mustn't mind my governor,' Ralph explained. 'He's an awfully rummy chap. He'll be all right when he knows you better.'

'I'd have felt I'd known him for years if he'd give me a chance to get busy with my supper. I can get very familiar on half a mouthful.'

'Well, if you don't mind, Texas, I think you'd better not come back in again. It might make my governor rather shirty. I don't know if he'll let me come down to the brick-kiln anyway.'

'But I told old Harry we were coming, and he'll have chestnuts for us.'

Ralph thought desperately.

'How late will you stay?' he asked at last.

'Coo! I'll be there all night. You don't suppose I'm fool enough to go home on a Saturday night to my uncle's. Not half. Just about now he'll be starting in to chase pink and green snakes with the poker.'

'All night?' Ralph breathed. 'Will you really be there all night? I say suppose we come frightfully late? I mean about twelve? Wouldn't that matter?'

'Not a bit. Harry has to be up all night anyway when he's baking. He's got to watch the fires. The bricks would be spoilt if he let them down.'

'Well, I'll try to get out after they're all in bed,' Ralph declared adventurously.

'You know which way to come?'

'Yes, rather. And I say, Texas, you don't mind if I bring my young brother with me?'

'What, the raspberry-faced kid who was stuffing down pudden in there?'

'Yes, his name's Roger. He's quite all right really. Only of course he's rather a kid.'

'All right. Harry and I won't eat him if he won't try and eat us. So long, kiddo.'

And to the strains of 'Everything in the Garden's lovely' Texas Bill retired from the inhospitality of Dream Days to a warmer welcome elsewhere.

'Where on earth did you pick up that young scallywag?' Mr Waterall asked when his son was back in the room.

'He's a friend of the Chilcotts.'

'Oh, another Reformed Child of Israel,' Mr Waterall observed in what he fancied was a tone of sardonic humour. His wife put a finger to her lips and nodded an anxious reminder of Phyllis's presence at the supper table.

'Isn't that the young man against whom good Mrs Gnat-head opposite warned me yesterday?' he continued. 'You'll want to be a bit careful how you make friends round here, Ralph. I didn't buy this place to turn it into a thieves' kitchen. By the way, talking of kitchens,' he said to his wife, 'you really must write and tell Donkin that we cannot wait till doomsday for him to put up this kitchen door. There's a draught curling round my legs now like a lasso.'

Mr Waterall jumped up from the table in sudden exasperation and rushed into the kitchen to see if anything could be done about it.

'What in fortune's name is this extraordinary contraption?' his family heard him exclaim.

'Oh, I forgot to tell you, dear,' Mrs Waterall said in a worried voice, rising as she spoke to join her husband. 'Phyllis and I found it in the sitting-room when we came back from our little walk, and we dragged it in here. We thought it must be a mistake.'

'But what on earth is it?' Mr Waterall asked. The perplexity in their father's voice had roused the curiosity of his sons who followed him into the kitchen.

Ralph at once recognized the machine for cramming fowls which he had seen at the Chilcotts'. His heart leapt joyfully at the welcome gift, but discretion warned him to say nothing.

'It looks like some kind of engine,' he observed. He thought of the sodden carcass of the rat, which, hidden beneath some of Bocock's moss litter, was waiting to be experimented upon. Then cunningly he added, 'perhaps it's something the workmen are using.'

'But the workmen haven't been near the place for two days.'

'Well, something they've sent out to use when they do come.'

'I know what it is, Daddy,' Phyllis suddenly exclaimed. 'It's something belonging to the Mr Chilcotts. I remember it now. I saw it standing outside their little house when I went to see how my darling little goat was getting on. And I was wondering what it could be.'

Mr Waterall looked indignant.

'Is there anything in Oak . . . by the way, I didn't tell you, did I, that I've decided to call this place Oak? I don't like Oaktown and I can't stand the Oak Farm Estate. So in future we shall call it Oak. Is there anything in this place that is not contaminated by these Chilcotts? And what the deuce do they mean by leaving their engines about in our cottage? First of all their cow walks into our kitchen, then one of their friends walks in and invites himself to supper, and now this confounded contraption arrives somehow and fills up the whole place. What's it mean? There's a limit to bohemianism. I'm not narrow-minded, but I must say I take exception to the casual way in which these Chilcotts are making use of Dream Days.'

'They may have thought it might be useful to us,' Mrs Waterall suggested. 'They really are extremely kind young men, dear.'

'Useful to us? What on earth could we do with an idiotic affair covered with wheels and tubes when we've not got the slightest idea what it's for? They come sneaking in here when there's nobody about and deposit this great clumsy contraption in our kitchen . . .'

'No, dear, it was in the sitting-room,' Mrs Waterall gently corrected. 'Little Phyllis and I dragged it out here.'

'That makes it all the worse. Whatever it may be used for, it's not a thing to put in the sitting-room of people you hardly know. In my opinion they're trying to play some clownish joke. Don't keep fiddling with those wheels, Roger. And Ralph, take your foot off that treadle.'

'I think it's something to do with this tube, Father,' his elder son suggested.

Mr Waterall picked up the tube and looked down at it. At that moment Ralph started the treadle again, and a lump of congested material, the relic of some long since fattened fowl, shot out and struck Mr Waterall a smart blow just below the eye.

'Did you know it was going to do that, my boy?' he asked his elder son, looking as stern as he could with a blinking eye.

'Why should I know?' Ralph countered indignantly.

'You've seen this infernal machine before, my boy,' his father pressed, as he wiped the dried remains of mash from his eyelid.

'I may have seen it at the Chilcotts'. So did Phyllis.'

A rage seized Mr Waterall. He rushed at the crammer, dragged it outside the kitchen, and flung it over on its side in the yard.

'To-morrow,' he promised, 'I shall go into the whole question with these Chilcotts. They must be made to understand that we are not quite the same as most of the other people who live down here.'

'Not to-morrow, dear,' his wife begged. 'I've invited both

these young men to tea to-morrow. I'm sure you'll like them very much when you meet them.'

Mr Waterall could not have said in front of the children what he would have liked to say to his wife, and there being no sanctum at Dream Days in which plain speaking could be indulged without the risk of being overheard, he said nothing. He merely sat down moodily in front of the Tortoise stove and asked in a hurt voice if there was nobody capable of remembering even to bring him his slippers at the end of a long and tiring day.

Ralph, thinking of the chestnuts to be roasted at the brick-kiln, was glad to hear his father confess that the day had been tiring. He hoped that he would go to bed early and sink into a stupor of sleep as soon as his head was on the pillow. So when at a quarter to nine it was suggested that he and Roger must be sleepy and that anyway it would be better for them to retire in order to give Phyllis, whose chair-bed was in the sitting-room, an opportunity to get off to sleep, Ralph leapt up with an alacrity that once more revived in his mother her belief in the victory of his better nature. Roger was so much taken aback by his elder brother's unusually pusillanimous surrender to bed that he could think of no better excuse to delay the loath-some moment of withdrawal than the loss of his handker-chief.

'Wait a jiffy, Ralph,' he implored. 'I can't find my nose-rag.'

'Roger dear, please,' his mother protested. 'I don't like that unpleasant expression. And never mind about your handkerchief now. You can get a clean handkerchief out of your drawer.'

'Come on, you fool,' Ralph urged, with a yawn.

'And, Ralph dear, please do not call people fools. Remember what the Bible says. It's not at all a nice word to use about the house.'

'Well, Roger's such a fat lazy hog,' Ralph explained in justification of the apostrophe.

'So are you a hog, you stinking pig.' growled Roger indignantly.

'All right, you cheeky young cad. You wait,' the elder brother threatened.

Whereupon Mr Waterall who had been dozing woke up to ask if this were Billingsgate, and the boys retreated to their room, muttering at one another like a pair of sulky terriers.

'I hadn't finished the chapter I was reading in *Chums*,' Roger expostulated when he and Ralph were in their room. 'I could easily have finished it if you hadn't got up at once.'

'If you aren't jolly careful I won't tell you why I wanted to go off to bed,' Ralph threatened.

'Oh, yes,' Roger jeered. 'Of course you've always got a jolly good reason for anything *you* do.'

Ralph was tempted to push Roger into the bath; but his desire to get the rest of the family quickly off to bed restrained him. He even denied himself the pleasure of tormenting his brother any longer and explained without more ado the reason of his strategic move bedward.

'I say, I'm awfully sorry, Ralph,' the penitent minor declared. 'I really am. Only you never said anything about climbing out and going to the brick-kiln.'

'Well, how could I, you young ass, when the room was chockful of people?'

'No, I know you couldn't. I'm awfully sorry. Really, I am, Ralph.'

'All right. Only next time don't be so beastly cocky, or I'll go without you.'

The boys undressed without further argument until Ralph suggested that Roger should have a string tied to his toe to prevent his falling off to sleep.

'Why can't *you* have a string tied to *your* toe if you're so afraid of going to sleep?'

'Because I thought of this rag, that's why, you fat-faced cuckoo,' Ralph replied.

'No, you didn't. It was Texas Bill who thought of it.'

'It wasn't, you liar. I thought of climbing out of our window when he said he was going to be at the brick-kiln all night.'

'Well, you wouldn't have thought of that if he hadn't thought of asking us to go to the brickfields.'

'He didn't ask you at all, you greasy little cadger,' exclaimed Ralph, staggered by his younger brother's assumption. 'I asked if I could bring you, and I told him you didn't stink too much.'

'However much I stank he wouldn't know if you were there whether I stank or not,' Roger retorted.

'Oh, shut up. I won't take you with me in a minute.'

'Well, then I'll shut the window and you won't be able to climb in again.'

'If you did that you'd be the dirtiest cad who ever lived.'

'I don't care. So would you,' Roger retorted.

And there had been enough in his threat to make Ralph cautious of driving his younger brother to extremes.

'All right. Pax. I was only ragging when I said that about the string.'

By nine o'clock the two boys were in bed, and their mother who had come into her room at a quarter past, expecting to have to appeal in a low voice for less talking and for the extinction of candles marvelled at the stillness. So still was it that she opened the door and peeped in to ask if they were all right. Two sleepy voices from the bunks mumbled their reassurances and she closed the door again, convinced that, whatever the discomfort of life in a small country bungalow might be, the moral effect of it on her sons would always make it immensely worth while. When their mother had retired, Ralph tapped on Roger's bunk.

'We were rather silly asses to undress,' he whispered. 'The mater didn't bring a candle in. I say, mind you don't go to sleep.'

'Rather not,' Roger promised. 'But I wish we could read. When do you think the pater will come to bed?'

'Pretty soon, I expect,' said Ralph hopefully.

There was a longish silence, and then Roger leaned over to know if Ralph was still awake.

'Yes, I'm drawing with a wax match,' Ralph said. 'Can't you smell the phosphorus?'

Roger in his anxiety to see what his brother was drawing leaned so far over that he overbalanced and crashed to the floor.

'Gently, boys, gently,' they heard their mother's reproachful voice murmur from the other room. 'I thought you were being so quiet.'

'Roger fell out of his bunk,' Ralph called back reassuringly. And then to Roger he whispered, 'Get into bed with me. That'll keep us awake.'

For some time the brothers amused themselves by drawing phosphorescent faces. Then unfortunately Ralph pressed too hard with his wax vesta, and when it flared up suddenly he let it drop on to his brother who leapt up and struck his head against the bottom of the upper bunk.

'Boys, boys, please go to sleep quietly,' their mother begged, 'I can hear Father getting ready to come to bed.'

This warning kept Roger from trying to avenge his brother's clumsiness, and they agreed to see which could count up to a thousand first under their breath, tremendous oaths of strictly honourable behaviour having first been vowed.

Six minutes later Ralph whispered 'one thousand' and Roger did not dispute his achievement. He had fallen fast asleep shortly after he had reached five hundred. Ralph decided to let him sleep while their father, who had just come into the next room, undressed. When he began to gargle his throat, as he always did last thing, he would seize the opportunity to wake Roger up again. So when he heard his father's liquid notes he dug Roger in the ribs, who shot up in bed with a stifled yelp, gasping.

'What is it? What is it?'

'Shut up, you fool. It's the pater gargling.'

'I dreamt I was in a railway accident,' said Roger.

'Well, don't go to sleep again,' Ralph whispered fiercely, 'because I jolly well won't wake you again.'

The two boys concentrated hard upon keeping awake, and prayed for the sound of their father's snores to come quickly.

'We'll have to throw the clothes off,' Ralph announced at last. 'I jolly nearly went to sleep then.'

So they pushed back the bedclothes, and though the chilly effect was unpleasant it certainly was easier for a while to keep awake. But there was no sound of paternal snoring. On the contrary he was evidently reading in bed, because there was still a golden streak under the door.

'Do you think it's nearly twelve yet?' Ralph whispered in his brother's ear.

Roger suggested holding up the blanket while Ralph struck a match and squinted at his Waterbury.

'My watch must have stopped,' said Ralph.

'Why?'

'Well, it's only a quarter to ten. Where's your Waterbury?'

'It's under my pillow.'

'Well, get it.'

But on Roger's watch being examined it confirmed Ralph's as an honest timekeeper. It was in fact only a quarter to ten.

'The pater may go on reading for hours yet,' Ralph muttered in despair.

'He reads such frightful tosh too,' Roger whispered, who was thinking regretfully of the unfinished chapter of that serial in *Chums*.

'Perhaps if one of us stood in the bath while the other stayed in bed,' Ralph suggested, 'we could take it in turns to wake one another.'

Roger, who felt convinced that he would be the first called upon to perform the less pleasant part of this experiment and that when it came to his elder brother's turn to do sentry go in the bath, he would decide that the experiment was a failure, argued that it would make too much noise.

'Are you boys still talking in there?' their father's voice inquired from the next room.

'I only asked Roger if we had to go to church to-morrow,' Ralph explained in an injured voice.

'Well, go to sleep. Your mother will decide that in the morning.'

For the next quarter of an hour the boys lay still and by the stern exercise of will-power kept themselves awake. At last that detestable streak of golden light vanished from beneath the door. Ralph leant across to breathe the good news in his brother's ear.

'Look out, you cad,' Roger grumbled indignantly. 'You spat in my ear then.'

'Well, you shouldn't grow such big ears,' Ralph retorted. 'And shut up, or the pater may light the candle again.'

Mercifully for the boys their father, exhausted by horticultural decisions, fell asleep fairly soon, and presently they heard his first snore. Beleaguered damsels in a castle heard not more joyfully the horn of a knightly rescuer.

'You dress first,' whispered Ralph, 'and then you can lie in bed while I dress. Only, don't go making a frightful row. We'll have to put our boots on outside.'

To Ralph lying in bed his brother's attempt to dress quietly sounded noisier than pigs being fed, for Roger bending hither and thither in the darkness to search for his clothes apparently could not move without uttering a loud grunt.

'Don't make such a beastly row, you fat porker,' he adjured fiercely.

'Well, I can't see to buckle my bags', replied Roger, with a loud grunt of exhaustion.

When it came to Ralph's turn he was so anxious to give a demonstration to his fat brother of easy, quiet, and rapid dressing that he dropped his vest in the bath, and in trying to save it barked his shins on the rim; and when he tried to open a drawer quietly to extract a clean vest, the drawer in coming out made a noise like one of his father's more passionately convulsive snores. However, in the end both boys were dressed, and the ticklish business began of getting out of a very small window without any sill to it.

At the cost of a certain amount of damage to a representative collection of cotoneasters which had been hastily planted underneath the window of the boys' room the business was carried through successfully, and the charm of freedom in this damp November moonlight shed a magic on the boys' mood as they crept round the bungalow and made for the lane. They negotiated the path without too many crunches, but the latch of the gate came up with such a loud click that they thought they were lost. However, the curtains of their father's room did not reveal his face, and they reached the lane in safety. Presently they were able to put on their boots and as they set out for the brickfield, not minding how much noise their footsteps made on the muddy road, they felt that at last country life was beginning in earnest.

CHAPTER NINE

THE two boys walked on arm in arm along the lane between the high hazel hedges. The elation of their successful escape evoked a series of almost affectionate confidences.

'I don't expect the pater will always be down here when we are,' Ralph began on an optimistic note.

'And if he is,' said Roger, 'he won't always be putting on so much side about his rotten plants and everything else.'

'He has been putting on frightful side since he bought this place,' Ralph agreed.

'But he puts on side about everything he buys. Do you remember when he bought that bike?'

Ralph groaned at the reminiscence.

'And it was a most frightfully heavy bike. It weighed thirty-six pounds,' Roger went on contemptuously.

In those days lightness was the quality which gave a bicycle modishness and style.

'A chap in my form this term's got a racer that only weighs seventeen,' Ralph announced.

'Good lumme, how fizzing!' Roger sighed enviously.

'And he thinks that if he takes off the bell he's got and puts on a Little Demon instead it'll only weigh a bit over sixteen and a half.'

'Good gum, how spiffing!' Roger ejaculated. 'What's his gear?'

'A hundred and two. He can scorch like anything.'

Roger who had never succeeded in getting a chance to ride a bicycle above fifty-six was lost in a dream of sublime speed.

'Do you think the pater will get us that pony he talked about?'

Ralph shook his head doubtfully.

'If he does he'll only get some rotten brute that Phyllis can ride. I don't know what we can do about Phyllis. She's more affected than ever.'

'It's Father's fault.'

'Yes, because she sucks up to him,' Ralph commented.

'Are there any gypsies round here?' Roger asked suddenly.

'Why?'

'I don't know. I was thinking if there were she might get stolen.'

'What would gypsies want to steal Phyllis for?' Ralph asked.

'Well, she's got a very pink face and they could stain it with walnut juice. That's what they do.'

'We'd only have to rescue her,' Ralph pointed out austerely.

'Well, if we rescued her she'd have to shut up being so affected.'

'She'd be more affected than ever. Especially if it was in the papers,' Ralph declared.

The odour of the brickfields began to mingle with the moist autumnal scents of the hedgerows on either side of the lane, and presently a tawny glow revealed the entrance to the kiln itself. The renowned Harry Gibbs came to the doorway and bade them welcome. He was a loose-limbed lanky man of about thirty-five with flaxen hair that looked bleached against the terra-cotta of his face and neck and sinewy arms. Lolling on a bench before one of the doors of the furnace which was open and glowing they beheld Texas Bill piping away on his whistle. An auburn cat was drowsing on his knee, and on a tray in front of the furnace chestnuts were popping.

'Hallo, here are the kiddos,' said Texas cordially.

The kiddos grinning shyly took their seats on the bench and started in on the chestnuts, after which they helped Harry Gibbs to stoke his furnaces and then settled down to hear some of his famous stories about the poaching he had done in youth and other delectable adventures of a similar nature. And after that Harry Gibbs who had a good tenor voice, sang to them old English folksongs accompanied by Texas Bill on his whistle. And after that Harry's brown curly-coated retriever came in from the woods with a rabbit in his mouth which with much complimentary tail wagging he deposited at his master's feet. Harry Gibbs spat three times into the furnace with a kind of ritualistic solemnity, and after slapping his corduroy-clad thighs declared that he was bothered if they wouldn't make a rabbit stew this very moment. So they routed about among the shadows of the great kiln and discovered all sorts of delicacies like onions and milk while Harry paunched and

97

skinned the rabbit and told a story of how he had once gone mining somewhere in South America and met a puma face to face and stared him out of his path. The expressions on the faces of the two boys revealed their happy, indeed their rapturous consciousness of the fact that they were now at least really leading the life of men.

'It's half-past eleven,' Ralph murmured to his brother in awe.

'Good gum!' Roger exclaimed in amazement at the combination of luck and daring which had conferred upon them this supreme experience.

At home when rabbit was put on the Waterall board it was the custom of Ralph and Roger to show every sign of a rapid and overpowering nausea induced by the mere prospect of having to contemplate partaking of such a disgusting dish. But the rabbit of the Waterall ménage in Orange Road which was wont to float like stray bits of kitten drowned in the water in which the plates had been washed was a different affair from this succulent creature whose plump and candid flesh peeped delicately from a milky stock fragrant with onion and parsley. And when the rabbit had been eaten with the horn spoons and the black two-pronged forks that lent it such an added savour Harry Gibbs produced a great china mug full of beer which was passed round like a loving-cup. To be sure, Roger nearly disgraced his elder brother by sniffing a lot of froth up his nose when it came to his turn; but after all in this company such an accident would only have added to the conviviality of the occasion. Finally, as the perfect crown for this glorious night Texas drew from his pocket a packet of cigarettes and handed them as a matter of course to Ralph and Roger, who tried to accept them with a suitably adolescent nonchalance, but beamed like children round a Christmas tree in despite of it.

The combination of chestnuts, stewed rabbit, beer, warmth, and silence necessary to enjoy the exquisite flavour of the cigarettes induced a drowsiness in Ralph and Roger which they tried to fight against as unmanly, but which stole upon them more and more potently. Time glided by in a dream. Ralph looked at his watch.

'I say it's two o'clock,' he exclaimed in a voice of awe. To have found himself on the moon would not have made him seem more remote from real life than to find himself awake and dressed at such an hour.

'I hope our governor's still asleep,' he said.

Had Ralph uttered this hope a few moments earlier, his governor would have been asleep; but at this moment he had just been wakened by a series of loud thumps on the front door of his country house. He had just sat up in bed, and asked his wife who on earth could be knocking at this hour.

'I can't imagine, dear, unless it's the police.'

Phyllis, who perhaps injudiciously just before she went to bed had been reading a story about the revolt of the slaves in Jamaica, now came rushing into her parents' room with piercing cries of alarm.

'The black men are coming after us. They'll murder us. Daddy.'

The thumps on the door redoubled in frequency and vigour.

'Did you actually see a black man, Phyllis?' her father asked in a voice that was distinctly tremulous.

'No, but I was reading about the naughty black slaves who murdered their masters and mistresses.'

'A little girl of your age shouldn't fill her head with such infernal nonsense,' said Mr Waterall angrily. 'I thought at first you'd really seen a black man.'

'I wonder if we ought to open the door,' Mrs Waterall quavered.

'The bolts are drawn, aren't they?'

'Yes, dear.'

'And the chains on?'

'Yes, dear.'

'Then wait a minute. I'm going to look out of the window and see who it is. Ralph! Roger! Come in here and look out of the window and see who's kicking up this infernal row. I'll tell you one thing,' Mr Waterall went on, turning to his wife, 'if I find either of those Chilcotts is waking us up in this abominable way, there's going to be trouble in Oaktown—I mean Oak. Ralph! Roger! Phyllis, don't stand there shuddering in your nightdress. Go and wake your brothers.'

'Oh, no, Daddy. I'm frightened,' she moaned.

'I'll go and wake the boys, dear,' Mrs Waterall volunteered.

'Fancy being able to sleep through a racket like this,' grumbled the head of the family. 'No wonder they're late for breakfast every morning.'

Whoever it was knocking outside he had seen the light in the bedroom, and he was now rapping almost as loudly on the window.

'Who are you?' Mr Waterall bellowed. 'What do you want? Good heavens, he's pulling down the window. He's going to climb in. Where are those confounded boys? Why don't they wake up? They must go and fetch Poley or Gnathead. I warn you,' said Mr Waterall to the unknown intruder in a voice which he tried to think was shaking with anger, 'I warn you that I have a revolver here, and that I shall not hesitate to shoot if you don't go away from the window at once.'

Then Mr Waterall turned to his wife.

'Give me a weapon of some kind.'

But she could think of nothing better than her own indiarubber hot-water bottle which her husband spurned as useless.

The unknown was apparently now trying to climb up and get into the room over the top of the open window. Mr Waterall suddenly remembered the story of Troppmann who had laid out a whole family with an axe, and he told his wife to go in and get the two boys out of bed. His intention was to retreat with the family by the back entrance and rouse some of the neighbours.

'The boys have gone,' Mrs Waterall wailed from the inner room. 'Their bunks are empty.'

Mr Waterall rushed to the window of his own room. That Ralph and Roger had dared to play a practical joke like this upon their father put out of his head all unpleasant ideas of wandering murderers with axes.

When, however, he pulled the curtains he saw looking down at him over the top of the window a large bearded face with a shock of hair, the face of the conventional Russian nihilist, but certainly not the face of either of his two sons.

'Where is my nephew?' it asked.

'How do I know where your nephew is?' Mr Waterall replied. 'I don't even know who he is. And I don't know who you are.'

'My name is Augustus Ryan,' said the intruder. 'What's your name?'

'Never mind what my name is,' said Mr Waterall, who was beginning to feel a little bolder now that he could see the intruder was not carrying an axe.

'I don't mind what your name is,' Mr Augustus Ryan declared. 'I'm looking for my nephew.'

'That doesn't give you the right to go round banging on people's doors and windows at this hour of the night.'

'Yes, it does,' Mr Ryan contradicted.

'Why does it?'

'Because I'm looking for my nephew.'

'What on earth leads you to suppose that a nephew of yours is in my bungalow?'

'Because he turned loose hundreds of pink and lemon-yellow rats in my room this evening and it has taken me nearly all night to clear them out again. And now I'm going to give my nephew a jolly good thrashing. My mother married his brother, so my brother was his father. That makes it my duty to see he behaves himself. If your nephew put pink and lemon-yellow rats in your room, you'd call him to account, wouldn't you? I'll repeat that remark. You'd call him to account, wouldn't you? I'll repeat it again. You'd call . . .'

'You're drunk,' said Mr Waterall contemptuously.

'What makes you think that?' asked Mr Ryan in a puzzled tone of voice.

'Get down from that window and leave the precincts of my bungalow.'

'Precincts? Did you say "precincts"?' Mr Ryan demanded.

'I did.'

'So did I,' said Mr Ryan; and he laughed so heartily at this triumph of elocution that he lost his hold on the window and fell backwards with a crash among some of Mr Waterall's crataeguses.

Mr Waterall took advantage of this to return to his terrified wife and daughter who were crouching in the back room.

'It's all right,' he said. 'Just a drunken lunatic. There's nothing whatever to get frightened about.'

'Nothing to be frightened about?' his wife exclaimed in what for her was a voice of something like indignation. 'A drunken lunatic has either carried off both our boys, or else frightened them out of bed, goodness knows where. A drunken lunatic is trying to get into the bungalow by climbing up the window. And you say there's nothing to be frightened of. Really, Robert dear, I think there's such a thing as being too calm sometimes. Listen!' she cried, 'there he is climbing up the window again. If he murders us, it will certainly be your fault for taking it all as a matter of course.'

'He's apparently got it into his head that a nephew of his is here.'

'There you are, Robert. Ralph! Roger! Where are you?' the distracted mother moaned. 'Depend upon it he thought they were his nephew. Drunken people always see two of everything. Oh, those poor darling boys, they must have been frightened out of their very lives.'

'Well, we can't do anything about it till they come back,' said Mr Waterall.

'Indeed we can. I'm going to get Phyllis into something warm and then we'll escape through the kitchen and go and wake up the Chilcotts and ask for help.'

'I won't have you going round to these Chilcotts. The proper person to wake is Poley who is in my service. Moreover, his bungalow is much nearer. I'll go back and keep this fellow's attention occupied while you slip away up the garden and across Hobday's plot to Poley.'

Mr Waterall went into his room to continue the interview with Mr Ryan whose shock head was once more leaning over the top of the window.

'What I was saying just now when my foot slipped was precincts,' Mr Ryan began. 'And now I hope you'll have the courtesy to give me back my nephew.'

'But who is your nephew?'

'I made that perfectly clear just now. I made it perfectly clear that he was the son of my brother's wife. When I retired from poetry and came down here to cultivate the soil my nephew came down too, and it was his duty to look after me. And it's not looking after me to bring lemon-pink rats into my room.'

'But who is your nephew?' Mr Waterall repeated in exasperation.

'You know, you really are an unusually stupid man. I believe you're the stupidest man I ever met. In fact you're so stupid that I shall call you Mr Stupid. Don't you understand that when a brother marries a wife and has a son that son is the nephew of that brother's brother? Well, that's my position. You see, my brother married beneath him. He married beneath him in two senses, his wife being a short shop-assistant, and when I came into this legacy and retired from writing poetry I felt it was my duty to my dead brother who had a seizure in the middle of the overture and fell back dying into the arms of the first clarinet at the Theatre Royal, Chatsea. Is that perfectly clear?'

'But who is your nephew? That's what I want to know!'

'You know, you really are an exceptionally stupid man, Mr Stupid. My brother was a conductor, and he married a short shop-assistant, and I felt it was my duty to bring up his eldest son as a gentleman. But he still has some bad habits. Putting pink and yellow rats into my bedroom is not the behaviour I expect from a nephew of mine. For which reason being myself one of the boys of the old brigade I feel it incumbent upon myself to punish him. Now then, Mr Stupid, I hope you won't keep me here hanging on to your window any longer, but that you will hand over my nephew without any further attempts at prevarication.'

It suddenly occurred to Mr Waterall that the name of the objectionable youth who had apparently expected to be invited to supper this evening had been Ryan.

'Does your nephew play the penny whistle?' he asked.

'He does play the penny whistle. He inherited his musical talent from my brother who was the conductor at the Theatre Royal, Chatsea.'

'Well, he came down hereabout half-past seven; but he did not stay.'

'This is a bungalow answering to the ridiculous name of Dream Days, isn't it?'

'It is called Dream Days, yes.'

'Well, that's where I was informed my nephew was. And you, sir, are called Waterall, I believe.'

'That is my name.'

'It's a terribly gloomy name, isn't it?'

'I had not thought about it as a particularly gloomy name,' the owner of the name replied with dignity.

'Hadn't you? You surprise me. It has cast a terrible gloom over me to think that anybody should have to go through life with a name like that.'

'Well, sir, I do not require your sympathy,' said Mr Waterall. 'And now I have told you that your nephew is not here, perhaps you can inform me if you have seen anything of my sons?'

'Your sons? Are they called Waterall too?'

'Of course they're called Waterall,' said the father of them irritably. 'What else would they be called!'

'Why should I have seen your sons? When the whole of my faculties are concentrated upon seeing my nephew it would be more than improbable that I should have seen your sons. In the first place how could I have known they were your sons? They might have been anybody's sons, by which observation I intend no reflection upon Mrs Waterall. The point is that if I had met two sons walking along the lane I should have said to myself, 'Hallo, there's a couple of sons," but I wouldn't have known they were yours. So your sons are missing too, are they?'

At this moment Mr Waterall heard an agonized whisper from his wife to pull the curtains while she and Phyllis ran through the bedroom to reach the kitchen and obtain help. So Mr Waterall pulled the curtains and hid from the eyes of Mr Augustus Ryan the flight of his wife and daughter. As soon as they were safely through he pulled the curtains again, for he did not want the shock-headed visitant to chase them up the garden and intended to keep him in conversation until they could reach the security of Fernbank.

When, however, he pulled the curtains there was no sign of Mr Augustus Ryan.

Mr Waterall dragged on some clothes over his nightshirt, paused but for a moment in the kitchen to pull on his boots, and hurried up the garden to rescue his wife and daughter. They were nearly across Hobday's half-acre when he over-took them, running as hard as they could through a jungle of decayed cabbage stalks.

'Oh, it's you Robert,' Mrs Waterall exclaimed in relief. 'I thought it was the cow.'

'If you'd thought it was that abominable creature like a drunken pavement-artist, I could have understood, but to think I was a cow is simply being hysterical,' said Mr Waterall fretfully, for one of his boots had come off in the clay and he had tripped on a sharp flint with his bare foot before he could stop himself.

'But we saw the cow, Robert.'

'Where?'

'In the garden.'

'Nonsense, you must have seen this fellow Ryan and thought he was a cow.'

'No, Daddy, really,' Phyllis put in. 'It was the cow. She was eating your lovely trees, and then she galloped away round the cottage.'

'Well, I object on principle to cows coming into our garden; but in this case the brute seems to have done us a good turn by ridding us of that drunken sweep who was making such a nuisance of himself. However, I think we had better rouse Poley now that we've come so far. I am a bit disgusted with the cowardice of Ralph and Roger in bolting off like that. They seem quite incapable of meeting any kind of little crisis that may arise. You remember the way I had to deal with the dog you brought back from the Dogs' Home?'

A minute or two later Mrs Poley sat up in bed and listened to a knocking on the door of Fernbank.

'Will,' she breathed, 'wake up and get the warming-pan.'

'What for?' exclaimed her husband who was still dazed with sleep.

'To hit 'em on the head,' Mrs Poley whispered savagely.

'Rats?' asked Mr Poley.

'Rats, no, you silly man. Burglars. Thieves.'

Mr Waterall rapped again upon the door.

'It's somebody wanting to come in, my dear,' said Mr Poley.

'That's what I'm telling you, aren't I? Get the warming-pan and give me the big saucepan.'

'Hush, my dear, it's a voice outside calling "Mr Poley". A burglar wouldn't say "mister". Who is it?'

'It's Mr and Mrs Waterall from Dream Days. We are extremely sorry to disturb you at this hour; but we have just had a very unpleasant experience with a drunken man.'

'Will,' whispered Mrs Poley hoarsely, 'give me my bed-wrap and put on your trousers. If that Blackham's come back, we'll sell up Fernbank and go to live with my sister at Charmouth. Family differences aren't pleasant but they're better than Blackham.'

Presently Poley unbolted the door and received the refugees from Dream Days.

'Will,' Mrs Poley whispered, 'pour out the cowslip wine. The poor souls are perishing with the damp.'

While the refugees were being revived and relating their tale, Ralph and Roger escorted by Texas Bill passed along in the lane below, and, after a good-night full of affectionate gratitude and admiration, they crept cautiously through the gate of Dream Days and regained their room as they left it by the window. Breathless they listened for a moment.

'It's all right,' Ralph whispered in relief. 'He's still snoring.'

The two boys were soon in their bunks and fell asleep almost instantly.

So soundly did they sleep that to their poignant regret they did not hear anything of the stirring events from which they were separated by nothing more substantial than a thin door.

At Fernbank it was settled by Mrs Poley, who sat up in bed and planned the operations like a von Moltke, that her husband should return with Mr Waterall and find out if all was clear at Dream Days before Mrs Waterall and Phyllis left the protection of Fernbank.

'It's strange,' she said, 'that the biggest blayguards always give themselves the biggest airs. There was that Blackham always boasting about the Prince of Wales, and now there's this Ryan, the drunkenest sot for miles around, though there's sots and to spare in this part of the country, this Ryan looking like a cannibal king and stopping everybody he meets to tell them he's a gentleman. "Thank God," I've said to Mr Poley a dozen times, "thank God I know what the gentry is and have lived among them, and if that grimy-looking mop's a gentleman," I've said, "I must be the Empress of India," and which of course I'm not nor ever pretended to be.'

'Will,' she went on, wagging a bulky forefinger at her husband, 'you do as I say and take the warming-pan, and if he so much as looks at you, just you hit him on the head without any nonsense. He'll hardly feel it with all that forest of hair, but it'll show him you don't intend to have any of his vulgarity about being a gentleman. They say he earned a living writing mottoes for those fussy fidgety crackers which I never could abide, before he came down here to live on the land. Yes, live on the land was a good name for it, for I've peeped over the gate with my own eyes and seen him fall flat on his face five times in the road before he turned the bend. And as for the mottoes, well, I've read a few mottoes, and more than vulgar some of them were. Well, I say I've read them, but looked at them with disgust would be nearer the mark. Now, get along, Will, and don't keep Mr Waterall hanging about. I never knew such a man for not being able to start. You'd better put on my sealskin coat, or you may catch your death.'

Poley had not ventured to disobey his wife since he had been engaged to her. So he put on the sealskin coat which was cut in the fashion of the late seventies and had been presented to her by old Lady Devizes. Nor did he forget the warming-pan, though when he and Mr Waterall were on their way to Dream Days, Mr Waterall urged him not to use it unless Ryan showed signs of violence.

'Just as well to have it though,' said Poley, who looked like Robinson Crusoe carrying something back from the wreck to his cave. 'Mrs Poley's always right. I never knew a woman who was always as right as she is. She's seven years older than me and she's seen a lot more of the world. But she can't put up with Hampshire. No, no. Hampshire hogs they always say, and Hampshire hogs they are. They wouldn't get the name of hogs if they didn't behave like hogs. And it makes other people hoggish. There's hardly anybody in Oaktown who's really from Hampshire as you might say, but they've got the hoggishness already. It's in the air. Hoggishness is in the Hampshire air. Mrs Poley's Dorset. I'm Kent. We're like fish out of water in this hoggishness.'

'By the way, Mr Poley, does that cow of the Chilcotts ever get as far as Fernbank?'

'It came once. It came once and looked over Mrs Poley's shoulder when she was peeling some potatoes in what we call the brewhouse. And she said without looking around, "Don't breathe down the back of my neck like that, Will. You know I don't like it." I'm bound to say I had to laugh, though at the time Mrs Poley was a bit huffy with me for laughing. But really the expression on her face when she turned round and saw that the cow would have made anybody laugh.'

And for the rest of the road between Fernbank and Dream Days Mr Poley was too much overcome by the recollection of that expression to do anything except chuckle to himself.

There were no signs of the cow when they walked cautiously round the bungalow and there were no signs of Mr Augustus Ryan.

'All seems quiet again,' Mr Waterall observed. 'We'll just take a look round indoors, and then if you'll kindly go and fetch Mrs Waterall I'll stay here. Oh, by the way, what is this machine? It was left here this evening by the Chilcotts.' He pointed to the prostrate crammer.

'Why, that's a chaff-cutter,' said Mr Poley. 'Wait a moment, though. No, it ain't. No, that's no chaff-cutter. I know what that is. It's a crammer.'

'A crammer?'

'It crams fowl with food to fatten them. Some use a crammer. Others use a bicycle pump.'

'Who could cram food into fowls with a bicycle pump?'

'Oh, that just blows them up. Makes them look plump. This pushes the food down their throats.'

'But why should these young men suppose that I have any use for such an instrument?'

Mr Poley shook his head. To him it was only another instance of that much disapproved Hampshire behaviour. A moment later he was to be offered another.

'Don't you have a back door then?' he asked.

'You may well ask,' said Waterall bitterly, as they entered the unguarded kitchen. 'That door should have been in place long ago; but Donkin the builder has dilly-dallied and the result is we have to exist in the greatest discomfort with smoking lamps and cows dropping in at all hours just because Mr Donkin has seen fit to dilly-dally.'

Mr Poley clicked his tongue.

'Too bad. Too bad. But there you are. What can you expect in Hampshire? You wouldn't find a builder like that in Kent. And you wouldn't find one in Dorset.'

When they passed through into the living-room from the kitchen, Mr Waterall looked at the table in the middle of the room and frowned.

'I don't remember seeing a poker on the table when we went out,' he said. Then he gripped Mr Poley's arm. 'Listen! Do you hear anything?'

'It sounds like snoring,' said Poley.

'A cow couldn't make a noise like that?'

'Not unless it was took ill.'

'Then it must be that drunken swine snoring in my

bungalow. Mr Poley, I believe he has actually had the insolence to go to bed in my room.'

With this Mr Waterall flung open the door and, holding the candle above his head, perceived deep in the very middle of the pillows what he knew could be nothing else than the shaggy hair of Augustus Ryan, though beheld thus there was little to show that it was part of a human creature.

A rage seized Mr Waterall, a rage such as in all his life he had never experienced. For a moment he was tempted to snatch the warming-pan from Poley and bring it down with a crash on that great tussock of hair; but instead he snatched from the washstand a cake of soap and flung it at the intruder. The snoring ceased abruptly. Mr Augustus Ryan sat up in bed, stared hard at Mr Poley, lay down again, and pulled the bedclothes over his head.

This was too much for Mr Waterall. He snatched the warming-pan from Mr Poley and prodded the intruder with the handle.

'Get out of my bed,' he shouted. 'Get out at once, you drunken scoundrel. What do you mean by sneaking in here and getting into my bed?'

'Take away that bear first,' Mr Ryan called from beneath the clothes.

'There's no bear here. You're drunk. You're in my bed, and you're drunk. If you don't get out, I'll fetch the police and have you arrested.'

Mr Ryan peered cautiously above the clothes and buried his head again.

'I saw it,' he called from underneath. 'I won't move from here till you take that bear away. I thought it was a bull when I saw it coming round the corner just now, but I perceive now that it is a bear.'

Mr Poley shook his head.

'He thinks I'm a bear. Fancy that! And there's the trash that go about Oaktown bragging that they're gentlefolk.'

'Isn't that the voice of that silly old woman Poley?' Mr Ryan asked from beneath the bedclothes.

'Vulgar and uncivilized,' commented Poley. 'Hoggish!'

'I'll stand no more of this,' cried Mr. Waterall, and seizing the bedclothes he pulled them back to reveal the prostrate form of Mr Augustus Ryan dressed in a Norfolk suit.

'You take one arm, Mr Waterall, and I'll take the other,' said Poley. 'And we'll have him out of here and into the lane in two two's.'

'No bear's going to hug me,' declared Mr Ryan, with which he jumped up, made a dart for the door leading into the boy's room, and rushed through. There was a sound like stage thunder followed by a splash.

'My God, I've fallen into a well,' the fugitive exclaimed. Then seeing Poley advancing with a candle he jumped out of the bath, made for the window, scrambled through, and rushed round the corner of the bungalow to reach the lane, crying as he ran, 'Look out for bears, everybody . . . there's a bear coming . . . look out, all!'

His footsteps died away up the lane; his voice grew fainter and fainter in the nebulous moonlight.

'I think we've got rid of him this time,' said Mr Waterall.

'Hallo,' he exclaimed flashing his candle on the bunks of his two sons. 'Why they're both in bed all the time.'

'And fast asleep,' Mr Poley added.

'Mrs Waterall in her agitation must have imagined the bunks were empty,' said the father.

'Fancy sleeping through all that,' Mr Poley commented.

'These boys of mine would sleep through an earthquake. Well, it's half past three, Mr Poley. I'm very much obliged to you. I think perhaps I'd better wait here and get you to escort Mrs Waterall and my little girl back. Somebody will have to remake this bed entirely. And that's a feminine job. By Jove, I wish it *had* been a bear. I wouldn't have put out a finger to save that ruffian from being hugged to death.'

'Hamshire hogs! Hamshire hogs!' Mr Poley muttered as he hurried off to fetch Mrs Waterall, a queer figure in that old-fashioned sealskin coat which Lady Devizes had presented to his wife twenty years before.

CHAPTER TEN

PERHAPS the atrocious behaviour of Mr Augustus Ryan made Mr Waterall more tolerant of the rest of humanity. At any rate, he did not agitate the feelings of his family by a discouraging reception of the Chilcotts when they arrived for tea on Sunday afternoon. Ralph and Roger decided that such cordiality was due to his longing for an audience to whom he could relate the adventures of the preceding night and to whom he could boast of his representative collection of shrubs. But then Ralph and Roger were feeling a little sore at having failed to wake up even when the uncle of Texas had fallen into their bath. To be sure, their escapade to the brickfield had remained a secret; but it had been a blow that on the one night they should think they had had the adventure of their lives the rest of the family should have had the adventure of theirs. Ralph was puzzled by the extraordinarily neat appearance of the Chilcott brothers in their Sunday clothes. He could not imagine how they had achieved it in that shack. It was as surprising as the change of the caterpillar in the chrysalis.

'I want to enlist your sympathy with a project of mine,' Mr Waterall was saying, 'I want you to support me in getting the name of Oak recognized for this place instead of Oaktown. My point is that it was originally Oak Farm. Very well, as soon as it ceases to become a farm it becomes Oak. By calling it Oaktown we expose ourselves to the obvious gibe that Tintown would be a better name. Indeed I understand that some of the Galtonians do employ that cheap witticism already.'

'Well, I'm always ready for a change,' Rehob Chilcott proclaimed. 'I've no patience with the stick-in-the-muds of this world.'

'Good,' said Mr Waterall. 'I've already spoken to Poley on the subject, and I've no doubt Gnathead will support us.'

'Kettlewell won't.'

'Kettlewell?'

'That's the retired major who's building himself a house in the middle of the coppice behind the old farm cottages.'

'Ah, I haven't met him yet.'

'He's a terror,' said Micha Chilcott with a broad grin on his porcine countenance.

'I venture to think he will not terrify me,' grandly prophesied Mr Waterall, who by now was beginning in retrospect to regard his encounter with Augustus Ryan during the night as comparable to the exploits of Jack the Giant Killer and such worthies of romance.

'It was Kettlewell who first started calling it Oaktown,' observed Rehob. 'And he's one of those bottle-nosed old Tories who'd like to put us all back in the Ark.'

'Well, I am myself what you call a Tory,' Mr Waterall admitted. 'But I hope I have a stronger civic sense than Major Kettlewell. We are off back to London tomorrow evening; but I suggest we hold a meeting of Oak residents sometime and pass a strongly worded resolution, declaring our unalterable determination to call what was the Oak Farm Estate, Oak, and, at the same time, demanding a post-office.'

The Chilcott brothers smiled at Mrs Waterall who blushed.

'I think I told you, dear,' she murmured, 'that I made a little mistake and posted my letters in the box which the Mr Chilcotts have fixed to their gate to save the postman walking all the way up the drive.'

'And as we were getting nothing but bills,' added Rehob, 'we didn't collect our letters for a week.'

'Yes, I heard about that,' said Mr Waterall a little frigidly. He did not approve of a wife of his behaving with quite so much stupidity. 'By the way,' he went on, 'perhaps my eldest boy told you a cow of yours has taken rather a fancy to our kitchen.'

'Yes, she's a friendly old soul, isn't she?' said Micha.

'I've no doubt,' Mr Waterall agreed. 'But as a matter of fact we have just planted the garden with a rather carefully chosen collection of shrubs and trees, and I'm rather anxious they shouldn't be eaten before they have a chance to display their full beauty.'

'Yes, you ought to put up a fence,' Rehob declared firmly.

'I hadn't thought of doing that just yet,' said Mr Waterall. 'Fencing is rather an expensive item, I believe.'

'Well, you really ought to do it,' Rehob advised. 'Hobday will have his bungalow built in another couple of months and you'll want to fence off his family. They'll eat more than our cow by what I saw of them. Then you're bound to get people on the other side of you soon. As a matter of fact Micha and I have got to fence our place, and you won't be troubled any more by the old lady.'

'The old lady? Is there an old lady then who makes a nuisance of herself in the district? We shall really have to press for more attention by the constable,' said Mr Waterall.

'No I meant our old cow, Duchess. And what are you going to do about your goat? I don't think she'll ever give any milk again.'

'Dear me, that's bad news,' said Mr Waterall. 'What makes you think that?'

'Mr Chilcott, you're not eating anything,' Mrs Waterall intervened quickly. 'Do try a piece of this cake. Phyllis dear, will you run out into the kitchen, darling, and get mother some more hot water?'

Phyllis tried to linger, but her mother outmanœuvred her by heaping cake on Rehob's plate until she was out of the room.

'Robert, dear,' Mrs Waterall murmured, 'won't you and Mr Chilcott talk about the goat together quietly after tea?'

'Oh, it's only that the goat is too old,' Rehob resumed. 'She must be fifteen years old if she's a day. Perhaps more. She'll never kid again.'

'Did I put enough sugar in your tea, Mr Chilcott?' Mrs Waterall put in, with an anxious backward glance over her shoulder in the direction of the kitchen.

'Well, what can be done with her?' Mr Waterall asked.

'Micha and I would keep her; but she's taken to eating our currants and she doesn't agree with the Duchess, so we can't keep her in the cowshed.'

'In other words we must get rid of her?'

'Well, she's really not worth her feed. Of course, there's just a chance that next spring she . . .'

'Mr Chilcott, please,' his hostess begged. Phyllis was coming back with the hot water, and this conversation simply had to be stopped.

'By the way, did you amuse yourself with the crammer?' Micha Chilcott inquired of Ralph.

'Oh, the crammer was for Ralph, was it?' said Mr Waterall.

'We thought it would amuse him and his brother, and we don't use it,' said Micha.

Mr Waterall nodded graciously.

'We were at a loss to know quite what it was.'

Ralph managed to signal to Micha not to say that he had known perfectly well what it was, and the topic of the crammer died away.

'Now what do you say to a turn round the garden?' Mr Waterall suggested to his guests. 'I'd like to show you what we've been doing in the way of planting. Are you going in for much in that way?'

'Only currants and gooseberries,' said Rehob.

'And a few dwarf apples,' Micha added.

'We're relying for our fruit on what my predecessor Mr Blackham planted,' said Mr Waterall.

'Well, the stuff he pinched from us was all right,' said Rehob.

'I don't quite understand you.'

'Blackham pinched every single fruit-tree he planted. He used to go round at night and dig up whatever he fancied on other people's plots,' Rehob said. 'Most of it came from old Gnathead opposite. He dug up all Gnathead's plums and planted hazel-nuts instead. Gnathead never knew the difference, and he asked Blackham how he accounted for his plums never flowering, and Blackham told him the buds must have been nipped. The apples were coming from us till I laid wait for him one night and plugged his spade with a charge of small shot. The peaches came from Kettlewell. In fact the only thing he ever bought for himself were a few penny packets of seeds.'

'Then all these fruit-trees are really stolen goods? This makes me feel a bit uncomfortable,' said Mr Waterall. 'Oughtn't I to restore them to their rightful owners?'

The brothers laughed and shook their heads.

'No, no, it's too late now,' said Micha. 'And anyway you're quite innocent.'

'It really would never have entered my head that anybody was likely to steal fruit-trees. However, I can assure you that these have not been stolen.'

Mr Waterall indicated with a gesture the thicket of Bocock's representative collections, the labels of which were fluttering in the wind. Micha and Rehob Chilcott looked at the dormant vegetation as one looks at a dormant baby and tries to think of a mildly intelligent comment.

'This little lot cost you a bit,' observed Rehob at last.

Mr Waterall agreed somewhat pensively.

'You may have to thin them out a bit in a couple of years,' Micha added.

'I'm hoping to turn my two boys into good gardeners,' said Mr Waterall with a glance in the direction of Ralph and Roger who groaned inwardly at the prospect of undergoing such a transformation. 'However, their brief holiday will soon be over now, and we shan't be back here till Christmas. Unless perhaps for a stray week-end just to see how Donkin is getting along with that kitchen door.'

When the Chilcott brothers had gone home, Mr Waterall announced that they were a much pleasanter pair of young men than he had been led to suppose.

'Radicals, of course, and faddists, but nevertheless they have common sense. By the way, don't forget, you two boys, that tomorrow I want you to pencil over all those labels.'

Such a task for the last day of this all too short relief from the burden of school presented itself to the boys as a piece of deliberate persecution.

'Father is a caddish brute sometimes,' said Ralph. 'I wanted to go up to Texas Bill's place and meet his uncle, because Monday is his best day usually, Texas said. I wanted to hear about last night.'

'Let's ask Mother to ask Father if we need do these labels on the last day of our exeat,' Roger suggested.

'Pooh, what's the good? She always has to pretend that he's right,' Ralph grumbled. 'I jolly well won't ever get married.'

'Why not?'

'Because I think being married makes people such asses.'

'It does rather,' Roger agreed.

'I bet you Phyllis marries some frightful ass and is absolutely awful. Why doesn't Father make her do these rotten labels? He only wants them pencilled over so that he can read them and go siding about and pretending that he knows the names of all these dirty plants.'

However, a telegram arrived early next morning from Mr Waterall's partner calling him back urgently to London, and the boys had the satisfaction of looking forward to a free day which would culminate in their returning to London by the seven o'clock train alone, it having been decided that until the kitchen door was in place it would be wiser for their mother to remain at Dream Days.

So the visit to Texas Bill and his uncle became feasible.

CHAPTER ELEVEN

WHEN Mr Augustus Ryan inherited a legacy of £5,000 from a great-aunt and abandoned the occupation of writing mottoes for crackers and words for popular songs, he had made up his mind to buy a little place in the country where he could write the real poetry, of the inspiration to write which he was convinced he had only been robbed by the necessity of earning a hard livelihood from a bed-sitting-room in York Road, Lambeth, conveniently situated in an old flat-fronted house between a public-house called the Adam and Eve and a public house called the Rose and Crown. He too had seen the advertisement of land for the million in plots from a quarter of an acre upwards, and he had bought half an acre just beyond the old Oak Farm itself, an Elizabethan house whose mellow beauty of red tiles and latticed casements bloomed amid the bungalows of Oaktown like a tea-rose among a litter of sardine-tins.

On this half-acre Augustus Ryan had caused to be erected a four-roomed bungalow of corrugated iron, felt, and match-boarding, varnished inside and painted green outside. On the gate which led up to the front door he had caused to be painted in Gothic lettering Mon Repos. In the saloon bar of the Adam and Eve he informed his favourite tow-headed barmaid that he had built himself a little nest in the heart of the country where he intended to live out the remainder of his days, writing an epic about the Spanish Armada. In the saloon bar of the Rose and Crown he informed his favourite tow-headed barmaid that he had carved for himself a little niche in an old-world spot where he intended to pass the rest of his life growing early vege-tables for the London market.

'So when next spring you receive a peck of peas, birdie, think of me.'

'Yes, when I do I will,' she replied. 'Let me see, Mr Ryan, you owe me for two double whiskies.'

'There you are, my dear,' he said, putting down the money. 'And I'll have another. Yes,' he went on, 'an early peck of peas picked with my own hand. There's a good refrain in that for a song. Did I tell you I was going to make myself responsible for my brother's eldest boy?'

'What's the poor kid done to deserve that?' the tow-headed barmaid asked.

'The kid has done nothing. I hear he's thoroughly idle. But if my brother had lived, he would probably have shared in this legacy. So I'm doing the right thing by his memory. But I'm not going to stand any nonsense. No, by George! I'm going to bring up that nephew of mine as he ought to be brought up. Did you give me that double whisky I asked for?'

'Give it you and watched you drink it, you scatter-brained thing.'

'So I have. I never noticed. That's me all over. Maiden meditation fancy free. I arise from dreams of thee. Spirit of poesy. Give me another whisky, there's a good girl. Yes, I've got ideals for this nephew. He's just fourteen. It'll be a great chance for him. It's a lovely spot. Far from the madding crowd's ignoble strife.'

So, to the relief of his widowed sister-in-law who had six children younger than Texas, Mr Augustus Ryan carried off her eldest son to Mon Repos and set to work on the task of turning him into a gentleman. As his only method for this was the application of a wangee cane, Texas Bill's social education might have been an extremely painful one if his uncle, luckily for him, had not been almost consistently incapable of hitting anything he wanted to hit ever since he arrived at Mon Repos. His nephew's chief duty was to see that he was never without enough whisky and gin to keep him in a condition of almost continuous intoxication, and Texas who enjoyed freedom did his duty well. He was walloped occasionally when his uncle was sober enough to do it; but, as the wallopings were usually for not having seen to it that the supply of whisky and gin was kept up, Texas recognized that he was paying the just penalty for his negligence. For a few months a melancholy housekeeper called Mrs Hawkins had attended to the domestic side of Mon Repos; but Mr Augustus Ryan's habit of singing over and over again all the popular songs he had ever written had increased her melancholy to such an extent that she had left his service, since when Texas had looked after the bungalow, which by the time Ralph and Roger visited it on this November day resembled those interiors which are suddenly revealed by earthquakes and typhoons. Texas could not be blamed entirely for this state of affairs, because his uncle in certain moods delighted to wrestle with the furniture. The furniture had suffered considerably, and indeed the only piece to put up anything of a show had been a large wardrobe which, exasperated by the behaviour of Mr Augustus Ryan, had fallen on top of him in the middle of a bout and laid him out for nearly a week.

When Ralph and Roger arrived at Mon Repos they found Mr Ryan, whom they had last heard of in their father's bed at three o'clock on Sunday morning fully dressed in a Norfolk suit, now at three o'clock on Monday afternoon at work in his garden wearing pyjamas and a dressing-gown. Such exquisitely paradoxical behaviour could not but excite their profound respect, and perhaps some of the regard they felt for Mr Ryan was expressed in their countenances, for Mr Ryan himself looked up from the serpentine trench he was digging and smiled at them.

'And who may you be?' he asked.

'We know Texas Bill,' Ralph explained. 'Is he at home?'

Mr Ryan pushed back a mop of shaggy hair from his forehead, blew out the stray bits of beard and moustache which had drifted inside his mouth, and addressed his visitors in grave accents:

'You know my nephew, do you? Well then, young gentleman, you know one of the chief examples of human ingratitude which this lop-sided world has to offer. And in response to your inquiry I can only reply that owing to that very ingratitude he is at this moment not at home. So far as his uncle is concerned his name may be Norval and he himself may be on the Grampian hills, though what the dickens for I have not the remotest idea. Do you smoke?'

'Sometimes,' said Ralph.

'A little,' said Roger.

'Then let us withdraw into my sanctum. I can offer you better weeds there than any you'll find out here. Were there weeds in Eden? There is a nice theological problem to occupy your leisure – that is if you have any leisure. I have none myself. I came down here, hoping to live out the rest of my allotted span in Arcadia. But I have had to spend my time wrestling with the soil, and when I am not

119

wrestling with the soil I am wrestling with the furniture. Could you step over that grandfather-clock?'

This question was addressed to his young visitors who were finding Mr Ryan's sanctum almost impassable on account of the furniture which was strewn about the floor in every attitude of collapse.

'Yesterday morning when I reached Mon Repos, after a night spent in hot pursuit of my nephew all over the countryside, I was set upon by my furniture, and for a few minutes I had a hard task to hold my own. There's one particularly aggressive wardrobe – a most dangerous brute – which half-killed me on a former occasion; but I managed to tie him up with a tablecloth, and after that I was able to settle the others. As in fact you see,' he concluded, pointing out the confusion on his floor. 'I had one bad ten minutes with the washstand when I got my head through the hole for the basin and the grandfather-clock was pounding me in the back with its pendulum. However, I managed to fling myself free of the washstand, and then I turned round and knocked out the clock with a devastating punch on the fleshy part of the hour-hand. The amazing thing was that earlier in the evening I had had to chase some hundreds of curiously spotted rats out of Mon Repos. I don't know where they came from. They were pink and yellow. I've never seen any quite like them before. At first I supposed my nephew had brought them in; but on consideration I really don't see how he could have found so many. So I think they must be part of the local fauna. Then later on I came in contact with a bear. At first I thought it was a bull. In fact if it hadn't followed me into a bedroom which I had borrowed for forty winks, I should have continued to think it was a bull. It was, however, indubitably a . . . I say, did you hear that?'

'I didn't hear anything,' said Ralph, looking round in some alarm.

'I was under the impression that I had said "indubitably". There you are again. I did say "indubitably". I've said it three times. I've given up keeping a diary for many years now. But if I had not given up keeping a diary, that's the sort of thing I should have made a note of.'

In spite of Mr Ryan's reputation as a severe educationalist, and in spite of his farouche appearance, he diffused a geniality which made the two boys feel perfectly at ease, and when he put on a purple smoking-cap with a gold tassel and offered them a box of manilla cheroots they accepted one apiece as readily as if they were made of chocolate.

'Put the big end in your mouth,' he advised, and by this advice he probably saved both boys from being sick, for the big end was so big for their youthful mouths that they were only able to keep the cheroots alight by puffing in the wrong direction.

'Ever blow soap-bubbles?' Mr Ryan asked presently.

They nodded. Had either attempted to speak, the cheroot would have left his mouth like a shell.

'I thought you must have by the way you're smoking those cheroots. If I had some clay pipes, we'd blow soap-bubbles now. By the way, what's your name?'

'Waterall.'

'Waterall? Then you must be the two sons your father is looking for. He was very worried about you round about three o'clock yesterday morning, and kept asking me where you were. But I was so busy looking for my nephew that I couldn't spare the time to help him to look for you. Well, if he loses you again tonight, tell him to come and knock me up at Mon Repos, and I'll try to explain where I last saw you. I notice you're admiring my bee-skeps. Do you know why I had to get them?'

This question was addressed to Ralph who was eyeing a pile of straw bee-skeps which were standing in a corner of the room piled one on top of the other like hats.

'Texas told me some bees swarmed inside you last summer,' Ralph mentioned, as if the incident were of everyday occurrence.

'Oh, I was terribly plagued by them,' Mr Ryan said. 'I couldn't get a wink of sleep during the day nearly the whole of last summer. In and out of my mouth all day from sunrise to sunset, and a continuous feeling in my inside that I'd eaten too much for tea. I used to have to sit by the hour in the garden with one of those bee-skeps over my head in the hope they'd be attracted to it and leave me alone. You remember the old rhyme?

'A swarm of bees in May
Is worth a load of hay,
A swarm of bees in June

121

Is worth a silver spoon,
A swarm of bees in July
Is not worth a fly.'

'Well, I added rather a neat little couplet to the end:

'A swarm of bees in August
Or else I'm sure to bust.'

'I daresay Texas has told you that my profession is poetry. But I've written very little since I came to live in the country. In fact that final couplet I recited for you just then represents practically the whole of my literary output since I left London. I intended to write an epic about the Spanish Armada. But somehow it has not yet been written. Of course Macaulay never finished his poem about it either. Funny thing two poets should both get stuck like that over the Spanish Armada.'

At this moment the snub-nosed face of Texas Bill looked round the door.

'What cheer, Uncle Gus? Been knocking the furniture about again? Hallo, kiddos, you here? Come on and give me a hand to put the room to rights.'

'Where have you been, Bill?' his uncle asked, jamming the smoking-cap down on his head and trying to look as severely dignified as he could in pyjamas and a dressing-gown.

'I've been away for the week-end like I said I was going.'

'Do you know I've been looking for you all yesterday night, or was it tonight? Never mind, the exact time is a matter of minor importance. But the point is that the father of these two sons kindly offered me the loan of his bed for a much needed rest, and I want to return his hospitality. Have we any tea?'

'Your whisky's out in the kitchen,' said Texas quickly.

'I did not mention the word whisky. I asked you about tea. I wish you had a better ear, Bill, for the finer distinctions of the English language.'

Texas, who was engaged in putting chairs on their legs and tables the right way up looked round indignantly.

'Do you mean you really want tea?'

'You will give us the pleasure of taking tea, won't you? Mr Ryan inquired of the boys.

'Thanks awfully,' they muttered.

'Well, there may be some tea left by Mrs Hawkins,' said Texas. 'But there's no milk and there's only some of last Friday's bread, and there's no jam, and there's no cakes, and there's no biscuits, and the last teapot we had you threw at that spider who kept winking at you from the corner.'

Mr Ryan ran his hand through his hair in perplexity.

'It looks as if we should have to fall back on the whisky after all,' he said at last.

'It looks like that,' his nephew agreed.

'Do you fancy whisky?' Mr Ryan inquired of the boys, who told him they had never tasted it.

'Well, you may not like it,' he said disconsolately. 'I remember many years ago now when I first tasted whisky I thought I'd put my tongue out of joint. It looks as if our tea this afternoon – or is it morning ... ?'

'Four o'clock of Monday afternoon,' said Texas.

'I was right then. I'm always pretty good at guessing the time,' said Mr Ryan. 'Yes, it looks as if our tea was not going to come within the scope of our modest household. Never mind. Stay on to supper,' he added expansively, his shaggy face lighting up with a warm-hearted hospitality.

'Thanks awfully,' said Ralph. 'But I'm afraid we've got to go back to London by the seven o'clock train from Galton.'

'You have?' Mr Ryan exclaimed. 'You mean to tell me that you'll be in London tonight?'

'We've got to go to school tomorrow,' said Ralph, a note of gloom in his voice.

'Ah, thank heaven, that *is* a place I've done with for good and all,' said their host. 'I wouldn't go to school again for anybody. And I'm very sorry to hear you've got to go, because I've taken a fancy to you two boys. I'm genuinely sorry you're going back to school. It's a place I wouldn't send a dog of mine to. Never mind. I shall think of something to cheer you up. I was a bit muddled when you looked in to call just now, but I'm getting clearer every moment, and depend upon it I shall think of something.'

The boys perceiving that Mr Ryan was becoming extremely abstracted in his manner, thought it was time to retire.

'Say "au revoir" but not "good-bye", life was not made for sorrow,' were his last words as the gate of Mon Repos clicked behind them.

Texas Bill accompanied the two brothers part of the way home.

'I never knew my old man so pleasant with anybody for a long time,' he told them. 'He's took a proper fancy to you two kids. Mostly when people come to our place he throws things at them till they go away. He's all right when he likes anybody. But it's not often he does. Well, so long. See you again when you come down for Christmas.'

But Ralph and Roger saw him long before Christmas. Indeed they saw him on the platform at Galton station three hours later with his uncle.

'Here we are again,' said Mr Ryan, shaking hands with extreme courtesy. 'When you said you were going to London by the seven o'clock train, the idea gradually came into my head that we would all go to London by the seven o'clock train. So all aboard!'

CHAPTER TWELVE

WHEN Mr Waterall had donned a Norfolk suit as an appropriate attire for a few days in the country, his two sons had suffered agonies of shame on his behalf. Had he ventured to appear in their company with as much as the faint shadow of Mr Augustus Ryan's eccentricity of demeanour and costume, his two sons would have been near to expiring of mortification. But then Mr Ryan was not their father, and although both of them considered his appearance 'rummy', they did not feel the least desire to disown his company nor did they mind how much the other occupants of the compartment stared at him. Yet Mr Ryan was wearing a Norfolk suit beside which their father's would have looked like a fine old English gentleman's. The material of it resembled the material of which thick woollen underwear is made, but any monotony in the negative grey of the colour was relieved by stains of green paint, red lead, blue ink, and the yellowish brown of burns. His stockings looked as if they had been knitted for a sufferer recently cured of a severe dropsy. One of his boots was laced up with a white cord used for pulling up blinds, which gave it the appearance of a very old pair of stays. The lace of the other boot finished half-way up the instep and was wired together at the top. A black inverness cape of what seemed ostentatious newness and silkiness added by contrast to the disreputable appearance of the Norfolk suit, and a large black sombrero on top of a shaggy head would have proclaimed Mr Ryan's connexion with the arts even if it had not been emphasized by a flowing bow-tie of claret-coloured silk.

As for Texas he was wearing the same shabby suit of dark-blue broadcloth in which he was always to be seen.

'Well,' said Mr Ryan as the train moved out of the station, 'when you two lads said you were going to London tonight you made me feel like Dick Whittington all of a sudden. And I decided that I deserved a brief holiday myself.'

With these words Mr Ryan drew from his pocket a very large pipe and lit it.

'Excuse me,' said a shrivelled woman in a corner of the compartment, 'but this is not a smoking-carriage.'

'Not a smoking-carriage?' repeated Mr Ryan. 'Well, that's a very extraordinary thing. I could have sworn I saw a "smoking" label on the window.'

He looked hard at the small shrivelled woman as if to suggest that she had somehow contrived to pull the label off. The small shrivelled woman sniffed under his scrutiny and observed to a stolid female friend with round shiny red cheeks, who was seated opposite, that it seemed funny the way some people did not look where they were going.

'May I inquire, madam,' Mr Ryan continued, 'if you object to the smell of smoke?'

And he filled the compartment with a large cloud as if to give her an opportunity of definitely making up her mind before she spoke.

'It makes my friend feel ill,' said the small shrivelled woman. Then she leaned across and screamed in the ear of her stolid friend opposite, 'The smell of smoke always makes you feel bad, don't it, Mrs Baxter?'

If silence and impassivity signify assent Mrs Baxter's affirmative was most definite, for she merely stared at her solicitous friend and continued to dandle on her tongue a large peppermint bull's-eye.

'Yes, of course, it does,' said the small shrivelled woman, 'it lays on your chest. People as smoke themselves think it's a pleasure for everybody.'

'Then am I to understand, madam,' Mr Ryan asked, 'that you wish me to abstain from smoking in this compartment?'

The small shrivelled woman pulled her veil down and sniffed.

'It's a pity some people have to be asked twice to do something what some people would do if they weren't even asked once,' she observed acidly.

'Never mind,' said Mr Ryan. 'If we are debarred from smoking, we are not debarred from eating. Not even good Queen Victoria herself can forbid her loyal subjects to eat. Bill, produce the supper. I was very worried about your tea this afternoon,' he continued, turning to Ralph. 'I was determined that you shouldn't go without your supper. So we bought a pork pie on our way through Galton. That's right, Bill, lay it all out on the seat. Got the bread? Only two knives? Never mind. We must eat with nature's knives and forks. Did you bring the corkscrew? This is just a pale East India ale. It wouldn't hurt an unweaned baby. Light, light as lovely woman herself. Your health, madam.' He bowed to the small shrivelled woman, who was making a self-important noise with her tongue and her teeth which sounded like a squeaking cork. The small shrivelled woman turned away with a sniff and gazed out of the black rain-smeared window-pane at the night. 'And yours too, madam,' Mr Ryan continued, raising his glass to the stolid Mrs Baxter, whose peppermint bull's-eye missed its footing and nearly slid off her tongue.

Ralph and Roger had eaten a large tea with two eggs each just before they started for the station; but they tackled that pork pie like a couple of Eskimos who had not tasted blubber for a week. It was a particularly good pork pie, without too much fat and with the space between the meat and the crust tightly packed with that peppery aromatic jelly, the flavour of which would have served the boys to illustrate what they might have imagined by ambrosia. The inside of the crust, too, had a softness and delicacy that caressed the teeth so alluringly that the teeth hesitated to strike and the crust was again and again reprieved.

'And what is the next course?' Mr Ryan asked when all that was left of the pork pie were a few flakes light as snow which lingered in the sheltered crevices of the basket.

'Bananas,' said Texas.

'Nothing but bananas? I hope you kids like bananas?' the host asked anxiously.

And when the boys only ate three apiece he was evidently worried by what he fancied was their indifference to fruit.

'Would either of you two ladies care to join us in a banana?' he inquired of the small shrivelled woman, who frowned at his invitation and glanced at the communication cord.

Finally Ralph and Roger wer prevailed upon to eat the last two bananas, and just when they had squeezed them down Texas remembered that there were doughnuts.

Roger drew a deep breath. He liked doughnuts almost better than any form of cake. Somehow somewhere he must pack away a doughnut inside himself. He drew another deep breath and managed it. Ralph, however, said he would have to wait a bit before he could eat one.

'Ever see me juggle, Bill?' his uncle asked.

'Well, I have and I haven't, if you know what I mean,' Texas replied cheerily. 'I've seen you going to bed with a lamp and it looked more like a Japanese juggler I saw at the Fulham pantomime than anything else. But you didn't think you was juggling.'

'Were,' said his uncle sharply.

'Where? Why, at the bungalow, of course.'

'Were. We were. You were. They were. Not was. I was juggling, but you *were* juggling.'

'No, I weren't.'

Mr Ryan gave up the niceties of grammar, and grabbing the three uneaten doughnuts began to juggle with them. After a few successful tosses the train gave a lurch, and the third doughnut landed on Mrs Baxter's bonnet, knocking it on one side in such a way as to give its owner the look of extreme disreputableness which a crooked bonnet can achieve so infallibly.

'If you can't behave yourself,' the small shrivelled woman snapped, 'I'll call the guard at the next station and make a complaint about you.'

But at the next station Mr Ryan declared that they must find a smoking-carriage, and the two women were left alone.

'Sometimes,' said Mr Ryan when he lighted up his pipe, 'sometimes the thought that a few hasty words in youth might have ended in my sitting permanently opposite a woman like that makes me shudder.'

He plunged down into the pocket of his inverness and drew out a flask, the contents of which he drained. Then he leaned back in the corner of the carriage and brooded upon the horrors of matrimony. Texas with a wink at Ralph and Roger produced his tin whistle. Conversation was not welcome to his uncle when he was in a mood like this. For the next hour he played tune after tune while the train jogged on towards London.

At Wimbledon, Mr Ryan recovered from his taciturn fit.

'After all, I did avoid marriage,' he said abruptly. 'Why should I mope like this? The real question before us is how to make the most of the time at our disposal while the night is no more than middle-aged. We shall be at Waterloo by a quarter to nine. Everything indicates the Canterbury Theatre of Varieties as the most conveniently situated place of amusement.'

'But I think Roger and I will have to get out at Clapham

Junction,' Ralph decided gloomily. 'We'll have to catch a train to Addison Road.'

'Such a notion verges upon the ludicrous,' said Mr Ryan. 'Tomorrow you two lads will be chained to your desks. Tonight you must make the most of the few miserable hours of freedom which a tyrannical educational system allows you. Song and dance at the Canterbury Theatre of Varieties followed by a light supper of fish and chips at one of my erstwhile houses of call in the Westminster Bridge Road. A brief visit to my old friends at the Rose and Crown and the Adam and Eve. A four-wheeler cab – and home, sweet home. That is my programme for the evening.'

'It's awfully decent of you,' said Ralph, 'but I think our governor would be rather waxy if we came home so awfully late.'

'Your father will be my concern,' Mr Ryan promised. 'True I cannot exactly claim him as an old friend; but I can claim that in the course of our short acquaintance we became intimate. The extremely hospitable way in which he put his bed at my disposal when that bear came round the corner of your bungalow touched me very deeply. Your own company happens to afford me genuine pleasure; but if your company were positively distasteful I should still feel it my bounden duty to repay your father's hospitality by entertaining his two sons to the best of my ability. The failure of the tea-crop this afternoon at Mon Repos was a great distress to me. I am anxious to atone for that failure. Say no more. The night is before us, though like myself it is unfortunately not so young as it was and as I should like to be.'

Ralph looked at his brother doubtfully.

'The only thing is that perhaps he'll think we missed the train, and he'd be rather waxy if he'd gone to bed and we woke him up.'

'Not at all,' Mr Ryan insisted. 'You must allow me to know better than you what your father is like when he is woken up suddenly by unexpected visitors. It may take a little time to explain just why we have woken him up. It took me a little time the other night. He was, if you will allow me to say so, a little slow in the uptake. But once he *had* grasped the situation, he immediately put his bed at my disposal in the most tactful way, and though I shouldn't dream of his doing such a thing again, you can rely upon me to make him understand fully the reason why, instead of arriving home at the hour expected, you have arrived home at what we may describe roughly as any hour. Say no more. We may be lucky enough to find Dan Leno occupying the boards of the Canterbury tonight. We may find Vesta Victoria who, as she says of herself in the columns of the *Era*, is a vesta who will strike anywhere. We may get a glimpse of Eugene Stratton. The prospect is illimitable tonight. Tomorrow your horizon will be bounded by the four walls of a classroom. Let us eat and drink today, for tomorrow we die, as it says in the Bible.'

Ralph tried to calculate the worst that could happen from yielding to the temptation. School was inevitable tomorrow morning. Roger and he could not be given more school than they were doomed to get already. They might be deprived of going down to Oak until the Christmas holidays; but while the governor was in the state of self-importance by the possession of a bungalow in the country, these week-ends might be a mixed pleasure. When the novelty wore off he would not be putting on so much side. Moreover, the country would be much more enjoyable in the spring and summer, and by then the escapade with Texas Bill's uncle would have been forgotten. The promised pony might be withheld; but that pony was in any case improbable and the certainty that Phyllis would have a claim upon it made the possession of it hardly worth striving for. There would of course be a row if they reached home after their father had gone to bed; but they would not have to face him unsupported. Indeed, it was likely that Texas Bill's uncle would draw the whole of the fire. Ralph could not recall that his father had ever expressed himself so strongly as he had over the action of Texas Bill's uncle in getting into his bed the other night. He would possibly be so angry at seeing him again that he would forget all about his sons. Besides, a chance like this to go to a music-hall might not occur again, and to forgo it out of funkiness would be a regret throughout all the weary months of school ahead. Hallo, here were the lights of Clapham Junction.

Roger looked at his elder brother inquiringly when the train pulled up, and Ralph scowled like a Bonaparte called upon to make a vital military decision about Waterloo.

'All right, you ass,' he said, 'don't make a face like a dying duck in a thunderstorm. We're not going to get out here.'

Roger in ordinary circumstances would have protested

at the comparison, but his elder brother's decision filled him with respect. He perceived Ralph in a glorious nimbus of audacity. He tried humbly not to resemble a dying duck in a thunderstorm, and as the train moved on towards Waterloo the hearts of the two brothers beat with that rapturous prelude to perfect joy which only schoolboys and lovers know.

CHAPTER THIRTEEN

THE entrance to the Canterbury Theatre of Varieties was an example of that mid-Victorian decoration which strove to produce in the spectator an illusion that he was being transported into another element. Quantities of shells embedded in the plaster of the walls of the entering corridors combined with a free use of ferns and cork to suggest a sea-change from the humdrum of terrestrial existence into something rich and strange. The very atmosphere laden with stale alcohol and nicotine had a kind of low-tide smell; and when at last the crowded auditorium was reached one had a sense of remoteness from the rest of the world which was not enjoying itself, a sense that all those hundreds of people who were laughing and whistling and drinking and smoking and joining in choruses had discovered a happy retreat conjured by magic out of the commonplace of laborious city life. One enters the modern cinema as one enters a municipal lavatory in obedience to a claim of the body. One entered a music-hall like the Canterbury, demanding and expecting entertainment. The music-halls did not always succeed in fulfilling what they set out to perform; but nobody ever left one of them without feeling elated or enraged by his experience. People leave a cinema as they put down a glass of water, because it is finished. They will drink again when they feel mildly thirsty, and the next film will taste exactly like the last.

On this night that Ralph and Roger visited the Canterbury Eugene Stratton sang 'Little Dolly Daydream', dancing about on the sanded stage with a blue lime following assiduously his lithe slithers and leaps. Vesta Victoria came running on, dressed as a little girl, to clap her hands and sing 'Our Lodger's Such a Nice Young Man'. Marie Lloyd in a big picture hat sang 'Everything in the Garden's Lovely'. And best of all Dan Leno reduced Ralph, Roger, and Texas Bill to three jellies of laughter by his account of a village fire-brigade and of the burning of a sausage shop. *You know what one sausage smells like when it's burning? Well, think of the smell of thousands and thousands and thousands of sausages all burning at once. And some of them not vaccinated!*

In the next seat on the other side of Ralph was an enormous woman dressed in spinach-green satin who was as much overcome by her laughter at Dan Leno as Ralph himself and who, to save herself from slipping down out of her stall, seized his hand and waved it delirously while with her other hand she thumped away at her chest to defeat the cough that her convulsions of mirth kept encouraging.

When Dan Leno had retired and his place had been taken by a befurred and energetic family of seven who were announced as the champion Sleigh-bell Ringers of the world, the enormous woman in spinach-green satin, after gradually wheezing back to her normal shortness of breath, produced a box of crystallized fruits from the grand canyon formed by her massive thighs, and offered them to Ralph

'And take a big one, ducky,' she urged. 'Don't peck about with one of those measly cherries. Take an apricot.'

This was the spirit in which to offer crystallized fruits Most people when they offered him crystallized fruits kept as forbidding an eye on the line of apricots in the middle as the dragon used to keep on the golden apples of the Hesperides.

'And pass them along to your friends,' the enormous woman added. 'Is that your brother next you?'

'No, that's a friend of mine. He's called Texas Bill.'

'Good sakes alive! Tell him to take all my apricots before he draws his revolvuar. And who's the apple-cheeked cherubine beyond? Five-fingered Jack or Deadwood Dick?'

'No, that's my young brother. His name's Roger.'

'Well, tell Sir Roger de Coverley to take the last apricot, and not be afraid. They can only be eat once. Here, lean over a minute, ducky, I want to ask you something.'

Ralph's head floated about on billows of spinach-green satin as the enormous woman leaned down and asked him if the gent with the hair was his pa.

'No, he's just a friend. He's the uncle of Texas Bill.'

'Is he now? Well, you often hear the saying, "There's hair!" But there *is* hair. Well, I saw the wild man of Borneo once, and I saw Jo-Jo, the dog-faced man from Siberia, only last week. But they were both behind bars as you might say. I don't recolleck seeing anybody out and about with more hair than what he's got. Ask him to have

133

a fruit. And he'll want to be careful, because they're very sticky, and if he gets one in that beard of his he won't find it again in a hurry. It'll be the old story of the needle and the haystack all over again.'

Mr Ryan, however, who had hardly had an empty glass before him throughout the performance declined the crystallized fruits.

'There you are, you see,' the enormous woman commented to Ralph, 'he won't risk it.' And as she spoke she beamed at Mr Ryan to express a sympathetic appreciation of his motive in refusing.

Mr Ryan smiled back and presently changed seats with his nephew.

'The mountain hasn't got to go to Mahomet this time,' observed the enormous woman, as she nodded a greeting.

'Have I had the pleasure of seeing you before?' Mr Ryan inquired.

'No, what you thought was me was the last time you saw the Albert Hall from the top of a bus,' she answered quickly.

'My name is Ryan, Augustus Ryan. This is my nephew Texas Bill and these are my two young friends, Ralph and Roger Waterall. We are just up from the country to enjoy ourselves for the evening. Perhaps you will join us, Mrs . . .' he paused on a question.

'That's right. It is Missus. Mrs Hamper, to be all Sir Garnet. But my husband went round the corner to have a drink two weeks after we were married, and I've never seen the artful dodger since. It was my own fault in a way, for I wanted to test his affections and I told him that I'd lost all my money. That's over thirty years ago now, but I've enjoyed every minute of it, and which is more than most wives can say. Would you really like me to join you for the evening? Because if it's just politeness, say so and don't be afraid of offending me. I felt a bit offended when my husband left me so abruptly. But I've taken everything very fellowsophically ever since. Yes, next morning, when I found he'd left nothing behind but his nightshirt I pulled myself together and said "Phœbe," which is the barmy name they gave me and which it took me the first twelve years of my life to learn how to spell, "Phœbe," I said, "you rung his affections down on the counter and they were base metal. What of it?" I said, "you've found out what you wanted to know. Why take on about it?" And with that I wrapped up his nightshirt in a brown paper parcel and put it at the bottom of a trunk where it remained for two whole years after which I gave it to a crossing-sweeper, who'd always touch his hat and give me a cheerful smile every time I crossed over the road, and what is more kept his crossing like anybody's hair-parting at breakfast. No, a woman like me who's lost a husband like that doesn't get offended very easily, so if you only invited me out for the sake of polite-ness I shan't worry. But there's my visiting-card in case this is the beginning of a life-long friendship.'

She fumbled in her bag and produced a large card which she handed ceremoniously to Mr Ryan.

'The idea was that we should visit a fish shop after the show is over,' said Mr Ryan.

'And a very good idea too,' Mrs Hamper declared. 'What's nicer than a nice supper of fried fish and chips? Unless it's sprats. I must say I'm very partial to sprats with a nice pint of draught stout.'

'Then you will join us?'

'Join you and enjoy myself too,' Mrs Hamper promised. 'Thank goodness, that bell-ringing party has stopped. You could hardly hear yourself speak. What I ask myself is where people like that practise. Very nice in the song when all the world goes ting-a-ling-ling, but a bit off just over your head. I had a friend once, a Mrs Bagshaw, who kept theatrical lodgings; but I never heard she ever took in sleigh-bell ringers. And in fact Mrs Bagshaw did have to give up letting rooms to theatricals, because just before her youngest was born she went into the room without knock-ing, her thinking she'd heard the lodger go out; but when she went in he was standing on the chest-of-drawers dressed in nothing but his vest and pants, hanging on to both his ankles and nodding his head at her between his knees. It seemed he was a contortionist, and this was the way he used to practise. Well, Mrs Bagshaw said it give her such a turn that she wondered little Jimmie arrived looking like a human being at all. She always vows she doesn't believe he would have if her other lodger hadn't have been a mes-merizer and mesmerized her into thinking little Jimmie would be all right. But even that had its drawbacks. Because once he'd mesmerized her, he was for ever at it, and her husband got jealous and said if he wanted to mesmerize anything let him try and mesmerize his fist, and there was a rare set out on the top landing. The last days of Pompey were a Pleasant Sunday Afternoon to the row they kicked up. After that Mrs Bagshaw gave up taking in theatricals, and a curate came to live with them, who was more faddy in one way, but much quieter except for the evenings he had his boys' club and they quarrelled over the bagatelle. Hallo, here's God Save the Queen.'

A few minutes later they were all sitting down in a fish shop which Mr Ryan declared was the best to be found anywhere on the south side of the Thames.

Texas Bill had been unusually quiet all the evening. He was puzzled by his uncle's prolonged geniality, and he could find no explanation of it. Texas had counted the whiskies he had ordered in quick succession at the Canterbury, and he knew that by now his uncle had reached the number when it was his habit to become violent and either wrestle with the furniture or try to knock into his nephew the elements of a gentleman's education. When the waiter announced that no sprats were obtainable this evening. Texas expected to see his uncle pick up the cruet and fling it at his head.

But all he said was:

'Dear me, no sprats? Have you any whiting?'

'Very nice whiting, Mr Ryan,' the waiter replied.

'Do you like whiting, Mrs Hamper?' she was asked.

'What's nicer than a nice whiting?' she replied.

'Whiting all round,' Mr Ryan ordered.

Texas could not understand it. He took out his whistle and played 'Genevieve' with so much emotion that a sombre man in a seedy frock-coat, who was sitting at a table in the corner and eating mussels, left his place and stood in the middle of the restaurant, listening.

'Come and join us,' Mr Ryan invited.

The sombre man nodded without uttering a word, and then turned away to fetch his plate of mussels. Texas wondered what his uncle would hurl after him, for he could not believe that the invitation was anything but a sarcastic comment on the sombre man's curiosity. Not at all.

'Bring another pint of draught stout,' Mr Ryan said to the waiter. 'That'll make six in all.'

Texas scratched his head.

'Are you feeling quite all right, Uncle Gus?' he inquired anxiously.

'I never felt better,' Mr Ryan declared. 'The fact is I'm thoroughly enjoying my little trip up from the country. Do you like the country, Mrs Hamper?'

'Oh, for an afternoon in the summer what's nicer than the country?' Mrs Hamper replied.

'But not all the time?' Mr Ryan suggested.

'No, indeed!' Mrs Hamper averred warmly. 'Time enough to be in the country all the time when the daisies are growing over my head.'

'Your last remark interests me professionally, madam,' said the sombre man, who by now had brought his mussels to their table. 'Have you any particular location in view for your last resting place? We have clients who like to choose in advance and, hearing you mention the subject, I venture to offer you the card of the firm of undertakers for whom I work, Messrs Cork and Cork. We should be happy to conduct the necessary negotiations with any cemetery . . .'

Mrs Hamper waved away the sombre man's suggestion with a large yellow silk handkerchief.

'For goodness sake, man, get on with your mussels. You'll be nearer to the daisies when you've eaten that little lot than what I shall be for a long time. Or I hope so.'

'Drink up your stout,' Mr Ryan urged. 'I ordered you stout.'

'Thank you, sir,' said the sombre man. 'Stout is a highly nutritious drink. I sometimes drink it hotted up with ginger when I return from one of our longer obsequies. Excuse me, young gentleman,' he went on, turning to Texas Bill, 'you were playing that touching old melody "Genevieve." I wonder if you could favour me with another old favourite of mine "Ben Bolt"? It begins "Oh, don't you remember sweet Alice, Ben Bolt?" You can't recall it? Do you happen to recall "Alice, where art thou?"'

Texas was able to oblige this time, and the sombre man wiped away a tear.

'Familiar though I have had to make myself with the melancholy finale of our mortal life,' he said, 'I am all too easily moved by any reference in poetry to the simple and beautiful name of Alice. It is the name of my beloved wife.'

'And you have lost her?' Mr Ryan asked sympathetically. 'Have another stout.'

'Oh, no, no, I have not lost her. She is as a matter of fact extremely well at the present moment, I am happy to say. But I never hear those songs without reflecting I might lose her. Only last week a neighbour of ours slipped at the top of her area steps and hit her head on the dust-bin.'

'Poor soul,' Mrs Hamper ejaculated. 'And killed instanter as they say, I suppose?'

'Oh, no, no, she wasn't killed. In fact except for an abrasion she wasn't hurt badly. But she might have been killed,' said the sombre man. 'It was a lesson to us all.'

Mrs Hamper prodded Mr Ryan in the ribs, and when he leaned over to hear what she had to say, whispered an urgent request to send old misery back to his own table.

'Cheer up,' Mr Ryan urged the sombre man, for in his present mood of geniality he could not bring himself to drive anybody away. 'And look here, Texas, don't play such sad tunes. Play something lively without any Alice in it. Still, I can sympathize with you over what might have been. I was feeling very depressed when we were in the train this evening thinking to myself that I might have been married and what a merciful escape I'd had. Being a poet I'm apt to let my imagination run riot on occasions. We all suffer from some weakness, and what's imagination with me is indigestion with another person.'

'I can't afford to smile,' said the sombre man. 'It would ruin me for good if anybody saw a smile on my face. I've got a very big reputation in the undertaking business, and without boasting I can say that I'm more run after as a mute than any one man in our firm. People come in and ask for my services special. I've heard our Mr Cork Junior say he reckons my presence on the box of a hearse is worth four extra plumes at any funeral. He says there's nobody can carry a crape veil round his hat with quite such a stylish melancholy as me. Slemmon is my name. "Can we have Mr Slemmon?" has become quite a byword at the offices of Cork and Cork. We do a very large business in South-east London, and we make a real feature of solemnity.'

The arrival of the whiting cut short Mr Slemmon's macabre reminiscences, much to the relief of Mrs Hamper who had been dabbling her large oval countenance uncomfortably with her yellow silk handkerchief.

'Well here's our whiting,' she exclaimed. 'And I'm bound to say I feel thoroughly glad to see them, for even though they're dead they look very lively, not to say frolicsome with their tails in their mouths, the saucy things. Enjoying your stout, ducky?'

The last question was addressed to Roger whose expression was almost as lugubrious at this moment as Mr Slemmon's.

'Not very much. It's rather sour,' he said.

'Well there, of course it is. Here waiter, bring a bottle of ginger-beer, or would you rather have a lemonade?'

Both Ralph and Roger on being pressed voted for ginger-beer, in which they were joined by Texas Bill, who for all his superior age and experience found draught stout too much for him.

'Now we mustn't be too long over our fish,' said Mr Ryan, 'because we've got to pop round to the Adam and Eve and the Rose and Crown before closing time.'

The sombre Mr Slemmon was invited to accompany the rest of the party to Mr Ryan's favourite resorts, but he excused himself on the plea of not liking to make Mrs Slemmon nervous by staying out too late.

'Then come and pay us a visit down in the country some time,' Mr Ryan pressed. 'We're true bohemians, my nephew and I. Liberty Hall, and all that sort of thing. Nobody will worry you to get up early or any of that sort of nonsense. And you look as if you wanted a change. Too much tombstone isn't good for anybody.'

Mr Slemmon thanked Mr Ryan gravely for the invitation, and then after putting on a pair of black kid gloves he glided out of the restaurant in search of his tram.

'Well, thank goodness, he's hopped it,' Mrs Hamper sighed. 'Why the Living Skelington was a Bank Holiday roundabout alongside of him. Well, you hear of people being as solemn as a mute at a funeral, and it's evidently a true saying. I reckon if you put him in the upper circle at 'Charley's Aunt' he'd give half the audience the jim-jams and upset the whole piece. No wonder he wasn't afraid to eat mussels. It would just properly tickle his fancy to know that some people think they're poisonous. Oh, you may depend he'd revel in it. It'd be better than a spoonful of vinegar to give them a tasty relish. I never thought to ask him if he had any children of his own, poor little souls. Just think what I may have escaped by losing my husband like that. He might easily have taken up with the notion of becoming a mute, for he was all the time chopping and changing about with what he would and what he wouldn't do. I remember only a week before we got married he took up with fretwork, and I couldn't get a word out of him edgeways, and I just had to sit there, gritting my teeth, instead of being cuddled as anybody might expect before they were on tap at all hours. But that was his way. Always had to be wrapped up in something new, and my novelty wore off very quickly when I told him I'd lost all my money. He looked at me the way a kid will look at an old doll. He was just a weathercock with a screw loose. The most frivolous-minded man you ever saw. A rolling stone, that's what he was. You know. Mad on hobbies and such like. And though he never did take it into his head to be an undertaker's mute, there's no knowing when he might have. And now if we're going to visit two publics before closing time we'd best look sharp. It's gone twelve already.'

Ralph and Roger were pleasantly thrilled by the prospect of visiting a public-house. Mystery still clung for them about such places. They had already solved one riddle tonight by visiting a music-hall for the first time. Now they were to solve another. Both boys were thinking of the effect they would produce upon their classmates tomorrow morning.

'What did you do during the exeat?'

'Oh, I went down to our place in the country, and I shot a bit, and I helped keep the furnace alight in some brick-fields, and I went to the Canterbury to see Dan Leno, and I went to a pub.'

Not a bad programme to carry through in the course of four November days.

However, the inside of a public-house was less interesting than they had hoped. Or rather the saloon bar was less interesting. The public bar looked much better from the brief glimpse they caught of it on their way to the refined sanctum of the saloon bar. At the Rose and Crown there was a fight going on, and the police were just coming in to deal with the affair. Ralph, Roger and Texas were all looking back longingly over their shoulders through the haze of tobacco smoke when the door of the saloon bar in which Mrs Hamper and Mr Ryan had already passed swung back and caught the three of them a rousing thump which made them feel sore for ten minutes. And at the Adam and Eve Roger, whose lesson had not been learnt, in looking over his shoulder, this time to see what became of an elderly woman in the middle of dancing a breakdown on one of the benches, caught his foot in a spittoon and crashed on the coconut-matting of the private bar at the same moment as over on the other side the elderly woman crashed among the sawdust of the public bar.

Moreover, delicious though ginger-beer may be, four bottles of it on top of whiting within an hour exceeds the capacity even of a schoolboy, and the drum-like condition in which the boys found themselves militated against their appreciation of the discreet comforts of the saloon bar. The increasing nearness too of their return home and speculation upon the reception they would get were beginning to preoccupy both Ralph and Roger, while Texas who had been awake all night for the last two nights with Harry Gibbs was beginning to feel a strong desire to fall asleep.

Two minutes before closing time Mr Ryan left the rest of the party for the purpose of shaking the hand of his old pal the licensee of the Adam and Eve. The others went into the street, expecting to be joined by him there; but after they had waited for about ten minutes there was no sign of Mr Ryan's reappearance.

'This looks like being a bit of a set out, this does,' Mrs Hamper declared.

CHAPTER FOURTEEN

THE gradual dimming or extinction of all the lights in both the Adam and Eve and the Rose and Crown soon produced that shadow of impenetrable exclusion which closed public-houses cast upon the human mind.

'Well, it's not in reason to hang about here till the Day of Judgement,' Mrs Hamper exclaimed at last. With this she advanced to a door labelled 'Bottle and Jug' and rapped upon it peremptorily.

'Now then, none of that,' said a young policeman who had been watching Mrs Hamper and the boys from the other side of the road. 'It's time you were moving along home.'

'We're waiting for a friend,' Mrs Hamper explained.

'That's all right,' the young policeman replied, 'but you can't stay mooching about outside public-houses after closing time.'

'Mooching about?' Mrs Hamper repeated indignantly. 'Who's mooching about? Speak for yourself, young man. When you've been a bit longer in the Force you won't be quite so quick to accuse people of mooching.'

'That's all right,' said the young policeman, the roses of wounded vanity twining round his cheeks. 'I don't want any argufying about it. You heard what I said. Move on.'

'I tell you we're waiting for a friend. He's inside speaking to the proprietor of this public-house. If you don't believe what I say, ring the bell and ask.'

'There's not going to be any bell ringing here tonight,' said the policeman. 'It's high time you went home. So come along. I don't want to have to do anything you'd be sorry for afterwards.'

'Perhaps you'd like to run me in?' Mrs Hamper challenged. 'Let me tell you that if you did you'd be very sorry for it. Very sorry you'd be. It's my belief that if you were to run me in you'd find yourself back running errands, and which is what you ought to be doing now.'

The young policeman flushed hotly.

'Look here, if I hear any more of it from you, I will run you in.'

'I believe you would,' said Mrs Hamper scornfully. 'And if

I was by myself I wouldn't hesitate not for a moment to edge you on into making such a poppy-show of yourself. But seeing that I have three children with me to look after, I'm not at liberty to give myself the pleasure of being run in just to hear what your superiors say to you at the police station. For if you did run me in, it's as sure as the rising of tomorrow's blessed sun that you'd be run out yourself.'

Then Mrs Hamper turned in majesty to hail a four-wheeler that was crawling along by the edge of the pavement.

'Get in,' she said to the boys. 'I'll drive you home myself.'

'But what about Uncle Gus?' Texas asked.

'Never mind about Uncle Gus. He ought to know better than to keep us all standing about like a troupe of sandwichmen on the kerb and getting insulted by so-called policemen who ought to be tucked up safe in bed and a nightlight burning to keep them from being frightened of burglars. My sakes, we shall be getting moved on by the Church Lads Brigade next.'

'But what about me?' Texas Bill asked. 'Where am I going for the night?'

'You'll come back with me to Hammersmith. I gave your uncle my card. If he fetches you, well and good. If he doesn't, I'll see you into the train for the country myself.'

Texas did not hesitate any longer, but jumped into the cab. He had been thinking that if his uncle did not turn up he would have to go home to his mother who was living in Dulwich, and the prospect of walking all the way to Dulwich at this time of night was not attractive. Moreover, he had no desire to find himself at home again with six younger brothers and sisters after the pleasant freedom of life at Mon Repos.

Ralph and Roger had no clear idea at present how they should explain to their father their arrival back home in the company of a very stout woman in spinach-green satin, hours after the arrival of the train from Galton. Still, after the way Mrs Hamper had dealt with that policeman they felt a measure of confidence in her ability to handle their father.

'I say,' Ralph suggested to Mrs Hamper when the cab was jogging over Westminster Bridge, 'do you think we need say anything about Mr Ryan to my governor? Could we say that you met us in the train and asked us out to the theatre? If Texas stayed inside the cab, my governor wouldn't see him when we get to our house in Orange Road, and I think perhaps he'd be less waxy if we came back with you than if we came back with Mr Ryan.'

'That's right enough,' Texas agreed. 'The kiddo's right. His old man hasn't much use for me, and he hasn't no kind of use at all for Uncle Gus since he went round to his place looking for me the other night.'

'Well, anything to make life a little easier,' Mrs Hamper agreed. 'And if it'll make life easier to tell a good thumping whopper, tell it. I don't hold with telling whoppers just for the sake of telling them like some people do, any more than I hold with taking medicine when you don't want it. But a good whopper at the right moment can clear the ground just like a good pill at the right moment. That's the way we see life at 22 Barking Terrace, Hammersmith.'

'Do you live at Barking Terrace?' Ralph asked. 'I know that road.'

'So do I,' said Roger.

'It's quite near St. James's School,' Ralph went on.

'Certainly it is,' Mrs Hamper agreed.

'And that's where I go to school,' said Ralph. 'But Roger's still at Randell's. He won't be able to go to St. James's till next September. He's too young.'

'Well, you only went to St. James's last September,' said Roger defiantly.

'What of it?' replied his elder, a certain truculence creeping into his tone. 'I'm not a kid at a prep school like you.'

'Well, you were.'

'Well, it wasn't such a stinking school then as it is now. So sucks!'

'Yes it was. It was more stinking,' Roger declared. 'So sucks to you!'

'Ha-ha, what sucks! You were there yourself when I was there,' Ralph cried triumphantly.

'Well, you went there first, and that's what made it stink. It doesn't stink now,' Roger declared.

This was too much for Ralph's dignity to stand.

He flung himself upon his younger brother, and they became locked in deadly combat, the old cab creaking and groaning as the struggle grew fiercer.

'Behave yourselves, you naughty boys,' Mrs Hamper commanded. 'Behave yourselves at once, or I won't ever ask you to tea with me at 22 Barking Terrace.'

Her words were healing as balm. The fight ceased.

'We're breaking the commandments one by one in this blessed cab,' said Mrs Hamper severely. 'And at this rate we'll end by breaking the poor old cab itself. I'm sure I heard the floor give a loud crack when you were dusting into one another. You must remember I'm a big-made woman, and this cab wasn't built yesterday. In fact to my way of thinking it must have been towed in behind the Ark. It's creaking now like a laundry-basket. I've had the floor of a cab come out with me once before in my life, and then I had to run along inside about a hundred yards before the passers-by saw what was the matter and stopped the driver. Ever since then I've sat very quiet in cabs, I can tell you, and I'll trouble you to do the same. Yes, I'll be very glad to see you at 22 Barking Terrace whenever you like to come round. I've often sat in my window and watched the poor little things hurrying along to school with their books and bags and what nots and thought a good spanking tea would do them more good than all that nonsense they stuff them up with in schools.'

Even Mrs Hamper's flow of anecdote dried up in the slow progress of the cab westward. By the time it had reached Hyde Park Corner the fares were all fast asleep. The smell of mouldy leather, stale varnish, dusty straw, sweaty horse-flesh, dank plush, and old wood which provided the atmosphere for the inside of a four-wheeler, always had a potent soporific effect in combination with the jog-trot motion. Even the gayest revellers, the wildest roisterers succumbed to its influence, and on Mrs Hamper and the three boys it acted like chloroform. Jog-jog down from Hyde Park Corner to the corner of Sloane Street. Jog-jog from Sloane Street along Knightsbridge. Jog-jog along the wide emptiness of Prince's Gate. Jog-jog by Kensington Gore past Kensington Palace. Jog-jog along Kensington High Street. Jog-jog past the gardens of Holland House. Jog-jog until Olympia's hideous conservatory affronted the night. Jog-jog up the pier-like straightness of Orange Road, half-way along which the mouldering driver pulled up his horse and sat hunched upon the box, working himself up into the right mood of resentfulness in which to examine the silver coins placed in a palm unwashed since the first mud-pie of boyhood.

'This is our house,' Ralph proclaimed, looking up from the pavement at the discouraging line of dark cliffs to which the late hour had turned the houses of Orange Road.

'Better knock at the front door,' Mrs Hamper advised.

Neither Ralph nor Roger nor Texas was tall enough to knock with any suggestion of peremptoriness. None of them could grip the knocker firmly enough, and their knocks had a slithery and elusive sound which was as utterly lost in the desolate length of Orange Road as would have been the noise of a parrot sharpening its beak on the bars of a cage. They had to appeal to Mrs Hamper to come and knock properly. The cab heeled over as she forced her bulk through the door, and as she alighted upon the kerb lurched back into uprightness with a shudder.

'You press your thumb on the bell,' Mrs Hamper said to Ralph, while I knock. And, Roger, you go down through the area gate and keep ringing at the back door.'

Five minutes went by. The driver descended from the box with much difficulty and inquired in a sulky voice of Mrs Hamper if he was going to be paid for waiting; and Mrs Hamper, who by this time was out of breath with so much knocking, wheezed back crossly that he had to take her on to Barking Terrace, Hammersmith, before his hire was accomplished.

What Mrs Hamper's knocking had failed to effect was apparently effected by this short, sharp, and wheezy conversation between herself and the driver. One or two windows were pushed up along the street. Night attire shimmered in the gaslight, showing that curious heads were peeping out on the chance of being eyewitnesses of a good murder. Finally a window in Number 315 went up, and the voice of Mr Waterall himself was heard inquiring if anybody was knocking.

'Yes, I'm knocking,' Mrs Hamper replied firmly.

'You? Who are you?' Mr Waterall asked, and he peered down from his window on the second storey in an attempt to solve the puzzle of that indeterminate bulk he could dimly descry on the steps of his front door.

'I'm Mrs Hamper.'

'No missing hamper has been left here. You've mistaken the number of the house.'

'It's us father,' Ralph interposed. 'Mrs Hamper brought us home in a cab.'

'Where on earth have you two boys been?' their father asked in angry astonishment.

'We went to the Canterbury,' Ralph announced.

'That's right,' Mrs Hamper testified.

'How in the name of heaven did you get to Canterbury from Galton? Why, it isn't even on the same line.'

'Not the place where the archbishop lives,' Mrs Hamper explained. 'The Canterbury Theatre of Varieties in the Westminster Bridge Road.'

'Tell him you met us in the train from Galton,' Ralph prompted in an agonized whisper.

'All right, ducky,' she whispered back. 'But I always have to get my breath before a really big whopper. That's quite correct, Mr Waterall,' she said aloud.

'What's quite correct?' Mr Waterall asked peevishly.

'Why, about meeting your two lumps of trouble in the train. You must lay the blame on me if they're late; but I invited them to join me at the Canterbury to see dear old Dan Leno, and being a lady they didn't like to say "no", bless their hearts.'

'I don't understand a word of this monstrous business,' Mr Waterall said angrily.

'Well, why don't you come downstairs and open the door?' Mrs Hamper suggested. 'Only for goodness sake, pop your trousers on, or you'll catch your death in this rore air. I'll never explain what happened if I've got to crane my neck and shout up at you like this. I had enough of craning and shouting this spring when I had the painters in at 22 Barking Terrace.'

'I can't make out anything of what you're talking about,' Mr Waterall grumbled.

'No, and you won't,' retorted Mrs Hamper with some heat, 'until you come down and open your front door like a rational being instead of yodelling away at me from the top of Mong Blong. I've got a four-wheel cab waiting, and I want to get home as soon as I've seen these two boys safe inside their own house. You'll make me swallow all my aitches in a minute if I have to throw my head much farther back.'

Mr Waterall's head and shoulders disappeared from the open window. In a couple of minutes the fanlight over the front door glowed pink, and the noise of bolts and chains was heard on the other side.

'He's pretty waxy,' Ralph muttered. 'I hope he won't go and squint inside the cab and spot Texas.'

'You leave him to me, ducky,' Mrs Hamper said. 'I'll smooth him down. You wait and see.'

She spoke with the majestic security of a heavy garden-roller about to pass over a refractory bump in a lawn.

The front door opened, and the figure of Mr Waterall in his overcoat, darkened the entrance.

'A quarter to two,' he said sternly. 'What is the meaning of this disgraceful escapade?'

'Now, there's no need whatever to be annoyed with these two boys,' said Mrs Hamper. 'The blame is mine. I invited them to keep me company at the Canterbury, and afterwards we had a snack, and here they are safe and sound.'

'I haven't the least idea who you are, madam, but let me tell you that I take the very greatest exception to your behaviour. You should know better than to invite a couple of boys out to a music-hall and bring them back at this ungodly hour.'

'Ah, we should all know better,' Mrs Hamper agreed. 'But we don't. And that's plain to anyone who reads his newspaper. Still, the world would be a dull place if we all did behave ourselves. My gracious! I often ask myself what we should have to read and talk about if it weren't for the wicked. We ought to show a bit of gratitude even to a murderer when you think of the way he keeps everybody interested. And I'm sure there's no harm in having a little amusement sometimes. The two boys thoroughly enjoyed themselves and if you let them pop off to bed quick instead of reading the riot act in your front hall they'll be none the worse for it in the morning. Goodness me, we're out of this world before we hardly know we're in it. You ought to have seen that undertaker's mute who was wolfing down mussels tonight. He was a walking lesson to enjoy yourself on this earth while you still can. Yes, it was a pity you weren't with us, for really dear old Dan Leno would have made a pillar-box laugh. I know I nearly laughed myself over into the next row of stalls. Besides, you couldn't expect a couple of kids like this to say "no" to a lady when I asked them.

'I certainly expect my sons to say "no" when strangers in trains invite them to go out for the evening without a word to their parents. For all I knew they might have fallen out of the train and been killed.'

'Well, I'm sure I'm very sorry if you were fretting after them,' Mrs Hamper said soothingly. 'But bad news always travels fastest, and you'd have heard long ago before this if anything had have happened to them. They were very unwilling to come, and in fact they wouldn't have if I hadn't been so persistent.'

At this moment the mouldering driver called surlily from the box to know if he was to keep his horse standing here all night.

'Now there *is* a disagreeable old body for you,' said Mrs Hamper. 'You don't want to be like him, do you?'

This was altogether too much for Mr Waterall. He slammed the door and ordered his sons off upstairs to bed.

'He can't do much now,' said Ralph to Roger when they had reached their own room and begun to undress.

'He might stop our pocket-money,' Roger suggested.

'Well, I bet you if he does Mrs Hamper will give us all the tuck we want,' Ralph prophesied.

Roger's eyes glistened eagerly.

'I say, do you think she would?' he exclaimed, and on this exquisite prospect he fell into a heavy dreamless sleep.

Not so Mr Waterall, who tossed about indignantly on his pillow, remembering a hundred stinging remarks he ought to have made to Mrs Hamper, but which he had somehow failed to think of at the time.

Three o'clock struck thinly from the travelling-clock on the mantelpiece of Mr Waterall's bedroom.

'Confound those boys,' he muttered to himself. 'They've wrecked my sleep for the night.'

He got out of bed, lit the gas, and settled down to try to read himself into a less irritable frame of mind with the help of a yellow-back novel about a mysterious treasure buried in the city of Lima. He had just turned a page and come face to face with a heavily cloaked figure in a sombrero who was lurking in one of the gloomy archways that are a feature of romances laid in Spanish America, when he heard the front-door bell ring.

He sat back in bed, wondering if in the agitation caused by that fat woman's arrival with Ralph and Roger he had forgotten to close the front door properly, and if the policeman on the beat was summoning him to perform his duty as a householder by doing so now. The front-door bell rang a second time.

Mr Waterall got out of bed again. Raising the window as quietly as he could, he peered cautiously down. He drew back inside with a start, for the figure on his front-door step appeared to be wearing a cloak and sombrero and to resemble the sinister assassin lurking in that gloomy archway of old Lima. And when the front-door bell rang for the third time Mr Waterall felt gooseflesh all over himself.

'I wonder if I *did* bolt the door?' he murmured.

A tremendous tattoo from the knocker fetched his heart into his mouth.

'Who the devil can it be at this hour?' he asked himself.

The bell rang yet again and sounded as if it intended to continue ringing until the grim visitor was answered.

Mr Waterall wondered if his best course would be to go upstairs, wake Dodsworth and Cook with the information that a murderer was trying to break into the house, and rely upon their screams from the attic window to rouse the policeman on duty. But then they might not scream. They might merely faint. The idea of shouting for help himself was distasteful, because if the cloaked figure were not a potential murderer he might present himself to his neighbours in Orange Road in rather a foolish light. However, there would be no harm in opening the window and letting the man below know that he was in a position to summon help. Yes, yes, the only thing to do was to demand what this strange visitor's business was and if he failed to give a satisfactory explanation of his presence, to shout for the police.

'I'll get a proper whistle tomorrow,' Mr Waterall vowed as he went over to the window and demanded in the deepest voice he could manage what was the matter down there.

The cloaked figure looked up and said in a voice that was only too bitterly familiar to Mr Waterall:

'I'm extremely sorry to wake you up again, Mr Waterall, but I have lost my nephew and I am anxious to know if you can give me any news of him.'

'Go away, you blackguard,' Mr Waterall shouted down in accents of really impressive wrath. 'What the devil do you mean by following me up to London to pester me about your infernal nephew? I've not seen your nephew. I don't want to see him. I don't want ever to hear another word about him. If you don't stop ringing my bell, I'll call the police and have you locked up as a public nuisance. Stop ringing my bell, do you hear?' Mr Waterall choked, for throughout this speech the bell had maintained its shrilling.

'Yes, I hear it,' said Mr Ryan. 'But I wedged it with a match, because my fingers got so sad and weary of pressing it without any sign that it understood and appreciated my advances. And now the match has broken off short, and all the king's horses and all the king's men wouldn't be able to stop that bell ringing. It'll ring and ring and ring and ring until it rings itself dry. But I hope it won't go on ringing for more than a week. It ought not to with any luck.'

A red cloud passed before Mr Waterall's sleepless eyes. Fortunately for him he did not possess a loaded revolver, because without doubt if he had possessed one he would at this moment have shot Mr Ryan where he stood. And then his eyes caught the swelling shape of the toilet-jug. He rushed across the room and bore it brimming to the window. The bell still shrilling through the house relentlessly stung him into an equal relentlessness. He saw that Mr Ryan was bending over and poking about with his bell. He saw that he could empty the contents of the obese toilet-jug upon his stooping form. And he emptied it.

'My God!' Mr Ryan exclaimed. 'Then it *was* a fire-alarm.'

With this ambiguous comment on the assault he leapt down the front-door steps and rushed along Orange Road in the direction of Hammersmith.

'Well, I finished him off that time,' Mr Waterall said to himself in a burst of self-congratulation. 'That's the way to deal with pests like him. Firmness. I don't think he'll come back looking for his confounded nephew in my house again. I allowed myself to be bounced by him down at Dream Days. But this time? No. Damn that bell! How on earth am I going to sleep with that noise blaring on all night? I'll have to go down to the kitchen and put some blotting-paper round it.' Mr Waterall laughed complacently to himself. 'Ha-ha, it'll take more than blotting paper, though, to dry that pertinacious vagabond. He must be soaked to the skin. He must be absolutely soused.'

Ten minutes later when Mr Waterall had reduced the shrilling of the bell to a muffled rattle inaudible up in his bedroom and when he was wearily hoping for sleep at last, the rattle and clang of a fire-engine's rapid approach sounded through the night.

'Hallo, I wonder where the fire is?' he thought.

He was soon to know, or rather he was soon to know where there was an alleged fire, for the engine pulled up immediately outside his own door, and Mr Waterall looking once more out of his window perceived helmeted figures hurrying up his own steps.

'Whereabouts is the fire?' one of them shouted up.

'I don't know,' Mr Waterall shouted down.

'We were rung up by the alarm at the corner of Orange Road,' said the fireman. 'And we were told there was a fire at Number 315.'

'Who told you?'

'A bearded gent in a black cape and big hat. He was dripping wet. We thought he'd been trying to put it out.'

'It's a hoax,' Mr Waterall really yelled. 'It's an infernal rascally hoax! There's no fire at all. None at all. I emptied a jug of water over a blackguard who was ringing my bell, and this is his degraded revenge.'

'Well, we'll have to send somebody over to see you about it in the morning,' said the fireman. 'What's your name, sir?'

'Waterall is my name.'

'Look here, I don't want any funny stuff from you,' said the fireman angrily. 'You'll find it a serious business calling out an engine on a fool's errand.'

'I tell you my name *is* Waterall!'

'Well, don't try watering us or you may get a taste of the working end of this hose.'

'Look up my name in the post-office directory if you don't believe me,' Mr Waterall challenged.

The fireman turned away.

'False alarm,' he called to the others. 'Back to the station.'

Then he turned to call up to Mr Waterall:

'And I hopes they gives you a fine as'll teach you to be less funny in future, Mr Water Everybody,' said the fireman bitterly.

As for Mr Waterall he lay awake for the rest of the night, planning how to revenge himself upon Mr Ryan.

CHAPTER FIFTEEN

ON the morning after their adventurous evening Mr Waterall solemnly deprived his two sons of all pocket-money until the end of the term. He also declared that they should not leave London for a single week-end and that the pony he had intended to buy for them should now never be bought. The last was the severest punishment, not so much because they had forfeited the chance to obtain a pony of their own, though they would greatly have enjoyed such a possession, as because of the way their father would continue to hold forth upon the wonders of this unpurchased pony. Unpruned by the restraining influence of hard cash Mr Waterall's imagination grew so luxuriantly round this pony that within a week he talked of it as an animal that could have given Pegasus 14 lb. and a beating in the Cesarewitch. It was to have been the swiftest, the glossiest, the most aristocratic and intelligent animal that ever was known. It was to have been capable of performing feats of speed, endurance and sagacity hitherto unheard of in the equine family. And this paragon they had lost entirely through their own fault. They had only themselves to blame for the dull pedestrianism to which they were henceforth doomed. Their father grew so fond of this vision of horse-flesh that presently he began to talk about it as if it had really once been in his possession. It was to have been called Swiftsure, and within a little while it had been called Swiftsure with a pedigree and performance behind it of classic fame.

'I noticed a pony trotting up Kensington High Street this morning,' their father would say, 'and by Jove, I couldn't help thinking to myself what a much better animal Swiftsure was. That pony I was going to get for you two boys would have run away from it in a few strides. It's a pity that you couldn't have behaved yourselves with common decency. You missed the chance of your lives when I had to give up the idea of giving you Swiftsure.'

'Do you think he'll ever stop jawing about that rotten pony he pretends he was going to give us?' Ralph asked in despair.

'I shouldn't think so,' said Roger. 'But when he starts giving us our pocket-money again, I'm going to begin saving up for a bike. There's one in a yard at the back of an old-furniture shop in Hammersmith Broadway for ten bob. It's a boneshaker, but it will do for biking at Oak. It's better than the stinking fag of walking everywhere. I asked the man about it, and he said he'd keep it for me till March. Well, if I get three half-crown tips at Christmas and save my fourpence a week in January and February I can easily buy it.

Ralph's prophecy that Mrs Hamper would take care that neither he nor Roger lacked tuck during the penury to which an unfeeling father exposed them had turned out truly.

'Young folk need lollipops,' she laid down as an axiom, and they wondered if she might not be the wisest woman that ever lived.

Barking Terrace was a row of semi-detached houses set back from Hammersmith Road behind a balustraded shrubbery, and thus combining the advantages of main road and a secluded bystreet. Each house had a long garden at the back with fruit trees and potting-sheds and many other amenities of rural existence. Mrs Hamper's garden was enriched by a rustic summer-house where she had promised the boys they should have some rare teas in the summertime. She lived at Number 22 with one servant, an elderly woman called Beatrice, which Mrs Hamper pronounced 'Beetriss'.

'I used to call her "Beet" when she first came to me twenty years ago, but she became so red in the face as she grew older that I didn't like to go on calling her Beet, for really if there was one thing more than another that she looked like it really was a beetroot. "Beetriss" is bad enough, and in fact I've once or twice had to put my hand up to my mouth as if I was gaping to hide a smile when she's come along from the kitchen to talk to me about something or other. I expect you've noticed how red in the face she goes sometimes when she's answering the door?'

'I thought she was hot,' Ralph suggested.

'No, it's not heat makes her red. I've known her bake all day and look as fresh as a daisy. But if she gets a bit excited she'll colour up like danger on the line. Marking clothes always excites her for instance. Just let Beetriss mark a dozen handkerchiefs and you ought to see her colour. Well, it would make a Turk stare. I had my lesson when the butcher's boy let out a great vulgar guffaw because he heard me call "Beet" along the passage to the back door. I was in two minds whether I wouldn't call her "Beattie" after that; but there again she'd have been at the mercy of anybody who liked a bit of vulgarity, and though she's nothing near as stout as what I am myself still she's what you may call ample and "Beattie" was just giving people an opportunity, they being what they are.'

Roger at Randell's Preparatory School had a half-holiday on Wednesday as well as on Saturday, whereas Ralph at St. James's had a whole holiday on Saturday. At first the two brothers used to go to tea together on Saturday; but, when Mrs Hamper pressed them to bring their friends, Ralph's dignity was endangered by having to sit down and gorge in the company of a lot of Randellites. So a convention was reached by which Roger and his friends partook of Mrs. Hamper's hospitality on Wednesdays, Ralph and his friends on Saturdays. Nor did Mrs Hamper confine her entertainment to the giving of rich teas followed by games and, before parting, presents of carefully chosen tuck to winners and losers alike. She would often take her guests to matinées at the Lyric Opera House, which in those days offered a fresh touring company every week and a pantomime of its very own at Christmas. A melodrama like *Man to Man* which included an escape of convicts from Dartmoor in a fog and the wrecking of a train to obtain suitable disguises irradiated with its magic the humdrum of scholastic life.

It was wonderful to emerge in the blurred gold of Hammersmith Broadway about five o'clock of a wet December afternoon and arrive home with Mrs Hamper to a sublime smell of muffins and crumpets and hot buttered tea-cake, wonderful to see in Mrs Hamper's dining-room the big mahogany table rainbow lighted with cakes and jellies, and the face of Beatrice glowing like a ruby as she pulled out the chairs for the boys to sit down and eat whatever they wanted when they wanted and for as long as they wanted.

Amid these comforts of an urban existence Ralph and Roger had no regrets for the deprivation of week-ends in the country, where Mrs Waterall remained through the rains of November, hoping every day that Donkin's men would fix the kitchen door. Finally this was done on 25 November, and on the following day Mrs Waterall locked up Dream Days and returned with Phyllis to London until after Christmas. She brought the unwelcome news that the Hobday house looked disturbingly close now that the framework was almost finished. Her husband, however, busy with checking the yearly accounts of various firms that patronized Messrs Wickham and Waterall, did not go down to Oak, and thus the hideous progress of the Hobday erection was not revealed to him.

As for Mr Ryan, after the night at the Canterbury he had spent a mysterious fortnight in London, the details of which remained for ever undivulged, and then he returned to Mon Repos to resume the education of his nephew. Texas himself had been entertained by Mrs Hamper in Hammersmith for a couple of days, an entertainment which he repaid by entertaining in turn her two pet bullfinches for whose pleasure he played a hundred simple tunes. His playing proved to be one of the things which acted as a caloric upon Beatrice, who would listen to him with a face as ruddy as the breasts of the bullfinches. On the third day Mrs Hamper took him to hear the Moore and Burgess Minstrels, after which she bought him a shiny waterproof, a heavy woollen muffler, half a dozen pairs of bootlaces, a long mouth-organ, a set of bones as used by niggers, and his ticket to Galton. Then she saw him off from Waterloo where she left him grinning in a railway-carriage at the sight of a bright half-sovereign nestling in a palm of most unfamiliar pinkness.

Back in Hampshire Texas spent four happy nights with Harry Gibbs in the brick-kiln before his uncle returned to Mon Repos and the usual course of life in Oak was resumed for him.

After Christmas the weather became seasonable, and when the Waterall family arrived at Oak to spend the rest of the holidays in rustic seclusion the countryside lay under six inches of crisp snow and every duck pond for miles around was frozen. Enchanting though the wintry scene appeared to the boys when they alighted at Galton station, the pleasure of it for their father was marred by his getting into the line of fire of a snowball fight between the platform paper-boy and the junior porter with the result that he stopped two large snowballs simultaneously, one with his back and the other much more painfully with his nose. He held forth in the fly all the way to Oak on the decay of manners among the youth of today and vowed that at whatever cost to himself his sons should be compelled to emulate the standards of his own early life.

'My nose is still stinging,' he said indignantly to his wife.

'I'm sure it must be, dear,' she responded tenderly. 'It was really a fearful blow. I wish you'd have let the fly stop at the chemist's.'

'Oh, it's not the pain that annoys me,' said Mr Waterall stoically. 'It's the confounded lack of any sense of decency or decorum in which these young ruffians of today positively revel. Such a thing as two employees of a railway company turning the platform into a bear-garden would have been unheard of in my young days.'

Mr Waterall's indignation with the present was not mitigated when they reached the bungalow and he saw the barbarous affair in corrugated iron that Hobday had erected.

'Why, it's hardly twenty paces from Dream Days,' Mr Waterall gasped. 'And the fellow has actually had the impudence to put in a window on the side overlooking us.'

Indeed, at this moment three of the younger members of Hobday's large family were rubbing their noses against the pane of this window in greedy curiosity about the inhabitants of Dream Days.

'He had the whole of half an acre on which to build his monstrous abortion . . .'

'Daddy, what is an abortion?' Phyllis asked.

'Hush, darling, don't interrupt Father,' her mother put in quickly.

'To build this great sprawling unwieldy barrack of corrugated iron,' Mr Waterall continued, 'and he must needs choose that corner of it which is as close as possible to our bungalow. It's a piece of deliberate insolence. It's an expression of contempt which I will not tolerate. I'll have Donkin out here tomorrow, and he shall put up a twelve-foot fence to shut out that abominable eye-sore. Look at those filthy children now. Putting out their tongues at us.'

'I don't think they're doing that, dear,' said Mrs Waterall. 'I think they're only licking the frosted window-pane. Children will often do that.'

'Well, I'm not going to spend my time watching disgusting brats licking window-panes,' Mr Waterall declared. 'So we'll have Donkin out and see what he can do. It was all very well for Bocock's young man to persuade me to plant those poplars; but how can half a dozen poplars contend with that vile tin eruption almost alongside of us?'

Mr Waterall was in such a rage that he walked into Galton himself that afternoon, and what is more he dragged his unwilling sons at his heels, in order to impress upon Mr Donkin the builder the necessity of at once erecting a fence of tall stout planks to shut out Hobday's window and the degraded intimacies of Hobday's back premises, where at least six of Hobday's children seemed to spend all their time shrieking among the parings of potatoes and discarded heaps of tea-leaves.

'He's a bit of a radical, is this fellow Hobday,' Mr Donkin warned his client. 'He may try to make himself a bit nasty. How would it be if you put up that tool-shed you were thinking of in front of his window? Then he couldn't claim that you'd put up a tall fence just for the purpose of shutting out his light?'

'But why shouldn't I try to shut out his light?' Mr Waterall demanded. 'He deliberately plants this despicable tin barrack within a foot of my boundary and not content with that he has the impudence to put in a window on that side, so that I cannot move in that part of the garden without being glared at by a herd of grubby-faced brats. What right has he to complain if I do try to exterminate his view?'

'Oh, don't think I don't fully appreciate your position, Mr Waterall,' said the builder. 'Still, you know what local feeling is. The Galton Rural District Council is full of radicals, more's the pity, and nothing would give some of them more pleasure than to interfere on behalf of what they would call a poor man's rights. If you just put up a fence they might hold it was deliberate obstruction, whereas if you built a garden shed you could claim that it was the only suitable place in the garden to put it. Then we can carry the fence along on either side of it far enough to do what you're aiming at. I don't want to press you into putting up a shed, but last November you did talk about putting one up, and there's no doubt you do want a shed. I could get the plans approved right away and we could get to work on it as soon as you'd passed the estimate.'

'Very well,' Mr Waterall decided. 'Let me have the estimate. But mind you, you mustn't keep me waiting a month before you start. Spring will be coming on before we know where we are, and I don't want every flower and leaf on the side of the garden to be picked by a swarm of snivelling children.'

'When are you going away, Mr Waterall?'

'Well, I shall have to be back in London during the first week in January; but my family will be staying on another fortnight.'

'Before they go, Mr Waterall,' the builder promised almost emotionally, 'I'll have Hobday's view cut off.'

Mr Waterall was so warmly appeased by the thought of Hobday's darkened room on that side of his hideous building that not merely did he take the boys into the Market Hotel and stand them lemonade while he himself drank a sloe gin, but in passing the ironmonger's he took them in and bought them each a pair of skates of the type that screws into the heel of the boot. In Hilton Jones's shop they saw hanging up a toboggan.

'Come along,' said their father. 'You've got your skates. What are you looking at now?'

There was a hasty colloquy in whispers between the brothers, at the end of which they announced that if their father would put down the money for the toboggan they were prepared to repay him from their savings on getting home. They hoped faintly that such businesslike behaviour would soften his heart and induce him to say that he would buy the toboggan for them himself.

'I don't know where you're going to toboggan round Oak,' he demurred.

'Oh, yes, there's a spiffing hill past the Chilcotts',' said Roger.

'And there's a more spiffing hill above that big hop garden, farther along the Basing road,' Ralph added.

'But you've never done any tobogganing,' their father still demurred. 'Surely to goodness skating is enough. If you learn to skate decently during the rest of the holidays you'll be lucky.'

Mr Hilton Jones smiled encouragingly. It might thaw tomorrow, and he was anxious to get rid of the toboggan before it fell to pieces with dry rot.

'Are you sure you have the money?' Mr Waterall asked his sons.

'Yes, Roger was saving up for a bike, but he'd rather spend it on a toboggan,' said Ralph. 'And I was saving up for a vivarium.'

'For a what?'

'A thing to keep snakes in,' said Ralph.

'Well, if you really want this toboggan,' Mr Waterall agreed quickly, 'I don't mind advancing you the money till you get home. But mind, you're to pay me back.'

The mention of the vivarium had broken down their father's resistance successfully, but at the same time it looked like ruining any chance of Ralph's finding himself with spare cash for some time to come.

The sight of Ralph carrying that toboggan through Galton was a temptation to every boy in the place to snowball him. At last a couple of big ones landed simultaneously just above the collar and melted rapidly down his neck. This was more than he could stand, and he caught one of the youngsters who had flung them full on the mouth with a beauty. Roger followed up his brother's retaliation fiercely; but unfortunately he missed the grinning youngster and hit on the ear an old lady who was passing along. She at once rushed at Roger with her umbrella to chastise him, and Roger flying from her wrath ran blindly into the Vicar who collapsed in a drift; and then somehow or other it seemed as if all the inhabitants of Galton were snowballing one another, except Mr Waterall who, gazing round for his sons, presented the desolate appearance of one of those figures swept by a snowstorm inside a glass paper-weight. A snowball hit him on the nose just where he had already been hit at the railway station. Another knocked off his hat. A third with a piece of ice in its heart caught him a thump on the back of the head and nearly stunned him. Mr Waterall saw the boys' toboggan lying at his feet. He began to use it now as a buckler against the assaults of the enemy, now as an early British chariot to mow that enemy over. Finally he brought it down heavily upon the spike of a railing, which gashed the bottom of the toboggan. By this time, however the snowballs had ceased to fly and the snowballers themselves were going about their business again.

'I'm afraid I knocked a hole in your toboggan,' Mr Waterall said to his sons. 'But I suppose it will go just as well.'

Ralph shook his head.

'We'll have to try and patch it up. Otherwise the snow will come through, and it won't be able to go so fast.'

'I suppose that means you boys will expect me to pay half for this toboggan?' Mr Waterall asked in a tone of slightly self-conscious jocularity, which to the quick ears of his sons seemed to indicate that he was not entirely convinced of the strength of his position.

'Perhaps we'll be able to patch it up,' said Ralph pessimistically. 'But we wouldn't have bought it ourselves if there had been a hole in it, would we, Roger?'

'Rather not.'

'And we can't take it back to the shop,' Ralph continued. 'We've got to have it now.'

'I suppose you're trying to suggest that I should pay for the whole of it?' Mr Waterall asked, still in that tone of faintly uneasy jocularity.

'We wouldn't have bought it with that hole in it,' Ralph emphasized. 'We wouldn't honestly.'

'Very well,' said Mr Waterall. 'I suppose I'll have to pay for the whole of it.'

'But suppose the hole can't be mended . . . oh, I see, you mean all of it,' said Ralph. 'Thanks awfully.'

'Thanks awfully,' echoed his brother.

The walk home was quite a pleasant one.

Ralph and Roger were touched by this revelation in their father of a sense of justice he was apt to keep too closely hidden. Roger was thinking about his boneshaker in the spring. Ralph was wondering if a toad and a grass snake would live at peace with one another in that vivarium which was once again within reach of his finances. Mr Waterall himself was thinking that after all it was better worth while to have a pair of sons like this than not to have any sons at all.

The crinching of boots along the white road; the occasional drip of snow melting from a leaf or twig under the rays of the wintry sun; the flutter of small birds' wings among the cold shrubberies of the houses on the outskirts of Galton; far away the cry of a shepherd on the down coming thinly across the stillness of the cold: this was winter indeed.

'Well,' said Mr Waterall to his wife when they were back at Dream Days, 'we've had a delightful walk, and these boys are lucky to have a father who provides them with every luxury. Skates and a toboggan, you see.'

'Oh, Robert dear, how very kind of you. And so soon after Christmas.'

'What did you bring for me, Daddy?' his daughter asked.

'What did I bring for you, my little piece of sugar and spice?' Mr Waterall parried. 'What *did* I bring for you?'

Phyllis rummaged eagerly in the pockets of his big overcoat.

'Ah, you won't find it there,' her father said, searching his mind for something that he might have given her.

'Oh, Daddy, where is it?' Phyllis begged to know in her voice of most profound affectation.

'That's the great question of the moment,' Mr Waterall said.

Ralph and Roger stood apart, cynical smiles upon their fraternal countenances. Unless the governor performed a startling feat of mental acrobatics, Phyllis was going to have one of the most notable sucks on record. Nothing that they could think of as likely to be in their father's pockets would be able to impose upon Phyllis. Even if he tipped her as much as five bob she would know the plain truth that he had forgotten all about her. Skates and a toboggan for her brothers, for her nothing. Perhaps this blow would do her good and remove some of the cockiness which so paradoxically permeated her feminine nature. The two brothers stood there like the chorus in a Greek tragedy watching a heroine go to her doom.

'You did bring me something, Daddy?' Phyllis pressed in sudden suspicion.

'Now would I go all the way into market without bringing back something for the dear little pig who stayed at home?' Mr Waterall countered with a jocose allusiveness that would have nauseated his two sons, had they not been so deeply preoccupied in contemplation of their sister's inevitable fall.

'Oh, please tell me what you brought from market?' Phyllis begged.

'I'm sure it's something far nicer than anything you could have dreamed of,' her mother suggested. 'Perhaps Father wants you to guess what it is.'

'That's right. I'll give you three guesses,' said Mr Waterall, who was telling himself that at any rate this would shed a light on the state of Phyllis's desires.

The boys looked curiously at their mother. By what process of wifely fatuousness, they asked themselves, could she have failed to perceive that her husband was being driven into a corner from which there was no escape?

'Was it a doll's perambulator?' Phyllis asked.

'No, it wasn't a doll's perambulator,' said her father decidedly.

'How could it be a doll's perambulator, you fat ass?' Roger demanded. 'You don't think that Ralph and me would wheel a stinking perambulator out from Galton just to please you?'

'Look here, Roger, would you oblige me by not butting into this guessing game?' his father said sharply. He felt inclined to add that if circumstances had led him into buying a doll's perambulator for Phyllis it would have been for him to say whether or no Roger wheeled it out from Galton. But a doll's perambulator sounded rather too elaborate a present to saddle himself with merely for the pleasure of taking Roger down a peg.

'Was it a fishmonger's shop?' Phyllis asked.

'A fishmonger's shop?' her father repeated. 'My little girl mustn't be silly. How could Daddy bring her a fishmonger's shop?'

'Well, Muriel Hapgood's father gave her a fishmonger's shop at Christmas,' Phyllis insisted. 'He did really, Daddy, with lemon soles and cod and such darling little lobsters and lumps of ice and . . .'

'She means a toy fishmonger's shop,' Ralph interposed in contemptuous elucidation of a mystery that was evidently beyond his father's grasp.

'No, it wasn't a fishmonger's shop,' said Mr Waterall more decidedly than ever. Even a toy fishmonger's shop sounded to him a good deal more expensive than a doll's perambulator.

'Who wants a fishmonger's shop?' Roger asked. 'Hapgood told me his kiddy sister's shop was rotten. He put a lemon sole on the bars of the schoolroom grate, and it melted away in a second. He said it melted quicker than a soldier in one of those rotten penny boxes.'

'Well, I think Georgie Hapgood is horrid to Muriel,' said Phyllis.

'No, he isn't,' Roger contradicted. 'Because she's nearly as affected as you are, and you'd jolly well let Hapgood hear you calling him Georgie if you don't want to get your head smacked.'

'He wouldn't smack my head, would he, Daddy?' Phyllis appealed.

'I'm sure he would never be so ungallant,' Mr Waterall replied. 'But don't let us talk about the Hapgood family now. You've still another guess.'

Phyllis thought long and deep.

'It wasn't a dear little kittie-wittie, was it?' she asked at last.

'Yes,' said Mr Waterall quickly, before his daughter had a chance to change her mind about such a practical and at the same time such an economical guess.

'Yes,' Mr Waterall repeated, 'it was a kitten.'

Ralph and Roger would not withhold from their father a grudging glance of admiration. Kittens were always to be had for the asking, and on such a cold day as this he would have an unanswerable excuse for not bringing it back with him in his pocket.

'But where is it, Daddy?' Phyllis pressed. 'Oh, Daddy, I want to see my darling little kittie-wittie. What kind is it?'

'Well, I suppose you'd call it a tabby really,' said Mr Waterall. 'You shall have it as soon as it can leave its mother.'

'Where is it now?'

'I tell you. It's with its mother.'

'Is it a boy kitten or a girl kitten?' she went on.

'It's a boy kitten,' said Mr Waterall.

'How did they know it's a boy kitten?' she still went on.

'Phyllis darling, don't ask so many questions,' her mother intervened. 'You'll tire poor Father. You may be sure that it will be a lovely kitten, and that's enough for any little girl to know. Was your visit to Mr Donkin successful?' she turned to ask her husband in order to change the subject.

Mr Waterall scowled at the Hobday abomination.

'Donkin is to start right away on the tool-shed and the fence. I've settled to put up the tool-shed now. We badly want a tool-shed. That lawn-mower must be put somewhere. And by the way we must get a place for Dodsworth or Cook. We can't be without a servant here always.'

'I don't think Dodsworth would like sleeping in a tool-shed, dear,' said Mrs Waterall. 'Cook might not mind. She's so very obliging. But Dodsworth has always been rather nervous of beetles.'

'Who's proposing to put either of them into a tool-shed?' Mr Waterall demanded indignantly. 'I intend to build a room on behind the kitchen. Donkin can get straight on with the building. Then I think we'll put on two more rooms on the other side at right angles. We can buy them all ready to put up and Donkin can build the brick foundation. The sitting-room will open out of our present living-room, and our bedroom can open out of that. We'll have french-windows for the sitting-room leading on to the lawn.'

'The lawn?' echoed Mrs Waterall timorously.

'Well, of course we're going to have a lawn on that side of the bungalow. Surely you realized why I left that space free from shrubs or trees? And why on earth should I take so much trouble to bring a lawn-mower down here unless we were going to have a lawn? March or April, however, is the best time for sowing lawns, they tell me, unless one does it at the end of September.'

Mrs Waterall felt somewhat overcome by the prospect of all these grand additions, and through her mind there may have passed a momentary regret that she had been so quick to offer to find the money for the new kitchen out of her own small capital. Had she been patient Robert would certainly have managed to find the money for the kitchen himself.

'Did you say that Mr Donkin had promised to do all this immediately?' she asked.

'Right away,' her husband answered confidently.

Mrs Waterall, with memories of an autumn spent with an unhung kitchen door did not look quite so confident.

'As long as the workmen are out of the place before you start on the lawn, dear,' she began.

'Of course they will be. I don't anticipate this job will take a month altogether.'

'No dear, I hope not. But workmen do seem to loiter about a long time when they once get into a place. In fact they never seem to get out, and I know you'd be irritated if they left their tools and buckets and things lying about on the new lawn.'

'I should be rather more than irritated,' said Mr Waterall. 'However, don't worry yourself. Donkin perfectly understands how essential it is to give that fellow Hobday a lesson. As far as I can gather from Donkin the fellow is a miserable agitator, which is just what I should imagine of anybody who would come and deliberately build a hideous erection like that almost on top of his next door neighbour. It was a gesture of social contempt. That's what it was. He was trying to demonstrate to the world that Jack was as good as his master. Well, we shall see. And now if you two boys intend to make the most of this seasonable weather,' he concluded turning to his sons, 'you'd better be off out of doors. It may thaw tomorrow. It probably will as I've bought you those skates and that toboggan.'

Mr Waterall spoke with the air of one who feels that he possesses a personality large enough to tempt the particular malice of Providence.

CHAPTER SIXTEEN

RALPH and Roger, who were only too glad to be out of the way of dry discussions about tool-sheds and fences and foundations, voted to test their new toboggan immediately, and they hurried out to make the most of what was left of the day before the swift winter darkness overtook them. Tomorrow morning would be time enough to seek a suitable duckpond and discover the joys of skating.

'Let's go and toboggan down the hill behind the Chilcott's,' Ralph suggested.

'Will it be all right if we toboggan on a road?' Roger asked. 'Suppose we biff into somebody?'

'Well, we can steer, can't we, you ass?' said his brother scornfully.

Roger did not reply. He was not perfectly convinced either of his own skill with a toboggan or of Ralph's.

'What a silly chump the governor was to bash this hole in it,' said Ralph when they started off along the lane towards their run.

'A frightful chump,' Roger agreed. 'Still we got it for nothing that way, and I'm frightfully keen to get that bike in the spring. I shall explore the country all round here.'

'A chap in my class said he'd swap two green tree-frogs and an ostrich egg which his sister's governess stuck together with only one bit missing after their skivvy knocked it over dusting,' Ralph informed his brother, for his mind had reverted to that vivarium.

'What did he want for them?'

'He wanted all my Brazilians and all my Chilis and all my Uruguays. He's gone dotty on South Americans. They're catalogued in Stanley Gibbons's at £4 3s. 8d. But I asked at that stamp-shop in Hammersmith Road what the man would give me for them, and he said one and twopence for the whole lot.'

'I think he's rather a chiseller,' commented Roger. 'A fellow called Barclay at Randell's had some three-cornered Cape of Good Hopes, and he told him they were fudges. But Barclay said his uncle gave them to him off old letters.'

'Well, I'm not dead nuts on stamps any more,' said Ralph. 'So I think I will swap them when I get my vivarium.'

'Are you going to put the ostrich egg in it too?'

'Good lumme, no, why it's an enormous thing.'

'What will you do with it then?'

'Keep it of course, you ass.'

'Where?'

'How do I know "where"?'

'I wonder if they eat ostrich eggs where they grow,' Roger speculated.

'Eggs don't grow, you fathead.'

'Well, you know what I mean. I mean where they're found.'

'I should think they'd be pretty mucky,' Ralph murmured pensively. 'Besides, everybody doesn't think about eating everything like you do.'

'No I don't think about eating everything.'

'Yes, you do.'

'Well, so do you if I do.'

'All right, but shut up talking because I want to think about my vivarium till we get to the Chilcotts'.'

'We might ask them to mend the hole in the toboggan,' Roger suggested.

'You ass, isn't that why I said we'd go to the Chilcotts'?'

The boys had not seen Micha and Rehob since the November exeat; but they found on arrival at the shack that the two brothers had already heard of the adventurous evening at the Canterbury from Texas Bill.

'I reckon you ought to get Mrs Hamper down here,' said Rehob, his florid freckled face puckering to a grin. 'She'd just about fit in with this landscape.'

'Well, we did ask her,' said Ralph. 'And I think she's going to come and stay at Wyatt's Farm during the summer holidays.'

'Mind you bring her along to tea at the shack,' Micha laughed. 'And I hope I'll be there when she first meets Uncle Gus at home. Now then, let's have a look at that injured toboggan of yours.'

A few minutes handiwork was enough to patch up the hole satisfactorily, and the two boys sallied forth to see what their toboggan could do.

Bent Hill, as the road was called which forked from the Galton road up past the Chilcotts' and the stucco house built by Lightfoot, the vanished solicitor, to an undulating parkland on the high ground above the scattered bungalows of Oak, was narrow and winding. For the first few runs the toboggan did not succeed in carrying Ralph or Roger beyond the ditch of the first bend, and even when this was safely negotiated, the ditch at the next bend always stopped them. Every trial, however, owing to the polish of the frozen snow on its under surface the toboggan moved forward more rapidly, and by the time the boys had been upset about twenty times in one or other of the ditches full of drifted snow it was starting off like a bullet from a gun. Finally, when by some happy miracle Roger had managed to pass both the bends in the road without upsetting into either ditch, it entered the straight where the road sloped down more steeply and swept forward faster and faster towards the lane from Oak which cut across the bottom of Bent Hill almost at right angles.

It was by now almost dark, and it was the habit of a retired naval lieutenant called Green accompanied by his housekeeper, a Mrs Rellie, and seven white fox-terriers to proceed at this hour into the bar of the Market Hotel, Galton, and remain there until closing time, after which, leaning upon his housekeeper's arm, he would return slowly and unsteadily to his bungalow in Oak and sleep until the following afternoon. Lieutenant Green's reason for walking so far to get fuddled was the quantity of rats that infested his bungalow, and the inability of his seven fox-terriers to keep them down. Once or twice the Lieutenant had seen rats of a pinkish hue; but generally speaking all the richly coloured rats in the neighbourhood invaded Mr Ryan's bungalow, and only the commonplace brown rats frequented Sweetbriar Cottage, the residence of Lieutenant Green. What these rats lacked in quality they made up for in quantity.

'At a low estimate,' the Lieutenant told a neighbour once, 'I should put the number of rats in Sweetbriar Cottage last night at over twenty thousand. My dogs couldn't begin to cope with them. They just sat still on the hearthrug and shivered. One enormous brute actually ventured to get right inside my glass and snapped at me when I tried to drink my whisky. Another got inside Mrs Rellie's teapot, and she never noticed it till I pointed out to her that its tail had wormed its way through the spout and was waving about at the top. So the only thing for us to do is to spend the evening at Galton, where I'm not bothered with these rats. Even there I had a bit of a shock the other night when I distinctly saw or thought I saw a lizard inside the siphon. But Mrs Rellie said it was just my fancy, and of course it may have been, for I never heard of a lizard getting inside a siphon before. I asked Mr Ryan if he ever had, and he said he hadn't, but that the other morning he had found his bath absolutely alive with adders, which must have been amazingly unpleasant. Still, there's one thing to be said for adders in a bath, alcohol is recognized as the finest antidote for snakebite, and so I do not anticipate any fatal results for our friend Ryan.'

It was upon Lieutenant Green, Mrs Rellie his house-keeper, and the seven white fox-terriers that Roger descended at express speed just as they reached the spot where Bent Hill joined the road to Galton. Mrs Rellie was so much accustomed to false alarms that when the Lieutenant seized her round the waist and dragged her headlong into the snowy ditch, shouting that an avalanche was falling upon them, she was at first inclined to suppose that he was mistaken, and it was only when a heavy object landed full on the back of her neck and drove her face deep into the snow that she began to realize he might be right, though actually the heavy object was Roger flinging himself from the toboggan before it carried him into the heart of the thick hazel hedge beside the road.

Before Roger had time to clear his mouth of snow and explain what had happened the noise was increased by the infuriated yelping of the dogs and the barking of a still more infuriated human being.

'Get down, you brutes, get down! Whose dogs are these? One of them has bitten a piece out of my overcoat. By gad, I'll sue the owners of them. Where are they? Lie down, will you. Lie down, you curs!'

The Lieutenant's dogs, supposing that the confusion had been caused by an attack and anxious to show their master that when there was something tangible to guard him against they were only too eager to guard him, had rushed wildly upon the approaching figure of Major Kettlewell, who was building in the middle of the coppice behind the old farm cottages a red-brick house much more like a real house than any other except the old Oak Farm itself. Major Wilberforce Kettlewell was a tall man with a turkey's neck, veinous cheeks, and a bottle nose, and he was on his way at this moment to his half-built residence where he intended to spend an hour admiring his own architecture by the light of a bull's-eye lantern. He was a retired major of the Volunteers, and as such he assumed a military deportment that was somewhat exaggerated. He was indeed very like the caricatures of retired colonels that were features of popular farces.

'Look here, if somebody doesn't call off these abominable curs,' he bellowed, 'I shall start shooting.'

Ralph, hearing the uproar at the foot of the hill and surmising that in some way Roger and the toboggan were responsible for it, started to run down with the idea of helping his brother escape the consequences. At his hurried appearance the dogs left Major Kettlewell and rushed yelping to attack him.

No sooner, however, was it fixed in their minds that Ralph was the danger than Micha and Rehob Chilcott came running along their drive to see what was the matter, whereupon the seven dogs at once left Ralph alone and started to attack them .

'Who do these dogs belong to?' the Major shouted. 'They're attacking the whole neighbourhood. They're making the whole road unsafe for foot-passengers. Somebody is going to hear about this.'

While he was talking Lieutenant Green and Mrs Rellie were extricating themselves from the snowy ditch, and now the housekeeper began to call off the dogs in a feeble voice:

'Spot! Bouncer! Jimmie! Tip! Joe! Battler! Dash! Good dogs, good dogs. Lie down, good dogs.'

'They belong to a couple of tramps,' Major Kettlewell shouted wrathfully when he saw the dusk-dimmed forms of Mrs Rellie and the Lieutenant emerge painfully from the ditch. 'Is that you, Mr Chilcott? I call you to witness that I've been attacked by dogs belonging to two wandering tramps. I'll summon them. I'll have them before the magistrates. What's your name, you fellow there?'

'My name is Green,' replied the Lieutenant with dignity. 'What is yours?'

'You heard him, Mr Chilcott?' the Major exclaimed. 'You heard the damned insolence with which he answered me? I shall call you as a witness.'

'I think you're making a slight mistake, Major. This is Lieutenant Green of Sweetbriar Cottage.'

'Is it?' growled the Major, peering through the darkness in the direction of his neighbour. 'Then he ought to know better than to loose a pack of undisciplined dogs at every pedestrian who comes along.'

'Somebody knocked me over,' said the Lieutenant. 'That's why they went for you.'

'They didn't only go for me,' said the Major. 'They went for everybody within reach. They rushed snarling and yapping all over the place, biting at everybody they could see.'

'They've been well trained as watch dogs,' said the Lieutenant. 'They stopped as soon as my housekeeper could get up and call them to heel. They wouldn't have got so excited if we hadn't been knocked over in the ditch by something rather like an avalanche which rushed straight at us.'

'I think perhaps it was me,' said Roger. 'The toboggan ran away. It's in the hedge, I think.'

'Who is this boy dashing about the public thoroughfare on a toboggan?' the Major demanded. 'Nobody has any right to toboggan to the public danger. Who are you, boy?'

'This is Roger Waterall, Major,' said one of the Chilcotts. 'And this is his brother Ralph.'

'Are you the people that bought Canadian Cottage from that scoundrel Blackham?' the Major asked.

'Our father did, yes,' Ralph answered.

'Well, tell your father that half the trees in his garden were stolen from my garden, and tell him that he ought to know better than to let his sons go careering all over Oaktown in a toboggan, knocking people down and exciting dogs to madness.'

With this Major Kettlewell set out again in the direction of his half-built house without so much as a 'good evening' to anybody.

'I'm most awfully sorry I biffed into you,' Roger apologized to the Lieutenant. 'But the toboggan went much faster than I thought it would, and I couldn't steer it round the corner.'

'Oh, that's all right sonny,' said the Lieutenant in the friendliest way. 'Now that I know what it was I don't mind so much. But some very extraordinary things have been happening to me lately, and for all I knew it might have been anything. Well, come along, Mrs Rellie,' he went on, 'we want to get into Galton as soon as possible. Good evening, everybody. Call the dogs, Mrs Rellie.'

'Spot! Bouncer! Jimmie! Battler! Joe! Dash! Tip! Good dogs, good dogs,' Mrs Rellie murmured feebly, for she was still feeling dazed by the force with which Roger's weight had rammed her face down in the snowy ditch.

'You'll make yourselves unpopular in this neighbourhood, young men,' said Rehob Chilcott. 'What became of the toboggan?'

'It's all right,' said Roger. 'I'll lug it out of the hedge.'

'Is it smashed, you ass?' Ralph inquired anxiously.

'No, it's quite all right,' said Roger. 'So keep your hair on.' Then his voice died away to a gloomy mumble. 'At least I think it is a bit cracked, perhaps.'

'You clumsy litle cuckoo,' cried Ralph. 'You've split it right up.'

'Well, I couldn't help it.'

'Yes, you could.'

'No, I couldn't,' Roger maintained. 'It was going too fast to steer it properly.'

'Steer it properly?' repeated Ralph with scorn. 'You couldn't steer it if it was standing still.'

'Well, nor could you. And if you'd been on it then and gone past the bend, you'd have done just the same as me.'

'It must have been cracked already to split up like that,' said Micha Chilcott. 'It was lucky thing you didn't do more damage than you did. Rehob and I will try to patch it up for you tomorrow.'

And this was successfully done again. But two days afterwards Ralph, tobogganing down the steep hill on the other side of the Basing road, crashed at full speed into an old hawthorn tree at the bottom and made matchwood of the toboggan, not to mention nearly making mincemeat of himself.

So Roger was avenged for his brother's criticism of his steering, and tobogganing gave place to skating on the duckpond at Wyatt's Farm, one of the pleasures of which was going into Mrs Poley's at Fernbank afterwards in order to drink her ginger wine and be made to feel, moreover, that one was performing a duty toward one's body in doing so.

'You can't catch your death after this,' Mrs Poley used to affirm in that mighty whisper of hers. 'If I'd only made a rule always to drink ginger wine in cold weather I wouldn't ever have lost my voice and been a martyr to my chest for all these years. It's a lesson to you two boys.'

It certainly was a lesson which Ralph and Roger learnt more pleasantly than most.

They asked Mr Ryan once if he ever drank ginger wine and he replied he would rather pour some treacle on a mustard plaster and drink that.

'There's only one place for ginger wine,' Mr Ryan declared, 'and that's in a kennel with a strong chain round its neck.'

CHAPTER SEVENTEEN

MR WATERALL had to return to London two or three days after his family arrived at Oak to spend the rest of the Christmas holidays there; but before he went he had the pleasure of seeing Donkin's men arrive with the material for obliterating Hobday's view of Dream Days. The very sound of his neighbour's name was an offence to Mr Waterall, and if he had not feared to gratify his sons unduly he might have changed the name Dream Days to avoid that intrusive assonance.

The day after Mr Waterall left, Mr Hobday called in person at Dream Days. He was a short thickset little man with stubby black hair and sallow cheeks in the middle of one of which was a large mole which gave him the look of a die or a domino.

'I've come to see what's going to be done about it,' he announced.

The boys were out skating. Phyllis had gone across to the farm for milk. It was not Poley's day for digging in the garden. Mrs Waterall was alone.

'Won't you take a seat, Mr Hobday?' she asked nervously.

'What I have to say can be said better standing than sitting,' Mr Hobday replied sternly.

So poor Mrs Waterall, who would have given much to sit down and still the trembling of her knees, felt that she must stand to.

'Mr Waterall has gone back to London,' she said.

'Just as well for him he has,' Mr Hobday snapped, 'or he'd have heard more from me than what he's heard from anybody for a long time.'

'I'm sorry,' said Mrs Waterall.

'So am I, mum,' said Mr Hobday fervidly. 'Because what I was going to say to him would have been worth hearing. However, there it is. And what I want to know now is what you're aiming to do about it?'

'Do about what, Mr Hobday?'

'Why, this trick of putting up a great hoarding a bare twelve inches away from my window.'

'We're building a tool-shed,' Mrs Waterall explained.

'It may be a tool-shed, or again it may not,' Mr Hobday continued. 'But tool-shed or deliberate obstruction there's an acre of ground to spare for either, and to put it right in front of my window is nothing more nor less than deliberate persecution. Now, you and yours, mum, may think that it's still all according to persecute the poor; but let me tell you that the day of the idle rich is over. Yes, mum, the downtrodden masses are rising in their thousands, and the days when people like you could build tool-sheds twelve inches away from a poor man's window are gone by. There was a time, mum, when a rich man could go to a poor man's house, haul his daughter out of bed, and use her as one of his baubles. There was a time when he could treat the poor in a way he wouldn't dare treat a dog nowadays. Before the glorious cry of liberty resounded in every humble cot throughout this land your husband could have built what he liked in front of a poor man's window, and if the poor man said a word on his behalf the law was there to help the rich man and grind the poor man down. Well, things aren't all as they might be yet, but the oppressed millions have risen at last, and there's some things, thank god, the rich can't do, and one of them is to put up tool-sheds to shut the light out of a poor man's window. Light is free, mum, light don't belong to the rich any more than what it does to the poor. I've as much right to light as what you have. And so I've just called on you like this to ask what you're going to do about it.'

'You must write to Mr Waterall,' said Mrs Waterall as firmly as she could. 'I do not interfere at all with anything in the garden. But you must admit, Mr Hobday, that you did build your house as close as you possibly could to ours.'

'And why not?' he demanded. 'I bought my humble plot of ground with the money I'd saved from years of hard work. And now I'm not going to have the right to build my humble home where I like on my own ground? That's a good one, that is. You send across and measure up my land and yours, and you'll find I'm a good two feet inside my own boundary. Play the game fair, mum. Don't make dirty insiniations against people who may be poor, but who'd scorn to take a blade of grass which wasn't their own, bought and paid for with the sweat of their brow.'

'I assure you I was not accusing you of building over on

176

our side of the boundary,' said Mrs Waterall. 'What I meant was that your window looks directly into our garden.'

'Well, and isn't it more neighbourly to look into the garden next door than try to shut yourself up and show your dirty snobbishness and pride?'

'All of us like a little privacy,' argued Mrs Waterall.

'And what privacy have the masses had all these years?' Mr Hobday demanded. They've had to live out their wretched lives under the eyes of them who considered themselves their betters. But you're not going to lead me astray into a political argument, mum. Another time, and I'll argue with you till you're hoarse, but what I've come to see you about today is that tool-shed you're putting up to shut out the view from my window. It makes that end of the room useless to all intents and purposes, and when a man has a family of twelve he can't afford to let a room go to waste. My five youngest but one are sleeping in that room, and I'm a bit astonished that a mother like you are should go and encourage anybody to deprive children of light and air.'

'It's nothing to do with me, Mr Hobday. I have no authority from my husband to deal with this matter. You must please write to him directly. I'll give you his address in London.'

To Mrs Waterall's intense relief Mr Hobday took his leave at this, and when she heard the gate click behind him, she sat down exhausted into a wicker arm-chair, hoping that she had not done the wrong thing in giving Hobday her husband's address. She presented a desolate picture, sitting there by herself in that matchboarded room, the chair creaking beneath her like a tree in a tempest. Country life was wonderful, but one had to get used to it. There seemed so many little complications at first.

A couple of days after this interview Mr Waterall saw beside his plate at the breakfast table in 315 Orange Road, two letters with the Galton postmark. The first was from his daughter:

> *Dream Days,*
> *Oak, Galton, Hants.*
> Jan. 8th

My dear Daddy,
We are very happy in Dream Days and we all miss you very much. It is still very cold and there is ice on all the

*water butts. The boys go skating all day. Roger has cut the
back of his head but it is nothing much he says and Ralph
is learning to do the outside edge and he has cut the back
of his head but it is nothing much he says. Dear Daddy,
when will the dear little kittie come? I am longing for a
little playmate. There is nothing more to tell you. Mother
sends her love and says will you excuse a letter but she is
very tired with housework.*

Your loving little daughter,
Phyllis.

Mr Waterall smiled and shook his head in self-reproach.
'Dodsworth,' he said to the parlourmaid, who came into
the dining-room at that moment, 'you don't know of any-
body near here who wants to get rid of a kitten, do you?'
'I don't sir, but I could make inquiries.'
'I wish you would. Miss Phyllis is very anxious to have a
kitten, and I agreed that she should be allowed to have one.'
'Yes, sir, kittens are very pretty when they play.'
'Very amusing indeed,' Mr Waterall agreed. 'And—er—
Dodsworth.'
'Yes, sir.'
'Not a female.'
'No sir. Any kitten, I suppose would do, so long as it
wasn't a—female?'
'Well, I believe as a matter of fact that Miss Phyllis has
a notion for a tabby.'
'Yes, sir, a nice little tabby. Cook could ask one or two
of the tradesmen when they come for the orders and they
could make inquiries.'
'Just so.'
Mr Waterall picked up his other letter, and Dodsworth
passed on. The envelope was a dirty green, the notepaper
was a dirty pink. The handwriting sprawled across the page.
'Hallo, it's from that blackguard next door,' he muttered
when he had looked at the signature.

The Emmporium,
Oak Farm, Estate,
Galton.
Jan. 8th

Dear Sir,
    *I have to inform you with the present that you are com-
mitting a nuisance by putting up a tolshed or other obstruc-*

*shion against the side of my ressidence and shop combined
and I herwith warn you that if you do not remov this unlawe-
ful ereckshion I shal be relunctintly compeled to tak legil
preseedings against you to alow me dew light and air which
is the berthrihgt of every Englishman. Furthermore I must
inform you that I have loged a complaent at the Galton
Rural Distric Cownsel and arst them to order you to remov
your tolshed to a more convenient sihgt. Trusting to hear
from you being agreeable to do what I arst without any
nastiness on both sides.*

I remane yours truly,
Albert Hobday.

Horticulturists in their vanity have long sought to produce a blue rose, and the hue of Mr Waterall's cheeks when
he read this letter from Mr Hobday was exactly the colour of
one of those so called blue roses. He had not heard the
fluency of Mr Hobday's tongue, and the bad spelling of this
letter added to his rage with the claimant's insolence.

'An ignorant guttersnipe,' he spluttered. 'An ignorant
guttersnipe who can't spell two consecutive words of the
King's English who has the audacity to write me a blackmailing
letter of this nature. Very well, we shall see,' said Mr
Waterall, as he brought down his egg-spoon with a thwack
on the pate of his boiled egg. 'We shall see what we shall
see.'

When he told his partner at the office that he must go
down into the country again on urgent business old Wickham did not look pleased.

'Im afraid this grand new country house of yours is going
to take up all your time, Mr Waterall,' he grumbled. 'I
understood it was just a little week-end cottage. But it seems
to be costing you a good deal of time and money.'

'Well, of course, there are always many extra expenses at
first,' said Mr Waterall.

'You'd have done much better to move into a little place
somewhere in the suburbs. You'll find it's a tidy expense to
run two establishments. How long will you be away this
time?'

'Oh, I just have to settle up this business with my next-
door neighbour. He complains that I am shutting out the
light from one of his windows with a tool-shed I am building.'

'There you are, you see,' Mr Wickham grumbled. 'You'll be involved in expensive litigation, and then you'll wish you had followed the advice of an older man.'

It was a pity that Ralph and Roger could not overhear their father being talked to like this and have seen with what meekness he was bearing it.

'Well, if you think it's better,' said the junior partner, 'I won't go down to Oak until Saturday.'

'I not only think it better, I think it is imperative for the proper conduct of our business that you should set an example to the rest of the office.'

Mr Wickham still wore whiskers of the kind known as Piccadilly weepers, which were trained as carefully as his own roses at Surbiton, and when he gazed monumentally at Mr Waterall over the top of his big mahogany table in the innermost sanctum of Messrs. Wickham and Waterall, the junior partner definitely quailed.

'Very well, Mr Wickham, I shall fall in with your wishes,' he agreed.

The senior partner let a whisker flow with gentle majesty through his fingers and nodded slowly.

'I am very glad to hear you say so, Mr Waterall,' he murmured. 'And by the way here is *The Poultry World* for this week, which I shall not require again.'

Then he bent over his desk, and the junior partner withdrew.

When Mr Waterall arrived at Oak on the following Saturday he found that Donkin had indeed done his work well, for of Hobday's Emporium nothing was now visible from the garden of Dream Days except the gable end of the obnoxious building, the rest of it having been obliterated by a stout wooden fence twelve feet high against which the framework of the tool-shed was already in place. When Mr Waterall had plumped for twelve feet he had not realized quite how high a fence of these measurements would be, still less how high it would look. He felt for one brief instant a sympathy for Albert Hobday. With such a fence towering not two feet away from his window he might as well not have any window in that end of the bungalow.

'But after all why should the fellow have put in a window at that end? He had plenty of space elsewhere.'

'Still, I'm afraid there may be a bit of trouble about it, Mr Waterall,' said Mr Donkin. 'Some of these radicals on the Galton Rural District Council have been getting up on their hind legs. They're coming out here again tomorrow, and I hope things will be all right.'

'Do you mean to say they could hold up the building operations?'

'They could do more than that, Mr Waterall. They might make an order to remove the fence and the tool-shed on the ground of deliberate obstruction.'

'Do you mean to say,' Mr Waterall demanded, 'that a handful of jacks in office have the right to interfere with private property to that extent? What on earth is the country coming to?'

'I'm afraid that's how things stand,' said the builder. 'And the best advice I can give you, Mr Waterall, in your own interest is to try and come to some private arrangement with your neighbour.'

'Do you mean a financial arrangement? Why, that's nothing but blackmail of the most impudent kind. I won't pay him a halfpenny, not one halfpenny.'

'No, there's no question of money,' said the builder quickly. 'But I happen to know that Hobday is very anxious to obtain a licence to sell beer to be consumed off the premises, and if any of his neighbours were to oppose the granting of such an off licence I think he'd find it very hard to get it put through. There's your chance, Mr Waterall. Make it clear to Hobday that if he presses to have this fence removed you'll bring forward strong opposition to his licence. Hobday's a clever fellow in his way, and I think you'll find him agreeable to compromise on those lines. You might hint too that your custom is not to be despised, and you won't buy so much as a loaf from your next-door neighbour unless he withdraws the opposition to your fence. Life, Mr Waterall is largely a matter of fitting one thing into another. That's been very much brought home to me as a builder.'

So Mr Waterall and Mr Hobday were fitted together, and with Mr Donkin acting as the tactful joiner, their differences were composed.

'I will go so far,' Mr Waterall offered, 'as to write a letter in support of Mr Hobday's application for an off licence on medical grounds. I consider that the inhabitants of Oak should be able to obtain such necessities as brandy without sending all the way into Galton for them.'

But Mr Hobday is only applying for a beer and tobacco licence,' the builder pointed out. 'He'll find it impossible to obtain a licence for spirituous liquors.'

'Well, if he ever applies for one he shall have my unstinted support,' Mr Waterall promised grandly.

By the time the interview was over he and his neighbour were become close allies. Mr Hobday said he was thinking of buying a little governess-car he'd seen going cheap and running people in from Oak to the station for two shillings, or sixpence less than they charged for the Market Hotel fly.

Mr Waterall replied that he and his family should make a point of driving in with Mr Hobday whenever they had occasion to make the journey.

And then Mr Waterall spoke of his strong desire to have the name Oak accepted as the name of their village instead of Oaktown or such an abomination as the Oak Farm Estate, which added a penny to every telegram dispatched. Whereupon Mr Hobday declared that he was ready to support Mr Waterall up to the hilt in his stand for justice against tyranny. And on this Mr Waterall asked why there was no post-office in Oak and furthermore why Mr Hobday should not fill the part of postmaster. By now Mr Hobday was ready to argue with anybody that Mr Waterall's twelve-feet high fence was exactly what he wanted, first because it protected him against the east wind, secondly because it gave him an opportunity to plant some espaliers of codlins with which he had been presented, thirdly because it kept Mrs Hobday from worrying about the children getting lost, and finally because it lent an air of dignity to the Oak Emporium.

'And let who will hear me,' Mr Hobday declared, as he drained the parting glass of whisky, 'I don't care who hears me, but I'm going to paint on the board above the door "The Oak Emporium" in red letters on a yellow ground. That'll show which side I stand. Isn't that right, Mr Waterall? Hearts of Oak are our ships. Hearts of Oak are our men. Steady, boys, steady?'

Having uttered this sentiment more often associated with the imperial ambitions of the extreme right than with the humanitarian aspirations of the extreme left, Mr Hobday saluted the other two, and retired.

'A fine fellow,' Mr Waterall observed. 'And I believe solid

at bottom. A certain amount of froth on the surface, but blow that away, and you reach the solid—the—er . . .'

'Just so,' the builder agreed. 'Clear away the rubbish and you get your foundations.'

'Just so,' Mr Waterall agreed. 'Blow away the froth, and you reach the—er—solid . . .'

'Just so,' the builder agreed.

On Monday morning when Mr Waterall walked into his partner's sanctum Mr Wickham asked him if he had avoided any legal unpleasantness.

'Quite easily,' said Mr Waterall, 'I only had to be a little firm, and as I expected, my neighbour at once gave way.'

Mr Wickham grunted.

CHAPTER EIGHTEEN

DURING the early spring Dream Days saw little of the Waterall family. It was decided that Phyllis's promise as a historian must not be prematurely cut off by allowing her to miss another term at school. Her chief link with Arcadia was the tabby kitten which she had been promised down at Oak, but which was ultimately obtained from a house some four doors farther along in Orange Road. Mr Waterall himself was too acutely aware of his partner's criticism to venture on more than an occasional week-end, and his wife was too much exhausted by her rustic autumn without a kitchen door to persuade him into one more week-end than was necessary until the bedroom which was to hold Dodsworth or Cook or both, was finished. As for Ralph and Roger, naturally they could not go down by themselves.

So it was not until the Easter holidays that 315 Orange Road was shut up, and the bungalow now three times the size of the original Canadian Cottage was inhabited for the first time by the complete household.

And certainly Mr Waterall had reason to invite a measure of congratulation from his family upon their father's success as an architect.

Phyllis no longer had to sleep on a chair-bed in the sole living-room. Mrs Waterall no longer had to cook for a family of four. Mr Waterall no longer had to sit in slippered feet at the mercy of the first person who knocked at the front door. And the boys could revel in the prospect of no longer sleeping next door to their parents, but of having instead for neighbours the amenable Dodsworth and their kiddy sister. Indeed, everybody was so pleased with the additions that not even his two sons criticized by so much as a glance Mr Waterall's pleasure as of a child's with a new doll's house when he kept opening the door which had been cut at the end of what was now essentially the dining-room to give access to the new sitting-room and walking backward and forward between the two rooms. And after he had savoured to the full the delights of this doorway, he walked backward and forward between his new bedroom and the new sitting-room, although the novelty of this compared with the relationship between his original bedroom and the original living-room was not so conspicuous. Finally, a little to the embarrassment of Cook he must needs walk backward and forward several times between her bedroom and the kitchen.

'Well,' Mr Waterall proclaimed that evening when his family were gathered round him at the supper table and the necessity of one or other of them having to get up at any moment to fetch something or remove something had been obviated by the presence of the deft-fingered and solicitous Dodsworth. 'Well,' he proclaimed, 'I think we may fairly say that we have settled down to real country life at last.' And it did not occur to any member of his family to point out that Dream Days was at this moment nearer the urbanity of 315 Orange Road than it had ever been.

After supper Ralph called Roger apart and confided to him his firm opinion that it was their duty to arrange a series of booby tricks for Dodsworth and Phyllis in order to celebrate the first night of their joint occupation of what until now had been the parental bedroom.

'Well, what can we do?' Roger asked. 'Fain I dressing up as a ghost.'

The reason for Roger's unwillingness to play the part of a spectre was the taste of phosphorus with which on the last occasion of his impersonation his brother had smeared his lips and thereby induced a severe attack of collywobbles.

'Who wants you to be a ghost, fishface? Good lumme, there are thousands of other things to do,' said Ralph scornfully. 'Only don't look so beastly mysterious, or they'll twig that we're going to rag them. I vote we go up to the top of the garden and think of something. Thank goodness, the pater's got another room to sit in now. It bored me frightfully to see him always sitting with his feet on the Tortoise stove in the dining-room.'

The brothers wandered up the garden, sniffing in the sharp scents of the April night, and as they sniffed rejoicing in the pledge they seemed to offer that the Easter holidays had really begun.

'I think it's going to be rather decent down here these holidays,' said Ralph.

'So do I,' Roger agreed.

'It'll be ripping, bringing up young birds in my breeding-cage,' said Ralph.

'Awfully ripping,' his brother agreed.

'And I'm jolly glad now I didn't get that vivarium,' Ralph added. 'I think a breeding-cage is much better.'

'So do I,' Roger agreed warmly.

They had reached the top of the garden, and the great sky of stars above them encouraged the expression of their profoundest aspirations.

'I vote we squat here for half a tick,' Roger suggested. 'I get rather fagged walking about after supper.'

'Squattez-vous,' Ralph bade him.

So the brothers perched themselves on the dewy bar of the wooden railings which marked the northern boundary of Dream Days and gazed at the scattered yellow lights of Oak, at the shadowy woods and slopes around, and at the scintillating heaven above their heads.

'I vote we try and bring up a lark,' said Ralph.

'And a jay,' suggested Roger.

'And an owl,' Ralph added.

'And some linnets,' Roger went on.

'And some bullfinches,' Ralph supplemented.

There was a silence while the two boys sat in an immense aviary of their own upbringing.

Then Ralph spoke with a sudden severity.

'Look here, you ass, we didn't come up here to jaw about birds. We can jaw about them any time. We came up here to think of what tricks we can play on Dodsworth and Phyllis.'

'We could balance a jug of water over the door so that it soaked them when they went into their room,' Roger suggested.

'Pooh, that's a frightfully stale trick. And it's rather a rotten one too,' Ralph decided. 'Because it usually goes wrong, and even if it works it simply means they get wet and squeal like stuck pigs and then it's all over.'

'No, it doesn't last very long,' Roger agreed.

'And the governor would try to be funny and make Phyllis think she's being ill-treated or some rot like that,' Ralph went on. 'He doesn't seem to grasp the simple fact that if she doesn't get ragged a bit when she's a kid she'll grow up into the most awful ass and do nothing but wriggle about as if she had about a million fleas crawling up her back.'

Roger sighed. The problem of his sister's future vexed him as intensely as it vexed Ralph.

'No,' said Ralph, 'the kind of trick we want to think of is something that will make Dodsworth and Phyllis go nearly dotty while we're simply catting with laughter all the time.'

'That would be awfully ripping,' said Roger, 'I hope we'll think of something.'

A silence fell while both boys clung to the dewy railing and gazed up at the stars in an almost painful meditation.

'Of course we could put some snails at the bottom of the bed,' said Ralph at last, inspired by the discovery of a snail wandering along the railing beside him. 'But that only means a few shrieks. It's not enough.'

'We could pepper the pillow,' Roger suggested. 'We should hear them sneezing.'

'We might do that for one thing,' Ralph agreed. 'But the principal joke ought to be something much more than that. I want to frighten them both into fits.'

'Suppose I hid under the bed and moved it up and down from underneath?' Roger asked.

'No, Dodsworth would only start saying you'd no business to be in the room when she was undressing or some rot like that,' he objected.

'What a swizzle it's so late, or we might have got a baby pig from the Chilcotts and shut it up in the wardrobe in their room,' Roger sighed.

'Don't be a fat ass, you ass. What is the good of talking about what we might do when we're trying to think what we can do?' said the elder brother crushingly.

'Well, don't be a fat ass yourself,' Roger retorted warmly. 'You lugged me all the way up here after supper to think of something, and whatever I think of you say it's rotten. You haven't thought of anything yet except putting snails in their bed.'

'All right, keep your hair on. I'm afraid it's too late to do anything really decent tonight,' Ralph admitted. 'We'd better just put the pepper on their pillows, and I'll shove this snail at the back of their bed. It *might* crawl over them in the middle of the night,' he concluded hopefully.

'Well, we might tie a string to a small tin box with some

of those air-gun slugs in it and then hide it among the bandboxes at the top of the wardrobe,' Roger suggested. 'It would probably sound rather like a rat, and they'd get into an awful funk when we moved it about.'

'Right-o,' his brother agreed, much to the gratification of the junior partner. 'And now we'd better go in, or they may suspect something. Lend me your nose-rag to wrap round this snail.'

'Why can't you use your own nose-rag?'

'Because I've got half a piece of nougat wrapped up in mine.'

'Oh, donnez me some,' Roger begged.

'All right, you greedy hog, I was going to. So you needn't cadge like that. We'll eat it while we're waiting for them to start sneezing.'

A good deal of strategy was necessary to arrange the bedroom in which Dodsworth and Phyllis were intended to pass such a disturbed night. The string attached to the tin-box was fastened to a long piece of black cotton, which it was hoped would escape notice in the light of a solitary candle and allow the conspirators to lead the string under the bed, across the floor of the doomed room, and so underneath the door of their own room. Then the box itself was hidden away at the back of a heap of bandboxes piled on top of the wardrobe which stood on the far side of the bed. Cook's attention had to be engaged in trying to extract a splinter alleged to have entered Roger's finger, in order to give Ralph an opportunity to secure the pepper-pot and thoroughly dust the pillows of the bed where Phyllis and Dodsworth were to sleep. Then the snail had to be placed in what seemed the most attractive position under the bed to tempt it into climbing up one of the posts and pursuing its slow course over the bodies of the sneeze-racked sleepless pair.

At the last moment, just before Phyllis was going off to bed, the two conspirators decided that it had been a mistake to pepper her pillow since by sneezing prematurely she might create a mood of suspicion and ruin the whole evening's entertainment. So Roger hurried in to dust the pepper off her pillow, in doing which he began to sneeze himself. Indeed he continued to sneeze with such violence for half an hour afterwards that his mother became convinced he was on the verge of having a bad cold and sent him to bed with a cup of hot gruel. While standing over him to see him drink she was luckily called away by her husband, thus enabling Roger to leap from his bunk and empty the noxious stuff out of the window without imbibing a single drop of it, and what is more receive the commendation of an innocent mother for his virtuous absorption of the lot.

'You were a cuckoo to sneeze like that,' grumbled Ralph, when he joined his younger brother in their bedroom. 'You might have mucked up everything.'

'Well, you shook a most frightful lot of pepper over Phyllis's pillow,' Roger said. 'It came up in clouds when I was dusting it off. I should think Dodsworth will nearly cat with sneezing.'

'I hope that snail will crawl up the bed all right,' said Ralph. 'I put a line of pepper on each side of it on the floor to keep it from crawling along in the wrong direction.'

'Well, if it crawls up on the bed and smells any more pepper,' Roger said, 'I should think it would bunk off as fast as it could.'

'Snails can't smell, you fathead,' Ralph scoffed.

'Well, if they can't smell, what was the good of putting pepper on the floor to make this snail go the way you wanted?'

'Shut up,' Ralph growled. 'Dodsworth's coming into her room. Phyllis was asleep when I came through. But she's bound to wake up when Dodsworth starts sneezing.'

'It's a good job Mother and Father are sleeping so far away now. If Mother heard Dodsworth, she might bring in some more gruel,' said Roger. 'My gum, it was the most stinking stuff you ever saw, Ralph. It smelt like paste.'

The boys continued to talk in an undertone while Dodsworth was preparing for bed. They fancied that an unnatural silence from their room might make her guess an impending fate.

'She's taking a frightful long time to get into bed,' Ralph muttered in a tone of disapprobation. 'What can she be doing wandering all over the room?'

'I hope she doesn't spot the cotton.'

'No, I couldn't see it, even when I stared quite hard. Ralph reassured his brother.

'I say. She yawned then. Did you hear her?' Roger asked alertly.

'If she yawns like that just when she puts her head down on the pillow,' Ralph gloated, 'she'll sniff up a frightful lot of pepper.'

'Perhaps she will. She yawned again then, I think.'

'She'll be standing by the bed now, looking at something,' said Ralph apprehensively. 'I hope she isn't looking at the pepper.'

'Perhaps the snail has crawled up on the bed.'

'Well, if it has, she'd surely make *some* row,' Ralph said. 'Perhaps she isn't looking at the pepper at all.'

'Hark, what's the noise?' Roger murmured.

A slow swishing sound filtered through from the room beyond.

'Good gum, I believe she's brushing the pepper off the pillow. No, of course, I know what it is. She's brushing her hair. She's sitting on the edge of the bed and brushing her hair. I'll bet you anything that's what she's doing.'

'If I felt as sleepy as Dodsworth,' Roger muttered resentfully, 'I jolly well wouldn't sweat to brush my hair like that. I wonder why women brush their hair before going to bed?'

'Because they're always thinking about what they look like. Hark, what's that crackling?'

'Curl papers, I think,' said Roger.

Ralph uttered an exclamation of disgust.

'Good gum, she won't be in bed for hours,' he groaned.

But as he spoke the light in the next room went out. Dodsworth was in bed. Twenty seconds later to the ravishment of the boys' senses she sneezed a sneeze that sounded as if a dozen dishes had fallen from a dresser. A moment later she sneezed again even more loudly, and this time the noise must have wakened Phyllis from a bad dream, for her brothers could hear her whimpering to Dodsworth who between her sneezes was evidently trying to assure her that some animal or other could not possibly be in the house, less still in their room, least of all under the bed.

'I think I'd better start to move the tin box about now,' said Ralph, getting cautiously out of his bunk. 'Then Phyllis will think it really is an animal, whatever animal the silly little funk is thinking it might be.'

'It's something got up my nose,' they heard Dodsworth explain.

'Not a mouse?' Phyllis asked quavering.

'Good gracious alive, Miss Phyllis, of course not. Whoever heard of such a thing?'

'Well, you said a mouse ran into a little girl's mouth
once when she was asleep.'

Dodsworth sniffed indignantly at the comparison, and
Phyllis whimpered:

'There it is again. Are you sure the cow isn't in the dining-
room, Doddie?'

'Certain sure and positive. First a mouse, then a cow,
whatever next will you be imagining? I never heard anybody talk so silly. Goodness! What can be making me sneeze
like this? It must be the hay fever. And depend upon it that's
what Master Roger had.'

'But it's not hay time yet,' Phyllis argued.

'Don't be so fretful and contrary. It's hay time in my nose.'

Ralph, who had been cautiously pulling the cotton in
under the door between the two rooms, had by now secured
the string and was beginning to twitch about the tin box
of lead pellets on the top of the wardrobe.

'Oh, Doddie, what's that?' Phyllis cried out in horror to
the exquisite delight of her two brothers. 'It's a rat coming
after us. It'll bite us. It'll jump down and bite us.'

'Will you not be so fanciful, Miss Phyllis,' Dodsworth
scolded between two sneezes.

'Damn!' Ralph exhaled in a groan. 'The beastly box is
stuck now.' He gave it a sharper twitch. There was a cascade
of hollow thumps and bumps culminating in the crash of
the tin box on the floor and a fearful scream from Phyllis.
Ralph leaned back against the partition, helpless with
laughter.

'Don't hold on to me so tight, you silly girl,' they heard
Dodsworth exclaim. 'You'll choke me in a minute. It's
only the bandboxes fallen down on you from off the wardrobe. I'm not surprised, the way I'm sneezing. Let go of me,
Miss Phyllis, don't be so hysterical. I'll get out of bed and
strike a light.'

'Don't leave me, Doddie, don't leave me,' Phyllis wailed.
'I'm frightened. I know there's a rat going to bite us.'

'Will you not act so silly and babyish,' exclaimed Dodsworth, exasperated by the clutch of Phyllis's arms round her
neck when she was being shaken in every fibre by sneezes. 'I
tell you I *will* get out of bed and find the matches. I'd be
ashamed if I was a big girl like you to carry on so.'

'Pull the box over to our door before Dodsworth lights the candle,' Roger warned his brother.

So Ralph pulled, and quietly though he pulled the faint noise of the box's progress was heard by Phyllis and set her screaming again.

'I hear it, Doddie. I hear it. It's under the bed. It'll eat our toes. Oh, Doddie, where's Father?'

Apparently Dodsworth had succeeded in breaking away at last from the agonized clutch of Phyllis, for they heard her tell their sister to lie still while she popped out of bed for the matches.

And then rang out one of the most blood-curdling shrieks the boys had ever heard, a shriek to which the screams of Phyllis had been the murmur of a brook. It was the kind of shriek to the effect of which on the surrounding landscape romantic novelists have devoted some of their most colourful pages.

And no sooner had Dodsworth shrieked once like this than she shrieked just as loudly all over again.

'I believe she's trodden on the snail with her bare feet,' Ralph whispered to his brother in a voice rich with awe of his own achievement.

And this proved to be exactly what had occurred. Dodsworth's screams roused Mrs Waterall and Cook and even Mr Waterall to hurry along and find out what was the matter.

In the confusion it was easy for Ralph to secure the tin box, and there was no evidence of any kind to connect him or his brother with the nocturnal disturbance.

'I vote we go birds'-nesting tomorrow,' said Ralph as he settled down in his bunk as complacently as the village blacksmith to his night's repose.

'Oh rather,' Roger agreed, he too cosily aware of deserving the best that sleep could give him.

CHAPTER NINETEEN

AMONG the most cherished rustic aspirations of Mr Waterall was a lawn at Dream Days. The lawn-mower which he had brought down last December had not once been used. It was now living with ample space at its disposal in the new tool-shed, and the owner of it longed to exercise his muscles in a more practical way than by pulling stirrups attached to elastic away from the door of his bedroom.

'It's good for the muscles, I know,' he said to his wife, 'but these physical exercises are fundamentally a waste of energy. Moreover, they are selfish because they do not benefit others. Now, quite apart from the valuable exercise I shall get myself from mowing a lawn there will be so many games that we can all play . . . tennis, croquet, badminton . . . oh, the prospect is unlimited. Besides, the garden on this side looks unpleasantly bare.'

This was true. In spite of the representative collection of shrubs Mr Waterall had acquired from Bocock's Farnley Nurseries, the half-acre on which the windows of the sitting-room and of his own bedroom looked, bore little resemblance to a garden.

'I suppose one must expect losses,' Mr Waterall went on. 'But I'm bound to say I never supposed that quite so many of the shrubs and trees I ordered last autumn would die in the course of the winter. I don't feel that Bocock's treated me quite fairly, and I shall not entrust them with the making of a lawn.'

The fact was Mr Waterall had found the bill for his autumn planting a good deal heavier than he had expected and the harvest of a spring blossom and leaf a good deal lighter.

'I don't like to accuse a reputable firm like Bocock's of deliberately swindling a client,' he went on. 'But I am bound to say that the appearance of our garden is not in the least like what I was led to expect when I walked round their Nurseries at Farnley last October. But let that pass. I am not asking for the impossible. I do, however, know a labur-

num when I see one, and I am disgusted by the anaemic looking clothes-prop which is apparently Bocock's idea of a
laburnum. In short, my dear, I have finished with Bocock. I
don't intend to order a lawn and be fobbed off with a few
square yards of decayed coco-nut matting. We live and learn.
I hear now of an excellent fellow in Galton called Bellamy,
and I propose to call him in and get this lawn properly
made. The boys and I will walk over and see if he can under-
take the job.'

Simon Bellamy was a courtly old gentleman of nearly
seventy who lived in a tumbledown low house covered with
ivy on the outskirts of Galton. Although a painted sign
appeared above a high hedge beside the house to proclaim
Simon Bellamy and Sons, Nurserymen and Landscape Gardeners, the old gentleman, except for the companionship of a
housekeeper almost as old as himself and a Russian poodle,
lived there alone.

His nursery was overgrown like the Sleeping Beauty's
palace, for he had not bothered to keep it in order for several
years now. And the large vineries were in the same state of
neglect, the vines untrimmed, the bunches of grapes
unthinned, rust and mildew everywhere.

Mr Bellamy at first declined absolutely to consider the proposal that he should lay out a lawn at Dream Days. He had
long given up active work he assured Mr Waterall, and why
his name should have been recommended as a good nurseryman was beyond his comprehension.

'As you see, sir,' he protested, 'the Nursery is a thing of the
past. It was a fine flourishing business in the days of my
father, and so long as my brother was alive it remained a
flourishing business, but when he died about ten years ago I
lacked the energy to carry on by myself. I have enough to
keep me till I die, and I am quite alone in the world.'

Mr Bellamy's sitting-room in which this conversation was
being held was in an aquarium twilight, for the windows
at either end looked into unkempt vineries and, though the
vines themselves were not yet in full leaf, the glass itself had
turned green and opaque. Mr Bellamy himself was so much
flustered by the unexpected visit that he was scurrying
round his dim room like an insect which had curled itself up
under a leaf and had been suddenly disturbed.

'I must apologize for this intrusion,' said Mr Waterall.
'But I was told that you were a man whom I could trust to

194

give me the best horticultural advice and I was anxious to
provide my little garden with the best doctor I could find
for it.'

What Mr Waterall's ponderous eloquence failed to affect
was effected by the mediation of the shaggy Russian poodle,
who took such a demonstrative fancy to the two boys that
Mr Bellamy's heart was touched.

'Why, Peter, I've never seen you make such a fuss of anybody before,' said his master. 'Do you think I ought to take on
the job of making this lawn?'

At this Peter jumped up on the table and begged, his
countenance expressing the liveliest assent.

'He's an awfully decent dog,' said Ralph.

'Awfully ripping,' Roger agreed.

'Yes, yes, a fine old fellow,' said Mr Waterall, a trifle
impatiently, for country life had not yet taught him to be
fond of dogs and he thought all this sentimental pretence
about consulting Peter was childish.

'Well,' said old Mr Bellamy, 'if Peter thinks I ought to
make your lawn I suppose I shall have to make your lawn.
All right, Peter, tell Mr Waterall that we'll come out tomorrow and have a look at the scene of operations.'

At this Peter leapt down from the table with every mani-
festation of canine delight, and then to the exquisite satisfaction of Ralph and Roger he leapt up at Mr Waterall and
licked him effusively on the chin. Roger, indeed, was so
much overcome by the humour of Peter's performance that
he had to pretend he had dropped something under the
table to afford himself an excuse to retire underneath
it and there roll upon the floor in a paroxysm of suppressed
laughter.

'Down, good dog! Down, sir,' Mr Waterall gasped when
Peter not content with leaping and licking his chin sprang
right into his lap and started to slaver his face all over with
affectionate thoroughness.

This was too much for Ralph, who joined his brother
under the table and rolled about upon the floor beside Roger
in spasms of agonizing mirth.

'Peter, behave yourself,' said Mr Bellamy, lifting a forefinger in admonition. 'He's a very intelligent dog,
Mr Waterall.'

'So I should imagine,' Mr Waterall observed, for at his
master's bidding the shaggy poodle had immediately ceased

to bathe the visitor with his caresses. 'I should like to have a dog myself, but unfortunately my wife and children are rather nervous of dogs.'

Such an outrageous statement turned the merriment of Ralph and Roger to indignation.

'We're not,' they cried simultaneously, Roger emphasizing his repudiation of the calumny by striking the table a sharp blow with the back of his head as he rose from the floor to contradict his father.

Whereupon Mr Waterall related the history of the dog bought for ten shillings at the Battersea Dogs' Home, and from that went on to the history of the goat, of the cow, and of Swiftsure the pony.

'Well,' said old Mr Bellamy genially, while the two boys champed their teeth in impotent wrath, 'well, you'll all get used to dogs when I bring Peter out to help with the lawn, won't they Peter?'

Peter's reply to this question was to hurry out into the hall and return with Mr Bellamy's hat and gloves, which he deposited at his feet.

'He wants to start right away now,' Mr Bellamy chuckled. 'No, not today, Peter. We'll go over to Oaktown tomorrow morning.'

'I shall look forward to your visit,' said Mr Waterall. 'Oh, and by the way, Mr Bellamy, some of us out at Oak rather object to its being called Oaktown. We wish it to be called Oak. In fact I'm summoning a meeting of protest shortly in order to put our case before the authorities. So, I hope you'll help the good cause along by avoiding the use of the objectionable name "Oaktown"?'

'Now you listen to Peter,' said Mr Bellamy. 'Peter come here, Peter, listen. Oaktown? Rrrats! Oak? Good dog, Peter! Now, Mr Waterall, just mention casually the name you object to, and hark at Peter.'

'You mean "Oaktown" . . .' Mr Waterall began. He had no sooner uttered the word than Peter started to bark furiously.

'That's right, Peter, we don't like Oaktown, do we?' said his master. 'But what about Oak, Peter? Oak, eh?'

At this Peter stopped barking, sat down in front of his master, and offered him a paw in solemn congratulation.

'Yes, that certainly is a most remarkably intelligent dog,' Mr Waterall agreed. 'Well, we must be getting back.

Tomorrow then, Mr Bellamy, you will come over and tackle the problem of the lawn at Dream Days?'

'Peter says we must. Don't you, Peter, old boy?'

The shaggy poodle wagged his tail excitably, and his master was committed to the laying out of a lawn at an age when, as he said to the two boys, he thought he should be under the daisies instead of over them.

So Mr Bellamy and Peter the shaggy poodle, became familiar figures at Dream Days, they and a deaf mute called Ricky, who with William Poley carried out the operation of levelling the ground under Mr Bellamy's supervision. Not that this supervision was inactive, for the old nurseryman used to take off his coat and hang it up on the young weeping-willow, which was almost the only tree from Bocock's that Mr Waterall was able to be sure of recognizing without looking at the label. And when Mr Bellamy had doffed his coat he would take his turn with spade or fork or rake or roller, a fine old figure with his white hair and black eyebrows and clear-cut clean-shaven countenance resembling a distinguished actor more than a nurseryman. Poley had a profound respect for him, and he often expressed himself strongly in favour of deaf mutes as workmen. He used to take the ever amiable Ricky off to tea at Fernbank, because his company gave particular pleasure to Mrs Poley.

'A wonderful woman, Mrs Poley,' he used to confide in the boys. 'At home with everybody. That comes of travelling round the world with old Lady Devizes. Indians, Chinese, Italians. She was able to get along with any of them, and she says it makes her feel as if she was abroad again when she sits there gesticulating and bobbing to Ricky across the table. I haven't known anything take her out of herself like that since she went to Maskelyne and Cook's at the Egyptian Hall on our way through London after the wreck. Oh, how she did enjoy herself at the Egyptian Hall, especially when they shut up a woman in a white silk dress in a coffin and sawed right through it. Of course they didn't really saw her through. It's what they call an allusion. But Mrs Poley turned to me where we were sitting in the half-crown seats and said she couldn't have enjoyed anything more if it had have really happened. But then, of course she's very highly strung, Mrs Poley is. Anything a little bit out of the usual goes through her with a regular twang. Many's the time she's said to me "Will," she's said, "my inside feels like a guitar this morning." I remember just after we were first married a lion escaped from a circus and Mrs Poley used to lie in bed and shiver all night, because ours being a butcher's shop she thought this lion was bound to make for us as soon as it got hungry. And then one afternoon a steamroller going through Maidstone got out of control because the fellow driving it was drunk and crashed into a stationer's shop farther down the street. Well, I'd got a particularly fine side of beef hanging up in the shop that morning and Mrs Poley made up her mind that the lion had smelt it out and was after it. As soon as she heard the noise she rushed upstairs like the wind, for of course in those days she was as slim as a gimlet, and hid herself in an old trunk in the top attic, and when I went up to tell her it was a steamroller and not a lion she fainted right off. Well, of course being young and newly married, I thought the right thing to do with anybody who fainted was to throw water over them. So I lugged the toilet-jug up from our bedroom and emptied the blessed lot right over her. My goodness, you should have seen the way Mrs Poley give it to me when she came round! Tut-tut-tut! She said I wasn't fit to have charge of anything so delicate as a woman, and I said "never mind, ducky, you'll soon be dry". Well, when she heard me call her "ducky", which was a pet name I had for her, that was too much altogether. "You're not fit to be married," she said. "A man who can see his wife sitting in a trunk full of water and then call her 'ducky' isn't fit to be married." And I've never dared call her "ducky" from that day. Now, don't you boys ever tell Mrs. Poley this, because to this day she doesn't know I did it, but I had to go outside and laugh to myself over the way she looked sitting in that trunk. Oh, and I laugh to myself at it nowadays sometimes, but of course Mrs Poley hasn't an inkling. Not an inkling. So for goodness sake don't you breathe a word to her about what I've just told you, or you'll get me skinned alive. But this deaf and dumb boy takes her out of herself. The other day when she made him understand by signs that she wanted him to pass the strawberry and not the raspberry jam, she was humming to herself all the evening. Oh, dear, what a pity she couldn't have had any little ones of her own. She'd have been the one to bring up children. But it's wonderful too the way old Mr Bellamy makes Ricky understand what he wants. Mrs Poley was struck by it just the same as me. "Depend upon it, Will," she said to me at once, "he's travelled too." I asked Mr Bellamy about it, but he said he'd never been farther away from England than Boulogne for the day and back. But that story won't suit Mrs Poley. She says nothing will ever convince her that he wasn't a missionary once. And I expect she's right. She's a rare judge of people. The first moment Mrs Poley put eyes on Blackham she told me he was the biggest blackguard she'd ever seen, and she was right. She says there's something about the way Mr Bellamy uses his hands that puts her in mind of a missionary who used to preach down in Dorset when she was a girl. And another thing, Mr Bellamy rubs the side of his nose with his first finger when he's talking to you. Have you ever noticed that? Well, Mrs Poley says this missionary who used to preach in Dorset had just the same trick. It didn't matter where he was, in the pulpit or anywhere. It's a habit they get from the natives in the South Sea Islands. And of course the moment she saw how Mr Bellamy could manage that poor deaf and dumb boy, that finished it for Mrs Poley. What a woman! Well, I've often said to her, jokingly of course, that I didn't know I was going to marry a walking dictionary when I tied myself up with her. But bless my heart, you boys mustn't keep me here gossiping like this, or there'll be no lawn made this year.'

With this Mr Poley would clamp his wife's straw hat more firmly on to his head, wipe his hands upon his sack apron, and vigorously attack the ground with whatever implement he held, chuckling to himself and winking tremendously at Ralph and Roger. And every time they would come within speaking distance of him for the rest of that day he would repeat 'walking dictionary' and bend over his spade or fork in an ecstasy of silent mirth, his countenance puckering with minute wrinkles in patches like a film of boiled milk on a cup of coffee.

On the days that Mr Bellamy did not walk out to Dream Days Peter would walk out by himself. He would push up the latch of the gate with his nose and trot up the path, his lips raised in a smile of welcome, his tail swishing to and fro like a mop. Mr Waterall had gone back to London when Peter first took to paying these unaccompanied calls, so there was nobody at Dream Days to discourage him. One of his chief pleasures was to run behind Roger on his boneshaker, of which by the way the successful purchase has not been recorded. Not that the boneshaker lasted long. On a fine May morning at the top of Bent Hill the boneshaker suddenly invented the free-wheel several years before it came into general use. Micha Chilcott who was feeding his chickens heard what he described afterwards as a noise like a run-away dustbin descending Bent Hill, and when he rushed to the hedge to see the cause of it he saw Roger go crashing past, his fat form looking like a jelly about to collapse. Bits of decayed pinkish tyre were flying in every direction. Spokes were snapping like the ribs of an umbrella blown inside out. Peter was tearing along behind and barking at the top of his voice to warn the rest of the world to get out of the way. The boneshaker disappeared round the corner of the road. Then a prolonged clangour as of falling gongs was followed by a loud rending noise, and silence.

Micha Chilcott and his brother hurried down their drive to pick up what remained of Roger and found him in the middle of the hazel hedge, the bicycle a shattered twisted wreck at the foot, and Peter running round in anxious circles with the saddle-bag in his mouth.

'Are you badly hurt?' the brothers cried in anxious chorus.

'No, I'll be all right in a jiffy,' said Roger. 'But I think there's a whitethroat's nest in the nettles on the other side of the hedge. Get hold of Peter, I don't want him to come through till I see. He may break the eggs.'

'I suppose you know your bicycle is smashed to smithereens?' Rehob asked.

'Yes, I think the chain broke at the top of the hill,' Roger puffed, as he extricated himself from the hedge and sought with concentration for the cunningly hidden eggs he coveted.

'Jolly lucky thing your neck isn't broken too,' said Micha. 'I made up my mind I'd find you in little pieces at the bottom.'

'It *is* a whitethroat's nest,' Roger cried triumphantly. 'Five eggs. What sucks for Ralph! He betted me I wouldn't find a whitethroat's nest before the end of the holidays. My gum, these nettles do sting. I'll walk along till I come to the gate,' he went on. 'I've got two eggs and I don't want to smash them, getting back through this rotten hedge.'

A minute or two later Roger appeared farther down the road advancing with care, a small greyish egg in either hand.

The shaggy poodle pranced joyfully to meet him.

'Get down, Peter, you ass,' said Roger. 'You'll make me smash these eggs.'

So Peter, to show that he could find something too, dropped the saddle-bag and picked up a piece of tyre which he turned over in his mouth with as much apparent pleasure as an American clerk turns over a quid of chewing gum.

'Well, I'm sorry about your bicycle,' said Micha Chilcott. 'It cost you ten shillings, didn't it?'

'Yes,' said Roger. 'But it was a most stinking fag to ride it. It was worse than walking. Only don't tell Ralph I said so, because he said it would be, and he's always so cocky when he's right. He'll be awfully sick when he hears about the smash, that he didn't see it, and he'll be awfully sick when he knows I've found a whitethroat's nest.'

'So on the whole you think you've had a successful morning?' Rehob Chilcott asked.

Roger nodded.

'I'd better bung these bits of my bike into the hedge, hadn't I?' he suggested.

'It might be as well,' the Chilcott brothers agreed.

So the remains of the boneshaker were decently concealed and not left to offend the eye as boots are often left by tramps in the middle of the country and the ends of iron bedsteads by nobody knows who.

CHAPTER TWENTY

THE Easter holidays sped past as swiftly as the Easter holidays always do, and just when the sweet of the year was at the sweetest Ralph and Roger had to go back to school. This was a much harder blow for them than it was for Phyllis whom her brothers suspected of actually enjoying the beginning of a new term. Phyllis was not called upon to forsake the search for birds' eggs at the very moment when searching for them was at the top of its attraction. In fact throughout the holidays she had shown herself steadily hostile to birds'-nesting, and had been for ever reading extracts from the ridiculous magazine she took in about kindness to dumb animals.

It was idle for her brothers to point out that they never robbed a nest of enough eggs to make the hen-bird desert it. The compassionate heart of Phyllis was tormented by the removal of these eggs, and she was always coming in to announce the arrival of some new bird in the garden in search of its lost treasures.

'Mother, isn't it wicked of Ralph and Roger to take two eggs from that darling little chaffinch who had her nest in the Chilcott apple-tree? It was such a lovely little nest, Mother, and the poor little birdie is looking for her eggs everywhere. I saw her, Mother, I did really.'

'Shut up,' said Ralph severely. 'We only took two eggs out of five. If you leave three eggs, a bird can't see that any are gone.'

'How do you know?' his sister asked.

'Because you can read it in any book about birds, you affected little ass,' Roger put in. 'Birds can't count. I suppose *you* think they can do decimals?'

'Now please don't quarrel, children,' Mrs Waterall begged. 'The holidays are nearly over. Don't let us spoil them by angry words. And, Roger, please don't use unkind names to Phyllis.'

'Well, she shouldn't jabber such rot,' said Roger.

'And look at all the little baby birds you've tried to bring up,' Phyllis argued. 'But every one of the poor little things has died.'

'Well, we haven't had enough practice yet,' said Ralph. 'You couldn't even bring up a real baby if you tried now. So shut your jammy mouth.'

'Ralph, Ralph,' his mother protested, 'there's no need to be personal. You can explain your point of view to Phyllis without becoming personal and horrid.'

But these arguments were silenced more effectively by the end of the Easter holidays than by any arguments their mother could find to bring.

The fatal Monday evening arrived, a golden May evening when the swallows were flying high and the prospect of London at the end of a two hours' railway journey was almost intolerable.

'Never mind,' said Mrs Waterall. 'I'm sure Father will let you come down for week-ends next term, that is if you will only be good.'

Peter had come down to the railway-station with Mr Bellamy to see them off. When the train puffed out, the boys leaning out of the carriage window, could see him sitting upon the platform and staring after it, his shaggy head cocked on one side in evident perplexity over such an unreasonable departure.

'Do you think he'll go over to the cottage tomorrow to see if we're going for a walk?' Ralph sighed. What did Phyllis with her dumb friends' leagues know about the real sorrows of dumb animals?

The two boys sat back immersed in gloom until Woking where a ray of cheer was cast upon their mood by the sight of a handcuffed man being brought to the train between two constables.

'I wonder what he's done?' Ralph speculated.

'Perhaps he's a murderer,' said Roger hopefully. 'It would be rather spiffing if we could see a murderer being arrested on the last day of the holidays.'

'That man won't escape, will he?' Phyllis inquired anxiously of her mother.

'No, darling, and even if he did he wouldn't hurt you.'

'I wish he would escape,' said Ralph. 'If he came into our compartment, I'd jolly well help him to hide under the seat, and if the bobbies asked him I'd jolly well say he wasn't here.'

'So would I,' Roger agreed warmly.

'Texas knew a murderer once,' said Ralph.

'Did he? How ripping!' his brother exclaimed.

'At least he didn't exactly know him, but he knew the house where he lived, and he saw him come out of it one day.'

'What did he do?' Roger asked eagerly.

'He didn't do anything, you fat ass. He hadn't murdered anybody then. But he murdered his wife afterwards.'

'How?' Roger gloated.

'With a razor. Texas says the blood dripped down through the ceiling on to the people in the room underneath.'

'Did Texas see the blood?'

'He did when it was dry. But it wasn't really red. It was more of a dirty brown.'

'How rotten,' said Roger sympathetically.

'Mother, don't let Ralph and Roger talk about murderers any more,' Phyllis begged.

Mrs Waterall looked up from her bag in which she had been trying to marshal the tickets.

'I didn't hear what the boys were saying,' she murmured abstractedly.

'They're talking about blood, and they're frightening me Mother,' Phyllis whined.

'Jolly good job if somebody murdered you,' Ralph observed.

'Ralph, I will not have you say such things to your sister. If you can't behave yourself, I shall really have to tell Father about you, and you know what that will mean. No week-ends at Oak for the whole of the term.'

Although Mrs Waterall did not tell her husband about this unpleasant conversation, as a matter of fact there were no week-ends at Oak, because Mr Waterall was called upon to pay Donkin's bill, which was not a light one and, which coming on top of Bocock's, made him feel it was vital to economize for a while.

'It's all very well for you children to grumble about not going down to Oak every week-end, but what about your poor father? He won't get down to his own country place until the middle of August, because he has to stay working in London to earn bread and butter for you while you're enjoying yourselves.'

'Why can't you come down until then?' Ralph challenged.

'Because Mr Wickham is taking his holiday during the last fortnight of July and the first fortnight of August, and

that being so I have to wait my turn. You boys expect everything to fall into your mouths, but when you reach my age
you'll realize that life is not quite such a joke as you seem
to think it.'

'We don't think it's a joke,' said Ralph. 'It's not a joke
to have exams.'

Mrs Hamper's garden was a refuge during those hot days
of the summer term, and to the great delight of the two
boys she announced her definite intention of coming down
to stay at Wyatt's Farm for the month of August.

'Not because I think there's much in the country, mind
you,' she said. 'But from what you tell me about the inhabitants of this place Oak it sounds to me more like the
World's Fair, Islington, than anything else. And certainly
if the rest of them are as funny as that fellow Ryan was I
should enjoy myself a treat. And I shall bring Beetriss with
me. We'll just shut up Number 22, and if it's burgled, well,
it is burgled, and that's all about it. But the policeman
round here is a very civil-spoken fellow and always knows
where he can come for a bit of supper. "Yes," I said to
Beetriss the other day, "on this beat just expresses what he
is." And didn't she colour up! Well, if she must marry anybody I'd as lief she married a policeman, for though they
have the reputation of being fickle-minded where the ladies
are concerned, with a sweetheart in every street just like a
sailor has a sweetheart in every port, I'm told that when a
policeman does settle down he usually makes a good
husband.'

When the news of Mrs Hamper's forthcoming visit was
brought by Ralph and Roger to Mon Repos, Mr Augustus
Ryan happened to be sober, and with dignified emotion he
rose from his chair and thumped his fist upon the table.

'Texas, my boy,' he began tremendously.

'Yes, uncle?'

'While Mrs Hamper is staying at Wyatt's Farm, I don't
wish to drink quite as much whisky as usual. Mrs Hamper
is a lady for whom I have considerable regard, and so long as
she graces Oaktown with her presence I intend to be her
cavalier. Get out my inverness.'

'What, in July? You'll be stewed alive.'

'Don't bandy words with me, Texas. Get out my inverness.
I intend to wear it when I go down to the station to receive
her. And Texas!'

'Yes, Uncle?'

'If you don't mend that patch in the seat of your breeches before Mrs Hamper arrives, I'll make another patch on the other side of them with the broom-handle.'

'Well, give me the money to take my breeches to the tailor,' said Texas. 'I can't patch breeches myself. Don't talk so wild.'

'Texas! Any more blasted impudence from you, my lad, and you know what to expect. Now, if you'll excuse me, boys,' he said, turning to Ralph and Roger, 'I'll go and lie down for a bit. I want to compose an ode of welcome to Mrs Hamper.'

A day or two later the boys went up to announce the date and time of Mrs Hamper's arrival and asked if the ode of welcome was finished.

Mr Ryan shook his head.

'Alas, I've only been able to manage one line. *'Hampshire in future shall be known as Hampershire.'* It's a very good line as far as it goes, but it doesn't go nearly far enough. The fact is since I came down here I've been vegetating. I've lost the knack of writing poetry. Good lord, when I think of the way I could write a hundred mottoes a day during the Christmas rush for mottoes in August, and now . . . And it's not as if there weren't plenty of rhymes to "shire". The dictionary is full of them. It absolutely reeks of them. But my day is over. I'm a back-number, and a tattered one at that, with half the pages missing.'

Poor Mr Ryan made this announcement about himself in a voice of such profound despair that the two boys had to turn away their heads to hide an embarrassment in the presence of such misery, and they felt quite indignant when Texas said heartlessly:

'Go on, it's only gin making you feel like that. You know it always gives you the willies. And if you make up on gin what you lose on whisky you'll soon be worse than the fellow we saw eating mussels that night after the Canterbury.'

Mr Ryan shook his head.

'Ah, Texas, my boy, what can you know of the secret sorrows which gnaw at a poet's heart? You're young, my boy. The world is before you. The glittering prizes of success are still within your reach. But for me what is there left? A few more years shall roll, as Shakespeare says, and I shall be gone.'

At this point Mr Ryan broke down completely and began to weep, the tears clinging to his beard as dewdrops to barley.

Ralph and Roger tactfully withdrew and left the stricken poet to himself, and to the strains of the *Dead March in Saul* being played by his nephew on the penny whistle.

But when Mrs Hamper arrived Mr Ryan was down at the station to meet her, no trace upon his countenance of the dejection to which he had so recently been the victim.

'So this is Galton,' said Mrs Hamper, as she surveyed it majestically from the Market Hotel wagonette which Mr Ryan had decided was the suitable vehicle to transport her to Wyatt's Farm. 'This is Galton, Beetriss.'

Beatrice looked about her dutifully, and then said in a low voice that Galton looked very nice.

'Beetriss is wondering if absence makes the heart grow fonder,' Mrs Hamper observed with an arch smile.

'Oh, go on now, Mrs Hamper, what a one you are to tease anybody,' protested Beatrice. 'I'm sure I wasn't thinking of any such a thing.'

'Now what about a little light refreshment at the Market Hotel just to carry us out comfortably to Oaktown?' Mr Ryan suggested.

But Mrs Hamper vetoed this.

'In London, yes. But not in the country. I've come down here to have a complete change. So has Beetriss. If we start pub-crawling the moment we arrive, we might as well have stayed where we were.'

Wyatt's Farm was exactly what a farm ought to be, at any rate for those who go down into the country in August to take apartments in a farmhouse. It stood well above the road in an amphitheatre of pasture and arable land surrounded by Squire Melville's woods. The rooms let to visitors looked out upon a garden surrounded by a mellow red brick wall and full of old-fashioned flowers, and the farmyard with its duck-pond and quadrangle of thatched barns, its dapple-grey horses and spotted cows and fat pigs and motley crowd of barnyard fowls, was just such a farmyard as you might see in a child's picturebook.

'And what a noise,' Mrs Hamper said, when Ralph and Roger came to call upon her the morning after her arrival. 'I woke up this morning, dreaming that I was on show for the fat woman at Barnum's, and my head was quite dizzy till I realized what it was all about. Cows mooing, sheep barring, horses neighing, fowls clucking, turkeys gobbling, ducks quacking, pigs grunting, dogs barking, pigeons cooing, rooks cawring, and Beetriss snoring. "Well," I said to myself, "Hammersmith Broadway on a Saturday night is a sweet lullaby to this." And when I hopped out of bed to give myself a sponge down I'm bothered if there weren't half a dozen earwigs playing touch-last in and out of the holes in my sponge. Oh, and that's not all, by any means. There was a spider waltzing round in my basin with legs like telegraph wires, and the water in the jug was alive with tiddlers. "Well," I said, "this is country life with a vengeance, this is." Then I looked across to see if Beetriss was awake. And laugh? Well, I really thought I should have to sit down with a bump on the floor laughing, for I'm bothered if there wasn't a grasshopper sitting on her pillow about two inches off her ear and looking at her as wise as a judge. "Beetriss!" I called out, "Beetriss!" "Yes, Mrs Hamper," she said, only half awake. "Beetriss," I said, "Look round and see what's sitting just beside you on the pillow!" And jump? Well, it would take a good hand at guessing to say which jumped farthest, Beetriss or the grasshopper. But she's all right now, poor Beetriss is. She's made friends with some chickens just hatched. But without a word of exaggeration, it was all I could do for a bit to keep her from taking the next train back to London. Of course I oughtn't really to have woken her up suddenly like that. It was really too bad. But that grasshopper . . . a whopper he was too and a most lovely green . . . sitting there with his head cocked on one side and staring at poor Beetriss, well, it was as good as a play, to see the way Beetriss jumped out of bed. Oh, and I'm forgetting the best of it. When she was putting on her slipper, out jumped the grasshopper again, and poor Beetriss clung to me like a kid in a thunderstorm. She had her troubles too, washing, because when she lifted the soap a young boa-constrictor bolted out and started off across the washstand at an alarming rate.'

'A boa-constrictor?' echoed Roger incredulously.

'Well, you know what I mean. One of those things all legs and back.'

'I expect it was a centipede.'

'I daresay it was. Or a velocipede if it comes to that.'

'They sting,' Roger announced seriously.

'Well, poor Beetriss never gave it a chance to practice on her, because she opened my umbrella and held it in front of her, which rather annoyed me because it's very unlucky to open an umbrella in a bedroom. But, as I say, she's quite happy now with these chickens. Dear little balls of fluff! So all's well.'

Ralph and Roger had seldom enjoyed themselves so much as they did when escorting Mrs Hamper round the bungalows of their various friends in Oak. In this they lacked the help of Mr Ryan, for whom the excitement of welcoming Mrs Hamper had proved too much and who in consequence for the first day or two after her arrival was quite incapable of getting even as far as the front door of Mon Repos. On top of that he developed an unfortunate belief that a man called Macintyre, of whom nobody had ever heard until now, was trying to steal his bungalow from him.

'I had a wicked night last night,' he told Mrs Hamper when she called upon him first. 'All night long Macintyre was digging away at the foundations, and I expected Mon Repos would collapse at any moment.'

'But who is this Macintyre?' she demanded indignantly.

'Ah, that's the question,' said Mr Ryan. 'I can't find out exactly who he is. That's my trouble. But he's been worrying me for years. I've never said a word about him before, but he's been at the back of my mind like a perpetual toothache almost ever since I can remember. You've never heard me mention him before, Texas?'

'No, that's a fact,' his nephew confirmed sarcastically.

'I've suffered from Macintyre in complete silence all these years, Mrs Hamper. And I wouldn't intrude on you now with my domestic troubles if I wasn't acutely aware of my grave discourtesy in not acting as your cavalier round Oaktown. But you see how I'm situated? I can't leave Mon Repos at the mercy of a man like Macintyre. He hasn't a scruple in the world. Not a single one. I might come back here and find he'd carted it away lock, stock, and barrel while I was out with you. And then where should I be? I wouldn't mind so much if the scarlet runners were more advanced. But you can't sleep under French beans.'

'Yes, but who is this Macintyre?' Mrs Hamper repeated.

'If I could answer that question,' said Mr Ryan solemnly, 'half my difficulties would be over. But he won't meet me face to face. He just sneaks about at the back of my mind.'

'But how do you know his name is Macintyre?' she asked.

'Forgive my seeming to criticize your common sense, Mrs Hamper,' said Mr Ryan with a sad smile. 'But how do you know that lettuce is lettuce? Or cows cows? Or water water? Macintyre is a natural phenomenon like lettuces or cows or water. And a very unpleasant natural phenomenon, I may add, in many respects not unlike water.'

'Well, I think you ought to speak to the police about him,' said Mrs Hamper decidedly. 'When people start digging away at the foundations of a house it's past the limit of common decency to my manner of thinking.'

'The police would never catch him,' said Mr Ryan with a deep sigh. 'Never. Macintyre is much too artful for such gabies. The only way for me to get the better of him is for me to stay here on guard. When I was writing my ode of welcome to you, I went out into the garden for a moment, and when I got back to my desk I found Macintyre had stolen every idea I ever had. The fellow's a bad 'un. Through and through. The other night he drank every drop of whisky in the house and sat on the roof all night, talking to an owl. Not a wink could I get while he and this owl were talking away to one another in an undertone all night. And talking such nonsense too. That's what annoyed me. Not that I blame the owl. No, in my opinion the culpable party was Macintyre. Well, you see how I'm situated, Mrs Hamper, and my only hope is that Macintyre will discover he cannot steal Mon Repos, and leave me alone for a bit. Then I shall be able to devote myself to your entertainment in a proper manner.'

Mrs Hamper told Ralph and Roger when they left Mon Repos behind them that in her opinion Mr Ryan was suffering from hallucinations.

'And in fact I'm beginning to wonder if there really is such a person as this Macintyre.'

The boys agreed with her, and gave her other examples of Mr Ryan's queer fancies.

'Thought the bees had swarmed inside him last summer, did he? That's what it is, I reckon. The sun touches him up, and then he gets fanciful.'

'But he's an awfully decent chap,' said Ralph.

'Awfully decent,' Roger echoed.

'Decent without the living shadow of a doubt,' Mrs Hamper declared. 'But a bit light-headed sometimes in spite of all that hair. Well, perhaps this aggravating phantom will vanish presently, though there's one thing I'd say and that is whatever Macintyre may be he can't be more extraordinary than some of the people living in this place. But I'm bound to say I enjoy meeting them. Where are we going this afternoon?'

'We thought you'd better go and see Mrs Gnathead,' said Ralph.

'Gnathead it is then,' Mrs Hamper agreed.

Allusion has been made to Mrs Gnathead's habit of receiving visitors inside the rustic porch of her front door and of never inviting them into Blackheath Villa. She had no chance of doing this with Mrs Hamper who advanced firmly and by sheer weight drove Mrs Gnathead gradually back into her parlour, which Ralph and Roger entered in her wake.

There was no reason that the boys could see why Mrs Gnathead should not have invited anybody into her parlour. It was an extremely neat little square room with a mat of Berlin wool on the round mahogany table in the middle and antimacassars over all the chairs. There was a framed photograph of the Hutton Road Primitive Methodist Sunday School Annual Outing in which Mr Gnathead as a superintendent was just visible in a corner, and there was another photograph of Mr Gnathead standing beside a wedding cake slightly taller than himself. There was a steel engraving of Doré's Day of Judgement, a chromolithograph of Belshazzar's Feast, and a photogravure of Daniel in the Den of Lions. And on a whatnot in a corner there was a box heavily encrusted with shells which at once attracted the boys' curiosity.

'Is that where Mr Gnathead keeps his agates?' Roger asked.

'Yes, those are Mr Gnathead's agates,' said Mrs Gnathead; but she did not offer to raise the lid. The boys looked hopefully toward Mrs Hamper, who apparently had not heard the question, her gaze being fixed upon the steel engraving of the Day of Judgement.

'Fancy being whisked up out of the grave like that,' she observed. 'You know, if we can go by what we read it'll be a big surprise for some people. I had one experience like that, and I can tell you I'm not looking forward to another. It happened at a fair shortly after my husband left me.'

'Oh, your husband left you, did he, Mrs Hamper?' their hostess interposed, her quick eyes darting all over Mrs Hamper's large form. 'How terrible for you.'

'Not at all terrible,' said Mrs Hamper. 'But I was telling you about this fair. A man standing alongside of me said "Going up in the swing-boats?" And I thoughtlessly said "yes", for I was feeling in the mood for a bit of fun. Well, I wasn't the size then I am now, or anything like it. Still, even then I was a tidy handful. But I might have been no bigger than a little liver-pill the way that man swung me up. He just caught hold of that thing like a bell-pull, and I shot up like a rocket. "Not so fast," I called out. "Faster!" he called back. And faster it was. "Not so high," I squealed. "Higher!" he yelled back at me. And higher it was. Oh, my inside! Well, I don't believe I ever did get back some of it. Up I'd go, and I'd see that fellow grinning at me from underneath. He was very dark and put me in mind of an organ-grinder. And then down I'd go, oh, and what a down it was, and there would be that grinning face on top of me. "Will you stop swinging," I kept calling out. And the only answer I got was a whoop like one of Buffalo Bill's Red Indians. Well, I think I must have partly lost consciousness, for the next thing I remember was that I was paying the man who owned the swings for both of us, and he charged me double because we'd been up so long. And when I looked round for that black-haired rascal he was swinging somebody else farther up the line. Yes, I never look at a picture of the Day of Judgement without thinking of that swing I had soon after my husband left me.'

'Left you, did he?' Mrs Gnathead said eagerly. 'Dear, dear, wasn't that terrible?'

'Not at all terrible,' Mrs Hamper replied brusquely. 'But that swing was terrible if you like. And when we're whisked up out of the grave on the Last Day, that's going to be pretty terrible if swing-boats are anything to go by.'

There was undoubtedly something in Mrs Hamper's manner which discouraged Mrs Gnathead. Driven like this away from her front porch where she had been accustomed to probe the secrets of all her neighbours she was at a disadvantage in her neat little parlour. She tossed as helplessly upon the breadth of Mrs Hamper's eloquence as a cork upon the majestic surge of the Atlantic. It was true she had learned that Mrs Hampers had been deserted by her husband; but there was little satisfaction to be gained from that when the deserted woman herself so evidently regarded the matter with a serene indifference, if not with a positive relish.

'A poky creature,' Mrs Hamper commented to the boys when they were outside the confines of Blackheath Villa. 'A poky creature. Just like one of those scraggy fowls of hers, scratching and pecking round the back door.'

'Well, she's usually more interesting than that,' said Ralph.

'She'd have need to be,' Mrs Hamper declared. 'I'm glad I left Beetriss looking after her fluffy little chickabiddies, because Beetriss might have started gaping, and that would have put me in the wrong. Because manners are manners whoever you're talking to.'

Mrs Poley was much more to Mrs Hamper's liking than Mrs Gnathead. There was a warmth of hospitality about Mrs Poley which made an instant appeal to the mistress of 22 Barking Terrace.

'Mind you, as between that cowslip wine of hers and cod-liver oil and malt, though there's little or nothing to choose, the old dear meant well. I should think the cow put its foot in that wine when it slipped. In fact it hasn't stopped slipping yet if my inside's anything to go by. And what was that other stuff she gave us? Mistletoe wine, was it?'

'No, elderberry wine,' Roger informed her.

'Travelled, has she? I should think that elderberry wine travelled with her. Or else the King of the Cannibal Islands gave it her for tattooing and she drunk it by mistake. Well, if I come out in a rash of purple birthmarks, you'll know the cause. It's a good thing we left Beetriss with her chickens, because she gets red enough now in the face already, and a glass of that wine might have fixed the colour for good and all, which would have been rather a pity now she's half made up her mind to marry this policeman.'

But the place she liked best was the Chilcotts' shack.

'Though, of course, partly that's due to them being young men, for the older I get myself the more I prefer the company of young men to that of middle-aged females.'

She could not understand why they proposed to spoil their care-free existence by building a conventional red-brick villa.

'You've got just what you want in this shack. I felt a bit nervous when I first sat down in it that when I got up it would get up with me, and I quite expected Ralph and Roger would have to be picking bits and pieces of it off me the way they have to pick the brambles. But that feeling soon wore off and I don't remember when I was so much at home anywhere as I am in this shack. When a place is just a little untidy it fidgets you, because you feel all the time you want to be tidying it up. But when a place is as untidy as this shack you just sit back and enjoy it, because you know that you couldn't tidy it up even if you spent the rest of your life trying to. You'll often hear people say that everything's in a glorious muddle, but this really is a glorious muddle. And yet, you know, Beetriss couldn't appreciate it. "Well, really," I said, "Beetriss, don't keep on so about it, or else you'll make me think you're finicky." But Beetriss is funny that way. It quite upset her when she started to put the tea on and found there was a sock inside the kettle. "Good gracious, Beetriss," I told her, "don't be so afraid of anything a little peculiar to your way of thinking. Anybody might suppose you'd found a black beetle in the kettle, jumping like that as if the sock was going to snap your head off." Well, I suppose we mustn't be too hard on Beetriss, because when she goes home she's got to say "yes" or "no" to this policeman of hers, and I daresay the responsibility of it all is a bit on her mind. Yes, I think you're making a big mistake,' she said to Micha and Rehob Chilcott, 'letting your father build you this new house. You're both too young to settle down yet, and you may find a new house a milestone round your necks. Whereas when you're tired of this shack, as you call it, you can just kick it away in a corner like a child's box of bricks.'

Ralph and Roger profoundly agreed with Mrs Hamper. They viewed with misgiving the preparations for a neat villa residence which were already in progress. Young though they were, they could feel that time was passing and that even now over the happy-go-lucky settlement of Oak lay the shadow of impending change.

'Too late now,' said Micha Chilcott. 'The old man's coming down here himself the week after next to superintend the building.'

The boys regarded him with sympathy. They knew what it was to have a father coming down the week after next.

'And I think we'd better have my beano before any of these other people do arrive,' said Mrs Hamper.

This beano, as Mrs Hamper called it, was to be a picnic given by herself in honour of those inhabitants of Oak by whom she had been entertained.

'I say a picnic,' Mrs Hamper had explained, 'because Beetriss and I would feel a bit funny giving people tea at our lodgings. Not that I've a word to say against our landlady; but the best-hearted landlady in creation can't help looking a bit surprised when you send out to make a third pot of tea, and if there's one thing more than another that I cannot abide it is surprised looks flying round when people are sitting down to enjoy themselves. Besides, a picnic's the right kind of meal for the country. And that's one good thing that can be said in favour of the country. You can eat and drink where you like. Now in London you couldn't lay out a cloth on the pavement and sit about drinking tea on the kerb. Or if you did you'd soon get moved on by one of Beetriss's intendeds.'

'Well, you can't go and picnic where you like in the country,' Ralph pointed out.

'Some farmers don't allow it,' Roger said.

'Well, since there's plenty of room,' said Mrs Hamper, 'we'll picnic where we're welcome. And as a matter of fact I've had my eye on the very spot for a long time. You know where the old boy with one leg who looks like Stanley the explorer lives?'

'You mean Colonel Diamond?'

'That's right. Well, up beyond him on the left there's a gate leading into a field and this gate has a label on it painted Elizabeth Place. There's no house. There's no drive. There's nothing except this field of grass and a gate. Well, Beetriss and I looked in the other day, and we settled that this field was the very place for our picnic. There's a lovely view inside. All the country you want for miles, and the farm-cart can drive right in with the eatables so that we shan't have to lug them all over the place. The best picnic in the world will be spoilt if you've got to lug the eatables too far. The right way to eat is because you want to eat, not because you want to get rid of what you're carrying. Do you know the place I mean?'

The boys knew it well, and they agreed with Mrs Hamper that it was a capital site for a picnic. Moreover, nobody knew who the owner of it was. He had bought the plot when the Oak Farm was first cut up, had affixed this label of

Elizabeth Place to the gate, and had not been seen or heard of since. Nobody even knew his name.

'Now then, let's make a list of the guests to be invited,' said Mrs Hamper to the boys. 'Well, we'll start off with your ma and your sister. Now don't you both start off by making faces. This isn't a private escapade for you and me. This is a bit of a social affair, and I shouldn't dream of not inviting your ma and your sister, and if your pa was down here I should invite him too.' The two boys unwillingly entered the names of their mother and Phyllis at the top of the list. They thought Mrs Hamper was overdoing the social side of the picnic.

'Now then we'll have old Mr Bellamy. Dogs at picnics are a mistake as a rule. But I'm bound to say his dog can keep itself to itself when it's told. The two young Chilcotts. Texas Bill and his uncle. That is if Macintyre will let him come. I'd like to have asked that Lieutenant Green and his house-keeper; but you've never taken me up to call on them.'

'Well, we don't know him very well,' said Ralph. 'We only spoke to him when Roger biffed into him on the toboggan.'

'Now put down the Poleys. Mrs Poley is wheezy. Very wheezy. But she can drive up with the food. If we ask the Poleys, we can't very well leave out the Gnatheads. The only thing is perhaps they won't come. Not that there's much chance of that. You can always count on those nosy little women going everywhere. Let me see, that makes fifteen in all with Beetriss and myself. Then there'll be Peter, and one of the boys from the farm to drive the cart. I'll tell you who I would like to ask and that's that fellow Bagnall who used to play the trombone in the Drury Lane orchestra. It's a pity he's given up playing the trombone now, or he might have played to us after tea. I've never heard the trombone played with a free hand. Usually the fellow who's playing it has all his work cut out to keep from hitting the cornet on the back of the head, and that must cramp his style in the oompah bits.'

'There's Mrs Bagnall and two or three kids as well,' the boys reminded her.

'I know there are. It would do poor Mrs Bagnall good to get out. She looks very mopy. Well, you'd expect a woman who'd been in the ballet to feel a bit depressed with nothing to do all day except watch her husband ripening tomatoes.

Still, perhaps fifteen is enough. So we'll leave the Bagnalls out.'

Mrs Waterall had never felt quite at ease over this strange large woman with whom her sons had struck up such an intimacy. She had not realized that so many of their afternoons in London had been spent in her company, and she was wondering a little anxiously what Mr Waterall would say to her when he arrived at Dream Days next week. Had she realized that Mrs Hamper was the woman of whose behaviour in waking him up last November he had written to her in such strong terms she would have felt still more anxious. The boys, however, had managed to divert that knowledge from her when it seemed likely to flow in her direction. In the end Mrs Waterall decided that she would have a bad headache on the day of Mrs Hamper's picnic and thus avoid what might seem like a commitment of her husband. To the immense relief of the boys Mrs Waterall decided that Phyllis could not go to the picnic without her. As some compensation for the disappointment she and Cook were to have tea together in the garden, to the profound derision of Ralph and Roger on their way to the richer delights of Mrs Hamper's picnic.

It was a pleasant sight for schoolboy eyes, that corner of the field where beneath a spreading oak-tree the cool grass was a polychrome of cakes and sandwiches, of jams and fruit and biscuits. Even Ralph and Roger, accustomed as they were to lavish notions of tea at 22 Barking Terrace, were amazed at the variety and splendour of the feast which the combined marketing of Mrs Hamper and Beatrice had provided. They gazed with proud affection at their hostess, and in that glance they seemed to arrogate to themselves a little of the credit for this wonderful occasion. They seemed to demand from the assembled company congratulations for having endowed Oak with this beneficent fairy.

'Come on now, sit down and start in before the flies eat up every blessed thing,' Mrs Hamper commanded. 'Now, Mr Bellamy, don't stand on ceremony. Come along, Mr Gnathead, you're not at a Sunday school treat. Pass Mrs Gnathead those cress sandwiches. Mrs Poley, will you pour out the tea up your end? Mr Ryan, tea disagrees with you, I know. So you'll find something that suits you better in that basket. Peter! Why, where's Peter off to know?'

The poodle was trotting down toward the gate, his tail

erect, his ears raised. A small man had just opened it and was coming walking up the field.

'Is this the long lost proprietor by any chance?' Rehob Chilcott asked.

'Never mind if it is. We'll ask him to tea in his own field,' said Mrs Hamper. And then over Mrs Hamper's own countenance crept an expression of some emotion very like horror.

'Mr Ryan, come over her a minute,' she called sharply. 'I want to speak to you.'

What Mrs Hamper said to Mr Ryan was not audible to the rest of the company; but immediately afterwards Mrs Hamper put up her green parasol and started to walk quickly toward the gate while Mr Ryan ran down the field ahead of her to meet the stranger, and not merely to meet him, but to run round and round him as hard as he could in small circles.

'Here, Uncle, come back and behave yourself,' his scandalized nephew shouted.

'Look out, Texas,' Ralph muttered. 'I think Mrs Hamper told him to do that.'

'Come off it,' said Texas scornfully. 'Why on earth would she tell him to run round a fellow like that who he'd never seen? Uncle! Stop it, will you?'

But Mr Ryan paying no attention to his nephew continued to run round the stranger as fast as he could, and it was not until Mrs Hamper had passed through the gate, climbed up into the farm-cart, and driven off down through Oak that Mr Ryan ceased to run round the stranger.

'Are you mad, sir?' asked the stranger, who was a dried-up little man with grey hair and grey mutton-chop whiskers.

'No, it's a picnic,' said Mr Ryan.

'Well, you're all trespassing,' said the stranger angrily. 'This is my land.'

'It is the long lost proprietor,' murmured one of the Chilcotts.

'No harm intended,' Mr Poley began pleasantly, but before he could say any more his wife broke in:

'Will, don't you interfere. You're only a guest. You ought to know better by this time than start interfering when you're only a guest.'

'Won't you sit down and have a cup of tea?' suggested Beatrice who felt that whatever may have induced Mrs

Hamper to leave the picnic in that extraordinary fashion she would wish her reputation for hospitality to be sustained.

'No thanks,' said the disagreeable little stranger. 'And I should be obliged if you will all clear out of this field. I've come down here on business, and I can't do business with a crowd of excursionists all over my field.' He lanced a vicious glance in the direction of Mr Ryan. 'Queer state things have reached when a man can't cross his own field without some clown trying to be funny.'

'Come along,' Mr Bellamy suggested, 'as this gentleman dislikes our company so much perhaps we'd better finish our picnic in the field on the other side of the road.'

So the guests gathered together the china and the eatables and the cushions, and started their picnic all over again.

But it was not a success. The arrival of the disagreeable little man, and the departure of Mrs Hamper had spoilt it.

About an hour later the farm-cart came back, but without Mrs Hamper, and only a message to ask Beatrice to join her as soon as possible at the farm.

'Very mysterious,' observed Mrs Gnathead.

When later on Ralph and Roger went round to the farm they were shocked to be told that Mrs Hamper had been called back suddenly to London. Much depressed they betook themselves to Mon Repos to see if Mr Ryan could provide a solution of the mystery.

'No mystery at all,' said Mr Ryan. 'It was her husband. She didn't want to meet him again. She told me to distract his attention while she got away. That's why I kept running round him. You remember that, if ever you boys want to distract a man's attention. He won't look at anything else. It's a cert. And the smaller the circles the more it distracts him. But of course it's always apt to annoy people. He was just getting ready to hit out when Mrs Hamper passed through the gate to safety. I wonder what he calls himself. Do you know I wouldn't be surprised if his name isn't Macintyre?'

Two days later the boys received a letter from Mrs Hamper:

> 22 Barking Terrace,
> Hammersmith, W.
> August 11th.

Dear Ralph and Dear Roger,
  Well, Beatrice and I got back safely, but what a set out

*it nearly was. And what a piece of luck that Mr Ryan
should have been so quick and kept his eyes off me. Well,
we've laughed at the poor man's fancies, but they've given
him real presence of mind in an emergency. After Macintyre
my husband was nothing for him. But fancy him turning
up at a picnic after all these years. Still, I might have
known if I'd thought that land for the million was just what
he would go in for. Just like him to go and buy a nice field
like that and then not go near it again till he was going to
try and sell it to somebody else. He evidently hasn't
changed since we were married. He hadn't changed much
to look at and I'm bound to say it was more of a puzzle than
ever what I once saw in him. Well, I'm bound to say I'm
glad to be safe back to dear old London, though I've had a
bit of trouble with Beatrice because now she thinks she'd
better not marry this policeman after all and which as I tell
her is nonsense just because I nearly walk into my husband
having a picnic in his field. There's one thing I would like
to know. Who was Elizabeth? Well, I'll see you both
when you come back after the holidays, and the next tea we
have together won't be quite so interrupted. Don't you ever
laugh at Mr Ryan again. Presence of mind like he's got
is nothing to laugh at.*

*Your loving old
Phœbe Hamper*

CHAPTER TWENTY-ONE

OPPOSITE the old Oak Farm was an old thatched barn
which was as fine a monument of an old vanished England
as any church. The days had gone by when the floor would
be covered with a golden sea of threshed grain, and they
would never return. It was abandoned now to the rats and
the bats, to the sparrows and the owls. No thatcher would
ever again set his ladder to its oaken sides and comb out the
glossy new straw with rhythmical movement; the roof would
gradually rot away; the rain would soak through and drip
from the huge rafters. The dry scent of hoarded grain would
be permeated with the dank odour of mildew and rotting
wood. It was what some would call an anachronism, that
grand old barn, what others more acutely would recognize
as a *memento mori* to the foolish people of England. It
stood there against the background of Squire Melville's
rolling woods as utterly obsolete as an old wooden battle-
ship. Ten generations of labouring men had served it. The
last of them was old Snell.

It was to this barn that upon a Saturday evening in
August Mr Waterall summoned the residents of Oak to
demand a fully equipped post-office and the immediate
abolition of the derogatory and telegraphically expensive
name of the Oak Farm Estate. He had been driven into
doing this by Major Kettlewell who had just sent a circular
letter round the neighbourhood, inviting everybody to
petition for the name of the Oak Farm Estate to be made
Oaktown officially. This letter had reached Mr Waterall in
London where he was beginning to wonder when his partner
was going to return from his holiday and set him free from
this August heat. He was so much annoyed by the Major's
calm election of himself to the position of leading citizen
that he made up his mind to give him a lesson.

'By Jove, I'll summon a meeting myself,' he cried aloud,
as he thumped the mahogany of his desk.

He wrote off to Albert Hobday to find out if there were
any objections to using the old barn for that purpose, and
on hearing from Hobday that there was none, he caused

bills to be printed at his own expense in London on which was announced:

A PUBLIC MEETING
of the residents of the
Oak Farm Estate will be
held in the
LARGE BARN OF THE OAK FARM
on SATURDAY, AUGUST 17th
at
6.30 P.M.
to protest against the lack
of postal facilities and demand
a suitable name for this rising
district.
ALL ARE INVITED
to attend and express their views
on this matter of vital importance
to a rising community
THERE WILL BE NO COLLECTION

A hundred of these bills Mr Waterall sent down to Dream Days and entrusted his sons with the task of affixing them in suitably prominent positions around the district.

It was not often that Ralph and Roger found themselves able to throw themselves with whole-hearted enthusiasm into tasks devised for them by their father; but bill-sticking did make a deep appeal. They had often envied the bill-sticker his brush and pail of paste, had often paused to contemplate a bill-sticker at work and thought wistfully to themselves how remote from their reach such a profession was likely for ever to remain. Now, by a rapid turn of fortune's wheel, their ambition was to be gratified.

Do your best boys, he wrote. *Call in anybody you like to help. I shall be with you on the afternoon of what I hope is going to be a historic Saturday in the annals of good old Oak.*

It would have done Mr Waterall's heart good to see the way his sons leapt from their bunks so early on that fine

August morning and prepared to sally forth with brush and pail and roll of bills to make the meeting known from one end of Oak to the other.

Cook was back in London looking after Mr Waterall. Phyllis was sleeping with her mother. Dodsworth was in the new bedroom off the kitchen. The room next to Ralph and Roger was occupied by the callow young of a pair of sparrows, who had obligingly hatched a late brood and thereby given the boys a chance to get some more much needed practice with bringing up young birds on bread and milk.

'Don't you forget to feed the sparrows in half an hour from now, will you?' Ralph put his head round the door of Dodsworth's room to remind her.

'Will you go out of my room at once, Master Ralph,' the bashful Dodsworth protested from under the blankets.

A moment later Roger thrust his head through her open window.

'And be jolly careful not to stick the match too far down their throats,' Roger warned her. 'Ralph choked one by doing that.'

'No, I didn't, you liar. It choked itself,' the elder brother contradicted hotly.

At this moment the penny-whistle of Texas Bill was heard playing 'Come into the Garden, Maud', and Dodsworth in a turmoil of alarmed pudicity at the prospect of her bedroom being used as a thoroughfare called upon Ralph and Roger to stop their goings on at once unless they wished to find all three sparrows dead when they came back to breakfast.

Out in the long light shadows of the morn and under the gaze of the bland early sun beaming above the wooded hills Ralph and Roger forgot the worry of bringing up young birds in the zestful prospect of bill-sticking.

They began with the new tool-shed at Dream Days, which in their anxiety to achieve perfection of technique they covered all over with announcements of the forthcoming meeting until it resembled a newspaper kiosk in Paris. When at last they decided that they were able to fix a bill well and truly anywhere, they moved across the road to Blackheath Villa and stuck one bill on the Gnatheads' front door, and another couple on their front windows. After that they plastered Fernbank, and just as they were finishing off the outside of the Poley's bedroom they heard sounds of movement within. Afterwards Mr Poley told them that Mrs Poley had woken him up to say that she could hear the tail of Hobday's pony swishing against the side of the bungalow and bid him get out of bed at once and chase the brute off their land.

'Did Mrs Poley mind when she saw the bills?'

'Not when she saw what it was; but at first she thought it was a Baptist meeting, and that did rile her, because she can't bear Baptists ever since she had an aunt who turned Baptist and had three hundred pounds in Government stock which it was always expected she intended to leave to Mrs Poley, who never went abroad with old Lady Devizes but what she brought back an album of views or something as a present for this aunt. Well, the silly woman goes and gets into a tank of water, calling out she was saved in a white silk dress, goes home, catches pneumonia, and dies a fortnight later before any of her relations could stop her leaving all her money to the Baptists. But Mrs Poley has always been staunch Church of England herself, and if she'd had her way she'd have cleared every dissenter out of the country.'

After plastering the immediate vicinity of Dream Days with bills Texas proposed that they should take the opportunity of exploring Major Kettlewell's house into which he was to move, it was rumoured, within the next day or two, the workmen having finished it at last. Major Kettlewell's was the largest of the only three brick houses in Oak. It occupied the middle of a coppice behind the thatched cottages of the old Oak Farm, and in his desire for the seclusion which he felt his superiority to everybody else in Oak demanded, the Major had only cut down just enough trees to clear a space for his house. A winding drive, entered through a gate nearly as grandiose as the Chilcotts', led up to the portals of Kettlewell House in their privacy of perpetual shade. Some of the sylvan charm of this drive was spoilt by a trio of large yellow notice-boards, on the first of which was painted in scarlet letters BEWARE OF DANGEROUS EXPLOSIVES, on the second BEWARE OF THE BULL, and on the third BEWARE OF SAVAGE DOGS.

When Ralph and Roger had seen these notice-boards for the first time they had been impressed, and it was not until Texas Bill told them that there were no explosives, no bull, and no dogs of any kind savage or otherwise, that they had ventured to explore the coppice and the Major's then unfinished house. It was this passion the residents of Oak had for inspecting the progress of his house and removing odds and ends from it which had caused the Major to put the red and yellow notice-boards.

Kettlewell House was always able to exhale an atmosphere of comparative permanency amid the mushroom habitations and ephemeral human beings of the rest of the settlement. At this quiet hour of the morning it dreamed in the heart of the coppice with what was really a remarkably good imitation of a small but dignified country house, and the impression it made on the boys was voiced by Ralph when he asked doubtfully:

'I say, do you think we'd better stick any bills on it?'

'We might push one under the door like they do with circulars in London,' Roger suggested.

Texas played upon his whistle 'The Bogey Man', adding scornful grace notes that stung with their implied criticism.

'I'm not afraid to stick bills on it,' Ralph protested.

'Go on,' Texas jeered. 'Of course you're afraid. Afraid of the bull, afraid of the bangs, afraid of the . . .'

'I'm not afraid,' Ralph denied hotly; and forthwith he affixed a bill to Major Kettlewell's newly-painted glossy green front door.

'Come on, let's see if we can get inside and have a jolly good look round,' Texas chuckled.

They found an open window and climbed into the empty house which smelt of fresh paint and varnish and size.

'Suppose old Kettlewell suddenly comes?' Roger asked.

'Don't be silly,' said Texas. 'It's hardly half-past six. What would he be doing here as early as this when he's moving out his furniture today or tomorrow?'

And as answer to this question there sounded outside a roar such as the mythical bull or the imaginary explosives might have made.

'What's that?' said Ralph shakily.

Another roar resounded without, and the quiet golden air of the morning was made hideous with hoarse cries of rage.

'I believe it's him,' Roger whispered.

The hoarse cries of rage were succeeded by a crash and a rattle.

Texas went down on all fours to approach the uncurtained window, peeped over the sill for a minute and ducked quickly.

'It's him all right. He's dancing about in front of the house with a face like a coloured supplement. My eye, he hasn't half got his shirt out. I reckon if he sees us there'll be foul murder done in the moated grange ere tomorrow's sun rise up beyond yon purple mountain tops. What? I reckon he'll slice us into rashers if we don't look out for ourselves.'

'You don't think so really, do you, Texas?' Roger quavered in a voice that seemed well on the way to become a sob.

'Don't be an ass, of course he doesn't,' said Ralph, but in his voice too there was a shakiness which belied such an expression of confidence. 'What's he doing now, Texas?'

Texas took another cautious peep.

'Tearing off the bill you stuck on his freshly painted front-door,' he said. 'We'd better get out the back way as quick as we can.'

But when they crept downstairs into the hall they heard the key fumbling in the lock.

'He can't do nothing if he does come in,' said Texas Bill. 'And anyway he can only catch one of us.'

Ralph and Roger were wishing with all their hearts that they were safe back in their bunks at Dream Days, and the jaunty Texas himself was beginning to whistle nervously under his breath instead of upon his pipe, when a rescuer appeared.

This was Peter, Mr Bellamy's shaggy poodle, who charmed by the fineness of this August morning, had left his master's house very early with the intention of barking outside the window of the boys' room until he had persuaded them to rise and go for a walk with him before breakfast. To his surprise when Peter had reached Dream Days after an easy rambling progress from the other side of Galton, during which he had dallied luxuriously over every smell he encountered on the way, he found that his young friends had anticipated his suggestion and had already gone out of their own accord. He followed their tracks to Blackheath Villa and thence to Fernbank until finally he traced them to Major Kettlewell's house. Peter quickened his pace along the drive as nose to the ground he found the scent getting fresher and fresher, and he was just going to look up and

bound forward with swishing tail to greet his young friends
when to his dismay he perceived a tall bottle-nosed purple-
faced military gentleman whose personality by no means
appealed to him.

So Peter stopped and said 'Woof!'

Whereupon the bottle-nosed stranger turned round and
rushed at Peter.

'Get out of here at once, you vile cur.'

Peter said 'Woof! Woof!' and then barked.

Whereupon this bottle-nosed and by now extremely anti-
pathetic stranger left off fumbling with the key and ran
several paces in Peter's direction, waving his arms and
shouting, 'G'out of here, you infernal brute.'

Peter said 'Woof!' three times, barked twice, and then
retreated down the drive for a few paces, looking back over
his shoulder to watch the movements of this objectionable
stranger, who supposing that he was successfully frightening
this disreputable dog out of his grounds stooped to pick up
one of the bill-stickers' brushes which he flung as hard as he
could in the direction of Peter, shouting at him more
abusive epithets.

'I'm damned if I'll stand that,' Peter barked, as he turned
round and rushed at his assailant with menacing growls.

The Major who had nothing in his hands except the
bunch of keys flung them at Peter as hard as he could. The
keys missed Peter and disappeared in the undergrowth
beside the drive. Whereupon Peter dashed forward, barking
so furiously that the Major ran to his tool-shed, on the door
of which was painted DANGER! DYNAMITE IS STORED HERE.
His intention was to arm himself not with a stick of dynamite, for that was as mythical as the bull and his own savage
dogs, but with a rake or a garden fork. This movement of
the Major gave the boys their chance, for their retreat down
the drive was no longer cut off. So they scrambled out of
the windows at the back of the house and ran for it, while
Peter harried the Major with furious barks.

'I expect he'll summons us,' said Texas Bill when they
were safe on the other side of Major Kettlewell's grandiose
entrance gate.

'What for?' Ralph asked.

'Bill-sticking, trespass, and burgling,' said Texas. 'Hallo,
here's the tyke.'

And Peter appeared, carrying in his mouth the brush

which had been flung at him, and which from time to time he tossed in the air to catch again with sportive skill.

'I vote we go back and have breakfast now,' Roger sighed. The serene emptiness of the dewy countryside was being ruined for him by the unquiet emptiness of his own inside.

'You nearly blubbed when Major Kettlewell put his key in the lock,' Ralph accused him with Spartan scorn.

'Well, you nearly blubbed yourself, didn't he, Texas?' Roger appealed. 'And shut up jawing. I don't care what you jaw about till I've had my breakfast.'

And Ralph was beginning to feel so hungry himself that he lacked the vigour to chastise his brother's weakness further.

'I hope Dodsworth fed the sparrows properly,' he said.

'I don't expect she did. I expect she's choked them the same as you did that one,' said Roger, in whom hunger was begetting a mood of pessimism.

'I didn't choke it. It choked itself,' Ralph contradicted, wearily this time.

A silence fell upon the three boys as they walked on towards Dream Days. Their minds were bacon-haunted. Even the pleasure of being able to invite Texas to breakfast with them was spoilt by this gnawing hunger. Only Peter was cheerful, as he ran before them, tossing the brush in the air and catching it again.

CHAPTER TWENTY-TWO

JULIUS CAESAR about to cross the Rubicon, Alexander the Great leading his host onward into the East, Napoleon Bonaparte mounting his white charger to pass over the Alps, Christopher Columbus embarking upon that fatal voyage of Western discovery, it would be among such moments that an analogy should be sought for Mr Waterall's state of mind when he left the offices of Messrs Wickham and Waterall at half-past twelve on the morning of the seventeenth of August and entered the hansom cab which was to drive him to Waterloo. On his way through the dusty city streets Mr Waterall asked himself why it had never occurred to him before that politics rather than chartered accountancy was the career for which he was intended. All these years he had been plodding along in order to earn enough to bring up a family in respectable comfort, and all these years he should have been training himself to fulfil the civic duties which through no ambition of his own were now thrust upon him.

'It is perhaps too soon for me to consider a parliamentary candidature,' Mr Waterall said to himself as the hansom jogged on. 'But there is no reason why I should not ultimately be invited to contest a seat. Tonight will show whether I have the power to swing an audience. I believe I have that power. What has been my previous experience of public speaking? Nil, or as good as nil. I proposed the bride's health when old Wickham's daughter was married two years ago. Everybody assured me that I made a most happy little speech, but people's critical faculties are dulled by the nuptial atmosphere. Everybody is hoping for the best and everybody wants to avoid anything like a jarring note. Then there was the presentation to old Richards, our chief clerk, to celebrate his jubilee of service with the firm. 'In asking Mr Richards to accept this pair of cuff-links I wish to assure him that they are symbolic of the many links that for fifty years have united him first to the fortunes of Wickham and Son and later to those of Wickham and Waterall, Chartered Accountants.' As a matter of fact I expressed it more neatly than that at the time. But I wasn't inspired by old Richards. In fact when I first joined the firm I really found him an infernal nuisance with his antediluvian obstructionism. No speaker can do himself justice who is not inspired by the subject of his discourse. That's where I ought to score tonight. I'm completely possessed by my subject.'

The solitude and luxury of a first-class compartment developed Mr Waterall's sense of his own political significance. His silk hat on the opposite seat, his white spats and well-creased trousers and frock coat and Ascot tie seemed to assure him of the occasion's genuine importance and taught him why members of Parliament feel that they ought to dress themselves as if they were going to a wedding when they visit their constituencies. Hitherto Oak had only seen him in the knickerbockers of rusticity. He must have seemed to his fellow-residents a mere unit of that million wanting land. Now he would be revealed as a personality. He would be recognized as an influence. There was a mirror let into the side of the compartment between views of Bournemouth and Swanage and other South-Western Railway watering-places. Mr Waterall rose to address the reflection of himself in that mirror.

'Ladies and gentlemen,' he rehearsed, 'I have taken upon myself to summon . . . no, to invite . . . summon might strike an unpleasant chord in the memory of some members of the audience . . . to invite you here tonight . . . this evening in order that you may signify in no uncertain fashion what is your will . . . or pleasure? . . . or desire? . . . why not all three? . . . your will, your pleasure, and your desire . . . I'll make a note of that.'

The orator felt in his pocket for his memorandum book, and the train rounding a corner at that moment he was nearly precipitated on top of his silk hat, which he removed for safety to the rack.

'When I look round me at this sea of eager faces I am filled with a deep sense of my own unworthiness. Who am I, that I should venture to offer myself as the spokesman of your most intimate hopes? Ladies and gentlemen, I do not wish to arrogate to myself a position to which I have no claim. Like yourselves I am but another humble seeker after the simple life our rude forefathers led. Like you I am sick of the artificial existence of the town and as often as I can flee to Hampshire with my family, there to commune with nature in a tranquillity which no city can give. . . .'

Mr Waterall gazed at his reflection in the mirror with frank admiration.

'By gad,' he declared enthusiastically, 'I'd no idea you could talk like that . . . a tranquillity and a contentment which no city can ever provide . . . God, ladies and gentlemen, made the country, man the town . . . I hope I shan't forget that last sentence when I find myself on the platform. Platform? I wonder, by the way, if there will be anything in the nature of a platform in that old barn? And chairs? I never thought about chairs. I can't just get up in the middle of a barn among a lot of people standing all round and start making a speech. The effect might very easily be merely ludicrous.'

The journey to Galton passed quickly for Mr Waterall. What between rehearsing sonorous periods of rhetoric, planning out what could be done to provide accommodation for his audience, and following his own future political career from the hustings to the House of Commons, from the back benches to a seat in the Cabinet, he was fully occupied.

'Minister for Agriculture,' he meditated. 'What an opportunity for a man with imagination and courage! Hallo, here we are running into Galton already. And very fresh and green the country is looking.'

Mr Waterall rather wished he had ordered the Market Hotel fly to meet him. He felt something a little incongruous, something almost undignified, in driving through Galton in Hobday's governess-car, wearing a silk hat. Still, Hobday was likely to be one of his stoutest supporters, and it would have been tactless to offend him.

'Fine weather, Mr Hobday,' he said cheerily.

'Grand weather,' the owner of the Oak Emporium agreed.

'Prospects good for the meeting tonight?' he asked.

'Why, I believe there'll be a good turn out,' said Hobday. 'Some of 'em was a bit huffy about the bills. They didn't quite like it when your boys pasted them over their windows. Old Mrs Felton up at Windermere Cottage thought there'd been a blizzard in the night when she got out of bed yesterday morning to draw her curtains. It gave the old lady a bit of a turn for the moment. But I think the only one who was really annoyed was Major. And Major *was* angry. In fact he had the police out from Galton.'

'Had the police out?' Mr Waterall exclaimed.

'Well it seems your two boys stuck a bill on his front door

and being fresh painted he couldn't get it off properly. He was blowing about all yesterday saying he was going to sue you for three coats of paint.'

'I never heard of anything so childish,' Mr Waterall observed severely. 'Of course, my boys had no business to stick a bill on his front door. But it's hardly a matter for the police.'

'Well, Major's one of them high and mighty Tories,' said Hobday. 'And as such he thinks his front door is a bit sacred. I don't know if he'll come to the meeting, but I reckon if he does you're going to get some opposition.'

'I hope he does come,' said Mr. Waterall warmly. 'Nothing would give me greater pleasure than to show up a pretentious snob like that. Police indeed! It's a post-office we want in Oak not a police-station. By the way, what about seating accommodation in the barn? How shall we manage about that?'

'Oh, there's plenty of old benches and bits and pieces of planking and one thing and another. And we could put two or three chairs up at one end where there's a kind of platform.'

'Ah, I'm glad to hear we can manage that,' said Mr Waterall with a good deal of satisfaction in his tone. In fancy he was looking down at that sea of faces under the thrall of his eloquence. Now my notion of the evening's programme – proceedings, I should say – is as follows. First of all I will explain to the meeting why I have taken upon myself to summon – to invite them I mean. I will then put forward my suggestion for a name coupled with a demand for a post-office. Then I will call upon you to speak, and after you . . .'

'I'll tell you who's down here for a week lodging over at Wyatt's Farm,' Hobday interrupted. 'The Reverend Nehemiah Chilcott. That's the father of Micha and Rehob. They tell me he's considered a big man in the preaching line. My idea would be that you should call on him next.'

'Very well, though he's not strictly a resident,' said Mr Waterall.

'No, he's not actually a resident,' the other allowed, 'but he's paying most of the bills for his sons and if they ever build their house it will be with the old man's money.'

'Well, I'm quite agreeable,' said Mr. Waterall. 'But I hope

he won't drag in a lot of religion. We don't want to stir up religious strife over a post-office.'

'And after the Reverend Chilcott,' Hobday advised, 'I'd call upon Major Kettlewell if I was you. That is if he comes. If you call upon him, and he hasn't the manners to go up on the platform, why then, he's shown his paltry spirit in front of everybody and they'll know what to think of him. I'm a Socialist, Mr Waterall. I look at people like Major Kettlewell as so much lumber to be carted away as quick as possible. But what I say is give such rubbish rope to hang themselves with. You and me don't see eye to eye in politics, Mr Waterall, but because I'm a Socialist and you're a Tory, that doesn't keep you from buying marmalade at my Emporium, or driving alongside of me like you're driving now.'

'Certainly not.'

'But Major won't put a foot inside my Emporium. Everything he has he has from the Army and Navy Stores.'

'Showing thereby an utter lack of local patriotism,' Mr Waterall observed sternly. 'Well, I've no objection to giving this Major Kettlewell an opportunity to expose his ignorance in public.'

'Then if I was you,' Hobday went on, 'I'd throw the meeting open to a general discussion, and after that put the resolution. And then I'll get up and propose a vote of thanks to you.'

'Well, of course, that would be very gratifying,' said Mr Waterall.

'And then we might proceed to elect a deputation to approach the proper authorities and put our case before them.'

'Capital, Mr Hobday. I'm not a man who pays idle compliments, but I must congratulate you on the extremely helpful way in which you are doing your best to make this meeting a success. I hope the time will come when you and I shall find ourselves both serving to the best of our ability on the Parish Council of Oak. I don't mind what a man's politics are when I meet a public-spirited citizen like yourself.'

'Well, I've struggled to bring up a large family, and I've had my knife pretty deep into the idle rich,' said Hobday. 'But when I comes up against an opponent as I can respect, well, I'm not going not to respect him because his position is better than my own. I'm not that kind of a man at all, Mr Waterall. When you met me fair and square over that little matter of the fence between us you didn't find me hard to convince.'

'On the contrary, I found you most reasonable,' Mr Waterall declared.

'And Albert Hobday's not the man to forget when he's been treated right. I'm with you thick and thin in this fight for what's only common justice when you come to look at it.'

'You think that there will be a fight?' asked Mr Waterall, whose nostrils were quivering like those of a war-horse that approaches the fray.

'It's my opinion there will be a fight,' Mr Hobday declared. 'You arst me for why, and I answer you that there's too many people in Oak with time hanging heavy on their hands for them to agree peaceably to anything.'

'Well, let there be a fight,' Mr Waterall declared enthusiastically. 'I shall enjoy a fight. Nothing worth winning in this world was ever won without a fight.'

'I believe that's true,' said Hobday sagely.

'I know it's true,' cried Mr Waterall with all the passion of a born political leader.

By now the governess-car had pulled up at the gate of Dream Days.

'Well, we shall meet on the field of battle,' said Mr Waterall as he alighted.

He walked up to the front door with the gravity of the occasion stamped on every movement he made. He frowned at one of Bocock's Siberian crabs which showed no sign of being aware by so much as a leaf that summer had now been here for quite a long time. He noted with corresponding approval that another of Bocock's Siberian crabs was sufficiently aware of its duty to have set half a dozen small fruits. Then he opened his front door.

'Well, here I am,' he proclaimed. 'And I hear we may expect a big meeting tonight.'

'Look out, Father, don't move,' Ralph cried.

'Stand perfectly still,' cried Roger.

'Oh, Daddy, don't move. Please don't move,' screamed Phyllis.

'What on earth is the matter? Is somebody taking a photograph?' Mr Waterall asked in a nettled voice. He felt that his family were not fully appreciating the historic importance of this moment.

'No,' said Ralph. 'But one of the young sparrows has got out of the cage and you might tread on it.'

'Good heavens,' Mr Waterall exclaimed irritably, 'you don't think I'm going to remain standing in my own doorway while you're looking for a sparrow? There are more important things than sparrows to consider this afternoon.'

With this Mr Waterall took a determined step forward, only to be pushed back by his own daughter who begged him to stay where he was and not tread on the poor little baby birdie.

'I don't want to tread on any baby birds,' he said. 'But I don't know what's coming over you, Phyllis. I hope the country isn't going to turn you into a great romping tomboy.'

'Well, please don't move,' said Ralph. 'Because there's only one other sparrow left now, and that's sure to die if it's left alone.'

'When you're my age, my boy,' said his father, 'and have had the anxiety and expense of bringing up children of your own you'll be less inclined to bother about bringing up sparrows.'

'There it is,' said Roger, pointing to the fledgeling crouched in a corner.

It was rescued, and the head of the family was allowed to move freely across his own floor.

'Well, what are the prospects for the meeting tonight?' he inquired with a touch of self-conscious anxiety.

'What meeting?'

'What meeting? Do you mean to say that you two boys have been plastering the countryside with bills and don't know that there is a meeting tonight in the Oak Farm barn?'

'Is it tonight?' Ralph asked vaguely.

'Can't you read?' his father spluttered. 'You boys don't seem to have as much brain between you as one of these wretched sparrows you're pampering.'

'Well, I forgot,' said Ralph. 'Major Kettlewell was here with a bobby because we stuck a bill on his rotten front door, and then Dodsworth choked a sparrow by giving it too big a lump of bread and milk. I can't think of everything at once.'

'This meeting,' said Mr Waterall sternly, 'is of a great deal more importance than Major Kettlewell's front door or these ridiculous sparrows you are murdering one by one. If you're not careful I shan't let you come to it and hear my speech.'

'Your speech?' the two boys gasped in horror. 'You're not going to make a speech, are you?'

'I am indeed.'

'Well, we needn't come, need we?' Ralph asked miserably.

'Do you mean to say you don't want to hear your father make a speech?'

Ralph and Roger stared at one another in dismay. This was a heavy price to pay for the pleasure of sticking bills up all over Oak. It was Phyllis, however, who succeeded in expressing their emotions, and for the first time in their lives they felt a faint regard for their sister.

'Daddy,' she said, 'I don't think I would like to hear you make a speech, because I think it would make me cry perhaps.'

'But I'm not going to speak about anything sad, my child.'

'No, I wouldn't want to cry because it was sad, but because you were making a speech. I'd be frightened.'

'Frightened of what?' Mr Waterall demanded.

'Frightened of what people would say,' Phyllis replied.

Mr Waterall withdrew into the sitting-room in an absolute dudgeon of disillusionment.

'You're tired and hot, dear,' said his wife soothingly.

'No, I'm not. But I was just thinking what a disappointment children are when they begin to get older. Even little Phyllis is deteriorating fast. She promised to be a sweet, sensible, healthy-minded child, but she is already being corrupted by the company of her brothers. There seems no kind of reverence for anything among the younger generation. When I look back on the way we regarded our father, how proud we were of him, how . . .' Mr Waterall stopped abruptly. On the vacant plot of ground beyond the level green of the lawn which Mr Bellamy had laid out for him he had caught sight of what looked very much like an encampment of gypsies.

'They've been here for three days now,' said Mrs Waterall wearily. 'I didn't like to worry you with a letter. Especially as apparently nothing can be done about it.'

'Nothing can be done about it?' Mr Waterall echoed

sternly. 'Do you mean to tell me that a parcel of wandering vagabonds can bring a couple of caravans almost on to our lawn and that nothing can be done about it?'

'It seems that the man who owns the next plot gave them permission to camp there.'

'It's obvious that this place is fast becoming a seething mass of glaring anomalies,' Mr Waterall declared angrily. 'I suppose that if I erect a fence to shut out that horde of squalid brigands the Galton Rural District Council would intervene on their behalf and say I was excluding light from them. What's that extraordinary-looking animal running about on the lawn?'

'I expect it's one of the gypsies' dogs, dear. They have several.'

'Good heavens, we might as well have built a bungalow in the middle of the monkey-house at the Zoo,' said Mr Waterall. 'Send one of the boys to chase the brute off.'

'I don't think that Mr Bellamy wants us to walk about much on the lawn during the dry weather,' said Mrs Waterall. 'He made a great point of that.'

'Oh, did he? Well, I had this lawn made to add to the amenities of Dream Days not to provide an arena for the dogs of gypsies.'

At this moment Dodsworth came in to say that a Mr Blake was anxious to see Mr Waterall on a matter of business.

'Mr Blake? Who's Mr Blake?'

'I think he's the owner of that plot,' said Mrs Waterall. 'He has called once or twice to know if you would like to buy it.'

Half an hour later there were signs of movement on the other side of the lawn. The gypsies were striking camp.

'Robert, are you sure you can afford to buy that extra land?' his wife asked anxiously.

'I can afford not to spoil the ship for a ha'porth of tar,' said Mr Waterall with tremendous conviction.

'Father, you are not sending the gypsies away?' Ralph burst into the sitting-room to ask.

'I am sending them off my land,' said Mr Waterall.

'Your land?'

'Yes, my land.'

'Well, let them stay till tomorrow because one of them is going to show me how to skin a rabbit properly,' Ralph begged.

'And one of them's going to show me how to lime gold-finches,' said Roger indignantly.

'Oh, Daddy, don't send the poor gypsies away. The woman's going to tell my fortune again,' Phyllis said. 'She told me yesterday I was going to have lots and lots of darling little babies when I got married. And I wanted to know how many girl babies and how many boy babies I was going to have. Don't send them away.

CHAPTER TWENTY-THREE

CURIOSITY rather than conviction or a desire to be convinced is likely to be the motive force which drives people into attending public meetings. The only settlers on the Oak Farm Estate (the chronicler must try by sticking to the recognized name not to prejudice the issue) who cared a jot whether it was to be known in future as Oak or Oaktown were Mr Robert Waterall and Major Wilberforce Kettlewell. There was not any real interest in the elimination of the clumsy name Oak Farm Estate, for hardly any of the settlers received enough telegrams during the year to feel the iniquity of having to pay a penny for those unnecessary two extra words or the exhorbitant porterage on telegrams brought out from Galton. And even the establishment of a post-office was not felt as a vital need by the happy-go-lucky population of oddities who had escaped to the Oak Farm Estate from the ever-growing complicacy of modern life. Nevertheless, in spite of this indifference to the issues at stake there was hardly one of the settlers absent from the meeting convened by Mr Waterall in the big barn of the old Oak Farm on that August evening.

Some came because a strong rumour had gone round that Major Kettlewell and Mr Waterall were likely to fight it out with fists before the evening was over. Some came because an equally strong rumour was prevalent that refreshments would be served free when the meeting was over. Some came because they had not had an evening off since they exchanged the soul-destroying demands of urban existence for the back-breaking demands of a country livelihood. Some came to stare at neighbours of whose extraordinary behaviour they had heard lurid tales, but whom they had not yet had an opportunity to know even by sight. Some came because it was a fine evening. And one came—it was old Mrs Felton of Windermere Cottage—because she had been told that it was a religious gathering, and church or chapel being so far away she thought it would be a nice opportunity to perform an act of worship. In addition to the settlers, there was a sprinkling of young farm-labourers from various farms in the neighbourhood, who made a habit of attending meetings for the purpose of shouting observations to the speakers, talking to one another in the back rows, and smoking cigarettes in defiance of the stewards. Finally there was the Press which consisted of a spotty-faced youth of seventeen with ink-stained fingers and a pencil he had bitten down to a pulp. To his four-line report of the meeting two days later in the *Galton Advertiser* no attention was paid at the time, and no attention need be paid now.

Hobday, with the help of planks, barrels, chopping-blocks, and hurdles had provided an excellent imitation of seating accommodation; and of the raised threshing-floor at the end of the barn he had made an almost lifelike representation of a real platform with two pots of ferns, a Union Jack, a table with a jug of water and five wicker chairs.

'You'd better come up on the platform with me, my dear,' Mr Waterall murmured to his wife as they passed from the spangled gold of the westering August sun into the austere shade of the old barn.

'Oh, no, Robert, please,' she protested.

'Well, somebody must sit in those wicker chairs,' he said. 'Hobday may be offended if we show no appreciation of all the trouble he has taken.'

'Well, I should ask old Mr Chilcott,' she suggested, 'and Hobday himself. But not me, please, Robert. I've never sat on a platform in my life, and I don't like to leave little Phyllis. She is feeling very nervous, and I've promised to let her hold my hand all the time.'

The Reverend Nehemiah Chilcott was a plump and venerable old gentleman dressed in a clerical frock coat. He had a long white beard, and like many old gentlemen with beards he considered it superfluous to wear a tie, supposing that the glazed surface of his dicky was sufficiently garnished by his white hairs.

'Mr Chilcott,' said Mr Waterall, the graciousness in his voice already betraying a tendency to be all things to all men, the effect of becoming a public character. 'Mr Chilcott, may I beg that you will do me the favour of occupying a seat on my right?'

Mr Chilcott indicated his willingness by an inclination of his venerable head and on reaching the platform sat looking down at the audience with the expression of a prophet faced by one of the periodic flirtations of the Children of Israel with strange gods.

'Mr Hobday, I think you'd better take the chair on my left,' said Mr Waterall, 'You're used to this sort of thing.'

'As you like,' said the owner of the Emporium.

Whereupon he stumped heavily up on the platform, sat down firmly in his wicker chair wiped his mouth with the back of his hand and looked fiercely across at the group of young farm-labourers shuffling their feet at the far end of the audience.

It should have been mentioned before that a considerable proportion of this audience consisted of dogs, some of whom had accompanied their owners, while others had just wandered in because the big doors of the barn were wide open. Among these dogs was Peter. There had been of course already a good deal of the low snarling and growling with which dogs express their contempt for each other's personalities and political opinions; but the quantity of dogs present was not revealed until the entrance of Major Kettlewell when every dog in the barn forgot to snarl at its nearest neighbour and barked loudly at the new-comer. Why all the dogs should have shown such resentment at the Major's appearance would have been difficult to say. Many figures outwardly much more eccentric than the Major had entered their seats without a word of canine protest; yet there was something about the way he came in which made every dog long to chase him out again. It was lucky that Lieutenant Green and his seven fox-terriers had not yet arrived, for they would undoubtedly have proceeded from words to action. However, they arrived later and they were too busy expressing their opinion of the dogs already there to notice the Major who by then had taken his seat.

'Shut up Peter, you ass,' said Roger.

'Can't I really put that bottle-nosed bounder out of the barn?' Peter asked.

'Lie down, Peter you, fool,' said Ralph severely.

'Every dog in the place agrees with me,' Peter grumbled, as he settled down unwillingly at the feet of the two boys.

'I think we might open the proceedings now,' Mr Waterall on the platform murmured to Mr Hobday. 'It's five minutes after the half-four.'

Mr Hobday agreed, and Mr Waterall produced from his pocket a hand-bell which he rang for silence. This started every dog in the place off again, for being unable to see from where they were lying what was happening on the plat-

241

form they decided unanimously to suppose that a door bell had been rung and that it was now imperative to fill the visitor's heart with terror of their sagacious ferocity and with awe of their noble devotion to property.

'I wish he wouldn't show off like that,' Ralph muttered to his brother. 'It's bad enough making an ass of himself by getting up and jawing, without ringing bells.'

'Ladies and gentlemen, or may I not say, fellow-searchers after the simple life . . .'

A loud 'Hear, hear,' from Hobday almost at his elbow nearly threw Mr Waterall off his rhetorical balance, and he bent over hastily to consult the note he had of his opening.

Ralph and Roger, blushing hotly at the parental spectacle, leaned down to bury their shame in Peter's shaggy coat. Farther along the row they could hear a faint whimpering from where Phyllis sat, clasping her mother's hand in an agony of filial apprehension.

Mr Waterall recovered from Hobday's sudden endorsement and proceeded more easily:

'I have taken upon myself to invite you here this evening in order that you may signify in no uncertain fashion what is your will.'

'Ask old Will Poley, if his missus don't object,' a voice cried from the back of the barn amid loud guffaws from the group of farm-labourers in a smoke-screen of Woodbines.

'Order at the back there,' cried Hobday.

'Order!' cried several members of the audience in front.

'Hogs,' whispered Mrs Poley to her husband.

'What can you expect, Maria? I told you before we come out that it would be all hoggishness. Pay no attention to them.'

'I do not want at this early stage of the proceedings,' said Mr Waterall, 'to introduce a note of bitterness, but I must ask those gentlemen at the back of the barn either to avoid the introduction of personalities or to leave the barn.'

'Hurrah, Poley for ever and free speech!' a concealed wag cried. 'Stand up, Poley, and show us your face.'

'You sit still, Will,' said his wife. 'Don't you dare move.'

'I wouldn't move a finger for such hogs,' Poley answered her, sitting poker-backed with dignity.

'When I look round at this sea of upturned faces,' Mr Waterall went on, 'I am filled with a deep sense of my own unworthiness. Who am I that I should venture to offer myself as spokesman of your most intimate hopes upon this momentous occasion? Ladies and gentlemen, I have no desire to arrogate to myself a position to which I have no claim. Like yourselves I am but another humble seeker after the simple life that was led by our rude forefathers.'

This remark was greeted by some stamping of feet at the back of the barn, but whether in approval of the poetical allusion or whether to express their surprise at hearing their relations called rude was not clear.

'Like you,' Mr Waterall continued, 'I am sick, mortally sick of the artificial conditions of modern city life and whenever I can flee with my family to lovely Hampshire, there to commune with nature in a tranquillity of mind and a contentment of body which no city can provide. God, ladies and gentlemen, made the country, but it was man ladies and gentlemen, man who made the town. But to pass from the poets and confront the grim facts of this workaday existence of ours. We are met here this evening to determine what we wish to be called. How many of us in later life have oft-times wished that we could have had a say in our names when they were first bestowed upon us by doting parents.'

At this point a very loud 'Hear, hear' rang out from that part of the barn where Micha and Rehob Chilcott were sitting; but, as both the young men immediately looked round to see who it was behind them that could have endorsed this opinion from the platform so enthusiasically, the Reverend Nehemiah Chilcott sitting with folded arms on Mr Waterall's right, was unmoved.

'Do not let me impute to our parents any neglect of their duties, ladies and gentlemen. Whatever names they bestowed upon us were given in the full belief that they were the names we ought to have.'

A cry of 'Shame' from somewhere near the Chilcott brothers again roused a suspicion that they were not in complete agreement with the speaker.

'But there have been parents,' Mr Waterall resumed, 'who have gratified their own love of eccentricity at their children's expense and there have been parents who have given to their children the first names that came into their heads. In some such spirit have those acted who propose to contaminate this lovely part of Hampshire with a name like Oaktown.'

Here Major Kettlewell leapt to his feet shouting 'Monstrous!' Much of the effect of his intervention was destroyed by the fact that he was sitting at the very end of a bench and that unknown to himself his seat upon it was the only thing that counterbalanced the weight of four or five children who were sitting at the other end of it. Consequently when Major Kettlewell leapt up to cry 'Monstrous!' at Mr Waterall's interpretation of the spirit in which the name 'Oaktown' had been chosen, the rest of the occupants of the bench collapsed in a heap on the floor. Not only this, but every dog in the barn which had been drowsing quietly through Mr Waterall's speech immediately started to bark furiously.

'Sit down, sir,' said Mr Waterall majestically. 'Sit down, sir. You shall have an opportunity later on to put your views before the meeting. There is no intention to curb the freedom of speech. We welcome discussion, but we will not tolerate interruptions.' Then he turned to the audience. 'Our friend takes exception to my use of the word 'contaminate'; but I appeal to you, ladies and gentlemen, is contaminate too strong a word for a name like Oaktown, a name which deliberately introduces into the sylvan atmosphere of Oak the harsh and discordant suggestion of city life? We do not want towns here. We have come here to avoid towns. And I say deliberately that for any resident upon the Oak Farm Estate to attempt to rob us of our rusticity will be strongly and justifiably resented. Not that I put forward any plea for such a clumsy name as Oak Farm Estate. Indeed, I will go so far as to say to my gallant friend down there, that if it were a question of choosing between the Oak Farm Estate and Oaktown I might be puzzled to know how to make my decision. Fortunately there is an alternative, and the alternative, ladies and gentlemen, is the simple yet picturesque monosyllable Oak. Surely there is no word in the language which appeals quite so-so—so——so . . . ' the speaker struggled to catch the resplendent adverb which was eluding the net of his eloquence . . . 'quite so much,' he gulped out finally, surrendering to the necessity that compels the orator to get on at any cost, 'which appeals quite so much to the deeper feelings of every Englishman. And whatever may be our different professions, occupations, and trades, we are all of us here, English men and women, and, let me add, we are all of us proud of it.'

Here the audience broke into that cordial applause which always greets a blatantly obvious statement reflecting credit upon itself. Even Major Kettlewell called out a bluff and gruff 'Hear, hear,' and Mr Waterall was just going to continue in a mood of refreshed complacency, when from the middle of the gathering bobbed up the hirsute face and head of Mr Augustus Ryan in the way that a seal will suddenly bob up from the middle of its pond at the Zoo.

For a moment Mr Waterall was possessed by an overmastering impulse to fling his silk hat at Mr Ryan, for there was something about that mop of untidy hair and untrimmed beard which roused feelings in Mr Waterall's breast not far from murderous.

'There will be an opportunity for you to address any questions to the chair later,' he said sternly.

'I've no desire to talk to any chair, now or later,' Mr Ryan insisted. 'I get quite enough back answers from my own furniture without talking to chairs I haven't met. What I wish to say is not meant for chairs. Far from it. What I wish to say is that I am of Irish extraction and that my nephew, Texas Bill . . .'

'Sit down,' Mr Waterall shouted.

'Thanks very much,' said Mr Ryan, his hirsute face and beard vanishing as he sat back in his place again.

'We were talking about the beauty of Oak, ladies and gentlemen, when we were interrupted by the shamrock.' Mr Waterall paused for a laugh but none was forthcoming, and he went on quickly. 'My contention is that Oak was the original name of this district. The Oak Farm. So called because it was the farm in Oak, not because it was built of Oak. When it ceases to be a farm what remains? Why Oak. What need to drag in 'town'? Already the wags of Galton have christened us Tintown. Let us beware that they do not presently call us Joketown.'

'Why shouldn't they call it Joke instead of Oak?' demanded Major Kettlewell angrily.

'They don't call it Joke Farm.'

'Why should they call it Joketown then?' the Major pressed.

'There's no analogy.'

'Never mind about analogies, sir. We're discussing facts.'

'Then discuss facts,' said Mr Waterall hotly.

'I don't intend to be bullied by you,' the Major rattled.

'And I don't intend to be bullied by you,' Mr Waterall retorted with dignified calm. 'I have convened this meeting in order to give the people of Oak an opportunity to express their opinion without let or hindrance, and I will not be deterred from carrying out my intentions by ill-timed interruptions. In due course as chairman I shall invite you to step up here on the platform and contribute to the discussion. Meanwhile, I must therefore ask you to abstain from interjecting irrelevant remarks from the body of the hall.'

'Hear, hear,' said Mr Hobday, who had been gazing fixedly at the Major throughout this interlude in the hope of conveying what he thought of him for dealing at the Army and Navy Stores instead of the local Emporium.

'What's in a name, ladies and gentlemen?' Mr Waterall resumed, 'You may say with gentle Shakespeare, "a rose by any other name would smell as sweet." That is true. Not even a name like Oaktown could successfully deprive this countryside of its loveliness. It could not rob the green from our hedgerows. It could not . . .'

'You're safe, Lootenant,' one of the young men at the back called out. But Lieutenant Green had found a seat with something to lean against and he was fast asleep.

'But though an ugly name could not destroy the beauty of Oak,' Mr Waterall continued, 'why should we repay the prodigal abundance of nature so ungratefully? Ladies and gentlemen, there is much more that I could say in favour of Oak as a name, much more that I could urge against Oaktown as a name. But there are other speakers beside myself here tonight, more eloquent, I know, though not, I venture to think, more sincere.'

Mr Waterall resumed his seat amid the applause which an audience finds it so difficult to withhold from anything that is finished. He had no sooner sat down than he rose again.

'Excuse me ladies and gentlemen, but in the emotion of the occasion I completely forgot that I had not said a word about the post-office which we all needed so much. I shall not detain you long, however. The arguments in favour of a post-office nearer than three miles away do not require elaboration by me. They can be appreciated by the lowest intelligence. In the middle of the night one of our loved ones is taken seriously ill. Where is the post-office? Three miles away. On an afternoon of wind and rain we are

246

anxious to communicate with friends, with relations, with our associates in business perhaps, and where is the post-office? Three miles away. In order to obtain one of those small mauve stamps which hold the likeness of our beloved Queen and which at the cost of one penny sends our message forth to the uttermost parts of the British Isles we must walk three miles. Ladies and gentlemen, such a state of affairs is not to be tolerated any longer. You will be invited to pass a strongly worded motion this evening, affirming your fixed and unalterable determination not to rest until the postal facilities to which, as citizens of this mighty Empire, you are entitled, have been granted to you. Do not the telegraph poles which connect Medworth with Galton pass some of your very doors? They do. And yet we are condemned to pay porterage of one shilling and sixpence on every telegram delivered in Oak. Not only that, but we have to pay an unnecessary halfpenny for the word "farm", another unnecessary halfpenny for the word "estate", another unnecessary halfpenny for the word "Galton", and a fourth unnecessary halfpenny for the word "Hants", because forsooth there is another Galton in the county of Worcestershire. But Oak, ladies and gentlemen, would be unique. Oak would require no Galton and no Hants . . .'

At this a bullet-headed little cobbler called Pluepott who had recently left Bedford to settle here and who had already shown signs of becoming the chief handy man for the neighbourhood, being an adept at everything from carpentry to bee-keeping, rose from his seat.

'On a point of order, Mr Chairman, why not?' he asked.

'Surely I made that clear?' said Mr Waterall. 'Because there would only be one place in the whole of these islands called Oak, and therefore the addition of Galton or Hants would be superfluous.'

'On a point of order, Mr Chairman, I still do not understand why,' Mr Pluepott persisted.

'Don't answer him,' growled Hobday, who regarded Pluepott with some jealousy as likely to become a serious rival. 'Don't answer him. He'd argue with the hind legs of a donkey.'

'I have given you a perfectly good explanation,' said Mr Waterall. 'And as I am sure that everybody else present understands perfectly well why Galton and Hants would be superfluous I do not propose to discuss the matter further.'

'But on a point of order, Mr Chairman . . .'

Mr Waterall rang his bell and every dog in the place started barking. When they had been cajoled or threatened into silence Mr Pluepott was still upon his feet, and Mr Waterall did not like to ring the bell for fear of starting off the dogs again.

'On a point of order, Mr Chairman . . .'

This was too much for Hobday. He rose from his seat and stepped forward to the front of the platform.

'What right have you got to go on blaring away when you've been ruled out of order?' he demanded.

'I'm not speaking to you, Hobday,' said Mr Pluepott contemptuously. 'I'm rising on a point of order, Mr Chairman.'

'How can you rise on a point of order when you're been ruled out of order. Be more civilized, Pluepott,' said his rival.

The Woodbine-smoking group at the back began to hope that there would be a fight after all and they cheered. 'That's right, Hobday, don't you be flummoxed,' they shouted.

'I call upon the Reverend Nehemiah Chilcott to address the meeting,' Mr Waterall said firmly. 'Perhaps he will be able to make the situation clearer to our friend than I have been able to. Mr Chilcott!'

Ralph and Roger looked across to where the Chilcott brothers were sitting. They felt genuinely sorry for them.

The old gentleman advanced to the front of the platform, and gazed down sternly at the audience. Then he cleared his throat loudly, thereby causing several dogs to growl and a small child to burst into tears, before he boomed out in a deep voice:

'Wandering sheep!'

The young men at the back baaed once or twice behind their smoke-screen, but something in the old man's eye checked them when he repeated:

'Lost and wandering sheep! Whatever name in your pride you give to this place where you have pitched your tents I beg you before it is too late to ask yourselves what is the name the Lord Jehovah has given to it. And I will tell you. The Lord Jehovah has sent me His unworthy servant to make known unto you that He will call this place New Sodom unless you turn from your abominations. Of what avail to petition for a post-office when one amongst you is seeking a licence to sell intoxicating liquor? Neither Oak nor Oaktown shall you be called in the ears of the Lord Jehovah, but Soak and Soaktown.'

Hobday leaned over and twitched Mr Waterall's coat.

'I know, I know,' the chairman muttered, 'it's very awkward. I'll try to stop him. Ahem! Mr Chilcott.'

But the venerable minister without turning waved Mr Waterall's interruption behind him.

'Lost and wandering sheep, come back,' he cried sonorously. 'Forsake strong drink. Seal the covenant. The Reformed Children of Israel abominate the juice of the grape. The Reformed Children of Israel . . .'

'Excuse me,' said Mr Waterall, 'nobody is more sympathetic than I am with the cause of true temperance, Mr Chilcott; but this is not a temperance meeting, and as chairman I must ask you to keep to the point at issue. We are debating a suitable name for what is now known officially as the Oak Farm Estate and we are calling upon the authorities to take immediate steps to provide us with postal, and telegraphic facilities. The question of the proposed off-licence is not upon the agenda.'

'The question of an off-licence may not be on your agenda,' said Mr Chilcott sternly. 'But it is on the agenda of the Recording Angel.' He turned again to the audience. 'Lost and wandering sheep . . .'

'I call upon Major Kettlewell to address the meeting,' said Mr Waterall. 'We have all listened with great respect to what the Reverend Mr Chilcott has had to tell us, but I'm sure that . . .'

'Lost and wandering sheep,' the old gentleman boomed out, entirely disregarding Mr Waterall.

'I should think Micha and Rehob are feeling pretty awful,' Ralph observed to his brother.

'Frightful,' Roger murmured.

'Major Kettlewell,' Mr Waterall called down. 'Will you take the platform?'

But the Major gave no sign of having heard the invitation, and the chairman tried once more to stop old Mr Chilcott.

'I must beg you, sir, to give somebody else an opportunity of letting us hear his views.'

'Obey the chairman's ruling,' Mr Hobday shouted angrily; but the old gentleman was impervious.

'Lost and wandering sheep, seal the covenant. The Reformed Children of Israel call you to return to the fold. You do not require a post-office to reach the Lord Jehovah . . .'

'Go down and ask his sons if they can get him off the platform,' Mr Waterall whispered to Mr Hobday.

'We can't do anything with him,' Micha and Rehob assured Hobday when he made his appeal. 'You shouldn't have asked him to stand up and spout. It's your own fault.'

'Lost and wandering sheep,' boomed that relentless voice again.

'I'll stand no more of it, Will,' Mrs Poley was heard to wheeze in her penetrating whisper. 'I'll not be called a sheep by anybody who isn't Church of England. I'm going home. You stay if you like, but I'm going home.'

Whereupon Mrs Poley rose majestically and left the meeting followed by her husband to the chagrin of Mr Waterall who had been counting on Poley's support for his motion.

For another ten minutes old Mr Chilcott held forth on the evils of strong drink, and he might have gone on for another half-hour if a bat had not left the upper glooms of the barn and started to flitter round and round him so close sometimes as almost to run the risk of being entangled in his venerable beard. Even Mr Chilcott's concentration was disturbed at last, and he was driven to take refuge in his chair and put a large red handkerchief over his face.

'Infallible,' Mr Ryan was heard to say. 'There's nothing like it for distracting anybody's attention. It's a pity Mr Waterall didn't call on me, I'd have stopped him in a minute if he'd asked me to. I'd have been up on the platform and running round that elderly gentleman till he'd have been glad to go home and sleep it off.'

'Well, ladies and gentlemen,' said the chairman,' 'I feel sure that some of you will now wish to hear a few arguments from the other side, and I have much pleasure in calling upon Major Kettlewell.'

'I'm not coming up on the platform,' snapped the Major. 'I decline absolutely to come up on your platform. Nothing will induce me to come up on your platform. I deny your right to summon the meeting at all. You are not the senior resident. You are not even a genuine resident at all.'

'What do you mean by that?' Mr Waterall demanded angrily.

'I mean what I say sir. I mean that you are a week-ender. A miserable week-ender. And for you to put forward your name in opposition to mine shows a most unneighbourly spirit. Not only did you call this meeting, but you caused a printed announcement of it to be affixed to my front door. You shall hear of that again, sir. Are you aware that I have already addressed a petition to the authorities, asking for the name Oaktown to be recognized as a fit and proper telegraphic address?'

'I refuse to accept the name Oaktown,' said Mr Waterall. 'I regard Oaktown as an essentially vulgar name. Oak, sir, Oak is the only name I will support.'

'Oaktown!' the Major roared.

At this moment Peter, who had been sleeping quietly at the feet of Ralph and Roger stirred.

'I say, Oak, Oak, Oak,' Mr Waterall shouted.

There was loud applause, not because the audience really cared a jot whether it was Oak or Oaktown, but because Mr Waterall had succeeded in shouting more loudly than the Major, who, enraged by what he thought was the tide of public opinion rising in favour of his rival, bellowed:

'Oaktown!'

It may be remembered that Peter had been taught by Mr Bellamy that Oaktown was a word of which he should show disapproval. On hearing it now bellowed forth like this by Major Kettlewell with whom he had already had a passage of arms this week, he rushed along between the benches and seizing Major Kettlewell's coat between his teeth he shook it with furious growls. It was not to be expected that the other dogs in the barn would allow Peter to occupy the centre of the stage without competition. Some attacked one another. Some barked wildly at the air. Some like Lieutenant Green's fox-terriers tore round after imaginary rats. To add to the confusion an owl, roused by the clamour, swooped down from where it was roosting and, bewildered by the light, brushed the heads of the audience with its great wings as it continued to swoop wildly hither and thither about the barn. Women and children screamed. The dogs barked more loudly. About twenty bats disturbed by the owl began flittering around with the original bat which had silenced old Mr Chilcott. One of them got caught in Mrs

Gnathead's bonnet. Gnathead in trying to knock it out, upset a plank on to the toes of about six young Hobdays. Mr Waterall on the platform rang his bell. The young men at the back shouted 'Yoicks!' and 'Tally-ho!' The dogs barked louder than ever, and above all the din the voice of Major Kettlewell was heard bawling at Peter to let go of his coat and threatening Mr Waterall with dreadful penalties for deliberately inciting a savage dog to attack him. Old Mrs Felton of Windermere Cottage was seized with palpitations, which were not diminished by the caving in of the lid of the barrel on which she was sitting and what looked in consequence like the probable attachment of the barrel to Mrs Felton for the rest of her life. Lieutenant Green produced a whistle which he began to blow as hard as he could with the idea of gathering his dogs to heel, but which sounded much more as if he were blowing for the police. Anyway his dogs paid no attention, but continued to scamper up and down after imaginary rats. Ralph and Roger were shouting at Peter to let go of Major Kettlewell's coat, but their shouts added little to the general noise because they were too much stifled by mirth.

'I didn't think this would be such a lark, did you?' Ralph observed to Roger.

'No, it's a jolly good lark, isn't it?' the younger one agreed. 'Look at that little funk Phyllis. She's blubbing like anything.'

'I've caught a bat! I've caught a bat!' Ralph cried in ecstasy.

'Where?'

'In my hat.'

'I say, how ripping! Let's tame it.'

'Of course I'm going to,' said Ralph. 'Look out, don't squash it with your great beefy paws, you clumsy hog.'

'We can put it in that canary-cage of Phyllis's,' Roger suggested. 'Do bats lay eggs?'

'Fish and find out,' said Ralph, whose knowledge of bats was not in excess of his young brother's.

And at this point the chronicler feels tempted to lay down his pen and to the kind reader who wants to know more reply ungraciously in the words of Ralph to Roger.

The farcical chronicles of Oak are not to be contained in a single volume, and if the history of Oak were to be brought down to the present it would merely fade out in a monotone of dull respectability. The post-office was achieved within a year; but the postmaster was not Hobday, who however did obtain his off-licence much to Mr Waterall's regret when he found it meant that every Sunday afternoon about twenty young men would sit along the hedge and on the stile opposite the gate of Dream Days drinking beer, this being the nearest lawful spot to the Emporium where they could be held to be consuming it off the premises. For two years the post-office stamped all letters Oak Farm Estate, which so much angered Mr Waterall that he would not use it and sent all his letters to be posted in Galton. However, the struggle between the supporters of Oak and Oaktown did ultimately finish in a victory for Mr Waterall's side some three years after that meeting in the barn which is at this moment breaking up in such noisy disorder.

Mr Ryan continued to provide amusement for the neighbourhood until a year or two later he fell a victim to a craze for going about without clothes, which ended in his buying a pony and riding down one night to Chatsea on it stark naked, and ultimately in poor Mr Ryan's being detained for some time in a mental hospital, while his nephew found a job far from buttercups and daisies in London. Micha and Rehob built their red brick villa which almost immediately caught fire and was burnt out. The disaster their father attributed to their having taken to drinking bottled cider with their meals. He refused to finance the poultry farm any longer, and like so many others of the first settlers they vanished from Oak. Hobday's Emporium flourished, and the eldest son runs it now; while Hobday himself, a firm supporter of the Labour Party, reads the *Daily Herald*, a very old man sitting in the sun and sheltered from the east wind by that twelve-foot fence. Mr Pluepott, his rival, caused him much anxiety for a long time; but ultimately Pluepott's wife died, and he left Oak to Hobday's supremacy. Old Joe Gnathead continued to try to make vegetable-growing pay, on the wrong side of the road, for several years; but the brickfields were closed for ever within a few months of this August and soon became a wilderness of birches and brambles.

The lawn laid down by old Mr Bellamy grew green and for many summers Poley mowed it. Then Mrs Poley died, and Poley returned to Kent where he now lives on an old age pension, a very ancient man indeed, but still able to read the headlines of his favourite paper, the *Daily Mail*.

As for the Wateralls themselves, well, of course, the children grew up and Mr and Mrs Waterall grew old; but quite half the trees from Bocock's Farnley Nurseries lived and are still alive, though Dream Days itself has long vanished, and a garden-city villa has taken its place.

Finally, the extra plot of land which Mr Waterall bought from Mr Blake in order to get rid of the gypsies that day of the meeting proved not to belong to Mr Blake at all, and consequently not to Mr Waterall. What is more the owner of it is still unknown, and to this day you may see in the middle of the sophisticated residential district of Oak half an acre of waste land covered in Spring with buttercups and daisies, all that remains of that derelict old farm, for even the great barn has been pulled down.

6155224   MACKENZIE, C.
823/MAC   Buttercups and daisies   F

Please renew/return this item by the last date shown.

So that your telephone call is charged at local rate, please call the numbers as set out below:

	From Area codes 01923 or 0208:	From the rest of Herts:
Renewals:	01923 471373	01438 737373
Enquiries:	01923 471333	01438 737333
Minicom:	01923 471599	01438 737599

L32b

2 FEB 1993

- 7 JUL 2004

1 2 NOV 2005

L 33